RITUALS

Books by Linda Gray Sexton:

BETWEEN TWO WORLDS: YOUNG WOMEN IN CRISIS

ANNE SEXTON: A SELF-PORTRAIT IN LETTERS

RITUALS

Linda Gray Sexton

Doubleday & Company, Inc., Garden City, New York
1982

All characters in this book are fictional
and any resemblance to actual persons, living or dead,
is entirely coincidental.

Library of Congress Cataloging in Publication Data

Sexton, Linda Gray, 1953-
Rituals.

I. Title.
PS3569.E886R5   813'.54
ISBN: 0-385-17301-6   AACR2
Library of Congress Catalog Card Number: 81-9839

Copyright © 1982 by Linda Gray Sexton

For A. E. Falute

Contents

Life is strange and changeful and the crystal is in the steel at the point of fracture, and the toad bears a jewel in its forehead, and the meaning of moments passes like the breeze that scarcely ruffles the leaf of the willow.

—Robert Penn Warren
All the King's Men

Prologue

DECEMBER 1980

One

IT WAS A VINTAGE YEAR. KATHERINE SINCLAIR ROLLED THE CRISP
stem of her wineglass between two fingers as she watched her
father. A tide of Bordeaux swirled against the thin bubble of
crystal. She waited, hoping that he would comment on her
choice, or raise a toast to her as his hostess.

The conversation at the table of fourteen eddied around them,
she at one end and her father at the other; the dry persistent
scent of wine mingled with the musk of Christmas lilies. She
scrutinized him over the expanse of starched damask and bone
china: his profile with its distinct features, his shoulders emphasized by the dark suit.

But Kirk didn't look at her. He kept talking to Paige, on his
right; he touched her small hand where it lay on the cloth, and
Kat's resentment began to build.

Her younger sister's blond hair looped in a gleaming crescent
over bare shoulders and back. The neckline of the black silk
curved in low against the high upward swell of her breasts, and
despite the cut of the dress, she wore no jewelry around her
small throat. When a man looked at Paige all he saw was creamy
skin and that magnetic rose-tinged descent.

Kirk drew their end of the table together in an intimate joke
that Kat could not quite hear. She watched Paige toss him the
next straight line as though they were juggling balls back and

forth between them. Once again she saw just how they both had the same dark blue eyes, set at a provocative slant against high cheekbones. Both were witty, both charming, both clever.

Kirk turned his shoulders slightly, and looked full in Paige's face: they did not hide their intensity, and from twenty feet away Kat could feel the turbulent current running between them. Rejection, confusion, and envy rose against the back of her throat, bitter as vinegar.

It wasn't fair, she thought, picking up her fork, it just wasn't fair. She'd been working on this meal with the staff all week long —a lot of time, love, and effort had gone into executing the exacting tradition of a Sinclair Christmas Eve dinner. The soup: a rich oyster bisque. The entree: standing rib roast, rare and only rare, flanked by roast potatoes and onions, broiled garlic tomatoes, and fresh green beans. This year Kat herself had carefully selected the wines from her father's wooden racks in the cellar.

In fact, she would have one more glass. It was sliding down so easily, and Kat felt less and less need to savor each sip. She had promised herself a limit of two glasses this evening, but there was so much she didn't want to see, so much she didn't want to feel, that a third glass seemed reasonable—particularly considering the quality of conversation offered by the young man to her left.

Skip Lowell was her father's idea of an excellent match, and Kirk had taken it upon himself to invite him tonight. Skip traded in old Massachusetts currency: from wealthy Pride's Crossing on the North Shore, to Exeter, to Harvard, to an up-and-coming position with the family-owned business. Since Kat had broken off with Aaron Salzer earlier in the year, Kirk kept pushing Skip at her.

But nothing could have interested her less. She had not really let Aaron fade from her mind yet, although they had been apart for nearly three months. The affair, full of argument and intense emotion, had begun a year ago, while they were seniors at Harvard. She sipped her wine quickly and imagined him here with her tonight, his familiar, slender hands maneuvering fork and knife in the European fashion, his dark eyes commenting silently, but with humor, on all that went on around them. He would have absorbed the scene and clicked all his impressions into the inner visual bank which so quickly emptied itself into his painting. He was an artist—a talented one in Kat's opinion—but practical as well; this year he'd begun at Harvard's Graduate School of Design, studying architecture as a safety measure against the future.

Her father had never liked him, had thought him uncouth—and he hadn't hesitated to point it out to Kat. In fact, it was totally beyond Kirk that Kat could fall in love with such a person. To Kirk, Aaron was a flashy, new-minted coin, straight from garish New York City. His family had money, but it was the wrong kind. He dressed carelessly and drove a secondhand Toyota. Kirk had been irritated by Aaron from the first time they met, and his intolerance had grown with time. He had been glad to see Aaron go.

Of course, Aaron would not have been comfortable in this elaborate setting either, Kat thought, with his old corduroy suit instead of something gray or dark blue. His usual attempts to start a rousing political discussion would have met with cold, damp disinterest. Subdued, he might have listened with loathing, as Kirk captivated the other end of the table with a racist joke.

But he wasn't here. He was gone. Kat traced the initials on her mother's heavy, simple flatware with the edge of a fingernail, trying to block out Skip Lowell's drone about the effect of world oil prices on his production costs. Sipping her wine, she looked politely, elegantly bored—or regal, sitting there with such an arch to her back. Against the deep burgundy of her dress, her collarbone drew an arrow of sharp relief. Her neck was long and fine, and her face had a sort of patrician interest to it; the long nose, the thin lips, the sharp jut of her chin, all softened in the muted light. Her short auburn hair even took on a gleam, waving softly around her ears, its reddish highlights accented by the rich color of her dress and the glass in her hand.

A sense of loss had been bearing down on her for hours, but she had continued to beat it back. Although the day had been filled with wrapping expensive gifts, an overwhelming emptiness drummed through Kat, a hollowness that the extravagance of cashmere sweaters, fine leathers, and good books could not offset. The Christmas tree lofted to the top of the cathedral ceiling, the hearth lit the room with orange fire, but Kat had felt only a barren cold from the moment she hung her mother's favorite ornament—a miniature piano—on the tree. All day long she'd curled her feelings tighter and tighter inside her like a secret forgotten scroll. The rest of the family hummed the traditional carols as they decorated the tree, and her mood had settled onto a new bottom shelf of depression. How could they be celebrating anything without her mother? How could she be celebrating anything without Aaron? It all seemed a blasphemy. She had shut herself in the bathroom with a large glass of sherry and sat woodenly on the toilet.

Was it just last year that they had all been right here, at the same table, with the same food and the same routine conversation? Had only the seating arrangement been different?

Last year her mother had been hostess of this table, her soft blond hair piled high on her head, her mouth bent in a warm smile. Kat closed her eyes to see Lily on a winter afternoon, at the piano: shoulders moving, arms moving, like a dancer, bringing forth miracles. The sound swelled through the living room, reverberating high up amid the beams of the ceiling. A fire had been lit and it burnished the high polish of the piano's walnut veneer, the soft waves of Lily's hair loose on her shoulders. It was in Kat's mind like a painting, the scene caught and held for all time. It was the beauty of their lives together, a ritual which encompassed them with its purity and clear uncomplicated meanings. Kat always pretended to read her book, pretended not to notice, as if she were listening to a record. But, curled in her wing-back chair, she'd really been studying Lily, watching the way she hiked one shoulder higher than the other for the crescendos, watching how she poured her body down into the keys, a funnel of energy. Her mother was so open with her music. Around her the world receded and there was only the sound Lily was bringing forth, each precise note falling into another till they blended together into a whole. Sometimes she would stop, biting the very tip of her narrow tongue, and shake her head, mark the sharp or natural, and play it over again. She was painstaking, meticulous. She made sure it was right. Kat listened, every afternoon from four to five. Darkness filled the winter streets but she did not notice, for this room was filled with light. The memory of these silent, shared hours—the sound of her mother's mind and heart—was a picture of something past but treasured. She drew it out now, needed it now, used it now.

But her mother was gone. There was only the emptiness of having taken her seat at this table. A question from Skip Lowell jolted Kat back to the present. She tried to snap herself awake with a reasonable answer, and discovered she was having trouble focusing her eyes. It was getting nearly impossible now to orchestrate the table conversation around her. She didn't want to be thinking about all these things, she didn't want to keep remembering last year and all the many losses, all that pain, all that grieving. She needed more anesthesia.

She emptied her wineglass.

For several weeks she had been trying to monitor herself, been trying to cut back. But now she realized dimly she was well on her way to being drunk again—now, just like last night, and the night before. But why, she wondered, straining to keep her eyes open, why couldn't she just stop? She certainly hadn't meant to drink so much tonight. Today had just been so upsetting and difficult that she'd needed the extra help.

But the small inner voice that commented on all her actions pointed out with a certain sharpness that being upset was just a standard excuse. Hadn't she been using it every day since her Harvard graduation, every day in the last six months, every day since she'd come home to live with her father again?

The queasy feeling in her stomach did not go away. Faces wavered in the candlelight, smiles stretched like elastic bands, words melted together in a solid stream. She could not hear. She could not speak. The sensation of falling, of sliding across ice into a danger zone, increased. She was sliding endlessly, she was unable to move, unable to call out, she was watching the black hole come up at her, the black hole where ice thins out to water.

Part I

MARCH 1980 –
DECEMBER 1980

Not out of vengeance have I accomplished all my sins but because something has always been close to dying in my soul, and I've sinned only in order to lie down in darkness and find somewhere in the net of dreams, a new father, a new home.

—William Styron
Lie Down in Darkness

Two

ALL HARVARD UNIVERSITY THERMOSTATS HAD BEEN SET BACK TO sixty degrees, and Kat fled the dank Widener Library reading room for her suite in Adams House. March was the most depressing month, she thought—the dregs of winter with no promise yet of spring. Bundled in a knitted afghan against stray drafts, she hunched over *Jude the Obscure* in preparation for a Victorian Lit exam the next day. Her roommate, Helena Gall, had just left for a late class in her usual flurry of disorganization, and Kat was grateful for the sudden quiet.

When the phone rang, she fumbled for it absentmindedly, still sipping her coffee, still caught up in Hardy.

"Katherine Sinclair please."

"This is she speaking."

"This is Dean Edwards. I wondered if you could drop by my office for a minute?"

Kat sat up straight in her chair. It wasn't often an undergraduate got a call from the Dean of Students. Maybe she was in trouble. Maybe something was wrong.

"Of course," she responded, nervous. "What would be a convenient time?"

"It would be best if you came right away."

Kat's breathing came hard. Jacket, shoes, out on the street. Every stone, every curb, every stoplight seemed tattooed onto

her vision. There had been something in his voice which
sounded a distant, urgent alarm in her. There was no real question in her mind what this summons meant. She did not doubt
that her life was about to change radically on the basis of one
short phone call. With all her reading as a literature major, she
had come to recognize the ubiquitous ringing as one of life's
hackneyed but significant mileposts.

The stone steps up to University Hall were hard against her
feet; the door swung out stubbornly under her hand. Numbly
she continued to grasp all the emotional defense she could mus-
ter. With the magical illogic that always accompanies shock, she
somehow felt that if she weren't caught unaware maybe it
wouldn't be true.

By the time she reached the third floor she was convinced her
mother was dead. In the dimly lit office, Edwards' face, grave
with his responsibility, confirmed it. Words were superfluous.

"My mother?" Kat asked, a tremolo in her voice.

The Dean grimaced in relief that he would not actually have
to come right out and say the words.

"How was it . . ." She paused and swallowed. "How did it
happen?"

"An accident, a car accident."

"She's been in three already this year," Kat said, talking aloud
to herself, wrapping her arms around her chest. "When?"

"This morning. The Concord police haven't been able to reach
your father. He's out of town. The housekeeper gave them the
university number."

Kat took it all in: they might have been discussing her grade-
point average. She walked to the couch and sat down carefully,
as if she did not want to jar herself. Edwards clearly didn't know
what to do with her, but his discomfiture didn't really matter to
Kat. She knew she should do something. She just wasn't sure
what. Right now it seemed very important to get home, to Concord, to Monument Street, to the house she had grown up in. If
she could get there, the bad news would evaporate like some
strange nightmare. She asked Edwards to call her a taxi.

The ride out was blank and silent. Kat was operating on some new plane of consciousness, some shut-down level which kept her breathing but did not allow her to think. She moved by rote, she spoke by rote. She was numb.

"That's eighteen-fifty," the cab driver said laconically as he pulled to the head of the long snow-banked drive. Kat paid him through the window, and walked up to the brightly lit stone house spread out before her. Overhead the pine branches were loaded down with a fresh coat of sleet and they clattered against each other in the wind like stiletto heels on pavement. It required a certain sort of courage to take out her key and unlock the door: she still half-expected to find her mother at the piano in front of the fire.

There was no one home.

She went to the den, set a match to the kindling, and poured herself a deep glass of scotch, trying to get warm. The housekeeper came in. She had been with the Sinclairs since Kat was a little girl, and still there seemed nothing she could do to help—not even dinner, for Kat wasn't hungry. She could not imagine trying to eat—eating belonged to another world, to another, a normal, place or time. She kept sipping her scotch, trying to burn away the frigid air locked inside her body.

After a while she put in a call to her father's hotel, but he was still out and she could hardly leave the news as a message. She used the grandfather clock in the foyer as a measuring stick for her calls: on the fifteen- and forty-five-minute chimes she tried Paige at Pine Manor. In between, she just sat and waited. She added more logs to the fire, refilled her glass, stared down the dark hall. The alcohol was not affecting her at all; there was no blurred relief from the present.

Paige answered her phone at a quarter to ten. Kat told her quietly and simply, with no elaboration. At first she said nothing. Then she wanted to know the details. Her voice was frozen, without inflection, like a straight line. She did not cry. When Kat asked her to come to Concord for the night, Paige said she was tired, it was late, she would come in the morning; Kat was too tired and too cold and too disoriented to push. She would wait for her father alone.

It wasn't until nearly midnight that he answered at the hotel. "Daddy?" How would she phrase it? The power and responsibility scared her.

"Kat, is that you?" Kirk asked in a startled voice. "Is everything all right?"

Kat stared at the dial on the phone, memorizing the letters numbly, trying to think of how to tell him, trying to get control of her voice. In the end, it all seemed ludicrously melodramatic, like something out of a soap opera.

"No, it's not all right. I think maybe you should sit down."

"What's happened?"

She could hear his fear washing through the wire. "It's Mom," she said. Her voice grew hoarse as she tried not to cry. "It's Mom. She . . ." A pause. Where were the words? ". . . She passed away this afternoon."

"What?" he said in shock, a harsh whisper.

"She's dead," Kat said at last. It struck her that saying it to him really made it so.

"What? Are you sure?"

"In the Buick. She hit a telephone pole."

"When?"

"This morning. When can you come home?"

"I'll be there as soon as I can get a plane." He paused. "Kat, are you all right?"

"Yes. Just come home. I need you."

There wasn't anything else to say. The pain vibrated between them, a tangible twisted thing. When she hung up the receiver, Kat looked at the face of the clock on the mantelpiece. It was eleven fifty-five. She thought, I'll never forget this, I'll never forget the time. This is the night I told my father that my mother was dead.

She crawled into her mother's bed and slept between sheets carrying Lily's scent. Sleep rolled in on her like a thick bank of fog. She did not dream.

She was sitting at the breakfast table Tuesday morning when her father came in. He stood, staring vacantly for a minute, and then gave her a hug with arms that trembled. He looked lost, as though he did not know what to say or do. "Did you call Paige?"

"Last night." She pushed the hair out of her eyes and continued to stir her coffee.

He sat down, but didn't unbutton his coat. His eyes were bloodshot, his beard showing silver bristles in the morning light. Even today it was a shock to see him in such disarray. "I'll go over and pick her up," he said in a blank voice. "There are a lot of people to call—so many to tell. Do you think you could start?"

She nodded, grateful to have something to do.

"Use your mother's phone book, and when I get back maybe we can finish them off together." He pulled his overcoat tight around his neck. "What about the funeral home?"

"I'll call them too."

"They'll need instructions. We'll have to go over."

She dug into the list, relieved once again to be working on something. She could see her father was going to need a great deal of help and support, and there was something reassuring in his assigning her a concrete task. The way they had instinctively divided up the responsibilities was comforting and familiar; the exchange tugged at Kat and with cool detachment she let herself recognize that the work she had taken on used to be her mother's domain. How many mornings had her parents sat right here, making their plans, assuming responsibilities according to the indelible rules by which they played. Kat could see her mother now, creaming her coffee with the small crystal pitcher, sipping from the bone china cup they'd given her one Mother's Day when they were children. Now she could see her pulling a pad of paper and her fountain pen toward her, the paper and pen she always brought to the table; and so she was ready for the day, ready for Kirk's thought or her own, or for what needed be done. She smelled of fresh lemons, and her blond hair d against the shoulder of her robe. That was a luxury she d herself—coming down to breakfast in her robe. In the she never frowned, or raised her voice. She was like a ting. Mornings were her forte.

her head free of the picture. How long will I remember? she asked herself, before stamping her foot down firmly on the trap door of memory.

Kirk and Paige returned at lunch time. Her sister's face was shut down, and she was unable to return Kat's hug. She was controlling herself; walling her pain off tightly within her, she made small talk as though nothing had happened. She kept getting up and going quickly into the bathroom. Kat could hear the water running in the basin.

In the den, Kirk put a match to the fire laid in the grate and then poured himself a scotch.

"I called Riverside while you were gone," Kat said quickly. "They want us to come down and go through the details."

"After lunch." Kirk moved to his chair.

"I don't know," she said directly, lifting her chin. "They seemed pretty insistent. Let's go and get it over with."

With a resigned sigh, Kirk downed his drink and picked up the car keys. Kat felt guilty for pushing him, but she couldn't bear to sit around the house when there were so many things to be done. They drove silently through the icy streets.

The funeral director greeted them at the door. Something in his hushed, hesitating posture made Kat feel as if what they were doing was vaguely illegal, or dangerous. His office was softly lit with a rosy light, the chairs plushly padded. He spoke in whispers. The atmosphere was filtered, muted, as though one could dilute the pain that brought people here. Kat had to repress her urge to jump up and down, to violate all the heavy phony silence.

"What was Mrs. Sinclair's date of birth?" he asked. Kat looked over at her father. His eyes had gone dim, his face slack, palsied. He looked like a very old man. Kat could tell that he wasn't listening. He wasn't really here. He was remembering. All those other trips to this place—once for his father, once for his moth, once for his brother. It was as if the sight of this familiar had brought the truth to him—someone else was gone, this, all the other losses were reverberating through h with its own peculiar and intense memory. Kat felt pain for his pain, and spoke up protectively.

"September 4, 1924."

The funeral director shifted his attention to the tall young woman before him. The other daughter would be of no help—she was very young, in shock, unable to make a decision. He was used to getting information from all sorts of sources. You never knew which family member would turn out to be the rock on which the others would depend. "And her parents' names, places and dates of birth?"

This stumped Kat. She wasn't sure of the dates. She turned to her father, but he seemed almost in slow motion. She made a few educated guesses, and told the director she'd check them at home.

He seemed more and more like a caterer setting up a cocktail party. The arrangements clicked off his tongue in precise, ticker-tape order.

"Which day are you planning to have your calling hours?"

Kat faltered. "Tomorrow?"

He nodded. "Will you have an afternoon and an evening session?"

"Do we need to?"

"It is customary, especially for a family as well known in the area as yours."

"All right then. Is a room available at that time?"

"Yes," he said, consulting a schedule on his desk. "The large reception area on the first floor will be ready for you. The funeral will be Thursday at the family church?"

"I suppose so," she said uncertainly.

He looked at her.

"It's St. Mary's, Concord Center."

"How many limousines will the family require from the church to the cemetery?"

"Do we need any at all?" Kat asked vaguely.

"It is customary—you don't want to have to worry about driving on a day like that. Each limousine seats five comfortably."

Kat made a mental count. "I guess two would be enough."

Then there were the flowers, the pallbearers, the minister, the newspaper releases.

"And you will bring a complete set of clothes tomorrow," he said.

Kat looked at him, confused. "Wasn't she brought in wearing clothes?"

The director raised an eyebrow. Questions dealing with the more graphic aspects of death were clearly distasteful to him. "We always discard the deceased's clothing. It would be best if you bring in something"—he hesitated, as if to emphasize the word—"fresh. High-necked, long-sleeved, full length. And don't forget shoes and stockings."

"What about underwear?"

Again he looked uncomfortable. "No, that won't be necessary. Now," he said, fingering his pen, "how do you intend to lay Mrs. Sinclair to rest?"

Kat looked at him, puzzled.

"I mean," he said smoothly, as if speaking to a child, "are the remains to be cremated or buried?"

She knew the answer to this question, and it was a relief not to have to worry about making the right choice. Her mother had had a horror of burial. "Cremation," she said firmly.

The director nodded and made a note on his pad. "Now to the matter of a casket. If you will come this way, you will be able to choose a style which you feel will best suit Mrs. Sinclair."

Kat got to her feet, and waited for her father and Paige. They followed him into a darkened room, and he snapped on the lights.

Here were coffins from wall to wall—plush, padded coffins lined with velvet and silk, coffins that didn't look in the least like coffins as far as Kat was concerned. Heavy mahogany cases, brass handles, satin pillows and bows. They looked like cribs for oversized infants. She wandered among them, overwhelmed.

"Why do we need a coffin at all if Mother's going to be cremated?" she finally asked, thinking aloud, running her fingers along the fine wood. The director looked tired.

"Well, you must have something suitable for the visiting hours," he said in a reproving tone. "People will be looking at the casket all afternoon and evening."

"Still," Kat said, getting pointedly insistent, "we wouldn't need a very sturdy one. It's only going to be burnt up anyway. Don't you have something simpler—a plain pine box?" She felt there was no dignity to all this opulence. It was offensive. Going out ought to be spare and uncluttered.

Her weariness over it all increased when the director, face placid, mentioned that the caskets ranged anywhere from $5,000 for mahogany with a lead liner, down to $1,000 for the pressed cardboard. Kat inspected the pressed cardboard; it was gray, and far less elaborate than the others, but it seemed less immoral too. It was less difficult to approach emotionally—more temporary, not such a permanent prison. She appealed to her father for his opinion, and he nodded in agreement, but she couldn't tell if he was really aware. Paige had gone to the window when they entered the room; stubbornly looking out into the street, she ignored their purpose.

"We'll take this one," she said.

The director showed them back to his office. Kat hoped they were finished; the weight of the afternoon was giving her a headache. She wanted to get away from the artificial atmosphere of the funeral home. She kept imagining rows of bodies lined up in the basement, sprouting leaves, limbs, and root systems like strange science fiction plants in the hothouse humidity, the carefully filtered light and sound.

"I'll need a signature," the director said, interrupting her thoughts. He held the sheet of paper in the general direction of Kat and Kirk, unsure of who would give him what he needed. Kat peered down at the sheet and looked up at him quickly. With resignation, she took it and sat down unsteadily in the chair which bumped against the back of her knees.

It was a form authorizing cremation. The director held out his fountain pen. The feeling of being underwater flooded through Kat again. She took the pen, read the sheet, felt the pain stoke up its glow inside her. She signed.

Three

THE COFFIN SAT ON A PEDESTAL LAPPED BY FLOWERS, ITS GRAY CARD-board barely visible under the blanket of daisies. Kat, Kirk, and Paige came into the long room from the far end. The walls were lined with rows of cushioned chairs, the borders defined by gentle light. Kat left her father and sister at the entrance, and slowly walked down the length of the room to the small kneeler in front of the shrine. She wondered whether she was supposed to pray. She didn't feel much like praying; in fact, the face of God held nothing for her. Life was too absurd, too mystical, too complex for Kat to believe a single giant power pulled the strings on divine whim or inspiration. She saw herself simply as a single being, governing and taking responsibility for her own actions. People who needed God, she felt, really needed a crutch. And so she only stood beside the coffin and rested her hand there.

She hadn't come with Kirk earlier that morning to see Lily for a last time. He'd gone alone. But now Kat felt a need to say more than a purely emotional good-by. Still, as much as she wanted that physical touch, that reality, she was afraid of it. She did not know what dead people looked like. She could not imagine her mother's cheeks and lips without color, her eyes blank as pennies. The figure in the box would be only a wax doll. Yet it would be as familiar and dear as her own palm. She simply could not cross the bridge between the memory of her mother's

warm face and the alien being in the box, and so she stood instead, trying to touch through layers of cardboard.

"Kat?"

She turned slowly toward the hoarse voice. Kirk stood beside
her.

"I wanted to tell you." He stopped. "In the red dress you
picked. She looked like a princess. A princess."

Kat looked into her father's eyes and it was like looking in the
windows of a house gutted by fire. "I'm glad," she said in a whisper, taking his hand and squeezing it. His carriage seemed fragile, limp, as he turned toward the entrance where their first
callers were arriving. Kat saw him flinch, as if seeing people
were more than he could bear. She stepped forward into the
awkward space his hesitation left, and moved quickly to greet
them. She would break the ice; she would warm up the room.

With a determined smile, she extended her hand. "Mr. and
Mrs. Lowell. Thank you so much for coming." She offered her
cheek.

"Katherine," the woman said in a subdued tone. "Is there anything we can do?"

How insane, she thought, as they made mechanical small talk.
As if there were anything anyone could do. Hours passed. They
were in a limbo where time did not exist. The clock rolled up the
afternoon and more people drifted in, wearing their sorrow like
admissions badges, offering their stock condolence—condolence
made stock only because language provided nothing more. Kat
was operating on remote control. She didn't mind. She saw dimly
that they came as much to be comforted as to comfort. She
steeped her own pain in theirs, and so forgot it for a time.

It was a cocktail party, and she was the hostess. She kept trying to draw her guests down into the room, but they bunched together like a herd of spooked cattle in the foyer. The room
seemed to tilt, listing to port, with everyone huddled on the star-
board deck, fighting the steep incline. Standing in the middle of
the room, she listened to the nervous noise on one side, and the
silent, solitary force of the body on the other. Except for a few

brave people, most of the guests seemed to pretend the coffin did not exist. They ignored it.

Then she saw Aaron's strong shoulder line cutting through the crowd toward her. He was here, she realized mechanically, he was here. They'd spoken on the phone Monday night and he, like Helena, had wanted to come out to Concord, wanted to hold her, comfort her—but she'd refused. She was afraid of falling apart. She had to keep things rolling. Now his fingers laced into hers, and for the first time that day she felt her own loss stinging behind her eyes. His tall lean body seemed a long straight line of power, and she just wanted to lean against him and breathe slowly.

Helena had come too, and she put her arms around them both in a three-way ring. Over their shoulders Kat saw other classmates, others who cared for her. She wanted to cry. "What time is it?" she asked instead.

"Nearly four," Helena answered. "When does this end?"

"Half an hour," Kat said, stepping back and trying to smile once again. "And then it starts all over at eight."

Aaron and Helena exchanged a worried look.

"Do you have to come then?" he asked.

She looked at them and felt they just did not understand the responsibility and the pressure on her. For a moment she felt angry, but she was too tired to be angry.

"We'll be with you then too," Helena said, taking Kat's hand again and moving close, as if to guard her. "And you can take a nap before dinner."

A nap. Sleep. Oblivion. It sounded wonderful. But so far away.

She saw a small room. Dark. No windows. Her mother lay on a long grating set into a low iron platform. Her breasts flattened to the side as she lay on her back. The weight of her feet rolled her legs out slightly at the hip, exposing the skin of her inner thigh. The eyes were closed. Even through the glass rectangle in the door, Kat could feel the heat rise like a sauna, building up to a deep crescendo. The skin ripened the color of copper. The eyelashes powdered onto the cheeks. The vertebrae snapped open like popcorn. Mouth, kneecap, and palm melted away.

Kat was struggling in the dark, sweating, twisted in the sheets as she tried to get away from the nightmare. She came awake, fighting up through layers of consciousness, running from the vision of the cremation. And then, with terror, she realized that she could not get away from it. Her mother was dead. Her mother would be cremated tomorrow. She lay in the dark, limp, tears running into her ears, and the taste of ash gritted against her teeth.

Four

"WHAT ABOUT THIS?" KAT ASKED AS SHE RUMMAGED THROUGH LILY'S armoire. She held up a brightly striped cashmere sweater.

Paige was stretched out on the chaise longue, leafing through the latest issue of *Cosmopolitan,* which she'd brought with her from the dorm. She eyed the sweater and shrugged.

"Well, how about this one?" It was a blue just the color of Paige's eyes.

"What is this," Paige exclaimed in sudden irritation, "a charity bazaar?"

"If you don't want any of this stuff," Kat snapped, "at least get off your ass and help me!"

"Yes, Massa!"

They stood together, folding and boxing, in silent angry tension. This was certainly not what Kat had envisioned. Yesterday's funeral had passed on a stiff breeze with nothing required of the family except to sit and wait for it all to end, and now she craved action, welcomed the task of sorting through her mother's clothing, papers, books—all the tangible, familiar evidence that Lily had lived. It had not occurred to Kat that it might be too soon for this, or in poor taste, or that Paige would not feel as she did. Deep inside her, an unconscious need shifted about, a need to bring up all she'd choked back at the public calling hours and funeral. A need to connect with her memories, to share with her

family in a private intense way. Last night had brought no relief: they'd sat in the library, each in a different chair. They'd
had their scotch neat and then gone to bed early.

At breakfast, Paige had resisted Kat's suggestions. The fact
that they had both lost their mother made her no less hostile toward Kat, and without saying a word, her feelings were clear.
Still, Kat had pushed, wanting and needing to share the loss, to
grieve together, to put her arms around her sister, to be held, to
cry.

But now, forced to the task, Paige held herself cool, as if to
punish her sister, or as if to take a stand from sheer perversity. It
was ironic, Kat thought to herself: they were doing exactly what
she'd wanted, but Paige had won by simply giving her nothing
of what she really needed.

Kat pulled open the top dresser drawer. It was full of pill bottles. "Damn. What about all this?"

Paige came over, curious, and peered around her shoulder.
Kat picked up one of the plastic containers. "Maybe," she
suggested facetiously, "maybe the drugstore'd buy them back."

"You're crazy," Paige said, reading the labels and weighing
the bottles in her hand. "This is great stuff—and a lot of it too."

"Sure," Kat said with irritation.

"I'm serious. There're enough downers here to keep my entire
class relaxed for the rest of the year."

Kat slammed the drawer. "I'm going to flush them all down
the toilet."

"You really are *prehistoric*," Paige drawled, with a scornful,
self-satisfied smile. She picked up her magazine and strolled out
the door.

"Damn you!" Kat burst out. "I hate you!" She twisted a silk
slip in her hands. Ever since they'd been teen-agers Paige had
been able to make her feel like an oddball, a misfit, an old maid
aunt. And, as always, while Kat lost her temper, Paige maintained her cool disdainful façade.

She was furious with herself for jumping at her sister's bait.
Even mentioning the idea of actually using their mother's pills
had been a setup, psychological sabotage, Paige's way of escap-

ing the work they had to do. Kat loathed disapproving of her
sister, of her ideas or actions, because it made her feel like a
mother—and she was not ready to be a mother. And, although
she couldn't admit it, part of her anger also flowed from a hard
kernel of envy—a sharp-edged envy that Paige dared to do exactly what she wanted.

She wasn't going to wait for her sister to cool off and come
back. She would get rid of those pills right now. She attacked
the dressing table drawers, drawers stocked like a library with
wholesale-sized jugs of sleeping pills, pain-killers, and tran-
quilizers. Kat felt a rush of anger at the physicians who were too
easy to get around, from whom Lily had wheedled large, permis-
sive prescriptions. She'd been clever; she'd been afraid of running out, of facing the world without her anesthesia.

Taking one bottle after another, Kat stood over the toilet,
flushing, for a solid half-hour, watching this chemical world spiral down into mushy confetti. The sheer quantity of the hoard
amazed her. It must be illegal, she thought vehemently—even if
every tablet and capsule had come with a prescription. Finally,
all the plastic jugs were empty.

With a sigh she returned to the big walk-in closet. She stood
surrounded by the smell and touch of her mother's nightgowns,
evening dresses, pants, suits, blouses, and underwear: she saw
Lily coming downstairs to breakfast in her blue silk robe, her
hair undone across her shoulders; Lily at the piano, shoulders
tense with effort, in the beige linen slacks; Lily entertaining, a
royal hostess, in the St. Laurent lamé; Lily slipping the cerise
satin nightie over her head before bed. She began to cry. Her
mother was gone. This would never be done. It was an endless
test of her endurance. It would press in on her, unfinished, for
days and weeks. No one would come to help her. All that was
left of her mother was this pile of lifeless clothing, and this endless job. Who will take care of us, she shouted silently at the
rows and rows of shoes, each paired to match a different outfit.
None of them would fit, she thought distractedly. She would
have to give them all to the Salvation Army. She kept sorting,
folding, heaping, like a lifer in a prison laundry.

And in the pockets of the clothing she discovered more pills. When she flushed them away she found even more, in side-flaps and change compartments of purses, of make-up kits and hand luggage. It was a swarm of endlessly multiplying shiny-backed insects. She kept flushing and flushing, determined to stamp them all out, as if ridding the house of them might bring her mother back. And there were small nips of scotch hidden in the closet too, airline-size nips—but these she set aside to take to the bar.

By mid-afternoon the closet had been reduced to a square cubicle with white walls, and Kat retreated to her mother's sitting room. She lit the fire, trying to warm up.

It was a beautiful room, with oak paneling, a fine oriental rug, and soft Matisse prints. It was her favorite room in the whole house. It was the heart of her mother. How many afternoons had she sat here reading, while Lily wrote letters at the roll-top desk?

She wandered over to the bar set that stood on a small mahogany cart near the french windows. These decanters had once been an integral part of her grandfather's library, and before that, of his father's library. Acquiring them had been one of the definitive family rites of manhood, and Lily had received them only because in her generation there had been no son. Kat reached out and picked up her favorite—the odd duck of the group. It was not stately, or heavily faceted. Instead it was squat, and round, of frosted glass with jungle animals etched on its face. It did not really belong with the set, but had been added by her grandfather on one of his European travels.

Mechanically she poured herself a small brandy and sat down at her mother's desk. She leaned her elbows on the blotter and looked up at the calendar filled with luncheons, doctors' appointments, and dinner dates. A leather tray held a stack of bills and personal correspondence. All this would have to be taken care of —more work and more responsibility for her. Her father would not deal with this; he had gone back to work today to avoid facing the empty house. "Maybe I should start on this," she said out loud. She sorted through the bills and piled them to one side.

She took the fountain pen from its marble base and wrote a short note on the bottom of a half-finished letter to Lily's old college roommate, explaining that her mother had died without finishing it. Perhaps Mrs. Rance would like to keep it as a memento.

She sipped her brandy again and then pulled open the bottom desk drawer to get an envelope. Here was her mother's stationery—boxes and boxes of cream-colored engraved informals, yellow monogrammed notes, elegant postals. She fingered one of the calling cards. No one would ever use any of this again. It was all such a waste.

The next drawer was full of bankbooks and receipts, and an old desire to trespass came over her. She ran her finger along the leather binding of the ledger. She had never before let herself succumb to this childhood deceit. Reluctantly, she pushed that drawer shut and reached for the top one. It had been locked for as long as she could remember. She pulled on it anyway, and then, suddenly frustrated, tugged even harder in an effort to spring the lock. It didn't move. She finished her brandy, and then, annoyed, she yanked the financial drawer open again and began to go through it. She picked up her mother's checkbook and rifled the pages, noting with shock the astronomical costs of running the house. "What am I doing?" she asked herself, slapping it shut resolutely. A small brass key bounced out of the pocket inside the back cover.

Without thinking, she tried it in the lock of the top drawer. It turned. She looked inside eagerly, expecting to find something like a treasured collection of naïve love letters. Instead, there was only a fire insurance policy, an inventory of her mother's jewelry, and a slender stack of checks bound together with a rubber band. She flipped through them in disappointment, and went to the bar to refill her glass.

Each check was made out to her father, the amounts varied from $20,000 to $80,000. Each had an IOU, signed by her father, attached for the corresponding amount. Each was drawn on her mother's brokerage account, and dated from three years back to the present. She added them up. They totaled nearly one and a quarter million dollars.

What did it mean, Kat wondered, sipping. Lily's parents had left her a trust fund with a considerable income. Kat's father was the majority owner in a shoe manufacturing business that had been in his family since the Civil War. Why would he have been borrowing money from his wife? It didn't make sense.

Kat pushed back her chair and began to pace. There must be some reasonable explanation, but she couldn't think of what it might be. Her mind was dull, yet she felt some urgent need to understand. Of course, over the years, there had been a few arguments about money, she reminded herself. In fact, most of them had happened right here in this room, at cocktail hour.

She could remember her parents arguing as far back as she remembered her earliest friends or her first birthday parties. The fights merged in her mind like one long experience, a regular ritual. There was no way to tell one from the other, why they started or how they ended. She remembered only how she felt.

When they began she was usually in her bedroom down the hall, reading before dinner. The sitting room during cocktail hour was an adult sanctuary. Little by little, very gradually, like a song slowly picking up tempo, her parents' voices escalated. At first a distant hum, then louder like an angry crowd, the words beating against the walls of her bedroom. She intently studied the intricate patterns of her wallpaper, the design of her rug. She rearranged all her top bureau drawers. But then she was drawn out, finally, against her will, into the hall, pinned against the stairwell by the voices, unable to leave, unable to stay. She was awash in their anger. She crept closer, hoping her presence would bring a magical halt.

The voices just got louder. It seemed her fear was worse than ever before, like a nightmare you redream and learn to dread. Their anger was death to her then, uncoiling like a snake, wrapping itself around the family. She peered around the corner. The room always looked the same, untouched by the emotion surging through it. The decanters stood, solid at the bar, the fire burned on, the lamps spread their warm light. On the walls the prints captured another moment, another time. Kat captured the scene before her and painted it in her head.

Her mother stood before the fire, her hands cutting the space in front of her, her voice cutting the air. A shattered highball glass lay at her feet, unnoticed. Her smooth face, furrowed with tears, glistened in the soft light. Her small frame vibrated with the power of her rage. Her mouth seemed to Kat an elastic red machine, spitting words, accusations, hate.

Kirk crossed the room, legs snapping like a scissors, face bitter as stone. He turned to face Lily. "Stop it," he said, "you're frightening Kat."

At the sight of her daughter, Lily moved quickly across to her desk. Kat felt awkward, intrusive, there in the middle of the room, in the middle of her parents' fight. She heard her father going down the stairs and went to stand hesitantly beside her mother. Now Lily was pulling out her checkbook. It was a bizarre time to be practical, Kat thought. She wanted to know what was wrong, she wanted to help. But her mother only asked if her homework were finished, if she had decided on the guest list for her Cotillion dessert party. Kat saw there was no place for her here in this world of adults; when would she be qualified to enter and to share? She felt sure once she graduated to the cocktail hour her parents' discord would cease, because, as an adult, she would cure it all. When, she wondered with longing, would she be a woman: have a checkbook, use Tampax, sip a cocktail slowly?

And then they went downstairs to dinner. Just as easily and quickly as it had gone awry, the world returned to normal. And they all pretended it *was* normal. Until it happened again.

So there were fights about money, Kat said to herself, what did that prove? Everybody fights about money. She heard her father come home from the office, go into the library and open the flue of the fireplace. Quickly banding the checks together with the worn elastic, she slipped them and the key back into their hiding places.

She went down to say hello, and kissed him, laying her cheek against his. He was kneeling on the hearth, striking a long match, putting it to the carefully laid kindling. It was his winter custom.

"Punctual as usual, I see," Kat commented, smiling at him. "How about a martini?"

"Absolutely." He sat down heavily before the fire in his favorite wing-back chair. Watching him as she mixed their drinks, Kat felt proud. He was so handsome—too handsome really, for a father. His silver hair swept back off a high brow. There were the strong well-defined bones of his face, the deep blue eyes. His only fault, Kat thought objectively, as she rubbed the rim of the glass with a lemon peel, was his height. From her five feet eight inches, Kirk's extra inch didn't seem quite enough. She could meet his gaze almost directly.

She handed him his glass, took hers, and settled herself in Lily's chair. He ran the ice-cold drink under his nose and sniffed appreciatively at the aroma of the very dry gin with its faint tinge of vermouth. Kat knew it was good. Some daughters brought their fathers' pipe and slippers. She'd always brought Kirk his martini.

"How was your day?"

"The usual. Bought off a few judges and took out a contract on my major competitor."

She laughed. "I see—they're driving you out of business as usual."

"Not to worry." He grinned. "The ruling class always wins." He held out his glass. "How about another fix?"

She mixed a fresh pitcher. She was starting to feel very relaxed, and the confusion of the day began to recede. As she poured, she rested her hand on his shoulder. He was responding to the attention; already he looked less depressed. All that tension she'd felt earlier was dissolving, all her grief damping down under the glow of the gin.

He smiled up at her. "Am I smelling what I think?"

"Your special pot roast," she said, nodding. "I had Mrs. George do it especially."

He clasped his hands behind his head and stretched his legs in front of the fire. "How was the . . . closet cleaning."

"Fine."

"Where's Paige?"

"I don't know. She left early."

He frowned. "Before you'd finished?"

"Before we'd started really." Kat shrugged. "But it's mostly done. Just one more day. Then I'll be ready to go back to school." It was out of her mouth before she'd even had time to consider it; she suddenly felt a need to get back to normal, to resume her life, to get away from the dark emptiness of the house.

Her father looked depressed again. "But it's so soon!"

"I'm fine—and the sooner I get back, the less work I miss." She hesitated. "You're the one I'm worried about. I don't like to leave you alone."

He twisted his wedding band on his finger. "Don't worry," he said lightly. "I know how to mix my own martini." There was a small silence.

"Dad?"

He looked up at her.

"I'd really like to have something of Mom's," she began nervously, "to remind me." She stopped and looked for a sign of understanding. He waited. "Could I take the bar set in her sitting room?" she asked in a rush. "Just the decanters? Then you could stop by for a drink every once in a while on your way out of town."

She could see the question hurt him.

"If you'd like to, you may."

"And you'll come by for a drink?"

"Why not? If the martinis won't come to Mohammed, Mohammed will come to the martinis."

Five

KAT BALANCED THE SHELF PRECARIOUSLY ON ONE SHOULDER AND tried to make a mark for the drill with a pencil. It was her first night back in the dorm, and building a bar for Lily's decanters was her top priority: she hadn't even unpacked yet. In Concord she had hoped that everything would return to normal once she was back in the safety of her room, but the minute she'd walked in and saw the afghan on the floor, her Hardy novel still open, she realized that the fabric of her life here had been altered. Nothing would ever be safe again. Her safety had been invaded.

The shelf just wasn't level, she decided, sitting down on the bed in despair. She'd wanted to do this on her own, but now it seemed impossible. She needed four hands. She got a drink of water, trying to calm down and tackle the problem intellectually. Her mother's decanters must have a home of their own.

The outer door of the suite slammed shut. Helena's voice called out her name and seconds later she appeared around the edge of the bedroom door.

"You're back!" She ran into the room and hugged Kat, her deep brown eyes and wide smile the best welcome Kat had seen in days. "I'm so glad! Are you all right? Can I help you unpack?" The words came quickly, tumbling out of her mouth like a descending run of musical notes. She ran her hand through her dark red curls in excitement. "Are you O.K.?" she demanded.

Kat laughed at this emotional bombardment, sat down on the bed again, and looked up at her roommate with relief. "I'm doing fine," she said wryly. "Now that I'm back with all your noise."

Noise was definitely a part of Helena Gall, and if you lived with her it became a part of you too. A bustle of endless activity and energy. She talked fast, she moved fast, she experienced fast.

They had been roommates since freshman year, when a computer had put them together in a tiny room with bunk beds. At first they had had nothing in common except that they both liked to sleep with their window open, and it had taken Kat quite some time to get used to Helena and her exotic ways. Her dress, her way of orchestrating her words with her hands, her tastes in décor, music, food, books—everything about her had seemed foreign.

But in spite of all their differences, Helena's warmth had been infectious, and she had no trouble getting around Kat's initial shyness. It wasn't long before Kat was fiercely loyal and knew the friendship would last the rest of their lives. They could talk to each other, deeply and intimately, about the most private things. Nothing happened that they did not discuss in detail—it was a friendship built on the immediacy of emotion, and the small trivia of a daily life together.

Helena had turned out to be a curious mixture: in her rainbow array of expensive clothes from Bloomingdale's, she preached socialist doctrine and talked of the corruption of capitalism. Kat nicknamed her the "socialist who wears silk shirts" during their second semester together, and it stuck. They had grown comfortable enough to tease, and spent most of their time sharing frustrations at being women in a male-dominated university, talking about literature and culture—and doing a good deal of old-fashioned girl talk, although as women of the modern era, they gave it a different name.

With a sigh Kat stood up and began to wrestle with the shelf problem again. Helena sat cross-legged in the armchair and pulled a box of Gitanes from her breast pocket. Kat smiled as Helena lit one of the strong French cigarettes. It still struck her as incongruous that her roommate had been born and raised in Houston, Texas, after her parents emigrated from Poland at the end of World War II. A prosperous fabric business had enabled them to give many things to their only daughter, including a year abroad in Paris.

Helena looked up, trying not to laugh as Kat struggled to keep the shelf upright. "What are you doing?"

"Trying to build a new home for these," she answered, her exasperation showing.

"Nice," Helena commented, still trying to keep her amusement under control. "Anything I can do?"

"They were my mother's favorites."

"I've been so worried about you ever since that funeral home." At last she jumped up to help Kat balance the shelf and mark the holes. "What a scene! Those people were so *rapacious*—they just lapped up your pain." Helena grabbed the drill and cut two clean holes in the wall, and they were silent while it bit into the plaster and sent up a small cloud of dust.

"It wasn't so bad," said Kat, going to her desk and handing her roommate the Phillips Head and two screws.

"Oh come on! You all looked like hell." She leaned into the screwdriver. "How's your father bearing up?"

"You want me to hold *your* shelf while you screw it in?" asked Kat sarcastically.

"Only if you get your elbow out of my face."

"You've got to understand," Kat answered finally, "that my family doesn't discuss sex, psychiatry, or death. We just don't talk about it. Here I am, back at the dorm. Dad went back to work the day after the funeral, and Paige went back to school on Saturday. Mom's dead and buried. A fact of life."

Helena shifted the screwdriver to her right hand. "I'd think you'd need to talk, to be with your family—when my brother died we stayed together. We had to."

"I guess my family's different."

"When he died, my parents could have won an Academy Award for emoting," Helena went on, almost not hearing Kat.

She shook her head free from the memory and attacked the other screw. "We sat shiva for seven days."

Kat moved to the desk again and began to fill the decanters with the gin, vodka, Bourbon, sherry, scotch, and brandy she'd ordered on the way home from class. "It's interesting," she remarked, getting out two glasses and pouring them each a celebratory martini. "After what your parents went through in the camps. You'd think they'd want to block out death—not dwell on it."

Helena looked up at the finished shelf. "If death becomes a way of life, you get used to it." She accepted the glass, sipped and coughed. "My God these are strong!" She wrinkled her nose. "For my mother, death was easier to face than my messy room."

Kat looked puzzled.

"What I mean," Helena said, setting her glass down, "is that for my mother, if my room was clean and neat, she knew she was here, in America. Not there, in Poland. She needed to see the little everyday signs of normality. After the camps she just couldn't deal with the small chaotic details of life—like my messy room, or a disorganized kitchen—but she was more capable, more accepting, of the things that might unhinge other people." She shrugged and sipped her martini again. "Have you seen Aaron yet?" she asked abruptly.

Kat began to unpack her suitcase, carefully smoothing and folding all the clothes that had been her mother's. The lemony fragrance that was Lily drifted through the room.

"I needed him on Wednesday."

"I could see it on your face." Helena stretched. "He called me last night because he was worried about you. He didn't want to phone Concord again. He doesn't like to bother your family."

Kat examined a small stain on the sleeve of one of Lily's sweaters. Instead of throwing it in the laundry basket, she folded it carefully and laid it in her drawer.

There was a knock on the outer door. "I'll bet that's him," Helena said.

Kat put down her drink, almost reluctantly. She was afraid to see Aaron, afraid he would ask her how she was, afraid she would tell him. She was afraid to come undone. At this moment, she suddenly felt that looking calm and sane might mean she really *was* calm and sane. She did not want him to break through her outer face; her lines of defense were too thin. She would have to be very careful, very controlled.

She opened the door and there he stood.

"Welcome back," he said, following her into the bedroom. He nodded to Helena. "Started without me, I see."

"And you'll finish without me," Helena said as she stood up. "I conveniently recall that I have a paper due yesterday."

He flopped down on the bed. "Glad to be back?"

Kat sighed and finished her martini. She felt trapped. "Better than sitting around in Concord feeling useless."

"I know what you mean." He ran his hand through his wavy hair, exasperated. "Ever since I saw you I've been feeling useless. This piece I'm working on—no dice."

"What is it?"

"Just a sketch. A woman at a funeral home. I couldn't shake it after Wednesday." He leaned forward, his dark eyes warming up. "But I couldn't even get past the charcoal stage." He got up and stood before her, running his index finger against the long, strong line of her jawbone. This was the line that had been defeating him, this solitary line around which her whole face pivoted, stark, clean, bare. He needed that line if he were really to do it right.

"You were surrounded by people, but you stood alone," he said, explaining with his hands, touching her face, her hair, her lips. "You who are so terrified of being alone were the most alone of all." He rubbed his palm against the curve of her cheek. The shadow falling from the cheekbone down into the sharp slope. It was the center of her face, the character of her face, the strength of her face, and the vulnerability of her face. It was too harsh to allow her real beauty, and yet gave her a quality of being different, of being on the edge.

"Would you sit for me tomorrow?"

"Sit for you?" she echoed, startled. She felt so vulnerable now, and his scrutiny made her uncomfortable. She knew he would not be drawing the outlines of her face—he wanted the outlines of her feelings. She was not sure she wanted him so close, not sure she wanted her emotions put down on paper where she would be forced to confront them. The pain was bad enough already. It was cruel, she felt, a cruel thing to ask of her.

She got out of her chair and poured more gin into her glass. Its dryness was finally numbing her a little. A silence stretched between them. She looked at him. "I don't think I want that."

"All I want is for you to sit still for half an hour."

"I know what you're asking! Don't be so casual about it!" She was suddenly angry. "I feel like I've swallowed some terrible thing, some huge terror, and it's waiting there inside me like a ghost. Like a shadow I can't get rid of." She paced up and down. "I can't remember the last time I saw her." She faced him. "I didn't get to say good-by. Understand? I didn't get to say good-by—and I don't want you painting that! Why should I let you paint that?"

Aaron put his arms around her, as if in apology. He didn't say anything. He didn't put words between them. He just held her and she began to let go. The silence around her was breaking, stretching, fragmenting into shards of sharp-edged emotional glass.

She let the sea flow down and out over both of them, warm and healing, salty, full of the life she had lost. Words pulsed out like blood from an artery. Memories bubbled up from childhood with their pungent aromas. Pain fell out of her like light spilling from behind a half-closed door, illuminating what darkness had hidden. Aaron listened and held her, and poured her another drink, and with the taste of gin came a brief freedom, an ability to feel, to talk, to let the hurt exist.

She lay beside him on the bed. His body was a comfort to her in this process she could not stop. Here was her pain—the mouth of her pain and the anus of her pain and the cunt of her pain. She could never escape it; she pulled her terror to her, felt its shape, ate it alive.

She touched Aaron's chest, his arms, his belly, and he absorbed her sorrow too, and made it his, and so they shared it.

She drew him to her raw edges, raw and open with the pain, and she cauterized them together with his touch. She felt her body come alive under him: her breasts, her belly, humming with the pain, glowing with the pain. It overcame her, it bloomed inside her; she let it obliterate her mind. She wanted to die there. She let his darkness overcome her, until she rested in his arms.

She might let him paint her, she thought. Sometime. But not tomorrow. She was not sure she could bear going through this pain again.

Six

THE LETTER FROM HER MOTHER'S LAWYER WAS WAITING WHEN SHE came back to the dorm for lunch. It had not been a particularly stellar day: Professor Kirby had been even more boring than usual in Fine Arts and Kat felt sleepy and nauseated with the sticky aftertaste of last night's brandy. She stared at the envelope. Having been back in the dorm for a week and a half now, she'd begun trying to develop a system for screening out the pain involved in living day to day, a pain which seemed to cycle through her these days with great regularity. She sat down on the marble step beside the mailboxes and braced herself against the wrought-iron balustrade. It was a brief letter and to the point.

Mason, Rutledge & Stone
Attorneys at Law
43 Tremont Street
Boston, Massachusetts 02115
March 16, 1980

Miss Katherine Sinclair
Harvard University
Adams House B-35
Cambridge, Massachusetts 02138

Dear Katherine:

It was a pleasure to see you last week, despite the sad circumstances of the day. We are all terribly grieved at the loss of your mother. She was a very special friend to me, ever since I joined the firm in 1954.

We will read Mrs. Sinclair's will on Monday, March 23, at ten o'clock. You are named as a beneficiary in the document, and it is important that you attend. I am also notifying your father and your sister of the date. I hope that this meeting will provide ample opportunity for us to answer any questions you may have regarding the disposition or execution of your mother's estate. If you have any difficulty in making this meeting, please let me know.

All my best,
Eliot Rutledge

Forgetting she had been on her way to lunch, Kat climbed the three spiraled flights to her room. What had all this to do with her and what questions could she possibly have? Once again, like the contents of Lily's desk, it hardly seemed her affair. But at the entrance to the suite she paused: what about the IOU's? As often as she put them out of her mind, she found herself returning to them—would they now become her debts, her responsibility?

Frankly she was tired of worrying about the issue. She very much wanted to let her mother go, but all these irritating details kept dredging up emotion, muddying the waters. In the past two weeks there had not been one clear day. Small things continually seemed to tug at her. She just wanted to forget, to lie down at night and no longer be filled with the ache. More and more, getting to sleep was an impossible ordeal, and she wanted to ask her doctor at the Health Services for a prescription, but she was afraid of her mother's old habits. Besides, a small snifter of brandy in bed seemed to do the job just as well.

Opening the door, Kat moved through the suite without calling to Helena. She wanted to be alone. Her life was like a beach strewn with wreckage: driftwood, ships' ropes and spars, sharks' teeth, kelp, starfish, sea hair, crates of opened lives, lost and found, all tumbled together in a tangle by the surf. She didn't know where to start sorting, or who to ask for help. She was beyond talking about it. Other people could not see that it was impossible simply to put it behind her. To forget totally. To resume life just as though nothing had happened. They could not see that death was a process, with all its necessary red tape, its wills and documents, its funerals and wakes, mementos and reminders. At best, she could stave off the knowledge that she had lost her mother for a few hours by burying herself in her schoolwork. But that left the rest of the day to pick over the tidal pools.

She sat at her desk for the better part of an hour. Her clear hazel eyes were disturbed, her thin lips compressed into a straight line. Sitting still, engulfed by her thoughts, was a new habit, and sometimes she could manage no more than this. At least it was controlled. It was the dreams that were really bothering her, the dreams she was trying to escape, the dreams she wanted to rub out. Last night she and Lily had gone to lunch at the Ritz. They had had vichyssoise and crab salad. They talked about Kat's English exam and about Aaron. Lily wanted to know more about him, she wanted to like him. She told Kat how she had first met Kirk, how they had fallen in love. Then her face grew lined and worn. She got up and left the table. Kat called after her but she moved silently toward the exit. The maître d' came toward Kat from the far side of the room, pushing a long dessert cart over the blue oriental rug. As he came nearer, Kat saw it was a long box, a satin-lined crib. And then it was Lily sitting up in her coffin, it was Lily with her eyes closed, her face pale and perfect, her mouth moving open and closed like an obscene fish. It was Lily reaching out for Kat, reaching out with her hands, reaching out with her mouth.

Kat had come violently awake, grappling with a fear so intense she thought it would kill her. She'd thought she would die there in the dark, alone. She'd tried to comfort herself: it was only a nightmare. But then she'd remembered. The loss flooded through her layers of consciousness, one by one. In the dark she remembered once again that her mother was dead. The pain was even greater than when she had first heard. And so it went, night after night.

There was a hammering at the door, and she opened it reluctantly. Aaron carried the familiar wooden paint box in his hand, dented and scratched, stained with paintstreaks and charcoal smudges. She had forgotten; he had come to sketch her, and now she wanted no part of it.

"Aren't you a little overdressed?" She regretted the bitchy tone in her voice right away, but didn't know how to stop it.

"Sure." He waved a paper bag in her face. "But don't worry—I've got my tux in here."

"Where have you been?"

"Meeting with my adviser," he said, stripping off his clean corduroys quickly. Kat turned aside, still a little shy at the sight of him so naked in the daylight. She watched him in the mirror over her shoulder. He never wore underwear. Secretly, she liked to look at him because men's bodies still seemed a combination of inconsistencies to her, and she had not seen enough of them to be bored yet.

Clothed, he moved into the living room. "Sit in the bay window," he instructed. "I like the angle of the sun."

Kat perched stiffly on the cushions Helena had made for the window seat. She always liked reading here: the window overflowed with philodendron, asparagus fern, coleus, and spider plants.

"Now move your head a little to the left."

At her left elbow was a large conch shell filled with soil and planted with different cuttings like a small terrarium. Helena was good with her hands, had a gift with green-leaved lives, Kat thought. She'd never had much experience with plants—her mother hadn't liked the dirt or the bugs. Now she felt there was no point to wasting time on a plant when it would only shrivel up and die in the end.

Aaron scowled. "Kat," he said, exasperated. "You're going to have to relax."

"Then stop watching me like a hawk." Springing up off the seat, she went into the bedroom, picked up her hairbrush, and started snapping it through her hair. He followed.

"What's going on?"

"Nothing." The air crackled with the static of her movements. "You're upset," he observed quietly.

"Don't project." She smirked. "What's wrong—are you on the rag today—"

"Look—"

"—or did your conference with Sanders get rough?"

"Quit fencing around. Come back out here. Let me get to work. *Please.*"

She sat down again, sunlight across her shoulders, glinting off her hair, emphasizing the shadow under her eyes. He sketched quietly, his pencil scratching against the paper. The silence felt less threatening now. She began to wonder how he was seeing her, how he was putting her down.

Aaron was once again absorbed with the angle of the jawbone. It was the line that eluded him. He made it rounder, softer; but that wasn't right either. He blurred it out, started over.

"You haven't mentioned your mother all week," he said, looking up at her. "Are you missing her today?"

He was so direct it took her by surprise. "I want her back," she answered without thinking.

He was quiet. She traced the outline of her cuticle with a fingernail. "There's nothing any more. I miss talking with her." She bent her head, fighting the urge to cry. "No—that's not right. I guess maybe we didn't really talk all that much."

Lily Sinclair had been a woman of very few words. She ran her household efficiently, measuring out time and attention judiciously, the way other women measure out their recipes. She and Kat shopped together, went to the ballet and museums together, planned social functions together. But Lily had always been a bit formal. Her manner carried a touch of professionalism—this was what she did for Kat because this was what a good mother did for her daughter. Kat craved something deeper, more intimate— the inner petals of her mother's life. She had sat quietly by her mother for years, hoping and watching for an opportunity.

It never came. Over time Lily had only become more and more fragile, more difficult to touch, more unreal—a human being who survived each day on a chemical cushioned relief.

"I'll never know her now," Kat said, talking to herself as much as to Aaron. "That's what really hurts. Not like the way I wanted to."

"But if it was never there, how can you miss it?" he interrupted. He had stopped drawing and the pencil rested loosely in his fingers. It seemed to him that what she was saying was basic to his drawing. If he could understand it better, he could find the angle of that elusive curve.

"But there were things that were good!" she said defensively. "Afternoons by the fire—we wouldn't talk, but we'd be there together. There was a link. Maybe not what I was looking for, but a link anyway."

"Give up that fantasy. Give up that illusion. Even if she was still alive, you'd eventually have had to give it up. It would never have happened."

He looked at the pad, and saw then that perhaps the angle where the jaw and ear joined was not curved enough. The connection had not been made—it was not what he'd expected to find, yet it was what was needed. "Tilt your head a little to the side." He went over to her and ran his pencil against the sharp ledge of bone again. Yes, he said to himself. He had been trying to make the line too distinct. It was an optical illusion that the line was sharp. He needed to show just how it joined the face, became a part of it, in a subtle soft curve. He returned to his pad and worked silently for a while.

Kat watched him as he drew, so absorbed. His hands were definite, reaching out and taking hold of what he saw. His mouth was tight with concentration, and she envied, for a moment, his sense of purpose, of drive. She wished she had something to feel so passionate about. His sense of direction was unfailing, one of the most attractive things about him. He was not good-looking in any classic sense—too many of his features were irregular for that. His long nose, which owed its bump to a tussle with a hockey stick, his dark hair never laying flat, his shirts continually untucked. He had a tousled appearance—as if he were always caught in mid-flight. But his eyes were so dark they had an extraordinary depth, with lashes and brows black and thick and straight. His whole face revolved around those eyes.

"I know how it feels," he continued, subdued, picking up a new pencil. "I know how it feels to give up a fantasy. I wanted my parents that way. I spent all of adolescence getting in trouble before I finally accepted the inevitable." He laughed bitterly and shifted the pad on his lap. "That's why they sent me to Andover —because my problems were inconvenient. They didn't want to deal with me."

Aaron's parents belonged to New York's beautiful set. Circulating with the financially successful, with chic couture designers, celebrities, the social elite, they dined out every evening and saw their children rarely. While Mr. Salzer concentrated on his real estate business, Mrs. Salzer worried mostly about which part of her body to have lifted next. She was a professional socialite who clothed herself only in designer originals and was courted—often paid—to attend social functions because her name on the guest list guaranteed a prominent mention of the gathering in the next issue of *Women's Wear Daily*.

"There's still a part of me that's angry, I guess." He shrugged. "But little by little I'm accepting the situation. In the long run, giving in is just easier."

Kat looked up at him. For all his nonchalance, anger had brought a flush to his translucent skin. She felt a surge of protective love. "How did your meeting with Professor Sanders go?" she asked, suddenly remembering.

"Fine." He shrugged and took up his pencil again. "Nothing new."

"Well, what did he say?" She started to fidget with the button on one of the cushions.

"I told you! Nothing." He looked up at the ceiling. "I'm sorry, I don't mean to be bitchy. I'm just tired of having him tell me what I already know."

"Sometimes that's what you need to hear," Kat remonstrated.

"Oh hell, I know I've got to make a decision! I don't need to be told that! I just need to make up my mind." He rubbed his fingers together and sighed loudly. "Sanders doesn't understand at all. He says being an architect will guarantee me a reasonable income and I can draw on the side. In my *spare* time."

"Can't you?"

"Sure I *can*. That's not the point. The point is, to do something seriously, you can't just do it with your left hand."

"So tell Sanders to forget it." She shrugged as if that could end the discussion. "Nobody can force you to spend five years in grad school."

"I've got to support myself somehow!" he said sarcastically, as if it were patently obvious.

The familiar irritation crept up her throat and she felt keenly her own ambivalence about the future. Once again, graduation day bobbed up as a deadline, a threat. He should be glad he's got so many options, she thought bitterly to herself. She pressed her lips together. "Aaron, we've been over this before—money isn't the problem. You've got money to burn." She rose and shook out her legs.

"But that's *their* money!" he said vehemently, slicing the air with his hand. "I want something of my own. It's not as easy as just deciding to draw. I'm not going to suck at the tit of my trust fund for the rest of my life."

"Well, it's easy to see why Sanders is pushing you—you're his golden boy and it'll look bad for the department if you shelve it now."

"I know," he admitted. "That makes it even worse. I don't like to let him down. And besides, he's right. The practical Aaron and the dreamer Aaron are arguing." He looked down at the pad on his lap and laughed. "Five years ago I was a fire-breathing radical. Look at me now—worried about making money."

Despite her jealousy, she suddenly found herself smiling at him.

"Listen," Aaron said, picking up his pencil. "The light's going. Give me ten more good minutes."

She consulted her watch. "You've got twenty. Then I'm due at a meeting."

The telephone rang. "Damn! Will you try not to talk too long?"

She nodded and picked it up. Her voice dropped; her face sobered. Aaron knew right away that her father was on the other end of the wire.

"Just fine," she said, twirling a curl around her index finger. "Nothing much is going on. Did you get the letter from Eliot Rutledge?"

"I guess Monday's the day," Kirk answered with a brittle gaiety which grated on Kat. "Will you be able to get away?"

"No problem." She gave Aaron an uncomfortable look. "How is your day going?" she asked her father.

"Just fine." He changed the subject quickly—too quickly. "I'm in a great mood. I just took Jim Powers for a hundred bucks in gin."

"Jim Powers?"

"Fellow works down the hall."

"Sounds like you're getting a lot of work done," she teased. Giving her an irritated look, Aaron stood and began to pace. Kat held up her hand, motioning for him to be patient.

"Just a couple of hands to pass a few slow hours," Kirk answered brightly. "Will you be home for dinner this Sunday?"

"Sunday?" Kat echoed, distracted. There was a short pause.

"Standing rib roast—your sister is coming out."

Guilt. She thought of him alone in front of the fire night after night. But she had planned a study session with Helena for Sunday.

"Of course I'll be there." She hid the conflict in her voice. Aaron stomped off into the bathroom with a sigh.

Kirk sounded pleased. "Maybe you'd like to get together for a drink tonight?"

"Can't. I'm off to a meeting about the publishing business and then Aaron and I are going to dinner and a double feature."

Kirk was silent. "*Spellbound* and *Rebecca*," she offered, trying to win him a little. "You must've seen those years ago."

"Well, in that case, I won't hold you up any longer. We'll do it another time. See you Sunday at five."

She hung up the phone slowly and looked mutely at Aaron, who came back to sit down with a sigh.

"What's up?"

She shrugged. "He sounds so forlorn." She tapped her finger against the cradled receiver. "Damn it—he makes me feel guilty!"

"What for?"

"We're going out. He's alone." She spread her hands as if to say the two facts were irrevocably linked, like the change of fall to winter.

"Stop being ridiculous. Didn't you say you'd go out there Sunday?"

"Yeah, and Helena's going to be mad. I told her we'd study together."

"For Chrissakes, Kat, stop making so much out of everything. Helena'll understand." He sounded annoyed. "Anyway, why did you say you'd go if you didn't want to?"

Kat stared down at him. Aaron made everything seem so clear and reasonable. But when she talked with her father she got confused. She couldn't tell which direction she was moving in.

She went to the closet, pulling out her red down parka.

"I'll wait here," he said. "As soon as you get back we'll go."

"Sure," she said, brushing her hair back from her brow with a wave of her hand.

Kat sat on a folding chair in a grim, dilapidated room—a room not brightened any by a procession of discouraging speakers. She wondered why she had bothered to come, what she had expected to find.

She looked up at the podium, depressed. The editor from Little, Brown certainly didn't fit Kat's image of the sleek professional woman. She was dumpy, dressed in an orange and blue batik print dress. Her hair clumped on the top of her head, she looked overworked and bored with the idea of answering questions from college students.

"What is the job situation?" asked someone from the front row. "For entry-level spots? Who do you hire?"

The woman smiled patronizingly. "We tend to look for people

who've worked at newspapers or magazines, or other book houses. Or we promote someone in house."

Kat wasn't sure she understood. The logic seemed circular. She raised her hand. "But how do you get your foot in the door in the first place?"

Ms. Josephs looked amused. "I started in the steno pool at Random House two weeks after I graduated from Wellesley eight years ago."

Defeated, Kat sank back against her chair. The rest of the discussion flowed by unnoticed. Her mind was busy, worrying the situation. Look at the competition, she thought. Practically every woman in the whole English department was here. She applauded perfunctorily with the others as the meeting ended, then made her way into the small circle around Ms. Josephs, waiting her turn. "I have one semester left before I graduate," she said. "Isn't there something I can do to prepare myself for an editorial job?"

"Look," the woman said. "I was serious before. I'm honestly only trying to help. It's a long time before you get to do anything really good. If you're really serious about breaking in, brush up on your typing."

The hard edge of cold stunned Kat as she walked back to Adams House. She was still digesting Ms. Josephs' last remark, not knowing whether to believe her, when she felt a push at her elbow.

"Wasn't that incredible!" Helena said.

"Yeah, eat two pounds of shit a day for three years and they'll move you up to window washer."

"Screw it," declared Helena. "I'm not going to wait around the back door for handouts."

"I don't know," Kat sighed. They had reached the front of the dorm, and were starting up the stairs. "The thing is, a meeting like that makes me feel desperate. I've worked hard, pulled good grades, gotten good recommendations. Now this woman tells me none of it matters anyway." She took out her key and unlocked the door. "Let's face it. I should have been a bio major or a chemistry jock." She stopped in the doorway. "And I know just what Aaron's going to say."

"That's exactly what I think," Aaron said carefully. "Nobody forced you to major in English. I mean really, for women who always talk so much about having careers, neither of you has done much real planning. Get out there and hoof it! And if you have to start at the bottom, then that's what you've got to do." He smiled at Kat. "After all, it's the same for me."

The two of them had been arguing for a half-hour while they had sherry in Kat's room. She was on her second glass now and it was helping her to unwind, helping her to vent her frustration over the meeting. "You're so typical," she flared. "Don't lecture me—I'll be out there pounding on doors with everyone else." She squinted at him angrily, knocking down the last of her sherry. At this moment she hated him. Why should she go to the movies with *him*? He was just like all the rest. Why had she thought he was different? She stood and steadied herself against the desk as she poured them another glass.

"Kat. I'm sorry."

"Great." She shook her head. Apologies don't help, she thought. How dare he attack her at this precarious time, how dare he assault her? She withdrew from him silently, viciously, wanting only to hit, stab, damage. She was alone, totally alone, and she told herself not to forget it again. The self-sufficient never got hurt. She wouldn't let go of her anger. Like the sherry, it insulated her. It felt good.

The phone jarred the silence. Kat grabbed it.

"Well," her father said in a querulous voice, "I see you finally decided to come home."

"It's six o'clock," said Kat, confused. "I was only out for about an hour." She paused. "Are you all right?"

"Tried to get you last night and the night before."

"Dad?"

"Just sitting here in front of the fire, and thinking about you," he said with that same brittle brightness to his voice. Guilt swept through her again. "Wanted to talk to my girl and she wasn't home. What are you doing tonight?"

"I thought I told you earlier, Dad. Aaron and I are on our way to a double feature. *Rebecca* and *Spellbound*. Hitchcock."

"Oh." There was a small silence. "Well, what about this letter —can you leave your classes on Monday to come to Rutledge's office?"

Had their earlier conversation been a dream? Kat wished she hadn't had so much sherry; she felt fuzzy and disoriented. He was asking questions to which he already knew the answers. It didn't make any sense.

"Don't you remember, we discussed this earlier?" she asked quickly. Confusion crowded her words together. "Of course I'll be there."

"Earlier," he repeated in a puzzled tone. "Earlier when?"

"This afternoon. You called me two hours ago," she prompted. "I did?"

"You'd just finished your gin game with Mr. Powers. You were still at the office." She waited. "Dad, is something wrong? Are you upset?"

"No. No, Kat. Everything's fine. It just slipped my mind that we'd talked. I've got so much to think about and keep track of these days."

Fear ballooned in her head. It was hard to think. He had no recollection of the phone call. Was he losing touch with reality?

"Well, it was nice to hear your voice," he said. "Hope I'll see you soon."

"Sunday for dinner. I'll be there by five." She hung up, uncertain that he even remembered the date, but she couldn't bear to ask him.

"What the hell's going on?"

Hearing the voice, she looked up. She had forgotten Aaron, who had gone out into the living room.

"That was my father," she said with difficulty, slumping into her desk chair and finishing her sherry.

"I figured that out for myself. What the hell did he want this time?"

"He didn't remember that we already talked on the phone today."

"Didn't remember?"

"Just what I said." She looked limp. "He didn't remember a thing we said, a thing we talked about. I had to tell him the same stuff all over again." Her voice quivered. "Oh, Aaron—what's happening to him? To us?"

He came and put his arms around her. All her anger was gone now. She was just plain scared; she wanted to be near him; she needed him to give her a reasonable answer.

"Did he sound drunk or something?"

"No." She wiped away a tear. "He sounded sort of . . . hysterically cheerful. I can't quite describe it, but the same thing was in his voice when he called this afternoon."

"Maybe he just had something to drink and got a little mixed up. He's working hard, he's got a lot on his mind."

"You're probably right." She didn't sound in the least convinced.

It would torture her all night long, she thought. How could she go to the movies now? She got up and started pacing. Aaron refilled their sherry glasses again.

"You've got to relax," he pointed out. "Getting raced over this isn't going to help anything."

She sat down beside him on the couch. She knew he was right, but the whole thing was so insane. She shivered. She was so tired, and even a little dizzy. Aaron stroked her hair, and she relaxed against him. His fingers played on the tender place at the back of her neck where her curls turned into down. He knew she loved to be touched there.

"How about a backrub?"

She wanted to say no, but he was trying so hard. Reluctantly she stretched out on the bed, face down. "Come on," he said gently, "take off your shirt." He helped her pull the turtleneck off over her head, and she pressed her skin against the cool quilted bedspread. She crossed her arms in front of her, and rested her head there. She tried to relax, but her mind kept churning. She could see Aaron out of the corner of her eye, see the way he was studying her, studying the slope of her slender waist as it flared out into her buttocks. She watched the lean muscles in his arms working as he began on her shoulders and the back of her neck, his strong fingers kneading the tension away.

It felt great, she had to admit it. She was starting to feel sleepy and warm, the sherry lying like a hot puddle in her stomach, and she raised no objection when Aaron began working her jeans down over her hips and off. His hands massaged her ribs, knuckling down over each vertebrae, relaxing her. He hesitated at the small of her back, taking an extra minute there, and then moved on, taking first one round cheek and then the other, pushing in deep against the bone. Kat began to feel a flush spreading up against her belly, the pressure from the rub moving her pubic bone against the mattress. Aaron's fingers gently squeezed the soft curve of inner thigh.

His weight shifted on the bed, and he moved on top of her before she could protest. The length of him lay over her, his mouth on her neck. Lifting her hair, he touched her earlobe. She felt herself slipping away, as though there were another person in her body. She felt herself getting ready for him. Slowly her legs moved apart. Now he rested just outside her. She was wet and he slid himself up and down against that wetness, over the small nub where her pleasure crouched, up and down until she broke the silence. She lifted her hips so that he sank down into her, slowly, and she expanded around him, opening herself up like wet, moist earth, sucking him in with all her desire. She could barely move. The pleasure was too intense. Her mind stopped working. She was only body.

He was strong inside her and she put her hand down to feel them where they joined. And she touched herself too, and began to feel her own heat overtaking her. She quickened their rhythm, and he moved with her, faster as the waves moved faster, and she hooked him, pulling him deeper, never wanting to let go. His stomach muscles tightened against her back, and his thighs tensed against her thighs, and she felt the quiver of him inside her, faint as a butterfly.

He lay on her quietly, kissed her neck again. She felt him receding from her, like the tide going out, sucking at rocks and shells. He rolled off her and propped himself on an elbow. She turned on her side and they faced each other.

"I guess we missed the movies," she said softly.

"Well, actually," he said in his most quietly exuberant tone, "the first feature just started. If you're not too hungry we could just eat popcorn and I'll fill you in on the plot."

She started to laugh as he bounced up from the bed and pulled on his jeans. He was trying so hard to cheer her on.

"You see, Ingrid Bergman's this psychiatrist who falls in love with Gregory Peck, who you think is a lunatic murderer . . ."

Seven

MASON, RUTLEDGE & STONE OCCUPIED THE TOP THREE STORIES IN A stately old Boston building on Tremont Street. The suite of Eliot Rutledge stretched across the front of the building, its busy noises muffled under thick old oriental rugs. The intricate sailing prints mounted on every available wall seemed to indicate Rutledge was a sailing buff, or else liked to pretend he was. A model clipper ship done in teak and ivory stood on the coffee table in front of the long velvet couch.

Against his surroundings, Rutledge himself was all the more undistinguished. Short, stumpy, and bald, his most distinctive feature was the cauliflower ears which protruded from either side of his wrinkled face.

Rutledge watched the three Sinclairs as he shuffled the papers on his desk, getting ready to begin the meeting. He was not looking forward to this. He'd been Lily Sinclair's trust officer for nearly thirty years—since she'd come into her large and complicated inheritance. He'd known both her children since they were little, and he had a certain protective urge toward them: Kat, sitting up so straight in her stiff-backed chair, trying to be brave, trying to be adult and responsible, trying to be the strong one; and Paige, looking cool and unperturbed, looking as though nothing had happened. He marveled at the magnificent mask she wore. But he also knew her well enough to see that her hands

trembled as she lit a cigarette, that beneath her cool smile her
eyes were really desperately sad. And then there was Kirk, subdued, clamping his teeth into his cigarette. Yes, he thought as he
cleared his throat to begin, they faced him like a trio of expect-
ant children waiting to hear the gypsy tell their fortunes.

Kat was not feeling well this morning, and she bit back a wave
of nausea as Rutledge began. The family dinner last night had
provoked her into drinking too much and she was just a little
hung over now. She had arrived in Concord a bit nervous and
apprehensive, unsure of her father's emotional stability. But the
evening had consisted mainly of a two-sided enthusiastic debate
about ice hockey—athletics being one of the passions Kirk and
Paige had shared for years. It was Paige, this time, who had
stood before the fire, mixing the martinis. Kat had been confused. She was glad to relinquish the responsibility she felt for
her father, yet at the same time she felt rejected and replaced.
Paige, in fact, *had* managed to make time for Kirk on Friday
night and she vivaciously compared notes with her father on
every last detail of their meal at the Ritz. All this had only
deepened Kat's sense of isolation. She had had more martinis
and then more wine than she intended, and by the time she went
back to Cambridge, her depression was acute. She had not
looked forward to seeing them again today, and hearing Kirk
had picked up Paige in Chestnut Hill on his way to town only
made her feel even more cut off.

"To simplify things," said Eliot Rutledge, looking up at them
over his glasses, "let's just say all this boiler plate means basi-
cally one thing. Mrs. Sinclair left her estate divided in thirds, one
part to each of you."

Kat looked over at her father in surprise. Once again, his expression had that bright, glassy quality to it. She had expected
her mother simply to leave it all directly to Kirk, and from the
look on his face, so had he.

"Mrs. Sinclair's portfolio will be split in three separate trust
funds, one for each of you. I have been appointed trustee, along
with State Street Bank."

"Mr. Rutledge," interrupted Kat with astonishment, "there are a couple of things I don't understand."

"Yes," interjected Paige, lighting another cigarette. "Can you tell us just how much money we are going to get?"

Rutledge coughed and shifted uncomfortably behind his desk; Paige's bluntness was growing with the years. His fat hands stroked the barrel of his gold Mont Blanc fountain pen, as he shot an embarrassed look at Kirk Sinclair—obviously thinking to himself that only a child would have asked such a question directly.

"Each trust will have equal proportions of blue chip stocks and bonds," he said carefully, "which generate an extremely generous income each quarter." He shuffled the papers in front of him. "Let me see. There are shares in Exxon, British Petroleum, Xerox, AT&T, IBM." He paused, as if he hoped this would satisfy her.

"But Mr. Rutledge," Paige persisted, "just what is all that worth?"

He sighed and gave in. "The liquid securities that we feel will remain after taxes in Mrs. Sinclair's estate amount to approximately four million for each of you, at current market value. Under the terms of the trust instrument, half of the girls' income is reinvested, half disbursed to them as beneficiaries. Assuming a rough return of twelve per cent on the present value of these investments, I'd say you two will each receive about $240,000 a year, after taxes."

It seemed stupendous to Kat. She had no idea of the value of so much money, could not imagine it, what it could do, or what it could buy. She had not expected any money at all, and she felt elated. Even more—relieved; it was so much that she didn't need to panic about nailing down a job before graduation day. She would never have to worry again.

She looked sideways at her father and was disconcerted to see the stunned expression still on his face. Of course, his $480,000 was much less than he'd been expecting, she realized. The old arguments, money over martinis, symphonies of anger coming at her through the floor—it all echoed through Kat again.

Rutledge went on calmly, ignoring the emotional turbulence coursing through the room. "The next matter which concerns us today is that of the seventh provision in the will. Here Mrs. Sinclair states that she forgives Mr. Sinclair any indebtedness due her from him at the date of her death."

"What's all that?" asked Paige.

Kirk quickly seemed to find his voice. "That's a reference to some personal business your mother and I concluded many years ago." He was casual but definite. He looked only at Rutledge. "How odd she should mention it."

Rutledge paused. His hesitation did not pass unnoticed by Kat, and once again she felt vaguely uneasy. Something was going on. She started to speak up, but then thought better of it. Not in front of her father, she decided suddenly.

Rutledge plowed on. "Finally, Mrs. Sinclair bequeathed the Concord residence—left to her by her father, including all furnishings and art—to you, Mr. Sinclair, and the old family summer house in Padanarum to the girls." He gestured to Paige and Kat. "Her personal effects—clothing, books, jewelry, and so on—are to be divided between her daughters equally. And there are several minor but generous cash gifts to the household staff." He pushed a button on his phone board and his secretary marched in on cue, carrying a large armful of documents. "These," he said, as he doled them out in small stacks, "are your copies of all the legal material involved at this stage in the settlement of the estate. When you have a minute you would be well advised to go over them in careful detail. We certainly want you all to understand everything." He smiled patronizingly at the two sisters. "Do either of you have any questions?"

"Not right now," said Kat, thinking quickly. "But I might after I go through all this. May I call you?"

He nodded congenially. "Of course."

You'll be hearing from me, Kat said to herself, as they stood and shook hands. Tomorrow.

Eight

KAT LOOKED AT THE SMALL FACE OF HER WATCH. IT WAS ONE-THIRTY now, precisely. She stood, put down her magazine, returned to the dining room hopefully, and then allowed the maître d' to seat her at Rutledge's empty table.

She had eaten at the Harvard Club many times before because her father was a member, but now she took an exaggerated interest in the smallest of details, as if to filter her nervousness through the familiar surroundings. Today, all this was a new arena. Today, she would take nothing for granted.

She studied the silverware, the flower in its bud vase, the closed grand piano, the pattern of the oriental carpet, the man on her left. Now it was one-forty. She wished suddenly that she had been late. Why did people always make you wait. All her life she had been prompt, or, as today, ten minutes early. To keep someone waiting meant you had the confidence to assume they would not leave.

She checked her watch again. One forty-five. The room was beginning to fill with middle-aged men in three-piece suits. This was the world of the business lunch and she was the only woman there.

She'd never been to a business lunch, had never dealt with sticky technical issues such as those she would raise today. Over the weekend she and Aaron had gone through the estate papers, and he'd helped her to pin point and define her questions. But all the minutiae was just an excuse, a cover, for the central issue —her father's debt. She flipped through the material in her brief-case, and checked once again to make sure she had everything she would need.

"Sorry to keep you waiting," Rutledge said, sitting down heav-ily in the chair across from her. A smile creased his pudgy face into a series of concentric circles. Damn him, she thought, he looks perfectly at home. And why not? Men have been eating lunch here for two hundred years. Women weren't even allowed as members until 1970.

She put on her best young lady's smile. "Not at all. I've been admiring the club."

"Dewars on the rocks, Mark," Rutledge said to the waiter who appeared at his elbow. He picked up his menu. "Katherine?"

"Martini, extra dry, with a twist," she replied without missing a beat. She crossed her legs, satisfied with herself, and smoothed the wool of the navy dress down over her knees. A martini was the most sophisticated drink. That was important today.

"How's school?" Rutledge asked conversationally. "You're looking very well." She was dressed smartly, more smartly than he'd ever seen her, he thought to himself. In fact, he was sure he'd seen that dress before; he was sure it had belonged to Lily. Over his menu, he judged that she'd even used a little make-up. Her presence had an aura more compelling, more sought after, more satisfying than mere beauty: it was class, he decided. She looked quite like Lily's mother—a strong-boned, powerful woman whom he'd met when he first joined the firm. Kat did not have the fragile beauty of her mother; it was Paige who had inherited that.

He liked this young woman, liked the air of intelligent naïveté which hung about her. He knew why she had asked him to lunch; he knew he could not lie to her; he knew he must simply try to avoid answering her questions fully. If she were as clever as he hoped, she would not need him to come right out and make everything plain. She would draw conclusions of her own, conclusions which had nothing to do with him. He had no intention of endangering his relationship with Kirk Sinclair, however much he distrusted the man.

"School's fine," she said. "I've finished my thesis, and now all that's left is my general exams." She consulted her menu. "How's the fish here?"

Rutledge pulled the chit toward him with a certain familiar pride, and wrote out their order: sole amandine, steak, another Dewars, another martini. Kat drew a legal-sized yellow pad from the leather envelope beside her chair and took out the Xeroxed copies of the trust accounting Rutledge had given her at the meeting. "I have just a few questions," she said, "and I know you're busy, so I'll get right down to it."

"There's no rush," he said.

"I'd just as soon," she said, anxious to get it all over with. "Take a look at page fifteen. On the bottom. Is this figure a total *after* the disbursement for attorney's and executors' fees? Or before?"

With a sigh he pulled out his copy of the document. No, he thought, he had not overestimated her. "That's computed after those expenses," he replied.

She made a note with her pencil. "On page twenty-five," she directed. This had been one of Aaron's questions, and she'd written it down carefully on her yellow pad. "When we sell stocks to cover estate expenses. What basis do we use for capital gains tax? Someone told me Congress is thinking of changing the rules."

Rutledge was surprised. "Did you ever consider law school?" he asked lightly. For someone so inexperienced, her questions were really remarkably incisive. "Don't worry—even if they change the law now, it won't affect any estate going to probate before 1983." He sipped his scotch, waiting.

This discussion, although not entirely trivial, was an obvious stall. One day, he thought, one day she would be a tough customer. But it took courage to ask about something you did not really want to confront, and he wasn't sure how much courage she had. He would volunteer nothing. He would use his silence, his perfunctory answers, as a defense against her curiosity. Then he would see what she was really made of.

Kat felt he was playing with her. She was fighting a gray panic. These minor points about trust figures were surely transparent. She felt skewered by his eyes, a moth on the end of a pin, twisting, turning, trying desperately to move onward. Suddenly she was angry. "Tell me," she said quickly, fueled by the slow flare of emotion, sipping her drink again. "Tell me about this debt. From my father to my mother on page eighteen of the will."

Rutledge's face gave way to surprise for only an instant. She had made the connection so suddenly, just when he'd been thinking she wouldn't be able to touch the issue. Still, her question was vague, without specific focus; now he must tell only enough to satisfy, not enough to pique.

"I believe the clause is quite specific," he said carefully as he forked up a bite of steak and smiled at a colleague across the room. "Your mother forgave your father several notes which she held."

"What sort of loans were they?"

"Business transactions, I believe."

Kat cut into the fish before her, and mulled this over. She noticed that his chin blended into his neck without a ripple. He was too clever, she decided. She would have to test him. "Do you know when Dad borrowed the money?" she asked, in an offhand way.

"He said the other day that it was quite some time ago."

"I was a little confused by that—what do you think 'quite some time ago' means?"

Rutledge was silent, studying the steak and potatoes on his plate, impassive. Kat could not tell what he was thinking. But this time the silence was her weapon.

"I don't know," he said uncomfortably. "Perhaps a number of years." He shrugged. "But of course, people have different ways of speaking."

Kat was ready now. "How many years? Ten? Twenty?"

Rutledge only stared at her.

"I would say six months ago was quite recent. Wouldn't you?" She kept looking at him, hard. She was tired of playing cat and mouse. "You were her trust officer—you knew every move she made. Are you going to tell me what's going on?" she demanded. "Because I found a stack of IOU's in my mother's desk. Lots of them—and they started only three years ago and the last one was dated this past October."

He ran his tongue over his lips. "I think it's very simple." He had not anticipated her actually knowing anything. What else did she have? "Your mother lent your father money."

"Why?"

"I assume he needed it."

"What for?" Her best young lady's tone gone, she was firing point-blank.

"I believe he used the money to reduce his business's bank loan balance."

"To reduce his loan balance?" She stopped to think for a minute. "You mean, to pay off loans?"

"Yes," Rutledge said unwillingly. He was beginning to feel angry that he had to deal with this inquisitive young woman. Suddenly she seemed quite headstrong.

"But doesn't that strike you as odd?" she asked, rubbing her temple in confusion. "After all, my father had capital of his own. Why, the business itself is worth a great deal. Why didn't he use his own money?"

"He did."

"I don't understand," Kat said. "If he used his money, why did he need Mother's too?"

Rutledge poked at his steak, not answering. When he looked up, he saw her clear hazel eyes register disbelief.

"You mean the debts were so great he couldn't cover them by himself?" A frozen calm settled over her. The feeling of panic ceased; the fear was a part of her now, a cold deadly part of her. She would know it all; she would not stop here. "You mean he sold out his own portfolio?"

Rutledge looked at her mutely. It had come anyway, he thought to himself, resigned. Despite Lily's precautions. She'd never wanted anyone to know of Kirk's financial difficulties, and now her daughter had unearthed it all. He felt sorry for Kat, sorry she had gotten her foot into this wasp's nest. She would never be able to look at her father in the same way again, he thought ruefully. Lily had wanted to protect Kirk from that.

"Business has not gone well for your father," Rutledge began quietly. "Having inherited the company while still young and inexperienced, he made a few bad mistakes. Mistakes cost money. And in recent years, the New England shoe industry has been leveled by imports."

Nausea. Another part of the world as Kat knew it was melting away. She'd always idolized her father's business sense. How could this be? Surely this was not true? She put her legal pad back in her briefcase. Mechanically she lifted her martini and finished it. "Thank you for telling me."

Rutledge could see she was just holding on. He did not want her to break down. "Frankly, I'm sorry you found out. Your mother never wanted you to know. Before he borrowed anything from her he sold off his own stock and the business itself borrowed heavily from an insurance company. But Sinclair Shoe was never profitable enough to reduce the principal on the loans. He took money from your mother to prevent the company from foreclosing and taking control. Now he'll have to come up with alternate funding."

Kat was silent.

"I'm sorry to have to tell you all this," he said uncomfortably.

She looked at him dully. "It's important that I know. So that I can decide what's to be done."

He did not understand what she meant, and he did not ask.

"Thank you for lunch. I'll be in touch." She stood, offered her hand briefly, and left the dining room. Rutledge looked down at his unfinished steak, cold with congealed fat, and picked up his knife and fork.

Kat hit the pavement with a fast hard step, and began to walk straight down Commonwealth Avenue. There was a lot of ice on the street, and heavy sleet melted against her cheeks and eyelids. She did not stop to put up her umbrella.

Once again life was pulsing through her like a swollen river in a narrow channel, drumming its way through, out of control. She wanted to still it, to push it aside. It was the enemy: she fought back the only way she knew how—by making her mind blank, as if she were retarded and knew no better.

On either side rose the townhouses of Boston's gracious Back Bay, quiet under the weight of the weather, their stone steps, leaded windows, and arched entryways coated with a veneer of shining ice. Once, several generations back, Kat's family had made their home here—before the exodus to the exurbs. Now the townhouses were split into apartments, and the old standard of living was a thing of the past.

A central promenade ran the length of the avenue, empty today of its usual dog-walkers and bench-sitters, and Kat crossed over to the glistening walkway. There was no one to bother her, and now she moved slowly. Even the cross streets, named alphabetically in descending order, carried no traffic or carriage trade. The electrified gas lamps were not yet lit, as it was still early, but the gray overcast made it seem as lonely and dim as four o'clock.

She lowered herself onto a wooden bench slippery with sleet, and looked around dumbly. Her vision seemed peculiarly intense. Each vivid detail held her mesmerized, like a sleepwalker or a child. The twigs on the forsythia bushes, the needled boughs of the evergreens, the stark veins of the sapling elms—she saw them all, all sealed in their fragile ice liner. All bent painfully under the new weight, pulled over toward their roots like unwilling dancers.

They will snap in half, she thought angrily. Going over to a small yew which was stretched nearly flat against the ground, she pried it up. Next she tried a young dogwood, but its spine was already cracked. Without thinking, she moved to the next, and then from tree to tree, from bush to bush, knocking ice off limbs with a clenched hand, not feeling the wet or cold. She was Joan of Arc. She did not think about what she was doing or why, she did not stop to wonder, to question, to reflect. She laid a blanket of ice, of silent ice, over her mind and over her fear; she steeled her will against the will of the storm. Somewhere between Gloucester and Fairfield she set her umbrella down to use her hands better, and she did not remember to pick it up again.

She released them all. At Exeter, she paused for a minute, before beginning on fresh ground at Dartmouth. None should die, she said aloud, as she wrestled with the ice. It slid off like a shiny snake's skin, and rasped against the ground. The branches boomeranged back against the sky. None should die. The avenue remained silent except for an occasional car sliding past. Boston had gone into hiding, and no one watched Kat on her strange dancing mission up across Clarendon, up across Berkeley. She was alone with the trees.

Commonwealth Avenue ended at Arlington Street, the Boston Public Gardens, and the Ritz. It was here, finally, that she noticed the gas lamps shining against the dim sky. It was here that she saw she had left her umbrella somewhere behind her. In an abstract fashion she realized she should call Aaron and tell him what had happened this afternoon. She would need to see him. He would help her decide what she had to do.

She crossed the street to the Ritz, with its line of yellow taxi cabs, and walked past the blue and gold doorman through the revolving doors, unaware of his startled glance. In the lobby, a large mirror reflected what he had seen: her hair plastered to her head, her cheeks and nose bright red with exertion, her clothing soaked and matted. She saw all this. She noticed, too, that the wool of her coat smelled like a wet dog. None of it registered, none of it mattered. She just headed for the bar, concentrating on locating a telephone.

She pulled off soggy leather gloves and dialed Aaron's number. Her fingers had no feeling in them at all. A busy signal buzzed against her ear, and she hung up. She leaned her head against the dial. She did not know what to do. A drink, she decided, a drink to clear her head. Her hands stung in the warmth now and as she climbed on a barstool she saw the green needles and bits of bark clinging to the breast of her coat for the first time. She brushed her hand over the surface furtively and then looked up. The bartender was standing in front of her expectantly.

"Extra dry martini, straight up, I guess." She looked around dully, and took her drink to a small table near the large plate glass window overlooking the sidewalk. She slumped into the warmth of the fabric-covered banquette and sipped; she did not notice the few miserable pedestrians who passed by just outside the glass. The steamed-over face of her watch said it was nearly four o'clock.

She got up to try Aaron again, feeling pressure, an urgent need to tell him what had happened. But the line was still busy, and she banged the receiver back onto the hook with despair.

Back at her table, there seemed nothing to do but order a new drink. As a waiter brought her a fresh glass, a tall woman with short, dark hair came in and sat down at a nearby booth. She ordered scotch on the rocks and turned to stare moodily out the window. "Bitch of a day," she said aloud to herself.

"The understatement of the year," Kat said, with a gloomy smile over her glass.

"The airport's closed."

"Along with the rest of the city."

"They *say* they might have one runway open by midnight," the woman continued.

"Are you trying to go someplace?" Kat asked. The gin was mellowing her a little by now; the problem was receding, pushed into some corner of her brain to be dealt with later.

"I'm waiting for a friend who's coming in from the Coast. That is, she *was* coming." She drummed her long fingers on the table top. "I'm Bea Daniels," she said, getting up and putting out her hand. "From D.C."

"Kat Sinclair."

"Join me?" Bea asked. "I'd be glad for a little conversation."

Kat hesitated for a minute, but she really wanted to be near someone, to talk to someone, and the fact that the bar was beginning to fill up convinced her. She was so alone, and as more and more businessmen filtered in it was increasingly uncomfortable to sit here as if she hoped to be picked up.

"What brings you to Boston?" Kat enquired when she had settled herself and her wet things at Bea's table. "Business or pleasure?" In the dim light she mentally catalogued her new acquaintance: late thirties, in a tailored suit, dark hair traced with a cobweb of gray, svelte figure.

"A little of both, I guess," Bea said. "I'm here researching an article I'm writing. But I'd hoped to connect with a good friend who was coming to town too. The snow's balled everything up."

"You're a writer?" Kat asked, as she popped the martini olive into her mouth, and ordered a third drink.

"Magazine articles."

"What magazine?" Kat asked, perking up noticeably.

"Freelance mostly. Right now, it's a city renovation piece, for the *Times* Sunday Magazine." She raised her glass and gestured with her other hand. "You're from Boston?"

"All my life."

"Well you know the renovation down at the waterfront. My piece is on the nation-wide trend to chic urban redevelopment. You know—Ghirardelli Square in San Francisco, Underground Atlanta, the Quincy Market in Boston."

"You're traveling around to see it all?"

Bea nodded. "I love it—traveling. Meeting new people, new places." She finished her scotch and gestured to a passing waiter. "What do you do?"

"I'm a senior at Harvard."

"A senior?" she echoed. "What're you planning for next year?"

"A job in publishing, I hope."

"Ah," Bea said, stirring her drink with her index finger. "Another moth to the proverbial flame. What's your strategy?"

"Strategy?"

"You know—how are you selling yourself? What have you got to offer?"

"Not much in the way of experience," said Kat, embarrassed. "I mean, just my degree."

Bea frowned. "Wrong," she said emphatically. "You *never* say that to anyone who's interviewing you. You *never* cut yourself down—that's basic. You *make* them believe you're better than every other poor slob off the street. Confidence." Bea fiddled with an earring and sized Kat up. "Got any connections?"

Kat laughed. "In banking, yes. In publishing, no."

"Well," Bea said, with a shrug. "Now you have me."

She spent the next hour dispensing free advice and anecdotes about the publishing business, and offered to pass Kat's name along to her contacts. Writing down a long list of names and addresses, Kat couldn't believe her luck. By five o'clock they were both very mellow; Bea was a great drinking partner, Kat decided—and disarmingly frank. She made no bones about admitting that she'd left her husband for another woman; that she was a practicing bi-sexual; that she had been waiting for her lover when the storm interfered. There was something cosmopolitan and risqué about her story, and it touched off Kat's hidden sense of adventure. She liked her own image, liked what she saw reflected in the mirror of the plate glass window. Here she was, sitting in the plush Ritz bar, heart to heart with a professional writer, pretending to be liberated, sophisticated, pretending to be unconcerned by these personal disclosures. The five martinis had brought down her inhibitions and she felt only an illicit sympathy, an illicit interest, as Bea talked about her new life. Her own problems had simply dissolved from her consciousness, and she forgot about calling Aaron after her last drink. There was a warm boozy companionship in being trapped together indoors, waiting. Her eyes shone, her cheeks flushed, her voice burbled out high and giddy. She had never felt more relaxed, more beautiful, more witty, more charming. She had made friends with a stranger, she thought to herself exultantly; this older woman was treating her as an equal, was impressed by her. Maybe she would find a job after all. She saw their conversation as intriguing, stimulating, intense, profound. It fulfilled all her fantasies. Bars really were wonderful places, she decided; look who you could meet when you weren't even trying.

She tried to flag down the waiter to order another martini, but Bea caught her hand.

"Hey," she said, "you look pretty looped already."

"No," Kat said, trying to focus on her new friend and failing.

She was slumped in the booth now and suddenly sleep overwhelmed her. She leaned her head back and closed her eyes.

"Come on," Bea said, throwing a bill on the table and stuffing
Kat's arms into the sleeves of her coat. "I'm sending you home."
Propping Kat on her shoulder, she steered her through the lobby
into a waiting taxi. "Listen, Kat," she joked, as she gave the cab-
bie the fare in advance, "I hope you don't make a habit of this.
You'd better give me a call when you wake up."

"Sure," Kat mumbled as the taxi moved off and she stepped
over the edge into oblivion.

Nine

LILACS AND WARM WEATHER AND PICNICS BY THE RIVER—SPRING
came to Cambridge. Kat and her classmates marched in caps
and gowns through the streets to the steps of Memorial Church
to hear their commencement ceremonies; and then dispersed, in a
blur of good-bys, to vacations before permanent jobs, or summer
jobs before graduate schools. Aaron was doing drafting for an ar-
chitectural firm in town before entering the Harvard Graduate
School of Design in the fall—a choice he had not made easily.
Helena had plunged right into the rank and file at Houghton
Mifflin as an assistant to an editor, but she wasn't kidding herself
any more about the typing.

Kat had decided to wait awhile before making plans, and
hadn't applied for anything at all. When the ceremonies in the
Yard were over, Kirk just packed her into the car, along with
four years of college living, and took her home to Concord.

Since her meeting with Rutledge in late March, Kat had put
most of her energy into worrying about her father, waiting for
his company to go bankrupt, and trying to decide what she
would do, what she would say. She wished he would confide in
her so they could discuss it openly and find a solution together.
This fear for her father was paralytic and to prevent disaster
seemed the only important thing now. She could not worry any
more about what she would do for the rest of her life, and she

and Aaron began to argue over her attitude—loud, violent arguments, arguments which went, for the first time, unresolved.

By mid-summer she was almost stuporous from the sun, from food and drink, and from the ever-growing need to protect her father. She was overcome with the lassitude of heat and water and light, and she loved the dulled narcotic feeling they gave her. She loved the tall screen of evergreens surrounding the pool for their gift of total privacy; she loved the idea that here, at least, the rest of the world was shut out. The July sun poured down like lava and when Kat dipped herself in the water, she could feel the heat steam off her body. She looked at herself critically through the clear water: since graduation she had been working on her tan full time, and she was brown. But could you ever be brown enough? she wondered idly, as she breast-stroked the length of the pool without getting her head wet.

"He's gone," Paige called, as she ran down from the house. "Break it out!" As if on command the five men and women on the far side of the pool began to peel their suits away from sweaty skin. Kat dove underwater, away from the sight of so many breasts and buttocks. She was embarrassed. She just wanted to be alone.

She came up for air and blinked the water from her eyes. "Are you sure he's gone for good?" she asked.

Paige looked down with a sarcastic smile. "You can't play eighteen holes in five minutes, you know." She stretched herself out on a chaise with defiance, next to her latest boy friend—a hairless young man with smooth skin.

Tamping down her anger, Kat swam to the other side of the pool and got out. She pulled her lounge chair to the far end, as far away from them as she could get, and tried to read. But their noise still crept into her space, catching at her, irritating her like a hangnail. Out of the corner of her eye she could see Paige holding court from a white chaise. Her lush brown body was evenly tanned, without a single strap mark, spread out carelessly under the sun.

Then she smelled it; the musky odor would always remind her of dormitory hallways, and its lure was too great. She hoisted herself up, walked over, and reached out for the pipe her sister was holding. "Great stuff," Paige said slyly.

Kat took a deep drag and it exploded inside her lungs. "What *is* this?" she asked in surprise.

"Thai stick," the hairless young man answered. "Opium grass."

Suddenly she was high. Like walking into a wall. She was flying. Above the houses, above the trees, above the clouds. Her body was very hot, her eyes electric, her mouth molten copper. It was so high she felt frightened, in a distant sort of way. She thought she might be losing her mind. With an enormous effort she got up as if hypnotized, and undid her suit. She mounted the diving board naked, and swanned into the cool gleaming water. It poured over her back and breasts. She swam like a dolphin, one perfect crisp length. Then she lay down in her chair on the other side of the pool, the sun burning its way into her lungs, her heart, her liver. She melted into the ocean of steady rays. Colored images danced on the screen of her eyelids. In her mouth, the sweet taste of butter-rum ice cream bloomed. She was stoned. Simply and utterly. And even though she was awake, she began to dream, as if asleep.

She dreamed the tree dream again. It was a tree she had never seen before, an old oak tree, fifty feet tall, standing guard on the very edge of a revolutionary Concord battlefield. She was a young girl, going down to her tree, the summer grass cool and damp under her bare feet. She rested her cheek against its rough bark, and put her small arms around its girth, around its strength, the power that flowed up from its root. She turned her face skyward. There was Paige, sitting high up, in the heart of her tree, hidden by its leaves, and she was laughing. She was laughing at Kat. Kat felt anger thicken in her throat, and she started climbing, hand over hand, toward her younger sister. Halfway up, the trunk began to shake and bend, the bark suddenly slippery and wet under her fingers. She was high over the ground now, slipping, trying to hold on, losing, shaken free, tossed out into the air. Paige's face spiraled away from her, smaller and smaller, a death's head of triumph.

She sat up in a hurry, sweating, anxious to wake, to get away from the ground coming up at her, and the sensation of falling. Aaron was standing at the foot of her chair, a stack of books in his arms, looking down at her.

"Good nap?"

"When did you get here?" she asked in confusion.

"Not very long ago. The tourist traffic in Concord Center is a bitch this time of year." He dumped the books on the ground and dragged a lounge chair beside her, draping his long frame over its slats. "I kissed you, but you were really out."

"What time is it? You're not supposed to come till two."

"It's two-thirty." He put his pale face up toward the sun. "Don't let me fry too long."

"You're whiter than a frog's belly."

He shaded his eyes. "Some of us work for a living, you know."

She took a deep breath and decided to let it pass. "How *is* life on the assembly line?"

He laughed. "A bore. Drafting—" he snorted. "—you can never do it right. All these prima donna architects with their precious designs." He took off his shirt. "Thank God it's only for the summer."

"So quit." She shrugged.

"I don't see how you can lie out here, doing nothing all the time," he remarked. "Don't you get bored?"

"Look," she said with an irritated edge to her voice, "don't beat on me. You're the one with the problem—it's a beautiful day and *you* bring your engineering books." She pressed her cheek against the towel morosely, weighted down by his disapproval. Why was he always picking at her, she wondered fretfully; hadn't she had enough this year? She sulked quietly for a while, annoyed each time Aaron flipped the page of his text, annoyed at his ability to concentrate. On the other side of the pool raucous laughter buoyed up and she watched the pipe making another round. She wished she could go sit with them. She would like another hit and a little light company. But Aaron would get mad. Still, she plotted, she could pretend to be going to the house for a soda, and maybe he wouldn't notice. She got up and put on her caftan. "Want a Pepsi?"

"Sure." He looked up with a smile. "Look, I'm sorry. Let's not fight today." He reached out and touched her hand.

When she came back with the Pepsi and lemonade, the dope was pushing her up again. She pulled off her robe and stretched out under the sun.

He grinned. "I take it your father's at the club?"

"Right." She poked him playfully. "And keep your eyes on *this* naked Sinclair."

"Don't worry—she may be blond and busty, but who can stand a woman with nothing but marijuana between the ears."

Suddenly Kat got a rush from the dope: she felt as if she'd swallowed the sun. An old song played in her head. *They call me mellow yellow,* she sang to herself.

"Did you get a chance to talk to your father yet?" Aaron asked seriously.

I'm just mad about saffron, she hummed. "Dad's O.K." *And saffron's mad about me.*

"That's not what I asked."

"I'll do it. When I'm ready," she said, swatting a mosquito from her leg. *They call me mellow yellow.* "It's not the right time yet."

"Why not?" He sat up. "As if I didn't know."

Electrical banana, it's bound to be the very next phase. "I'll know when. I don't want to humiliate him."

"It's time somebody stopped worrying about his pride, and got down to financial reality. Or else let him tackle all this on his own."

Silence.

"Kat?"

They call me mellow yellow.

"Earth to Kat? Where are you?"

"That's right. They call me mellow yellow."

Aaron reached over and grabbed her wrist. "What did you say?"

What had she said, she wondered in silent panic, had she said something aloud? "Did I say something?" she asked, squinting at him. Now the urge to laugh came over her hard and fast; she pinched her thigh in an effort to regain control.

Aaron's face cleared in sudden understanding. "I hate it when you're stoned."

"What makes you think I'm stoned?" Laughter started to leak out the corners of her mouth.

"A fool I may be, but blind I'm not. And stop giggling. It's not funny."

"There's plenty on the other side of the pool." She smiled and winked. "And I'm sure my sister wouldn't mind an extra mouth on her pipe."

He sat back in his chair and silently ran his finger back and forth over the edge of his book. Kat found herself wishing he would just go away. Why did he always have to ruin her fun? "What's your problem?" she burst out. "Don't you know how to relax?"

He looked at her speculatively. "It's not that at all. You just know how to relax a little too expertly and too often to suit me."

"Listen!" She was trying to think through layers of cotton. She blinked hard as if to clear her head. "It's been a hard year. I'm entitled to do anything I damn well please."

He sat forward on the edge of his chair and looked at her earnestly. "Kat. I know it's been tough. But you've got to pull yourself together."

She was silent. A nest of mourning doves called out from the weeping willow nearby, the only sound in the July air. Suddenly, she felt overwhelmed with self-loathing.

"Why are you so mean?" she said, crying.

"Kat, I'm not mean. I just love you. I'm *worried* about you—can't you see?" He pulled her to him. "Look, I'd just feel a lot better if you made a plan. A simple plan. For both of us."

"What kind of plan?" She wiped her nose, watching him.

"Well, we could get an apartment together—in the fall?" he suggested.

Her eyes were wary. "Do you mean it?"

He smiled at her. "Of course I mean it. And by then you'll be ready for a change. You'll be dying to get out and away from your family. You'll be ready to get a job, and start on something constructive. Something to focus your days around."

"I am being constructive now, you know," she bristled. "I'm taking care of my family. Organizing the house. Helping my father—"

"I know, I know. But there's not much future in it." He saw her face growing stubborn again. His criticisms came as threats to her. "We'll figure it out together. I promise." He got up and spread his towel on the grass under the cool willow. "It's hot," he said, "come lie here with me." She moved obediently beside him, and they lay there quietly for the rest of the afternoon, watching the leaves' pattern shifting on their skin, listening to the sad, everyday sound of the doves above them.

When the sun was low over the trees, Kat stretched. "Time to check on dinner."

Aaron opened one eye to look at his watch. "I didn't get a damn thing done." He sat up and rubbed the prickles in his arm from where Kat's head had been.

She stood up. "Will you stay?"

He laughed. "Sure. Might as well declare the day a total loss."

"I'd better tell Mrs. George." She pulled on her terry cloth caftan. "Dad should be here soon."

Kat walked around the pool, past the sleeping bodies and up the hill to the house. She entered the large kitchen, cool with its marble counter-tops and dark wood. Kat loved this kitchen—its efficiency, its warmth, its atmosphere of nurture. Mrs. George was laboring over a cold poached salmon. "How's it going, Mrs. G.?" Kat put her arms around her shoulder and surreptitiously sneaked a carrot. She crunched loudly into the nutty orange.

"Oh, Katherine," the housekeeper said in her Irish lilt. "Still stealing my ingredients like always." She gave Kat an affectionate look. "It's a nice piece of fish tonight—a good idea. Your father likes a cold fish on a hot night." She wiped her hands on her apron. "Have you picked the wine yet?"

"I'll do it in a minute." She watched Mrs. George take the herbed mayonnaise out of the refrigerator and scooped up some on the end of her carrot. She smiled in satisfaction. "Have you finished the raspberry sherbet?"

Mrs. George laughed. "Yes, but you keep away from it!" She began slicing a tomato. "What's the final count?" She sighed. "I notice your sister's friends are still here."

"I'll go check. At the least, Aaron and I will keep Dad company."

She went back down the hill, humming, in a good mood again. She liked running the house. She liked working with Mrs. George, making sure the meals were up to her father's standards. She wondered how much longer he could afford to keep up those standards; would they have to let the housekeeper go? She pushed the question aside firmly—she wouldn't think about it now; she'd wait till a better time.

At the pool Paige and her cronies were just rousing themselves from their stupor. "It's four-thirty," Kat said. "You'd better put some clothes on before Dad gets home."

Paige looked up at her lazily. "Cool your jets." She turned over on her other hip.

Her tone infuriated Kat. "Are you going to be here for dinner? Mrs. G. needs to know."

No answer.

"Paige?"

"Yeah?"

"Are you going to be here or not?"

"Don't get your bowels in an uproar. I'll let her know."

"Tell me now," Kat said in a deadly tone. By this time Paige's friends were watching the tug of war, amused at the way she was manipulating her older sister.

"Give up," Paige said over her shoulder. "You'll never be the perfect wife."

Kat looked as if she'd been slapped.

"If Dad's martini isn't made and his dinner on the table, it won't kill him to wait." Paige flipped onto her back and looked up at Kat with a certain superiority. "You'll never be Mom. Why try so hard?" She grinned, mocking.

It reminded Kat, in a sudden flash, of something else she knew well, but couldn't place. The words hurt her, exposed her, humiliated her. She hated herself. She hated Paige. Turning on her heel, she walked back to the house. Paige had never intended to stay for dinner; she had just been setting Kat up once again, almost diabolical in her psychological cunning.

Kat had wanted only to keep the family together, to create a sense of unity in the months since Lily's death—but Paige had fought her every step. She wanted to believe that Paige just resented her efficiency, that Paige was jealous, but rationalizing didn't help. Of course, nothing about Paige could really surprise her any more. Things never changed, she thought irritably, remembering all the times Paige had played one of them off against the other in front of their friends or their parents. When was the last time they weren't at odds? She stopped at the doorway into the house and leaned her head on her arm, thinking of the moment when her feelings for her sister had burnt into this acrid residue.

Maybe there had always been confusion, resentment, and hurt between them. But then Kat had seen for the first time, with utter clarity, how Paige moved the family around like chess pieces. With a deep sigh, she thought of that afternoon five years before.

Her sister had successfully routed a long line of tutors by being too stubborn to learn French, and so Lily and Kirk had asked Kat to help out for a few weeks. Kat had thought the session went well. She'd been so careful not to be too critical, played it light, joking, but still to the point. Paige seemed to deal well with her suggestions and corrections. She'd laughed at her mistakes, let a companionable air spring up between them. They were comfortable together and Kat felt elated. It had seemed there was love between them that afternoon.

Paige had pulled the session to a halt by suggesting that she go upstairs and tackle her French homework alone—calling on Kat with any specific questions. Kat had been pleased that Paige was willing to try on her own.

That night was one of those evenings when her parents had spent a long cocktail hour. They were glassily bright over dinner.

Kirk asked Paige how she liked Kat for a teacher. Resting her chin on her hands, Paige looked out wistfully from under that wave of blond hair. She looked so vulnerable, Kat thought, so helpless. She saw the sympathy slide across her parents' faces. She was really too dumb to be taught, Paige said, and she didn't blame Kat one bit for getting impatient and cutting their session short.

Kat hadn't been able to move. In disbelief she'd watched her parents move to shore up Paige, trying to encourage her, to bolster her ego. Kat felt their backs turn toward her: she had been cheated; the afternoon had no validity, no truth to it. What she'd felt had been made cheap. What had mattered to her had not mattered to her sister.

Hate had come into her then, brilliant and hard like a precious stone, and her heart had wrapped itself tightly around it. She'd wanted to yell at them, to set them straight. But she'd only sat frozen, trapped in her ego like a wounded child—self-righteous, angry, full of humiliated pride. She'd let them go on thinking what they wanted.

And so, just like that, in that small moment, in Paige's small lie, something inside her had kicked over, a brand-new engine. Kat shook her head now, trying to get free from the picture of that dinner table. She set her shoulders back and went on into the house, selected the wine, told Mrs. George to set three for dinner. Then she went to the porch.

The ice bucket was filled, the decanters shone out amber and clear like beacons. She lifted the martini pitcher and began the nightly ritual. This was her job. She didn't care what Paige said. Family rituals were the anchor. They were all that mattered, and she would continue to observe them all.

The sun was burning itself out against the faces of the green leaves, fading down slowly into the horizon, drawing the heat with it, leaving behind a cool breeze. The porch was suffused with the particular golden light that comes only in summer. Kat stood, humming, mixing the tall frosted shaker of martinis.

Mrs. George had set their dinner table here in the dry coolness of the balsam firs, on the screened bluestone porch. It looked down over a rolling slope of manicured lawn, down into a small pond fringed with fern and fiddlehead. Beyond, there were the tall woods, which hid the stables and paddock from view. The family often ate here in summer: on quiet nights deer came to drink from the pond or lick the salt blocks, pheasant to scratch for the corn Kirk scattered daily, rabbits to look for sweet clover. Dusk was past the hour of humans but before the hour of predators.

Kirk strode onto the porch, his hair still damp from the shower, looking cool in whipcords and a crisp sportshirt. The ruddy tan across his cheekbones made his eyes all the more blue, his hair all the more silver.

Kat poured the ice-blue gin. Her yellow sundress accented her own deep color, and she felt an inner satisfaction; she stood outside herself, observing the scene laid before her: the characters in their costumes, the interplay, the nuances of light, time, expression. It would be a lovely evening.

"How about Aaron?" Kirk asked, motioning to the two flared glasses. Aaron was reading, sprawled uncomfortably in a wicker chair, his long legs stretched out before him. Kat watched her father take in the rumpled shirt and jeans, the raw unappealing band of color across nose and cheeks.

"Come on, Aaron," she said, irritation edging her voice, "join us."

He put his book down and smiled. "Pepsi's fine. Really."

Kat shrugged and turned back to the bar in frustration. Sometimes he was so obstinate. "How was the golf?"

"Seventy-eight." Kirk sat in a wicker chair next to Aaron and crossed his legs on the ottoman with a satisfied grunt. "Where's Paige?"

"She took off with some friends—movies and dinner."

Kirk nodded. "How's the job going, Aaron?"

He stretched and set down his book again. "Nothing to cheer about." He got up and took another Pepsi from the bar.

"A real clean-living man you've got here," Kirk observed with an indulgent smile. "Well, I'm not ashamed to ask for a refill."

He handed his glass to Aaron. "Seems to me you're lucky to have any job at all. Everybody's got to do scut once in his life."

"I agree," Aaron said coolly. "And I like to work. But that doesn't make it any more interesting."

Kirk took his martini. "And your parents? I thought they wanted to stake you to a summer abroad."

Aaron sipped his Pepsi, watching Kirk over the rim of his glass, weighing the question. "That's their idea, not mine. Besides, I'm tired of sponging off them. I wanted to make some money on my own, in a job where my family didn't pull the strings."

"So this is your 'independent venture'?"

"You might call it that." He shrugged. "It's important to me."

"Yes, at your age I thought it terribly important too. It's a phase that passes with maturity."

Kat took Aaron's glass and her own to refill at the bar, and she could see the dark glint in his eyes. He didn't like being toyed with, or not taken seriously. His pale skin flushed around the angry flare of the sunburn. She wished her father would lay off.

"Yes," he said, from beneath a mask of innocence, "I guess you know all about independence, what with owning your own business and all."

The ice dropped into the shaker with a noisy clank. What was he doing, Kat wondered in horrified silence? Surely he wasn't going to say anything stupid? Mrs. George came through the porch doors then, and Kat turned to her with relief, grateful for the interruption.

"Well, cooled down a mite, hasn't it now?" she observed with pleasure. "Dinner is ready anytime, Katherine."

Kat looked at her watch, savoring her responsibility. "Anytime you're set, Mrs. George. We might have the soup now." The housekeeper turned back to the kitchen. On Saturday nights she always cooked and served them herself, providing a more relaxed, intimate atmosphere.

Kat went to the round glass table at the far end of the porch, and waited to be seated. Kirk pulled out her chair and planted a kiss on the top of her head as she sank into the wicker. Aaron

was on her right, her father on her left. She noted with approval
the centerpiece, low and elegant, of rhododendron blossoms and
tiger lilies.

They began with vichyssoise. Kat still felt unsettled, afraid
that Aaron might reintroduce the topic of Sinclair Shoe. She was
furious with him for playing such games in anger, and she intended to tell him so as soon as they were alone, but for now she
steered the conversation to neutral topics, like sculling carefully
down a broad river. It was an art, she decided as she downed
her glass of wine quickly in an effort to relax. She finished her
vichyssoise. Aaron had eaten only a few spoonfuls, and she remembered now that he did not care for cold soups. Mrs. George
brought on the fish.

Kirk spooned the green mayonnaise to one side of his salmon
and took a careful taste. Pleasure lit up his face. "Excellent." He
turned to Aaron. "Kat really does a remarkable job, don't you
think?"

"I'll have to take your word for it," he said, forking up a bite.
"I like my fish plain."

Kat refilled her wineglass, annoyed at his attitude. Aaron was
immovable on the subject of food, even when Kat did her best to
cajole him into a new taste or texture or spice. His palate was
simply limited, inexperienced, naïve; at college it hadn't seemed
to matter, but now it rankled. She felt it was all part of his deliberate rejection of sophistication that he would not partake of
martinis and vichyssoise.

"Where do you think Kat should start looking for a job?" he
said, shifting the subject abruptly.

"A job?" Kirk said, turning to her, startled. "Are you going to
look for a job *now?*"

"Well," she said uncertainly, "eventually, but just when I
don't know." She threw Aaron another angry look and emptied
her wineglass: why was he throwing bombs tonight?

"I should think," Kirk said with a serious expression, as he laid
down his fork, "that you'd want a little vacation. Aren't you enjoying yourself, Kat?"

"Of course I am. And I do want a vacation." She ran the hem

of her napkin under her fingernail. "But in the long run—I suppose I'll have to look for work."

"Well, for now there's plenty for you right here. I need all the help I can get, what with your mother—" He broke off dramatically and picked up his fork again.

"But, Mr. Sinclair," Aaron pressed, relentless, determined. "Surely you agree that Kat should look beyond merely running a house?"

Now Kirk was angry. He set his shoulders in a very straight line and drew his mouth into a narrow smile. "I think my daughter's best interests are to remain close to her family during a very difficult time."

Kat picked up her wineglass and swallowed hastily, searching for something to say which would cover the ensuing awkward silence. And then, at the bottom of the hill, she saw the rabbits. She'd thought they were not coming tonight. It was late dusk, bordering almost on darkness, far beyond their usual hour.

"Look," she said in a whisper, pointing. Aaron and Kirk turned to see the family of eight just emerging from the shadow of the woods. In the fading light the doe hesitated, scenting the air, and then moved out toward their favorite grazing ground. The babies followed behind her, bouncing up and down, chasing each other in wide loops despite their mother's alert caution. As they left the cover of the trees, the doe and buck nudged them into a large circle. Settling into the clover then, they began eating in earnest.

"Aren't they adorable? They've been coming ever since spring."

"But it's so late," Kirk said, a frown drawing his eyebrows together. "Very unusual."

"Why?" asked Aaron.

"At dark," Kat answered, leaning forward, "there're bigger animals around."

"Why so many all together?"

"It's a family, stupid!" She made a face at Aaron. "See? That one's the mother, that one's the father, the rest are the babies."

Kirk refilled their glasses; Kat could see he had forgotten the interchange with Aaron. She relaxed. In companionable silence they sipped their wine, watching the circle of rabbits feed. The noises of the wood, settling down for the night, came across the grass to them. There was, Kat felt, a harmony she could put her finger on in the ritual of the quiet feeding, a moment of order encircled by the rabbits, their sleek fur glinting with the soft color of the sunset, their long ears relaxed against their backs. She experienced a keen nostalgia over the rabbits, as if they were old friends, or the dolls she'd played with as a child.

A dark shadow dropped from the tree-line of the woods, like dead weight. It moved in silence above the lawn, last light blazing its rippling wingspan with fire. It circled in on the rabbits and they flattened against the ground, as if in a high wind. Seven broke rank, led by the panicked buck, scrambling for the woods. One, left behind, waited for the inevitable, alone.

A sharp, wild cry hung in the air then. Primitive, an echo of fear. The muscular wings beat the air, and it flew away again to the treetop with a brown bundle clenched greedily in its talons.

"What was that?" Aaron asked, horrified.

"Broad-winged hawk," Kirk answered. "Damn shame—but it was too dark." He picked up his wineglass.

Kat put down her fork, appetite gone. The loss seemed as if it were her own. She pushed the hair from her face with a damp hand. "But it isn't fair!" she burst out, looking as though she were going to cry.

"Of course it isn't fair," Kirk answered with a small degree of irritation. "What is? But that's the law of the woods! It was too dark."

Aaron nodded. He could see Kat grieving, fighting her emotions as she finished her wine quickly. She can't bear it, he thought. She can't accept the inevitability of things. It seemed to him that to be without such an acceptance left you vulnerable. He could see Kirk accepted these facts in just the way he did, and used them as the handle of the bat he swung at the world.

Aaron wanted to reach out to Kat and touch her, to explain all he saw. But he did not. The chink of cutlery to china resumed. They went on, eating their meal with precise, neat bites, preserv-

ing the law and order of the dinner table. She would not understand yet. She was not ready. She still demanded that life be fair.
She stood on the brink of discovery and it attracted him in some
raw, instinctual way. It was like the pull of a sketch in progress,
a space where interpretation, shaping, movement, and growth
were needed. The look on her face was what he had tried, and
failed, to capture when he'd sketched her that past spring. How
and when would it change, he wondered.

The night pressed cool and dark against the wire mesh of the
screen. Balancing her brandy on the window sill, Kat looked out
to the trees, the rocks, the shrubs. The wind was moving, lifting
each leaf tenderly, taking away the stain of the day's heat.

She heard the side door slide open and then closed on its well-
oiled hinges. Her father walked out onto the drive. It was late.
Aaron had gone home some time ago. Often she came to the
window to listen to the night when it was warm and she couldn't
sleep.

Kirk stopped in the middle of the curved driveway, put his
head up toward the sky. Kat was just beginning to feel as though
she were spying when her father's knees buckled, and he
slipped, without a sound, down onto the macadam. Frightened,
she pressed her face hard against the screen, trying to see
through the night. He did not move. Without stopping even to
put a robe over her thin nightdress, she ran from the room, down
over the stairs, heart pounding, heart spelling death, all the way
to the front drive, out the door in a blur, to stop it, to forbid it
from happening.

When she reached him, out of breath, his eyes were open. He
was lying flat, on his back, in the driveway, a brandy snifter in
one hand, looking to the sky.

"Are you all right?"

"What're you doing out of bed?"

"I saw you fall. I thought—" she paused. "What're you doing
down there?"

"Looking at the stars through the trees," he said.

She turned her face up and saw now, as he did, the boughs

moving in the wind, the leaves against the cold diamonds of the stars. She lay down, in relief, beside him, as if it were ordinary to lie on cool macadam in a sheer nightgown at 2 A.M. She sipped from his glass, realizing dimly that he must be quite high.

"Orion," he said, pointing. "The hunter. See his belt and sword? And his hound? That's the Dog Star—Sirius."

Kat looked over at him, his profile outlined against the dark green of the night. "How do you know all that?"

"When I was a kid," he said dreamily, "I had a telescope. I was going to be a navigator. Steer the world by the stars."

They lay there, side by side, touching shoulders, the smell of brandy mingling with the smell of the dew damp grass, watching the sky above them revolve on its jeweled axis. The wind played on the bassoon of the oaks and the bass of the pines. The limbs of the tree above them kept tempo, a strong-armed conductor, and the shifting leaves changed their view of the stars like an endlessly turning kaleidoscope—new design upon new design.

"I planted this tree, you know," said Kirk after a time.

"You did?"

"When we first moved into the house, your mother and I," he said, getting to his feet and swaying a bit. "There were no trees here. Your grandfather hated trees. He said they cluttered the view."

No trees here, Kat echoed, following him. She couldn't imagine it. Now the thick, lush lines of trunks seemed as integral, as permanent, as the earth itself. She felt the land beating its life out around them, embracing them as they weaved across the lawn. Kirk stopped to touch the rough bark, to see his imprint.

"But I made it back to what it was. Before they built the house." He turned to her and his eyes glistened in the dark. "The trees—" he hesitated. "The trees are like God to me. They don't compromise, they just endure."

Kat was quiet; she did not want to break the intimacy of the moment. Her father was so open and vulnerable. She drank it in.

"They're proud," he said, running his hand over the smooth bark of a crabapple the way one might stroke a prize horse—with admiration, with deference, with need. "Lily said I was extravagant. Too many trees, she said." He looked around him. "But I said we could afford it. It was important. She could have her pool. I'd have my trees."

Kat reached out and took his hand. To her surprise, he held on tightly. "Things were easier then. What I wanted, I took. Before—" He looked at Kat, the brandy letting him say it. "Before the business began to go sour." He leaned against her. "I had to borrow to keep it. But without her money, they'll be taking it anyway." He drank heavily from the snifter. "The notice came Friday."

This was it, she thought, the trees spinning away on the harsh burn of brandy. "I know, but we'll fix it. We'll fix it together," she said.

"Your mother and I were bad with money," he said, turning to her to explain. "Like a bad habit—we didn't know how to say no to ourselves. A vacation. A fur coat. Whatever. And the business —I just never had the feel for it my father did. I hated borrowing from her. But she didn't mind. What good was money if you didn't use it, she always said."

He was talking to himself now, deep into his past, without defense. Kat held his hand and listened. The brandy was with them in the soft night, letting them be together, without restraint, blurring distinctions, blurring caution. He held his life out to her now and she could not refuse it, could not refuse its painful truths. She sat with him instead, under the trees, under the lace and the stars, side by side, thigh to thigh, and she loved him as a parent, and she loved him as a child, and she loved him as a man. But with the love, there was also the anger, the disillusionment, the pain, the pity. As she wanted to take care of him, so she wanted to be taken care of. And in this time a thought came to her which she tried to push aside: her life would never be the same again. She cried out in her heart for the old, safe ways, but they were gone. The new intimacy was not what she had expected. Only she could help her father now, and she would never be a daughter again. She would have to give him what he needed.

Ten

IT WAS ANNOYING HER. IT WAS PRYING UP UNDER HER EYELIDS. SHE put her head into the pillow, but it was too late. She was awake.

Late morning sun washed the room in a wave of eye-aching light. She lay still, squinting, and surfaced gradually; some left-over, unfinished emotion pressed down on her, but she could not place it. It ran through her mind again and again, like a neon banner whose head follows its tail.

Funny, she thought, frowning, but she couldn't remember last night all that clearly. She recalled the dinner table quite well, and she remembered being outside with her father later. But as for what came in between—her mind was a smooth white wall. It was as if her memory were a sieve, and certain events had just filtered through while others had stuck on the mesh, accessible for this morning's contemplation.

The blank annoyed her, disturbed her, and she drew her brows together in exasperation before finally giving up. She didn't like not knowing where she'd been, or what she'd said. But, she told herself, stretching her toes into the cool space at the bottom of the sheets, at least she did remember the impor-tant thing: her father had finally admitted his need for help, and she would have to act on it today.

She went downstairs to brunch, and a headache started to hum at the base of her skull. Her mood accelerated from

grouchy to irritable. As she stepped out onto the porch she gritted her teeth and slumped into a chair. Kirk looked up over his
morning paper.

"Hair of the dog?" he asked, holding up a pitcher of bloody
marys.

"The very idea," Kat answered, with nausea. "How about
coffee?"

Reaching for the silver urn, he poured for her. As he handed
her the cup, she found it difficult to look him in the face. It was
like being embarrassed, as if they had shared something forbidden. "Late night," she said.

He nodded noncommittally, and went back to his newspaper.

She thought of his voice last night, and his broken confession.
The tension drummed inside her head. Over the rim of her
coffee cup, she watched him and wondered how he could carry
off this face of normality, wondered if she dared bring up his
need. He might get angry. He might tell her to mind her own
business. It was like leaning over the edge of a diving board,
considering how cold the water would be. But she knew she was
going to do it anyway. She had waited long enough. "Dad?"

He looked at her.

"I've been thinking," she began, sliding her cup around in its
saucer, "that seeing how the company's having trouble, maybe
I—" She stopped short at the expression on his face. He looked
like she'd slapped him. And then, violent anger, an electrical jolt.
Kat felt she would short out on the current. But, suddenly, like a
mime changing masques, he was under control again.

"I was tired and depressed last night," he said. "I made it
sound worse than it is. They'll extend the loan. By the end of the
week it'll all be squared away."

"How can you be sure? If you can't make the payment—"

"Honey," he interrupted, "I've been a businessman my whole
life. We'll get the extension. The company will come around—all
we need is a little time."

"Oh, Dad." She sighed and pulled a daisy from the centerpiece. "Let me help." She leaned forward and took his hand.
"Let me pay what you owe."

He slid his hand away from hers to light a cigarette and she pitied him. She could see the full weight of his failure press between his shoulders like the edge of a blade. As he lifted his coffee cup, his hand shook. He put it down.

"That's out of the question," he said finally.

"Why not? She should've left the money to you in the first place." She began pulling the petals off the flower, and they littered the table like limp snowflakes.

"Listen to me," he said quietly. "I'm your father."

She looked at him then for the first time really and his face seemed old, very old and resigned. His eyes were watering. She sat back in her chair, defeated. He was fragile and she had hurt instead of helping. She had threatened his pride, his nobility, his integrity. There was the bitter taste of wishing she had not spoken, nor been so clumsy. Looking down, she saw that she had stripped all the petals off the daisy. The bare yellow head seemed ugly now, and she snapped it from the stalk.

"What are your plans today?" Kirk asked with a casual air, as if she hadn't brought it up.

"Nothing concrete," she answered, pretending to turn to the paper. "Helena's probably coming over." She had tested the current: clearly the direct approach was out. He would never take anything as long as he could see it. But there were other ways—if she were clever.

Eliot Rutledge sighed. He'd just sat down to his noontime dinner when the call from Kat Sinclair had come through. Here she was again, projecting herself into the middle of things, and disturbing him on a Sunday. He cleared his throat. "There's a point to all this, Katherine," he said. "Your mother put me in charge of your money for a reason. She didn't want you wasting it."

"Loyalty to my father is hardly waste."

"Investing in a losing proposition like Sinclair Shoe is as foolish as going to the racetrack. I told that to your mother years ago. If you understood—"

"Of course I don't understand! Why don't you explain the situation instead of presuming to make my decisions for me!"

"All right," he sighed. His dinner was cold by now anyway, and he had to get this straightened out once and for all. "A few years ago your father borrowed 4.75 million in mortgage money from the Security New England Insurance Company for plant modernization, and another 2 million on a three-year term basis. He thought that would turn the business around. The mortgage was for twenty years at 8 per cent, and the 2 million was at two points over prime—or about 10 per cent in those days. What that boils down to was a total monthly payment of about $80,000.

"But things got worse, not better, and your mother began to help out with the monthly payments. Then the recession of '79 came and fixed things for good. Can you follow all this?"

"I think so," Kat said uncertainly.

"The insurance company had a choice. They could have thrown Sinclair Shoe into bankruptcy, but that meant getting stuck with an antiquated plant that would hardly be worth thirty cents on the dollar. They'd really had inadequate security for the loans to begin with, so they decided to give him two more years on the 2 million at the same interest, but they demanded he put up additional personal collateral."

Kat was silent for a minute, trying to sort out what he'd just said. "But when we had lunch at the Harvard Club last spring, you told me that he sold off all his stock before taking any of my mother's money. What else did he have to put up?"

Rutledge paused a minute, and then cleared his throat. "The house," he said. "Your mother let him put up your home in Concord."

Kat put her head against the cool wood of the bookshelf over the desk. One by one she saw all the large gracious rooms in her mind, her mother's sitting room, the warm kitchen, and the grounds, rolling under the weight of the resplendent trees. This land, in a town of pre-revolutionary houses and taverns, a town of colonial colors and dimensions, a town of history. And this house, which was her history. It couldn't be lost, not now, not after all these years. She was trying to think; she was confused. There had to be a way out. She must not let go, she must fight this. But their house! How could he! Suddenly her confusion gave way to anger; anger and determination. "Well," she said in an even tone that surprised her. "If they're going to foreclose on the house, why can't I pay off the principal?"

There was a shocked silence at the other end of the line. "That's over two million dollars, Katherine."

She paused, her mind clicking over options she barely understood. "Couldn't we get the insurance company to extend the loan again?"

"Doubtful. They might conceivably refinance."

"Meaning what?" she asked, feeling hope fade.

"Meaning that instead of the old interest rates on both loans—which incidentally cost your mother nearly $400,000 last year—they might extend the loan for 2 or 3 per cent extra."

"How much would that be?"

"$200,000."

She was silent. "That's a lot of money."

"To say the least," he observed dryly. "And it's hardly a sure bet."

"But I do have the money to do it."

Rutledge didn't answer.

"I understand your objections," Kat said finally. "But I'm not sure *you* understand. I can't think of a better way to spend my money. And Mom would approve—she helped Dad out for years, didn't she?"

"Helped him yes. But she *left* the money to you and Paige."

Kat was silent again.

"She did it for tax reasons, of course," Rutledge went on, "and in fact we never discussed it from any other viewpoint. But in my opinion it went beyond that. She was afraid if she left it all to your father there would be nothing left for *you*."

The argument was a dead end from which Kat saw only one way out, and so she gathered herself. "Mr. Rutledge," she said with firmness, "nothing you've said has changed my mind and I still need your help to carry out my plan."

"As your trustee I can block your moving on this entirely," he said dryly.

She paused and decided to try an appeal to his fatherly in-

stincts. "Look. You can leave me in the lurch to botch things up
on my own, or you can help me do it right. But either way, I'm
going to do it. You see," she said, tensing her shoulders, "you
may control the funds in my trust, but you have no control over
the jewelry my mother left me. Or the real estate."

Despite her innocent tone, the threat was clear and Rutledge
could see he'd been forced into a corner. "Let me think over-
night on this," he said at last. "I'll get back to you tomorrow."

"O.K.," she said, uneasily. "But at least call the insurance
company and find out their terms. Let them know there's a possibility Dad can meet the debt—don't close the door."

He sighed. "I'll call in the morning. Is there anything else?"

"No. That was all."

She hung up the phone, and her hands began to shake. Never
before had she tried to manipulate someone so powerful. She was
too insecure, too precarious, for these games. She was not good
at turning anger and charm on and off like a kitchen faucet, and
she cursed the complications in her life, the injustice of it, the
turmoil. The sums he had named were staggering, but to Kat it
was all vague, all monopoly money; she had no conception of its
value, what it could buy, how it ought to be handled. She only
knew it would rescue her father. And so, taking a long breath,
she stood and turned away from the phone. She would do it if
she had to, she thought. She would sell her mother's jewelry, or
the house in Padanarum. It would kill her, but she could do it. If
Rutledge made her.

"I agree with him," Helena said at last. "It's not your responsibility. I know you want to help, but your father'd die of shame
if he knew what you were thinking of."

"But I love him," Kat said, "I owe him."

"Love does not equal debt," Helena replied, gesturing vehemently with her hands. "Give him love, give him emotional support, but don't confuse it with money." She looked over at Kat.
"For God's sake don't castrate him."

Kat slumped back in her chaise and closed her eyes. Of all

people, she'd thought Helena would understand. "He took care of me." She sighed. "Now it's my turn to take care of him."

"You might as well put him in a nursing home."

Kat stared at her friend, and then lay back quietly in the sun. It was a breathless hot day, a day for burning—the kind she loved best. Her tube of Bain de Soleil was getting low, but she squeezed the corners and got out a little bit more of the cerise-colored grease. "You don't know the history," Kat said wearily. "You haven't seen his face." She sat up again and looked at Helena. "Tell me this: is it wrong for a wife to help her husband?"

"It depends," Helena said quietly, taking out her box of Gitanes. "But then, you're not his wife." The acrid odor of the French cigarette drifted in the air.

Her words bit hard into Kat. She was so angry she was afraid to speak.

"Kat?"

She did not answer.

Helena thought perhaps she'd gone too far. "I haven't done my run today," she said. "How about doing a couple miles around your bridle path?"

Again she did not respond. She wanted no part of Helena's peace offering. She was angry, justifiably angry.

"Oh come on," Helena urged, as she pulled a pair of Nikes from her tote bag. "You haven't been riding in weeks and it'd do you good. This sun's leached up enough of your energy already." She sat down on the grass and began touching her forehead to her knee. "A little exercise'll pick up your spirits."

"So. In addition to being a psychiatrist, suddenly you're a salesman?" Kat glared over at her. "Yesterday it was Aaron, today it's you. Just leave me alone and go jogging by yourself—you're the exercise nut! Maybe by the time you've finished torturing yourself we'll both have the brains to cool it."

Helena shrugged and went off toward the woods. Alone with her anger, Kat repressed a spark of envy as she watched her go. Her friend's exercise campaign had done great things for her body. Her arms and legs were muscular and lean, her abdomen flat. Uncomfortably Kat avoided looking at herself: this year, for

the first time since high school, she'd had to buy a larger size
bikini. She tried to ignore the new shape of her ass, the extra
weight on her upper thighs. At first, looking in the fitting room
mirror, she'd blamed the Italian designers for cutting such
skimpy bottoms this year. But by now she knew better. After all,
she was twenty-one—no longer a teen-ager. There was no exercise that would make her sixteen again, she rationalized. She
might as well face the fact that it was all downhill from here.
Last week she'd started the Drinking Man's Diet: one thousand
calories a day, over five hundred of which were a large allotment
for liquor.

She went into the house and returned with an iced pitcher of
lemonade, two tall glasses, and a bottle of Smirnoff, which she
took off the tray and stood to one side of her chair. Pouring herself a glass of half and half, she lay back and loosed her bikini
straps. The sun had just passed its zenith. It burned down hot
and harsh and the heat flushed up the length of her body. She
wished she were alone, without Helena or Mrs. George or anyone to bother her: she would like to lie greased and naked under
its power, like some Egyptian princess. Her mother had wor-
shiped the sun too, had adored baking under its voluptuous heat.
In winter, when she and Kirk weren't away on vacation, Lily
would set a chaise down in the shelter of the snowbanks on the
back terrace and line it with a mink coat. She could stay as tan
as if she'd spent a month at a Caribbean resort. The first time
she'd invited Kat to winter sunbathe with her, it had been a
graduation into a select club, admission into the narcissistic
world of womanhood. Kat had been twelve.

Now there was nowhere she could escape from these memories; they haunted her, waking and dreaming. Depression came
down on her fast. She felt she was fading into grayness, like an
old color photograph left too long in the sun, her strength
bleached out by emotion. She wanted only to be immune to her
own feelings. She turned on her side and sipped again from her
glass.

Helena jogged her way down the pine-needled path, hopping

over the small stream beds that crossed occasionally in front of her. There were frogs sliding on the moss-covered stones, birds jostling each other in the branches above, and the sunlight dappling the tree trunks—but she ran on almost without noticing, a frown on her face and a crease between her highly arched eyebrows. This furrow deepened as she ran, legs flashing white against the bark of trees, arms swinging in an energetic arc. She was thinking about Kat, rhythmically taking the problem apart piece by piece. Kat had worried her in the months before they'd graduated, but now her concern increased. She felt, in truth, alienated from her best friend. They had always been able to talk about anything, but slowly, over the spring and summer, Kat had moved into a private place where no one else was allowed. And even when they did talk, she reflected, Kat seemed only half there. She had never seen her friend so unhappy, so torn apart, and yet so determined to keep up a brave face. This insane plan to help her father by keeping the truth from him struck Helena as another refusal on Kat's part to look at plain facts.

Somehow she would have to change Kat's mind, make her see the never-ending cycle of distortion and depression. She finished the circuit and trotted back into the yard, flopping breathlessly down under the willow tree. Kat brought her a glass of lemonade. "Thanks," she said.

"Are you all right?" Kat asked. "You sound like you're having a heart attack."

"Fine," she panted. She was sweating freely in the sun, her thin cotton jersey sticking to her wiry athletic frame. Pulling a towel from her tote, she smiled.

They sat there quietly, the noises of midday stretching around them: mourning doves, breeze through the maple branches, a cicada with its buzz-saw whine, a lawn mower somewhere distant. Honeysuckle and rose wafted on the air.

Kat sipped her vodka and sank against the chair, savoring the faint sour taste of lemon, enjoying the sounds; relaxing, she gradually forgot her anger, her worry, everything that bothered her. She became buoyant in her own mind. Little by little the pressure began to slip away. She closed her eyes. She could really sleep, she thought.

Helena got up and came to the tray to refill her glass. Returning to her chair, she reached into her tote and pulled out a cotton shirt she was embroidering. The dragon on the back was only partially outlined in flaming orange, green, yellow, red, but it would be stunning when it was finished, she thought with satisfaction. She threaded the needle with floss and began to work, the sun flashing against the steel.

Kat looked over, roused from her stupor by the play of light. The colors of the floss licked up at her like flame.

Helena was watching her, thinking about the bottle of vodka by Kat's side. She made up her mind: it was better to alienate Kat than sit silently and watch her self-destruct. "You've got to stop it," she said at last. "You've got to forget about taking care of your father for a while and start worrying about yourself."

"You just don't get it, do you?" Kat asked, anger returning. She didn't want to wake up from the lull of the sun to defend herself again. "I have to do it. I've never loved anyone so much in my life. Except my mother. And he needs me now like he never has before."

"Is this what you want? Wasting away at home like a teenager? What about your career?"

Kat gave her a look of barely kept fury. "There's plenty here to keep me busy. You'd be surprised at how much work it takes to run a house and staff this size. Keeping the family bills and stuff. It's a full-time job."

"Who are you kidding? Look," her voice softened. "It's never too late to start fresh. Even I'm going to look for something better. The job at Houghton Mifflin is just too boring, and I'm not sure I'm cut out to be an editor anyway, so I'm thinking about applying to business school next year." She was talking with excitement, swept away by her new ideas. She wanted to share them with Kat, to encourage her to strike out, to try something new. "Then I'll try the business end of publishing. Maybe I can make a real dent there. And a little money too." She stopped short, bothered by the pinched expression on Kat's face.

"Enough," Kat said. "No more advice." Helena's ambitions threatened her. Here she was, still at home, making a career out of caring for her father, thinking that someday, if she pushed herself, she might find enough time and energy to apply for a job. For Kat, any job in publishing was a goal, a height to be stretched for. And now came Helena, leagues ahead, already moving toward something new. Her fear increased, her despair increased.

"But maybe you'll like publishing better than I do," Helena revised quickly, watching her expression. "Maybe you could take on some part-time work—like free-lance proofing, just to see." She looked at Kat frankly. "It's important to keep your hand in the game. Besides, aren't you going nuts just sitting here day after day?"

"I'm fine," Kat said, forcing a bright smile. "Look at my world. I mean, it's really disintegrated this year. But you see, I'm a very strong person. I've taken over running the house, helping my father, working with the lawyer. It's hard work—could someone who was coming apart do all that? I tell you, Helena, I'm in control."

"And that's why you put vodka in your lemonade in the middle of the day?" Helena said. "To keep in control?"

"Oh, for God's sake!" Kat snapped, springing up out of her chair, and going to sit at the end of the diving board. "Drop it!"

Helena nodded mutely. She couldn't win. Kat had dragged her out here for the day so they could talk, but she wasn't really ready for it yet. For a minute Helena watched her drag her toe through the water of the pool, wearing that martyred expression, and then she took up her embroidery again. She thinks I'm picking on her, she said to herself, turning the shirt in her hands. The dragon's eye gleamed pure gold under afternoon sun. Next time she would have to wait until Kat came to her.

Eleven

WHEN THE FALL CAME AARON TOOK AN APARTMENT ON IRVING Street, just around the corner from Harvard's Graduate School of Design. His space was the top floor of a well-maintained, old frame house. The backbone of Cambridge was houses just such as this, wooden monuments of a time past, of a time when building meant building, not pouring concrete. Aaron found particular satisfaction in the oddly shaped rooms, the oblong irregular windows, and the uneven hardwood floors that spoke out underfoot.

His drafting table stood in the living room, in a book-lined alcove fronted by a large casement window. To the left, his Luxo light craned its neck to one side. Apart from these items and a rug, the room was empty of furniture.

Kat moved tentatively down the hall into the kitchen. It was cozy, with plants at the curtainless windows, a marble sink and counter-top, and glass-fronted cabinets. Aaron's modest stock of new terra-cotta stoneware lined the shelves, and a pegboard on the wall housed his new skillets and saucepans. It seemed undeniably the place Aaron lived even though he had been a resident for only a few days. It must be the fastidiousness with which he had done everything, she thought: the pegboard just so, the dishes in symmetrical piles, the plants outlined in the large-paned windows. Aaron was not the sort to leave his walls empty either: in the living room he had already hung several oils and a few sketches; in the bedroom, her portrait; in the kitchen, a bright tempera mural.

Today was the first time Kat had seen Aaron's apartment. He'd discovered the place only last week, and moved in immediately. School started two weeks from now, and he wanted to be completely settled in by then. He came up behind her, and put his arms around her waist. She leaned into him.

"What do you think?"

"I like it," she said, after a moment.

"Change your mind about moving in," he whispered against her ear.

She slid away from him and wandered down the hall to the bedroom. On the threshold of the large room she noted the new brass bed and unstained maple dresser. "You must've spent a bundle."

Aaron shrugged, disappointed that she hadn't commented on his placement of the sketch of her. Of course, he remembered, she'd never really liked it. She hadn't appreciated the sharpness of its lines. But still, he'd wanted to please her, he'd wanted to hang it there. "It's not nearly finished," he said, looking at the bare floor. He gestured down the hall. "No rug. No couch. But you can only do so much at once. There's still too much empty space." Again there was the implied question in his voice—her furniture, her belongings, he'd left room for her. She turned away from it.

"What about dinner?" she asked.

"Chicken, broccoli, fruit. Simple stuff."

They went back to the kitchen. At the windows the plants reflected the last red of the sun, and patterned the floor with shadows. Kat liked this room best of all.

"How long does this take?" Aaron asked, holding up a pale rubbery chicken wing.

Kat paused, embarrassed to admit that she didn't really know, and then nodded to the *Joy of Cooking* on the shelf. "You bought it," she said, "so use it."

As he skimmed the index for baked chicken, she added, "And

check broccoli too." He looked up at her with a grin and they both started to laugh. "At least we're both in the same boat," she said finally. "I hope it's edible."

Kat began to cut up salad vegetables, surprised by the symmetry of round peppers and onions, long carrots and cucumbers. She liked the heft of them in her palm, the precision of chopping, with its pungence and sense of accomplishment. Aaron poured red wine into his new glasses; Kat admired the large round globes and thought privately that their size was their best feature.

The chicken sizzled in the oven and Aaron basted it meticulously. He was instinctively handy and efficient, and Kat wrapped her arms around his waist in appreciation, as he laid out the stainless steel on the butcher block table. His backbone pressed into her breasts, her cheek. She just stood that way, holding him, content to be there. Since they'd left school, love had not been so clean, so uncomplicated. This was just pure feeling, flowing fluid and relaxed.

The evening seemed to have a slow rhythm of its own and neither of them wanted to rush it. They sat quietly sipping wine, and when the chicken was finished they let it rest on the cutting board for a while. They talked of nothing important. They avoided talking of anything important. They did not want to argue. Quiet was needed now, as after a long walk in the desert. They ate the chicken on the reddish-glazed plates, its buttered skin crisp over the cooled flesh. The dry wine went down easily and made Kat's head light. The salad gleamed with its simple vinaigrette. The meal was basic and delicious.

The kitchen grew dark in stages as the shadows spread across the floor in a pool. When they could no longer see one another they moved to the living room. Kat emptied the last of the bottle of wine into her glass and brought a new one in with her. A cool breeze funneled between the two windows on opposite sides of the room. Outside rustled the thick leaves of giant elms.

They sound just like the trees at home, Kat thought, as more wine slid down her throat and her mind started to wander. What was her father doing now? Eating alone? Reading alone? A small discontent seeped into her stomach and she took more wine to blur it out.

Aaron watched the expressions crossing her face. "What're you thinking about?"

"Dad," she said, looking over at him. "I don't like leaving him alone on the weekend."

Aaron felt his resentment surge again: she had to drag Kirk into everything all the time. Her father and her guilt. "He's a grown man, Kat." He cracked his knuckles. "And not your responsibility." He bit down on his next thought. He didn't want to argue over this again; still it seemed to Aaron that Kat acted as if her father were really her child. He hated how she was handling her life—this obsession with her father, this need to take care of him struck him as abnormal. When she'd secretly assumed Kirk's debt last month, Aaron had fought her decision, tried to talk her out of it. He'd thought it a giant mistake, a move away from reality to reach into Kirk's life behind his back and rearrange everything. It was like a mother fighting her kid's battles, and it grated on him that Kat should be so possessive over someone other than him. She let her concern interfere in places that should be supremely private.

He watched her begin to open the second bottle of wine. "Do we really need that?" he asked.

She looked over at him, almost as though she'd been anticipating the question. "One more glass," she said with her most coaxing smile, although she was already quite high. "Come on, don't be a stick in the mud."

He controlled his emotions again, unwilling to risk a fight. "O.K., but let's watch it." He smiled and leaned down to kiss the inside curve of her elbow. "I'd like to stay awake for a while longer. You know."

"Sure." She filled her glass to the brim, just in case he gave her trouble about pouring another. She tilted her head back and closed her eyes.

"What've you decided about looking for work?" he asked as he leaned back against the wall, pulling her to relax against his knees.

She drew away. "That's uncomfortable," she said irritably, wanting to sit without talking and ride the high. "I haven't had much time for that stuff, Aaron. You know Dad and I have been planning this party."

"That's a great set of priorities," he replied, trying to keep his voice even.

"Let's not get into a thing about this."

Her tone set him on fire. Or was it the way she narrowed her eyes, that sure sign she was getting sleepy from the wine. "Maybe it's time someone did get into a thing about it!" he said angrily. "Maybe it's time someone got you looking straight!"

She tried to cut him off then, but he was sliding down a mountain of stored-up emotion. He would have it out. He would say all he needed to say. And then it would be done. And then he would have peace. At least it would be "yes" or "no."

He stood and towered over her, gesturing with his arms. "Get out of that house. Find some work. You're drowning and I'm not going to hang around and watch it any more!" The threat spread out in the air like gas. She curled herself into a tiny tight ball at his feet, as if his words were kicks she could protect herself against. She took a long hard drag of her wine. Then she looked up at him, fear on her face, in her eyes. "What do you mean?"

He sighed. "You're drowning, or you're drying up. You're turning into a neurotic, depressed, obsessed person. And," he added, pointing at her glass, "you're drinking too damn much. I can't take it any more."

Kat looked at him steadily, trying to concentrate on him and speak coherently. "I don't drink any more than other people." She shook her head. "You just don't drink enough."

"That's warped," he said, running his hand through his hair. "Drinking isn't a contest."

"Don't be a bore."

"Let's not get distracted here," he said in his firmest tone. "If you weren't at home with your father, I don't think you would drink as much. That's another good reason to move out of there and find a job." His eyes narrowed. "As if the first reason alone isn't impetus enough."

Now she made her eyes as cold as stone. She was unjustly accused. She wanted to do something dramatic, to make him pay, to make him sorry, to draw him back to her. But she could think of nothing. She only knew that he had threatened to leave her, and that she would be alone. She started to cry, tears sliding down into her wine. The room was weaving around her now, but she lifted her glass again stubbornly, determined to prove him wrong.

Aaron stood and watched her, silhouetted by the street light; he refused to comfort her, refused to give in. But when she looked up at him the light from the window illuminated her need, and he sat down and held her, his anger run dry. She felt so soft, so fragile, as if her bones would break, from her pain, from his hands. Slowly her crying stopped and she slumped against him. Around her the clean white walls moved up and down like the deck of a ship. She stretched her eyes wide, trying to stay awake, but all she wanted now was the sweet oblivion. And, she thought drowsily, his touch was so quiet.

When Aaron looked down, her eyes were shut, the lashes in sticky clumps against cheeks streaked with tears and rouge. She was not beautiful, but he had never seen her look more vulnerable. Some buried part of him responded silently, like an echo following the first call. He could not help himself. He loved her, and he hated her. He was tied to her, and he wanted to be free. Never had he been more torn. He rested his chin on the top of her head, and cried silently. He did not know if they would survive each other.

He picked her up in his arms like a child and carried her to the bedroom. He undressed them both in the dark and slid in beside her. He turned to hold her as she slept, limp, in deep unconscious dreaming. His penis rose against the pressure of her hipbone and his hand instinctively reached for her breast. Then he sighed and closed his eyes. Tonight, in this bed, there was no room for that sort of loving.

Morning. It was morning, Kat thought as she cracked one eye open to the darkened room. Around the edges of the blinds, sunlight tried to get in. Beside her, Aaron slept on, with his head under the pillow, his body curled on the very edge of the bed. Kat was grateful for this silence. She hated talking to anyone before breakfast.

She wondered what time it was, and what time they had finally gone to bed. The humming in her head might mean they had been up all night. And the thirst—if she got up, would she wake him? She decided that thirst was better than talk.

Depression had already stamped itself down on her day and it wasn't even lunch time yet. What was the matter with her? Nothing had happened, nothing gone wrong. She pushed her chin into the pillow, feeling fretful. Then it came to her that they had fought last night: he had been so angry, so set against her. But she couldn't remember why. There was a curious black hole in her memory, a gap between the beginning of their argument and now, as if someone had taken a scissors to her brain. What about getting into bed? What about getting undressed? What about any of those normal nighttime rituals? Why couldn't she remember them? Had they made up after they'd argued? Why did they argue to begin with?

A strange sense of dislocation came over her, and she was afraid. Why couldn't she remember such simple things? And she tried it over and over, the way a maddened rider sets his horse to the same fence, but she couldn't break through. It was no use. There was the start of the argument, and then Aaron growing upset, and then it was as if the vivid picture faded out into dull gray static.

Beside her, Aaron scissored his legs together in the kick which meant he was awake. He rolled over and inspected her through a half-opened eye. He didn't say anything for a while, and she didn't know what to do. She was afraid she might give herself away.

"Are we going to talk about it?" he asked finally.

"About what?" Kat faked, stalling for time. She would have to be careful, she would have to make noncommittal remarks. He must not know about her dark spots. She moved her bare legs away from his under the covers. She could not bear to be touched, even by his skin. All he had to do was ask one pointed question. She moved to get out of bed, but he grabbed her arm.

"About last night."

"Well," she said, after a pause, looking for a nonchalant reply. "You know I don't start these fights. I don't like fighting."

"Neither do I," he said, taking her hand. "But I can't bear you hurting yourself. It's worse than fighting." His dark eyes asked her to understand, and forgive. "That's why I'm pushing you."

Once more she was afraid. She had to know what had happened, what had been said. He was speaking as though a decision had been reached.

"Tell me again," she said flippantly, "just what is it you think will cure my life of all its ills?"

"A simple job. Getting on with your *own* life." He reached out and stroked her arm, as if to soften what he was saying. "I meant it too, Kat, what I said about my leaving. I'll go if you won't help yourself."

That was it then. She remembered it now. She really was up against the wall, trapped. How would she find a job? Who would want her? She would blank out in an interview, she would forget her name.

She wanted to push him away and scream that she didn't need him; she wanted to stitch his skin to hers with a fine permanent thread so he could never go. His hand folded onto her shoulder. She was no longer sure why she needed him so much, or if she still loved him, but she knew one thing for sure—she had to do what he asked. She might be afraid of a job, of an interview, of a boss, of all that would be required, but she was more afraid of being alone. She felt Aaron bonded her to some solid earth— maybe it was the past, with all its comforting safety, or perhaps it was the future and all that might be, someday. For now, she only wanted to brush her teeth, and think about all this later. Wordlessly, she pushed herself out of bed.

Aaron watched her naked back cross the room, and he wondered.

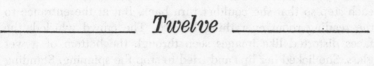

Twelve

THE RIVERSIDE SUBWAY CAR LURCHED AROUND THE CORNER INTO COP-
ley Station and Kat tucked the engraved business card back into
her pocket. Three nights ago she'd searched for several hours,
and finally found it in her jewelry box, but only by steeling herself had she been able to make the call. There was no way
around it, though, no way out. To ask Bea Daniels for a favor
was a move forced upon her; after Aaron's ultimatum over the
weekend, she *had* to find a job.

She climbed the stairs out from underground, and paused for
a moment on Boylston Street. Once again anxiety crept in on
her. She didn't understand it. What was there to be afraid of?
She tapped her foot impatiently, pushing away the feeling that
something bad was about to fall in on her, and told herself to get
going and take control of her life.

The day was cloudy, crisp, there was a crowd pressing by her,
all the reassuring signs of humanity, but in spite of this she felt
very alone. Tension in her throat made it hard to swallow. Of
course, Kat thought as she walked, turning her head so the wind
wouldn't blow her hair and breathing deeply in an effort to
quench her nerves, Bea had sounded pretty surprised to hear
from her. Although she'd been cordial enough over the phone,
Kat was now constructing a million disastrous conversations all
ready to happen within the next brief half-hour. She mistrusted

her luck and her life; she was certain nothing good could happen to her. And, if it did, she expected there would be a string attached.

She pushed open the heavy main doors of the Boston Public Library, and climbed the central staircase, locking her knees on each step so that she couldn't turn back. But at the entrance to the reading room everything blurred. The crowd whirled, the faces distorted like images seen through the bottom of a wet glass. She licked her lips and tried to stop the spinning. Standing there like a fool, she wanted only to turn and leave. Surely everyone was staring. And then, like a life preserver thrown into the air, a waving arm snagged her vision.

She was as attractive as Kat remembered from that hazy afternoon, her smoothly clipped dark head bent over the stack of books before her. As Kat crossed the room, Bea's angular face took on a genuine smile of welcome. "Hello, Kat," she said, extending her hand. "Good to see you again."

"I nearly missed you," Kat began quickly, feeling awkward. "It's such a big place and—"

"I was glad to hear from you," Bea said, interrupting Kat's nervous flow of small talk. Her eyes were candid and looked directly into Kat's as she leaned back in her chair. "It's been a while. I'd almost given up."

Kat sat down across from her, on the very edge of her chair, clutching her purse in her lap. "I'm sorry," she said. "I've just been ferociously busy."

"With what?"

"Things're humming," Kat said, brushing a stray hair off her cheek. "What assignment's brought you back to town?"

Bea hesitated, wondering why Kat had evaded her question, and caught up for a minute in inspecting her friend. She was very tanned, and dressed in a buff linen dress with matching jacket, but Bea instinctively felt that underneath all the gloss there was trouble: Kat looked heavier, and very tired. There was none of the excitement that had sparked from her the first time they'd met, none of the almost childish, refreshing enthusiasm which had lent her a sense of buoyancy. That day they had laughed in the face of depression, but now she seemed worn thin, creased, and very nervous—her hands even trembled a bit. "A fine set of articles," Bea said, finally returning to Kat's question. "I'll be here for a week or so."

"Which magazine?"

"*Ms.* It's women's health care." She shuffled through her papers. "From natural childbirth to DES daughters to the women's health collective. Boston's *the* place."

Kat nodded. "Are you done here?" she asked, glancing at her watch. "Let's go over to Friday's and talk in comfort."

"All right." Bea wondered what the hell was bothering Kat as she stuffed her papers into her maroon leather briefcase, and picked up two books. She stood. "Got to check these out on our way."

At the circulation desk, while the clerk took her card and stamped a due date, Bea kept watching Kat and remembered her own days as a young writer, the nerves that used to take her into the john. Maybe it was nothing more than that.

As they walked over to Newbury Street, Bea linked her arm companionably through Kat's. "So," she resumed, hoping to distract her young protégée, "the article on childbirth techniques is my current project. Do you realize that most hospitals have just begun using birthing rooms, and the services of midwives? I mean, the attitude of the medical establishment is positively medieval!" She went on to describe the new techniques, new breakthroughs, but again Kat tuned out on her. Bea began to feel discouraged, wishing Kat would open up about whatever was eating her so that then they could relax.

Friday's was one of those places with a long glass front overlooking the sidewalk, like a European café. The name was prominently displayed in zippy neon letters across the front entrance. Inside, the brass bar rail and stools and small tables with cane chairs were battled for by the crowd. You could stand at Friday's for a long time during rush hour. The lighting soft, the overhead fans turning lazily, it was the perfect meeting place for Boston's hungry singles.

Because it was still a little before five, Kat and Bea did find

stools at the polished wooden bar. Kat sat down, dangling her
feet to the bar rail like a little girl in a high chair, and immediately signaled the bartender to ask for a giant bloody mary.
Then she took off her jacket and settled back. Once again the
machine in her mind cranked itself up, and she began to fan-
tasize how she should bring up her problem, how she would put
it, just so, to Bea.

Bea sipped her scotch, and looked at Kat appraisingly. "So,
kiddo," she said, "what're you so nervous about?"

"Does it show that much?" Kat asked, jolted by her own trans-
parency, but smiling at herself after all.

Bea didn't answer, but just looked at her, waiting.

"I need a favor," Kat said, shoving aside all her carefully
planned words, and just blurting it out.

"For instance?"

"A job."

"What about the names I gave you last winter?" Bea asked in
honest surprise.

Kat looked embarrassed. "I never really got a chance to call
them. Anyway, now I'm looking for something different."

"What do you mean?"

"Part-time work. Free-lance. You know, something with flexible hours, like proofreading or something. No heavy duty."

"Why did you change your mind?" Bea asked, running her
finger around the inside edge of her glass as she tried to hide her
disappointment.

Kat could see her dismay and she shrugged. "I need something extra. To keep busy."

"Extra?"

"Well, that is, I'm taking care of my father, running the house
and all. But I think I should have a little something on the side."
She said it elegantly, with a little wave of her hand, almost as if
it didn't really matter to her.

"Taking care of your father?" Bea looked incredulous. "I just
don't get it, Kat. When we talked before you had a lot of ambitions—"

"Don't get me wrong," Kat interrupted. "This is just temporary."

"Forget about temporary," Bea said, coming to life at last, having made up her mind to speak out. "Look for a real job. Something that interests you."

"It's just not the right time for that."

"Why not?" She felt she had the right to ask; after all, Kat had come looking for her help.

Kat finished her drink and waved to the bartender for a refill. "I know what I want," she said firmly, feeling the vodka taking hold. "To ease into it. This's been a hard year for me." She looked up at Bea to see the effect of her words. "So many things have gone . . . wrong."

Bea reached over and laid her hand on Kat's. She felt almost guilty for her anger at the girl.

"With my mother gone, my father needs me a lot more. And," she said, looking wistful, "I guess I need him more too. I just want to relax with something productive, but not too strenuous."

Bea smiled her encouragement, responding to the poignancy of Kat's confession, but still she wished she could urge her forward. She was concerned—all this living at home and being dependent on her father was not healthy. Surely it was time Kat got on with her own life.

She ordered them another round of drinks, pushing her feelings down. At this point the best thing she could do for Kat was to cheer her up, and so she entertained her with story after story: her latest exploits, her latest articles, her latest lovers— male and female alike. They laughed together like best friends and Kat perked up considerably. The vodka was helping elevate her. Once again, she was enthralled by Bea's openness. This time she asked for details, the nitty gritty, and she felt she had grown up. As she drank more she did not mind it when her knees touched Bea's under the bar. She felt free, she felt daring; it was a raucous fine time.

"Got to go to the john," Kat finally said, standing up with an effort. She threaded her way through the crowd to the bathroom. She went into the stall and shut the door, but when she tried to hover above the toilet seat as she'd been taught, she couldn't keep her balance. She was so relieved to have it all over with that she didn't mind if she was a little bit too high. Once Bea had agreed to give her a hand in looking for work, she'd stopped worrying. When she washed her hands, she squinted at herself in the mirror hazily. She'd got what she'd come for. Aaron would have to shut up now, she thought. She would get a job. In fact, she decided as she brushed her hair, she would make sure this bargain was closed before going home today. Nothing would stand in the way of Bea's doing her this favor. She smiled at her reflection and concentrated on keeping her lipstick brush steady. And if she had one more drink, she'd be high enough. High enough to remember very little of it afterward.

Kat stretched her arms high over her head and crossed her legs under the bar. "Know what?" she asked. "This's been a really nice afternoon. A little rocky at first, but now, it's all just fine." She put her glass back on the cocktail napkin. "After all my trouble with Aaron, it's good to talk with someone understanding."

Bea smiled. "I'm glad too." She finished her drink. "Where're you off to now?"

"Nowhere in particular. Why?"

"Want to have dinner?"

"Great idea," said Kat, pointing her finger in the air for emphasis.

They paid the check and made for the door. Out on the sidewalk they discovered the weather was about to change. They made a dash for the Ritz, only two blocks down, where Bea was staying again, but halfway there the rain came down in a solid wall. By the time they crashed into the lobby, laughing hysterically, they were soaked through. The faces of strangers were wheeling around Kat now, and she realized that she was really quite drunk. Dimly she felt Bea propel her forward into the elevator, and then off again. She unlocked the door and ceremoniously ushered Kat in as if she were a bellboy looking for a big tip. Her parody sent them off into a fit of giggles. They felt like schoolgirls on vacation.

"Look," Bea gasped finally, clutching her mouth, "I've got to go to the john. Pour, will you?"

Kat filled two bathroom tumblers half-full of whiskey and added an ice cube to each. The straight huskiness of the Chivas was nice after all those bloody marys. Suddenly she was very, very tired. She sat down on the edge of the bed. Bea emerged from the bathroom in her stocking feet. "Where's mine?" she asked.

Kat gestured to the bureau. "My shoes are squishing," she announced, peering down at her feet. "I'm soggy."

"You look like you've been wading in the river, for Chrissakes. Here." Bending over, she tugged at the wet leather and pulled both shoes off, throwing Kat a warm towel to dry her feet. "Your dress is wet," she observed with an owlish blink. "Here, put on my bathrobe, and we'll dry your dress by the radiator."

Kat finished her drink and trundled across the room to pour a refill. "Could I do that?" she asked, feeling for the first time a tinge of doubt.

"Why not? I'm not wearing it." Bea started to laugh again. "No one's wearing it. Why not you?"

"Does that make sense?" Kat asked, putting her head to one side. Bea opened the closet and gave her a silk kimono with a sash. Kat went into the bathroom, unzipped the damp dress, and put the robe on over her slip. It felt good to be dry, to be cared for. She knew what she was doing and she felt wonderfully free —except maybe a little dizzy, she conceded, balancing herself against the porcelain sink as she peered into the mirror. She used Bea's brush to fluff the damp curls off her forehead, and then went back to the bedroom.

"Much better," she said, sitting down on the bed again.

"Have to keep you warm. 'Starve a fever, drown a cold'!" They started laughing again, and Kat collapsed against the headboard, warm and sleepy and comfortable. She tried to stay awake by focusing her double vision on the flower arrangement in front of the fireplace, fighting the urge to close her eyes. She had to finish

this, finish what she'd set out to do. She dropped one leg over
the edge of the bed so that it touched the floor, to moor it so it
wouldn't spin. Everything was warm and blurred and hazy. She
wanted to pay her debt and get it over with, but it was easier
not to think. She just wanted to rest her eyes for a minute. Time
was not easy to hold on to. She felt Bea move, and then she was
fighting sleep again, or maybe she had drifted off, when Bea's
cheek touched hers, soft as fine linen. Bea's mouth was sweet
with scotch. Somewhere inside, Kat knew she should stop it. But
it was beyond her now, out of her control. She had wanted it to
happen. She had asked for it, or at least allowed it. Now it was
here. She wished she had not come to this place, and she put her
hands out as if to make herself heard, but they just hung in the
air, useless, like broken wings. She was weighted down, at the
bottom of a deep well, pinned under the force of the spinning
room.

Bea's face moved above her. Her hands, gentle and persistent,
swam through Kat's vision. She was slipping in and out of focus,
watching this orchestrated dream. And she saw that, after all, it
was warm and close and familiar, like watching yourself in a
mirror. And it was easier to lie there. The whiskey made it easy
to do nothing at all. She closed her eyes.

Then they slept. When Kat woke later, the room was dark,
and still rocked around her like a seasick ship. Bea didn't move.
Kat crept from the bed, pulling on her dress, carrying her shoes
and jacket, crept out the door to the elevator.

Her head hurt. She was dizzy, dizzy from the liquor, nauseated from the liquor. She loathed the thick taste on her tongue,
her unfamiliar body. Why had she done this? How had she gotten here? She wanted only one thing now—to be sick, alone, in
her own bathroom.

Thirteen

LITTLE, BROWN CAME UP WITH KAT'S FIRST PROOFREADING ASSIGN-
ment: a book on the techniques of Alpine skiing. She set her teeth
edge to edge and thought that Bea's connections had brought immediate results. For the first time since she'd been six, the second
week of September had come and she was not in school. There
was no excitement over a new art class, or the anticipation of
Nineteenth-century Fiction with her favorite professor. There
were only the interminable lines of type stretching in front of
her, requiring so much—or was it that they required so little?
Making a caret and indicating the missing letter in paragraph
two in the margin, she pressed down hard on the point of her
blue pencil; it snapped. For the fourth time in an hour the plastic sharpener ground her lead into blue dust. The novelty of cor-
recting faulty copy and inverted quotation marks was, without
question, already gone.

It had seemed quite appealing at first, and when she'd begun
the job two days ago, she'd savored her own image: sitting here
on the porch in the sun with the long white galleys and her pencil ready for the mark. To accomplish something in a clearly
defined way, to say, "I must finish this page before three and the
next chapter by five," to give definition, a beginning and end to
her days—this was what she longed for. She was not prepared for
the tedium. She did not have the sort of small remote control

brain requisite for such exacting work, and so, periodically, she sat back in her comfortable chair and nodded off on a daydream, watched the breeze stir up the soft branches of the firs, listened to the growl of the housekeeper's vacuum cleaner inside the house. Or, when the wind was right, hummed with the gardener as he weeded and pruned in some bed she could not see.

The pages littered the glass table in front of her and she sighed, thinking that she had never had much patience. Ten long years ago—was it really ten?—those intricate piano scales had been the test. Her mother sat beside her on the bench, her dress and grooming as carefully maintained as a valuable work of art: each piece of jewelry complimented the next; her blouse and slacks contrasted not only in color, but in texture too; her fine blond hair was bound against the nape of her neck with a silk scarf; her fingernails were almond-shaped and clear as ivory. Even the smallest detail was important to Lily.

Kat watched with envy as her mother rippled over the intricate arpeggios. She tried so hard to imitate all those perfectly rounded notes; she pretended her hands were her mother's smooth instruments. But somewhere, perhaps right in the middle of a crescendo, she would hit F-sharp instead of F, or G instead of A, and Lily's brow would tighten, just a little. Kat would plow up a whole step, wishing desperately for that perfection, aching, aching to bring a smile of approval to her mother's face. And in her striving, she inevitably made another mistake. Lily said nothing, waiting, it seemed, for the next musical travesty. Kat wanted to apologize. She wanted to feel the absolution of her mother's cool palm against her cheek. She needed her mother to reach out and reassure her. But there was nothing except the sweaty clumsiness of her fingers: drop and roll, drop and roll. The metronome clicked like a bomb, marking the time Kat could not keep. She struggled through to the end, swallowing against her own loathing, wanting to cry, while her mother sat in silence, hands arranged perfectly in her lap, holding the stemmed wineglass in a delicate grasp. And each day there was this ritual hour of mother-daughter torture because Lily required it.

No, Kat sighed. Playing with words, with these intricate rules, logistics, signs, was no different from that. She hated it just the same. I am not suited for this, she thought, as she checked her watch again. Although it was only four o'clock she was tempted to stop anyway. She looked to the long yellow pad on the other side of the table, a pad covered with lists and notations for the party. That was what she wanted to be doing. Planning her party. The best party ever given in this house. A party to shame all other parties. A party for her father's sixtieth birthday.

Since the company had regained its financial balance, Kirk's mood had improved considerably, and he'd allowed Kat to talk him into the celebration, even though a year had not yet passed since Lily's death. It was time they came out of hiding, Kat had said, anxious to hostess such an elaborate event, and his birthday was a perfect excuse. Hours had already been spent in search of new and exotic menu ideas, pages filled with guest lists, and Mrs. George driven to distraction with Kat's obsession. She had ordered hundreds and hundreds of imported spring flowers to supplement those she would use from the Sinclair greenhouse, had even asked the gardener to string tiny electric lights through all the bushes and trees. She craved magic; she craved accolades. It was as important to her as the debutante ball—for she was coming out as the mistress of the Sinclair estate, the woman who managed her father's life. And they would all see how beautifully she fit here, and her father would be at her side.

The wind moved the pages of the galley beneath her hand. She had to finish this, she thought with desperation, looking around as though someone might come to her rescue. Then the idea of a beer took her all of a sudden, with violent appeal, and by the time she got to the refrigerator, she was salivating. She grabbed an iced Heineken and went toward the cupboard for a glass stein.

"Isn't it a bit early?" Mrs. George asked, looking up from her cutting board where she was peeling onions.

"It's daylight-saving time," Kat said, stopping short and deciding that she didn't need the stein after all. "If it weren't for the government, it'd be five o'clock."

She hurried out to the porch, sealing her lips around the rolled edge of the bottle to suck down the cool gold tang. Now she could finish her work. Now she could concentrate. It made it all less boring, it made her feel safe. She would finish; it wouldn't be so hard. The long columns of type were less tedious, or maybe she just cared less, but in any case, the time was passing and she no longer wanted to scream. The letters, the pages, her pencil, all relaxed into one. She sucked again on the bottle, looking for more magic, and saw, with sudden apprehension, that it was halfway gone. It had to last as long as she was working. She sipped now as if it were gold, as if it were the last water on a desert island, and the dwindling line of froth in the bottle obsessed her. No matter how slowly, how carefully, she drank, it kept getting lower and lower. She needed an endless jug where the line always stayed the same. There was only one solution, she thought angrily: get another bottle. She still had forty-five minutes of snowplows and stem cristies to go, and the dregs in this one were warm. A new bottle. Ice cold. Crisp. The aroma filled her mind. She couldn't put it aside. She had to have it.

She deserved a new one, she thought, as she padded down the hall in her bare feet. She had been hard at work. There was an infinite number of reasons why she deserved that second beer.

She peered in the kitchen door, and seeing Mrs. George was nowhere about, hurried across to the refrigerator, stepping carefully around the squeaky floorboard. With stealth, she opened the door, and eased two bottles from the shelf.

Now the work zipped by, and her eyes skipped from line to line like a stone across water. There seemed fewer and fewer errors than before, and she turned the pages faster, eager for the end of this chapter, her pencil in one hand, her beer in the other. She was flying, she was skimming down the long hill to the finish line, and elation filled her.

And then Paige strolled out onto the porch, heading straight for the bar. Ice, gin, tonic, lime, in a tall glass. Kat eyed the damp white shirt clinging to her sister's back, the high color in her face. She tapped her pencil tip on the edge of the table. She rarely went to the club, except when she took Kirk up on his occasional offer of a golf lesson, because she'd never really enjoyed it. Sports were not her forte. "Been at the club *all day?*"

Paige held the glass against her cheek, and the tonic bubbles spread a fine cool mist over her face. "I'd like to give Dad a *real* game Saturday."

Kat finished her bottle and reached for the next, going back to the galley again, making her little blue footprints across the page. She wanted very much to look official and efficient.

Paige came and stood behind her, reading over her shoulder. "You missed a typo," she said, pointing, "here. And here's another."

"I just haven't gotten there yet," Kat lied as she penciled in the corrections. "Enough for tonight." She shuffled the pages into a pile and put an elastic around them.

"Why are you doing this?" Paige asked, moving to the other side of the table and sitting down. "Aaron's on your back?"

Kat felt the taunt and held her beer close. "I like it," she said. "It's something to do."

"C'mon, Kat. Golf, tennis, parties. There's plenty to do." She shrugged. "The benefits of the leisure class."

Kat ignored her and dragged again on her beer.

Paige reached out to the yellow pad and flipped through the pages. "What's this?"

"It's for my party," Kat answered, stretching across the table and plucking the pad from Paige's grasp.

"Your party?"

"My party for Dad's birthday," Kat amended. It occurred to her now that in the zeal of her planning she'd forgotten to prepare herself for Paige. It was supposed to be her night, and Paige wasn't going to horn in on it.

"I bought a dress for it today," Paige said, eying her over the ice in her glass.

"Oh?" Kat tried to sound disinterested.

"I'm having it altered." She smiled with absolute confidence. "You'll love it."

"Getting it let out?"

Paige threw back her head and laughed. She tossed her long

blond hair across her shoulder. "No," she said, "cut down." She
ran her finger across her cleavage. "And slit." She ran her finger
up the side of her thigh.

Kat took another hit of her beer, trying to quench the long
slow thirst that had started when Paige first began talking about
the party.

"I can see," she said, eyes narrowed, "that once again subtlety
has eluded you."

Again her sister's head went back and again she laughed. Kat
wanted to drive the blue pencil into the taut creamy skin of her
throat. "Sorry," Paige said, grinning, as she looked with amusement at Kat's chest. "I forgot you're the jealous type."

Well, thought Kat, as Paige sauntered back into the house, if
she's going to ruin my party, I deserve another drink. She went
to the bar, and filled a double old-fashioned glass full of gin, forgetting the ice, topping it with tonic. She needed to go high,
higher. She needed to get away from Paige's taunts, away from
her face, her breasts, her tongue. In her mind, Kat saw Paige
waving her body like a flag, a sinuous, undulating red flag.

She lay down on the sofa, gin in her mouth like water. She
was planning her defense in the haze of self-justification and
self-pity which the alcohol so neatly provided. Tomorrow she
would buy a new dress, she decided defiantly. A new dress better than her sister's. An elegant dress, with class. A new dress, so
that her father would love her better. And dreaming of the magical transformation it would bring her, she fell asleep, her drink
still in her hand.

_____ *Fourteen* _____

SLEEPING AND WAKING SHE DREAMED OF THE PARTY, HOUR AFTER hour, all through the rest of September. It was the core of each day, an object fixed in her mind, a piece of iron sculpture that she turned this way and that, inspecting each detail, every line and curve. The kitchen staff had been running mad with her incessant directives, and Aaron had simply stopped coming by, as if waiting for the siege to end. The proofreading she had promised to finish by the first of October lay incomplete on her desk.

Kat saw none of this, so consumed was she with her planning. Somewhere deep inside her a voice had spoken up, a voice which warned that her life should not be this way, that the planning should not overrun all her time, that she should take control —and each night she promised herself that tomorrow would be different. Each day she rose, intending to spend only a few hours with her plans, and then, inexplicably, it was five o'clock. Time for cocktails. The way the days slipped by nagged at her. But she put her worry aside, just as she pushed aside Aaron's concern for her. She did not know how to help herself.

By the time the weekend for the party arrived, her anxiety had reached an electrical dimension. She ran from one task to the other, accomplishing very little. Friday afternoon every window and door was opened to fill the house with crisp autumn air; Mrs. George's preparations in the kitchen were double-checked;

at least fifteen minutes went to admire a leftover sample of the elegant invitations she'd had engraved at Shreve's; and then, once again, the handpainted place cards, which had come that morning from the calligrapher, were checked.

A delivery man arrived with a package—the beautiful new dress she had found on Wednesday at Charles Sumner's on Newbury Street. She'd bought new shoes, bra, panties, and slip at Bonwit's. She would be as pristine and perfect as a bride. And her mother's emerald necklace, lifted from its usual home at the vault, would match the deep green of the dress. As she unpacked the long fall of silk and hung it in her closet, she projected her own image in her mind, considering modifications, wondering, would she be perfect enough?

Helena's phone call late that afternoon forced her to emerge from the maze of her own thoughts. On the brink of calling the florist to change the centerpieces for the fifth time, Kat did not want to chat right then, but her best friend was, as usual, very persistent. When she learned why Kat wanted to cut the conversation short, she flatly refused to hang up.

"Ridiculous," she said. "Stop being so obsessed and get out of that house! Be at the Brattle in time for the six o'clock show."

"Are you insane?" Kat snapped, barely able to control her temper. "Have you any idea—"

"No, and I don't really care either. Meet me at five forty-five." And with that she hung up, short-circuiting Kat's arguments.

Even then, Kat wasn't going to go, but when Mrs. George began to bark with exasperation at her meddling, suddenly she had an impulse to get out and away from the waiting and the suspense. And so she went, leaving the house in its state of undress, went into town with the windows open, the radio blaring, dodging heavy traffic—all in a vain attempt to stop her mind from continuing its relentless agitation.

Helena was in the foyer of the Brattle Theater, tapping her foot and flipping the pages of a coming attractions leaflet. "Just in time," she said, handing Kat her ticket and ushering her through the door. "It's about to start." She hurried down the dark aisle and found two seats at the front of the theater. "What took so long?"

"Had to change some instructions with the caterer," Kat whispered.

Helena groaned. "If I hear one more word about this party—" She stopped short and settled back to watch the titles for *Sons and Lovers* move across the screen.

The Brattle was one of the frayed and battered theaters in Harvard Square that catered to student demand and ran old classic films—Bogart, Chaplin, Garbo, Bacall. *Sons and Lovers* or *Women in Love* played there at least once a year, and Helena and Kat—literature majors to the core—always made a point of going. Kat looked over now and saw that Helena was engrossed in the story as usual—but her own mind whirled on like a tornado, picking up new ideas and spitting them out, combing over the old ones, cultivating her fine obsession. She couldn't let it go, couldn't put it down, not even for a favorite old film, and she shifted about in her seat, crossing and uncrossing her legs, until Helena finally leaned over.

"Are you O.K.?"

"Fine," Kat said absentmindedly. "Just hungry and thirsty."

"I was thinking about a soda too."

"Not that kind of thirsty." She shifted again on the worn and lumpy seat. "I wish they sold beer at theaters the way they do at ballparks."

Helena just looked at her—with a queer expression, Kat thought. But now that she'd spoken of it, the idea of a drink plagued her, and she couldn't wait to get out of the theater to a restaurant. It was so hot in here. The itchy velvet seat pricked the backs of her legs. She bit her fingernail and kept seeing a tall, iced martini, kept tasting a tall, iced martini. The movie she had once loved seemed endless now, and she berated herself for getting talked into coming again. The dialogue irritated her, the worn, scratched film irritated her, the popcorn gritting under her sandals irritated her. How could she ever have enjoyed this? She felt glad to have escaped college life with all its ragged activities. She was glad to be an adult at last.

But an hour later, they were sitting in their familiar wooden booth at the Wursthaus—the place they used to hit for midnight bologna sandwiches during exam period—and Kat was glad, after all, that she had come. There were the brightly colored decorations, the links of sausage looped over the bar mirror, the bar list cut in the shape of a blue beer tankard. Kat summoned the waitress at once. "An extra dry martini, on the rocks, with a twist." She paused. "A double. And I mean as dry as the desert." She looked up into the bored face of the waitress. "Or I'll send it back."

"I guess I'll have a beer," Helena said, staring at Kat with a probing, puzzled expression. "Whatever you've got on draft."

The waitress nodded and moved off. Kat picked up her fork and fingered the tines, trying to relax.

"How's work?"

Kat shrugged, loathe to tell Helena how boring it really was. Helena had warned her and now Kat couldn't bear to give her the satisfaction. "I think I'm good at it."

"How about Aaron?"

The waitress put down their drinks, and Kat let the gin slide down her throat in a long slow line. Tonight she would limit herself to two drinks. She didn't want Helena on her back. "Aaron?" she repeated, setting her glass down. "He's just the same as always."

"But now that you've got the job—aren't things going a lot smoother?"

Kat took another long sip and frowned. "I don't know." She sighed. "It's just—he pushes me so to be ambitious. He thinks proofing's a waste of me. Free-lance work isn't a real job to him."

Helena licked a line of head from the edge of her beer mug. "Do you really think it is?" She looked down into her glass then and shook her head. "Kat, I'm sorry. I don't mean to push you either. But both Aaron and I care—a lot—and that's why—"

"You girls ready to order?" interrupted the waitress.

"Chicken, lettuce, and tomato, on rye," said Helena.

"Another double martini, extra dry," Kat began.

"Rocks, twist?" the waitress asked.

Kat nodded. "And bologna on white with mayonnaise." She winked at Helena. "For old time's sake. Want another beer?"

Helena shook her head. "I'm fine."

"I'm tired of Aaron harping at me," Kat said, draining the bottom of her glass as the waitress left. She was buoyed up now on that nice warm glow, and it was a glow that almost made her forget. "How I sleep, how I work, how I make love, how I talk, how I drink. I don't know." She pulled her mouth into a bitter smile. "I just want a little peace and quiet. All we do is fight."

"Look on the bright side," Helena urged. "You got the job with a minimum of effort, and at least you two are still together."

Kat's drink and their sandwiches arrived. "It was a good thing I met Bea," Kat said, trying to talk with her mouth full. "I mean —without her—I'd've had a lot of trouble. She really went to bat for me."

"You lucked out," Helena observed.

Something in her dry tone irritated Kat. "You make your own luck," she said, tilting her glass up. Slowly the tables around her began to revolve, like a merry-go-round, she thought abstractedly; the music overhead was sliding in and out of her ears, the wooden bench felt slippery and hard under her. She looked up dizzily and saw Helena waiting for her to continue. "I mean," she went on, her chin thrust forward, "nobody handed that job to me. I worked for it." And she began describing to Helena just how hard she had worked, how hard it had been to call Bea that first time, how difficult everything had been for her this year. She spoke vehemently and waved her hands in the air.

Helena put down her sandwich, wondering what had set Kat off on this bewildering rampage. She was obviously high—but that wasn't particularly surprising considering the size of those drinks. It occurred to Helena now exactly why Kat had been so preoccupied at the movies: she'd just been waiting to get here, and get her hands around that first martini. Aaron was right to be so worried about her. "Kat," she interrupted, "maybe you'd better not finish the rest of that."

"Nonsense." Kat drained the glass, as if to prove that her hand was still steady enough to reach her mouth. "S'very good. In fact"—she waved her arm for the waitress—"a third would be even better."

Three doubles, Helena thought to herself. Three doubles—that wasn't three drinks, that was six. Now she realized that by trying to stop Kat, she had only dared her into going further. Her drinking was stupid and selfish, and it wasn't like Kat at all. Helena knew this girl nearly as well as she knew herself, and she was confused by this uncharacteristic incoherence, this stream of self-pity. But then a few words in the deluge of slippery syllables caught her ear—something about the woman who got Kat the job.

"You think it all comes so easy?" she was saying. "You think I got *lucky?*" She spat out the word sarcastically. "Let me tell you —I groveled! And for what!" She stared with belligerence at Helena.

"What are you talking about?" Helena asked in astonishment. "Groveled how?"

"You pay for what you get," Kat declared. She raised her eyebrows and lowered her voice. "I paid her all right. One afternoon in her room at the Ritz."

Helena thought she would throw up; she couldn't believe it. "You went to bed with her?"

"Went?" Kat threw back her head and laughed, loud and staccato. "Not like buying for cash, you know—s'like an old bad debt. I'll have to keep on . . ." she drank again ". . . paying."

"That's disgusting," Helena said in a flat tone as she pushed her unfinished sandwich away from her. "Where's your pride and self-respect? Do you hate yourself that much?"

Kat's eyes were thin, hostile shards of light. "First Aaron, now you. I should've known. Can't win." She started to cry, but the tears rolled down her cheeks unnoticed. "Y'think I did it because I *wanted* to? Was all I could think of, was a way out. Now you criticize too."

"No one held a gun to your head." Helena leaned forward on her elbows and spoke vehemently, loudly, as though that would make Kat hear better. "You could've found other ways. You were just too lazy, or too dumb. Or maybe too drunk."

"Don't you talk to me!" Kat hissed. "You can't push me around!" Opening her purse, she grabbed a ten-dollar bill and threw it on the table. "I don't want you. I don't *need* you."

Through the coils of her anger, Helena saw she was ready to stalk off and knew they could not end this way. She reached her hand across the table, but Kat threw it off.

"A little late," she sneered. "D'you think I'd forget what you said. You looked at me like I was a whore!"

"I didn't!"

"No excuses now. I'm going. You won't have to sit with someone you despise."

She rose from her seat clumsily to find Helena standing directly in her way.

"Sit down and let's talk like adults." For a moment the tear-streaked face hesitated. "Besides," Helena urged, "you've had too much to drive now anyway."

The remark hit Kat like a door slamming shut: a final slur, a final dare. Why did no one see? She shoved Helena aside and wove her way out between the tables, crying with a despair she had never touched before—despair at being so maligned. The hell with them then; she would go back where she belonged, back to her father, back where she was understood and loved. Tomorrow night she would do what she was best at. They would all see. She would prove Aaron and Helena wrong. She would be on her father's arm, and she would be his perfect match.

Fifteen

DRIVING HOME HAD BEEN A FEAT OF EXPERTISE. THE WINDING ROAD to Concord shimmered and rocked under the car, and finally, in order to block out the doubled yellow line, Kat had simply shut one eye. The next morning her hangover seemed more like a terminal injury, and even her depression about Helena and her worry about the party that evening dimmed next to the thirst, nausea, and headache.

The day melted into a flurry of last minute tasks, and at six o'clock she went upstairs to dress. The hot bath rich with Badedas relaxed her a little, but the martini balanced on the edge of the tub did more. Looking up at the ceiling, tiled in contrasting blue mosaic stones, she lathered her arms and legs and decided that tonight would be different. She was going to be careful; she would have to be unless she wanted a repeat of last night's performance and this morning's queasiness. She would watch herself: a few discreet cocktails, a little wine with dinner, and that was all.

She submerged for a while, hoping that the bath would soak away the remains of last night's spectacle. If only the hot water could cleanse her mind as it did her skin, if it could just lift away the particles of memory and diffuse them into the indifferent steam. There was a lingering taste of shame about the whole affair, but she could not possibly admit, even to herself, that Hel-

ena's points were well taken. Remembering Helena's words, all
that she had said, all that unnecessary cruelty, Kat could not put
it from her mind. And what was worse—tonight she would have
to face Helena and speak with her as though nothing had happened.

And when she saw her for the first time, what, Kat wondered,
scooping up bubbles and rubbing her elbows, would they say to
one another. For her part, she would pretend to be cordial. She
would wait for Helena's apology.

At her walnut vanity, she made up her face, rouging her
cheekbones subtly, darkening her lash line with a smudgy charcoal pencil, and then mascara. Out of her dresser drawer came
the new uplift bra, which gave her more cleavage than biology
had willed. She would be composed and graceful, she decided as
she bent to shake her breasts into the cups and fasten the strap.
The green silk slipped on, cool and smooth. She turned in the
mirror, admiring the way the deep skirt encircled her waist, the
way the sheer straight sleeve emphasized the length of her neck
and her slender arms. The neckline cut a smooth half-moon
against the tanned skin of her chest, and she thought with satisfaction that the new bra certainly improved matters.

A new thought interrupted her session with the mirror, and
she spoke aloud to her reflection. "What if she tells Aaron about
Bea?" She stood motionless while her mind raced in a tight circle, like a dog with a scarf in its teeth. But no, she thought
slowly, relief coming to her gradually, Helena's code of ethics
wouldn't allow it. Kat's confession would be protected by their
unspoken pact as women, and there were some things women
simply kept to themselves. Her mother's emeralds were cold
against the base of her collarbone as she fastened the choker and
realized that to greet Helena would be harder than she cared to
think about.

Finishing her martini, she saw it was a quarter to eight. She
paused, spraying a fine mist of her mother's lemon-scented perfume on her wrists and neck, wondering where Paige was. She
hadn't seen her all day. Once again she wished that her sister
would just stay away. Concentrating hard, she outlined her lips

with a pencil, and then applied color and gloss, forcing herself to
stop worrying about Paige, trying to bully her brain into letting
go of the anxiety. She stood and surveyed the lines of her new
gown, the fine glow of her make-up, and then, with a deep
breath, she turned to go downstairs.

The September evening was a rare sixty degrees. Kat swept
through the house like a queen inspecting her court. Everything
was in place. The trees and shrubs, strung with lights, shimmered as if under a million small candles, as if it were Christmas. The warmth of the orchids, tiger lilies, and dahlias from the
Sinclair greenhouse spread through the polished rooms. Kat had
left no margin for error. It was a perfect creation.

On the patio stood the raw bar: its rows of oysters and littlenecks stared up naked as eyeballs, the shrimp curved head to tail.
Silver clamshells holding a spiced cocktail sauce were set into
the bed of crushed ice, and the yellow of a hundred lemons
garnished its border.

Kat felt queasy just looking at them all, remembering the cold
slimy feeling of the only oyster she'd ever eaten. Her father had
insisted she try one: it was her twelfth birthday and she'd cried
as she gagged it up, that horrible live animal coming back whole
onto her dinner plate. She'd never eaten an oyster since, always
seeing her father's face, how he'd laughed and how she'd hated
him.

She went back into the house to check the living room, long
and elegant, with its vaulted ceiling and high-arched windows.
Down the five stairs leading into the room, and to the right, a
linen-draped bar was tended by four attendants; champagne and
white wine lay cooling in large tubs of ice; there was every
imaginable bottle, every imaginable mixer, every imaginable
garnish—from onion to olive to caper to cherry. A dance floor
had been laid at the far end of the room, just in front of the
stone fireplace, and an eight-piece orchestra quietly tuned its instruments.

She stood silently, hands by her side, scenting out the mood
of the room, the atmosphere, the pulse of the painting she had
drawn. She saw the room anew, as if she had just entered, as if

she were a guest here for the first time. And it was the roses she
saw now, masses of roses, scarlet roses, head to sleek head, long-
stemmed in crystal vases, almost wicked in their luxury, in their
voluptuous color. They highlighted the oriental tapestries on the
walls. They contrasted with the dark wood of the windows and
floors. They were a force unto themselves.

Through the kitchen door, she could see the rows of salad, of
condiment, and dessert. Maids streamed in and out, carrying
cold hors d'oeuvres and glasses to the bar. The house hummed
like a hive, with the kitchen as its center, and Mrs. George, face
harried with exertion, barking orders left and right, was in her
element. Kat came in anyway, determined to check everything,
to ensure nothing would go wrong. Her mother had done it precisely this way, moving over each preparation, tasting a bit here
and there, like a hummingbird hovering to sip at occasional
flowers; Kat imitated her now, remembering her mother's tempo
as she proceeded through the kitchen. She checked the last minute garnishes and intricate seasonings until the housekeeper's patience was gone.

Her father did not see her at first as she came back to the living room and stood in the shadows of the hall. She was silent,
watching him as he leaned on the edge of the grand piano; she
watched him like a voyeur. The line of his arm was so fine
against the polished wood of the instrument, the strength of his
shoulders subdued under the formal evening clothes. Her love
was an expanding force; it pressed out against her rib cage till
she thought her spine would snap. For a moment he stood there,
still as a portrait, and then he sighed, turned toward the door,
and saw her.

She moved with a hesitant step; she felt shy; she was giving
him time to form an opinion. Her dress rippled as she walked,
and the soft sleeve and neckline contrasted with the angularity
of her face. It was not at all the effect of lazy sensuality she had
tried so hard to achieve. Instead she had merely emphasized that
appealing vulnerability inherited from her mother, that unexpected combination of softness and sharpness—like biting
through dark chocolate to find a salted nut.

And on his face there was love and approval and admiration. She wished she had a camera. "Happy Birthday," she said, even though she really wanted to say far more.

He bowed from the waist, a formal gesture, as if Kat were a great lady. "Your mother would be proud."

"People should be here soon," she said, clearing her throat.

"Relax." He lit a cigarette. "You've done the work. The staff does the rest." He paused for a moment and his eyes dimmed as he bit down hard into the filter tip. "Your mother knew—how to let go of a party, and let it gain its own momentum." He piped it into an ashtray. "A great hostess. Give up the helm and let the party drift where it wants."

"Yes," she said, not at all sure she could unwind for even a minute.

The invitation had read eight o'clock, so naturally everyone was late the requisite half-hour. Kat watched them as they filled the rooms, the bright colors of the women's gowns accentuating the black and white formality of the men, the laughter, the sparkle of family jewels. The staff moved on efficient feet, balancing great silver trays of hors d'oeuvres, wine, and champagne as easily as if they were stacks of laundry.

Having welcomed her guests, Kat scanned the room for her father, and saw he still had no drink in his hand. Excusing herself, she made her way to the bar. "George," she said to the bartender, "two martinis, please. Precisely as I told you earlier."

In a few minutes she had her choice of two slender V-shaped glasses. She picked up the iced crystal and tasted it tentatively, prepared to send it back. She would not take her father a wet martini. But it was excellent after all and so she pressed through the throng to Kirk's elbow, nodding and smiling. The band picked up its first tune of the evening, a gentle waltz, and Kat handed her father the drink.

"Are you sure?" he asked, jerking his head in the direction of the bar.

"I gave him a lesson this afternoon."

He sniffed the fine aroma and sipped. "You certainly did." He smiled and winked at her. "Almost as good as yours." He gestured to the couple with whom he had been speaking. "Kat, you remember Doug and Martha Winfield?"

"A long time ago," she said, extending her hand. "Nice to see you again."

Mrs. Winfield smiled. "You've grown into quite the young lady. A marvelous party, my dear."

Kat accepted the compliment with a smile and linked her arm through her father's. "Dad, what would you say to a dance?"

"Will you excuse us?" Kirk bowed and guided Kat to the dance floor, moving her smoothly into the simple pattern. Kat was no more comfortable on a dance floor than she had been at the piano bench, and the last few weeks she had practiced every day in front of the full-length mirror in her bedroom. The effort had paid off, she realized, because she was managing to avoid her father's feet. Still, she wondered, as she made a grace step, why Paige had inherited all her mother's co-ordination.

"Relax," Kirk whispered, and she smiled up into his face. To hold him so near, to feel his chest rise and fall—suddenly she was overwhelmingly happy, safe, encircled by the broad sweep of his shoulder and the length of his arm. Faces swirled by and as the music slowed to a finish, she saw Aaron and Helena at the edge of the crowd. Her father released her and gave her a full court bow, which she returned with a deep curtsy. Laughter and applause came up to her in a warm wave of sound.

Buoyed by a surge of confidence, she crossed the floor to her friends and gave Aaron a hug because she was scared to look at Helena. When she turned to her at last, there was reservation in her friend's face; she might be willing to forgive, but she would not forget. "When did you get here?" Kat asked breathlessly, to cover her anxiety. "I'm sorry I wasn't at the door."

Aaron shrugged. "This is quite a party. How many do you have?"

"Around two hundred," she answered, arcing her arm through the air as if to encompass the crowd, as if to take credit for it. Something in his voice made it sound as if he did not count himself as part of it all, as if he were standing outside it. Kat didn't like his tone, and she felt Helena's eyes moving over her face. All

this scrutiny made her nervous. "That's a lovely dress, Helena—
I've never seen it before."

"Yes you have." She looked at her with a raised eyebrow.
"That graduation party last year—in the master's residence."

"Of course," Kat answered, feeling caught in an insincerity.
"I'd just forgotten."

"I was worried about you last night." Helena spoke bluntly.
"But I take it you arrived home unscathed?"

Kat looked over quickly to Aaron. She didn't want him to
know. "No problem at all," she answered, forcing her face to
smile. "So," she turned to Aaron and linked her arm through his.
"Could I bully you into a dance?"

But a hand pulled at the sleeve of her dress before he could
answer, and she turned to see one of the maids. "In the kitchen,
Miss Sinclair? Mrs. George would like to see you."

"I'll be right there." She turned back to Aaron and Helena.
"Try and find someone to talk with, I'll be back in a second."
She left them, annoyed that they so obviously felt out of place.
These were her two closest friends: why couldn't they make an
effort to enjoy themselves, loosen up and get a little involved?
She wanted them to admire her party, to applaud her effort. As
she pushed open the kitchen door, she realized that she was
angry with them and their discomfort. It was not what she had
planned at all.

"I just wanted to check," Mrs. George began, interrupting her
train of thought. "You'll still be wanting dinner at nine-thirty?
Your mother used to change it at the last minute sometimes—
after getting ahold of the mood of the party."

"But then the lamb would be overdone," Kat said in bewilder-
ment. Change had not been included in her schedule, where everything was clocked down to the minute.

"True. Of course, your mother designed her menus to be a bit
more flexible."

Kat looked crestfallen, and insecurity overwhelmed her. Had
she made the wrong choice?

"Now stop worrying," Mrs. George soothed her. "It'll all be

fine. You've done a marvelous job and we'll serve just like you planned. Go on back and enjoy yourself."

Back in the living room, Kat asked for a refill at the bar. This would be her last martini of the night, she promised herself as the bartender mixed the pitcher. Two were enough. Tonight she would not renege on that limit. She had a great deal to do, a lot of responsibility—too much to get mushy and incapable. Besides, she was really quite mellow already.

Her father did not seem to be among the boisterous crowd, and she had just decided that he must be on the patio, when her eye caught Aaron lounging against the wall in a corner on the far side of the room. Already his bow tie was knocked just a little askew, and she knew it was only a matter of time before he began to look thoroughly crumpled. She felt a surge of compassion for him then; she had been a good hostess to everyone but Aaron. She knew how he hated this kind of party—the sort which must surely remind him of his socialite parents—and suddenly she was sure that if she could only get him to smile everything would be right again. They would have a good time, like last year, if she made the extra effort, and so with a smile, she started toward him to ask him to dance.

As she reached his side, she felt the crowd turn around her—murmuring, rippling under the force of a single object. Everyone was watching the entrance to the room, staring at Paige, who stood on the uppermost step, silhouetted by the hall light.

Her dress was a skin of scarlet, sheathing every curve. Strapless silk, cut low. A slit parted the side of the narrow skirt. She wore no bra, and under the thin material her nipples rose subtly erect. Her hair was piled on her head in an ordered disarray, and roses of the same flaming hue as those Kat had chosen for this room were tucked into the shining golden loops. Around her neck she wore the twisted strand of diamonds that Lily had left her. She waited there, draped against the doorjamb, framed by the tall vases of roses, letting everyone look at her. She smiled. The force of the room was hers.

Jealousy blazed through Kat. Never had her sister looked more stunning; never had a whole crowd turned to stare like this. How

does she do it? she shouted silently. How can she get away with
the color and cut of that dress? And no underwear—it seemed
cheap, or sick. But even as she thought this, she knew it wasn't
true. Paige had too much of Lily's class to look compromised:
she was chic, and stunning in a way Kat could never hope to imitate. It was simply an exploitation of her assets, even if it was an
exploitation to which Lily would not have resorted.

Kat turned away, angry, and looked over at Aaron, who was
watching Paige with amusement.

"Good God," he said.

"Rather hard to ignore, isn't she?" Kat said bitterly, sipping
her drink. Her glass was halfway empty now, and she tried to
slow herself down.

"If you like her style," he conceded, trying to pass off Paige's
impact as he looked into Kat's face with sympathy.

"Let's dance," she said, switching the subject.

He was not a particularly accomplished dancer, not a master
of specific steps, but his rhythms and instincts were good and
they moved together in a graceful imitation of the intricate patterns. As they turned to avoid bumping into another couple, Kat
saw her father and Paige part the crowd as they came out onto
the dance floor. Closer range did not diminish her sister's mag-
netism. Kat took in the tiny feet and ankles, which moved with
expert precision, and saw that against his young daughter's delicacy, Kirk looked quite imposing. It was almost as if they had
been practicing together, Kat thought, envy as plain on her face
as a tattoo.

"Hey!" Aaron said, as he held her back from him so he could
see her face. "What's going on?"

"Sorry," she said, having missed the beat and stepped on his
foot. "It's time for dinner. Let's go see."

Kat led him off without waiting for his response, eager to escape from the sight of Paige and Kirk, and stopped to retrieve
her drink from the window sill where she'd set it down. "Damn,"
she said, looking about to find it gone. "I'll have to stop and get
another."

A threatened expression crossed his face.

"Listen," she said, with a bit of impatience, "I've only had one other tonight, and this one was barely touched." She shut her mouth down tight. She didn't mean to sound so defensive, but a confrontation now with Aaron over drinking was out of the question. Distract him, she thought, just distract him. She took his hand and led him toward the dining room.

Everywhere there were candles. All the furniture had been removed except the long buffet tables, leaving the room open, with the lavish food on the linen its sole spotlight. A white-capped chef carved the roast saddle of lamb, pink and moist under his shining blade, and the pungent aroma of rosemary and garlic drifted to Kat and Aaron where they stood in the doorway. There were trays of intricately cut vegetables—tomato roses, oval potatoes, julienned carrots. Cold asparaus spears lay napped with hollandaise sauce. Kat straightened with pride as she sensed Aaron's astonishment.

"You arranged all this?" he asked.

"That's why I've been so busy," she said, turning her face up to his.

But he did not answer, and she felt once again that faint aura of disapproval emanating from him; to forestall any comment, she pulled him toward the tables. "Come on," she urged, "you must be hungry."

Aaron filled his plate and they found their places at one of the tables in the library. Helena wandered in and Kat watched them eat as she drank her martini. No one said much. There was just an awkward silence which Helena kept trying to fill with small talk. Every time Kat lifted her glass she could see them grow tenser and more watchful. The sensation of having been robbed, or cheated, built inside her and her anger at them all increased: Aaron and Helena, who refused to enjoy themselves; Paige, who had taken the party from her.

Helena continued to try and draw Kat out, to keep her talking instead of drinking. The gravity of the situation—the extent of Kat's fantasies about her father, her mother, and herself—had never been more clear to Helena. She had lost her friend, and she looked to Aaron, hoping to find reassurance in his eyes—but there was none. He seemed desolate, and alone. She pushed the food around on her plate, determined to find a way to break through.

Kat couldn't bear Helena's obvious concern and the useless conversation any longer, so she excused herself and went back to the living room. Her father and Paige were making the rounds of the guests, arms linked.

Kat went to the bar and got another martini; she no longer cared about limits or watching herself, or tomorrow morning; she cared only to ease that ache, that anger. Perhaps what hurt most was her father's blind inattention to her: the fact that he didn't miss her in the least, didn't come to tell her how much he was enjoying all her careful preparations, the food she had spent hours planning. Nothing.

Now Paige and Kirk were standing before the special surprise Kat had created for him—the chocolate table. It was in addition to the more ordinary dessert table on the other side of the room: a table laden with small chocolate pastries, chocolate tortes, dark chocolate nuts and fruits, chocolate liqueurs, cappuccino. But Kirk didn't even seem to notice, he was so caught up in introducing Paige. It was easy to see it now, she thought, easy to hate them. She narrowed her eyes and swallowed again.

Aaron appeared at her elbow. "Have you eaten anything yet?" he asked, eyeing her fresh drink suspiciously.

"I'm fine," she said. "Have you had any dessert? Chocolate there," she pointed, "or Grand Marnier soufflés here," she gestured with her glass, and then downed the rest of it. She could tell he was getting tired of the noise and distraction of the other people; he was not a party person. She had turned her back and was watching her father and Paige again when Aaron put his arms around her waist. They stood, linked for a minute. Then he said quietly, "Come home with me tonight."

"Tonight?"

"Yes. Now. Sneak out the back door with me right now. No one'll notice." He put his chin down on top of her head. "It's been so long."

She stiffened and pulled away. "That's just like you, Aaron,"

she said, without turning to look at him. "As if I'd leave my own
party. Desert my guests." She walked over to the dessert table
and ordered a coffee liberally spiked with Kahlúa. How dare he
suggest no one would notice she was gone. By now she was a little drunk, just drunk enough not to care about provoking him.
She was sure he'd marked the slightly uneven way she'd crossed
the room. Maybe she wanted to make him mad, make someone
pay some attention. Maybe that was why she poured the liqueur
in her coffee with such a flourish. When she finally glanced over
her shoulder, she was just in time to see him turn—turn and leave
the room. He was going, and suddenly she very much wanted
him to stay.

Aaron walked through the crowd and the brightly lit house,
outside, to the circular driveway, where he'd parked his car. He
felt only conflicting currents of anger and despair. She had left
him nowhere to go. She had backed him into a wall, and surely
this was the end. She had succeeded in freezing him out,
trapped him into surrendering. He bent to unlock the door, and
dropped the key in the dark. As he stooped to retrieve it, someone came up behind him.

"Don't go," Kat said, her voice near to crying.

He wanted to take her in his arms and heal the wounds, but
he had done it too many times before. Nothing ever helped.
Nothing changed. He did not turn around. He did not want to
see her face.

She caught his arm.

"Let me go," he said. "I'm tired."

"But it's still early." She didn't understand. Her brain was
wrapped in cotton batting and he was talking to her, but she
couldn't understand what he was saying. If only he would turn
around and face her. His words struck at her dully, off balance,
without piercing the skin. He said something about her father,
about the money, the house, the booze. What did it matter, she
wanted to scream at him, she needed him, needed his arms. She
was so confused—he couldn't be going now. This wasn't the way
it was supposed to be.

"Don't go," she said, having no words left. There was no lan-

guage. His shoulders were shaking, and she saw numbly that he
must be crying. She heard him say that she would have to
choose, choose between him and her father, between him and
booze. She couldn't listen any more to the assault of the words.
She turned from him, from his wet and angry face, that face he
wouldn't bring around to her, and started back into the house.
The dark surrounded her as she ran from the choice he had set
out. And even in her drunkenness she knew that truth equaled
danger, that to know the truth would require facing it, changing
herself, her life—all those things she dreaded most. She stumbled
into the back entryway and stood in the dark hall, her spine
pressed hard against the door, as if she had just escaped a terrible adversary, as if she could shut out choice behind her.

She started to cry, and the sound of the Toyota's engine
roared past the barricade to grind against her ears. She shut her
eyes, but the sound continued in her mind even after Aaron had
gone down the driveway. It was a sound she had heard before,
she thought dizzily; she needed to pin it down, and know why it
mattered. A car starting somewhere, a car starting in anger, in a
night of anger.

Yes, that was it. Her mother. On a holiday evening. Perhaps it
was only last Christmas. Or any Christmas. Lily had been alive.
She had been hostess that night for the traditional Sinclair dinner, and she'd conducted the meal effortlessly, balanced precisely, as always, on the edge of her chair. Her back never
touched the solid wood. She never bent her head to her food,
never spilled a drop of soup, never lost a crumb on the way. She
made it look easy.

Kat remembered how her mother had captivated the man
seated to her left, and she'd strained to hear what they were saying, but they were only talking about hobbies. He said he liked
to dabble in commodities; Lily said Kirk spent his free time gardening. Her fingernails tapped the edge of her wineglass. It
wasn't what they were saying, Kat decided. It was how her
mother was saying it, how she listened in that absorbed way,
how she responded—as if he were the only one with whom she
discussed such intimate affairs.

Lily's high-necked green dress emphasized the smallness of her features, her delicate face and hands, her hazel eyes. Her mouth was set in a gentle careful curve. But even her beauty did not begin to equal the impact her eyes made—eyes that reached out, eyes that betrayed an inner vulnerability, a softness, a need. When you looked at her you could not help wanting to protect her. This was her power, and she knew it.

Lily glanced at her elder daughter, and as Kat looked down into her mother's polite company smile she saw the weariness beneath the marble cheekbones. She saw the subtle pain in her eyes, that voiceless appeal which she had never understood. What was her mother really thinking? Kat wondered. She kept watching, mesmerized by the fluid motions of eating and drinking, caught on the gleam of the cutlery, on the gleam of light coming from her mother's blond head. She wished she could look like her mother; she wished men would stare at her the way they stared at her mother; she wished she were sophisticated like her mother. That inimitable way she held her champagne glass, for instance, the way she stroked its long fluted stem with her fingers. And when she lifted it to sip, she was the essence of pure chic; she might have been a color advertisement for Dom Perignon.

Kat looked down at her plate. She could hear her mother's voice flickering across the table like musical lightning, and her mind clicked down unknowingly on the sound, an automatic tracking device. She began to listen carefully to Lily's voice. She listened to the enunciation of the words, the way her mother's tongue pushed out each soft vowel, the way the consonants stuck against her teeth. She heard the subtle slur, the addition of letters not there. Lily had slipped a bit. No one else would notice. But Kat had noticed, and the anxiety started pumping in her stomach. She wanted to take her mother upstairs and put her to bed, take her away before her father noticed.

But of course Kirk already had; he was already aware, Kat saw, as she watched him click his knife against the side of the fragile plate. His jaw was a tense wire, his smile stretched pale. He knew the signs too well. There was something supremely irri-

tating to Kirk about that doting look in his wife's eyes, something which ignited fear and anger in him. Kat watched him listen to their talk about the stock market, about commodities and
this man's recent success. She knew he resented her mother's
fawning tone, the way she sounded impressed; he was thinking
that she ought to know better. He frowned. He tried to concentrate on his roast beef.

Kat could smell it coming on—the way you can smell a thun-
derstorm as it approaches, the way the wind turns the leaves un-
derside up before the rain. She looked up and down the table at
the two of them. She wanted to put down her glass and look
away from her mother, but her mother gleamed like a spinning
object. Tension began running down Kat's sides. Time and space
tightened around her, and for a minute she could not remember
what year it was. She might have been a little girl in her best
velvet pinafore, or she might have been a teen-ager in her first
silk dress. The scene spanned her lifetime.

Finally Lily stood to signal the end of the meal, and for a moment Kat hoped that perhaps the situation wouldn't get out of
hand after all. But as she watched her father pour cordials from
the crystal decanters in the living room, she could feel his anxiety stretch out toward Lily in a thin hot line. He was in suspended animation. He was waiting.

Slouched down in her chair, Kat watched her mother slip a
small gold pill case back into a hidden pocket in her dress. She
wanted to be someplace else, any place else. Her head pounded
and she pressed her finger tips hard against her temples.

"Darling!" Lily called out to Kirk, "some music, please!" She
swayed slightly, as if to an imaginary rhythm, her eyes wide and
staring, her lids with a faint droop. Without a word, Kirk turned
and chose a Sinatra recording. He knew that arguing would only
make her worse. Lily asked her dinner partner to dance, and
wound her way into his arms like a snake without a spine. The
other guests pretended not to watch; after a decent interval they
began to leave, one by one. Kirk saw them out and came back to
the living room where Lily leaned on the mantelpiece in front of
the fire. "Let me put you to bed," he said gently.

"Bed?" Lily cried, twirling gaily. Tangled in her long green skirt, she bumped into Kat. "It's early! Let's take a drive!"

Kat steadied her mother by the elbow, turning her head from the strong smell of stingers. "Please," she said, "it's late."

"Yes," said Kirk, taking Lily's other arm in a firm grip. "Let's get her upstairs."

"Don't you speak to me like that," Lily said shrilly, slipping on her words and throwing off their hands.

"Lily, come," Kirk began.

"It's bedtime," Kat entreated.

"No," she hissed, recoiling. "I know you two. You always want to put me to bed. You always want to get me out of the way." Her face twisted sideways and the tears slid noiselessly down her cheeks. She was like a toy top spinning down to the end of its string.

Kat ran out of the room. She had seen it all before. It was a nightmare that never ended, the world turned upside down, the world underwater. Paige was in the den, watching a late night rerun of "Columbo."

"So?" her sister asked. "Are they fighting yet?"

Kat sat down. "I hate it!" She twisted her hands into a rope and beat them against her knees. "Why is she getting worse—"

There was a crash from the living room, and then running feet, hitting the floor hard and unevenly. The back entry door slammed.

Kat waited without speaking. Paige watched the television, but as she lit a cigarette her hand shook. From the garage, Lily's car roared into ignition, a car starting in anger, grinding into life. "Don't worry," Paige said, looking at her watch. "They'll call before Peter Falk solves this one."

But it was one o'clock before the Concord police phoned. They were as familiar with picking up Lily Sinclair as they were used to reuniting stray dogs with their owners. At least two or three times a year they found her pulled onto the shoulder of the road, passed out behind the wheel. They never booked her but just watched over her until her husband arrived. It seemed more

sad than dangerous. And of course, Kirk was very generous with
the officers when he came down to the station.

Paige went off to bed. Kat waited by the fire, waited for her
father to bring Lily home. She needed to wait. Her mother
would return tonight from that blank unknowable place, and she
had to see her. She needed to see it was true. Once more she had
not lost the mysterious connection, and she could breathe again.
Her life was still intact.

But that was then. That was that year. Now it was Aaron roar-
ing off into the night, and she was the one who crouched here in
the dark, avoiding the inevitable, avoiding the painful. And her
life, what of her life? It was not as easy this time, not a mere
matter of waiting for someone to return. In the dark, there,
alone, in the midst of being drunk, Kat saw her mother running
away from the house and all it symbolized. She laughed at the
irony: would she spend the rest of her life running into the
house, slamming the door behind her? A new generation had
picked up the thread; now she and Aaron did the arguing, now
she played the role of the drugged and dangerous woman. The
rituals had been handed down, as carefully preserved as a secret
family recipe. Would she execute them faithfully?

Staring into the dark, she felt the tears coming cool and strong
from her eyes, she felt there were no answers, no way to say, "Yes
this is right and that wrong," no way to say simply, "I must go
with Aaron and leave my father behind." Or vice versa. She
could see the end of none of this. She wanted desperately to be
told what to do, where to go, how to accomplish the everyday
living of her life. She wanted it to be easy, rhythmic, natural.

She caught her breath. There were no solutions now. Now
there were only her guests. There was this task she must finish.
And by tomorrow Aaron might have changed his mind, by tomorrow she would have talked to him and solved the problem.
She was being melodramatic; everything would be all right. She
brushed her palms across her cheeks, and pushed herself out of
the dark passageway into the bright glitter and noise of the
party.

Sixteen

SUNDAY, MONDAY, TUESDAY, WEDNESDAY. KAT WAITED FOR AARON
to call.

In the beginning she told herself she didn't care, and that she
wouldn't accept his apology anyway. Still, despite her defiance,
she never left the house, accomplished nothing, ignored her
proofreading. In a state of suspended animation she tried to
deny he mattered.

But at night she dreamed of his face, his hands, his eyes—with
all her defenses down. In those dreams he was always going
away: on a boat, a plane, or even worse, dying. The thought of
his leaving made her claustrophobic, as if someone had shut her
in a small, black closet. In the dark she remembered him only as
strong and vigilant, and she knew she had no one to blame but
herself for this loss. He was a mirror into her, and even as she
resisted his ability to show her what she did not want to see,
some instinct told her she would be less without it. There had
been times when she'd fantasized she'd outgrown him, but now,
alone in the nights, she knew she could never outgrow that
steadfast face with all its pain and all its truth.

She would not believe that he did not love her any more.
Surely emotions did not change so fast, and what was so much a
part of them three months before must still be there. Love did
not just die, like hate. In the Sinclair family, love had been un-

conditional; in spite of anger, in spite of the vicious tongue, you could always assume there was love underneath. There was no crime great enough to kill love.

On Thursday she gave in and called him at last, determined to have him back. His voice was guarded, and she could not tell how he really felt about her. They talked briefly about his work, before Kat humbled herself by saying she was sorry about last Saturday. For a minute he did not reply, and then, his voice cool, he agreed he was sorry too. He had not wanted it to end that way.

Her desire to have him back was desperate now, beating inside her like a raw bird's heart, and she felt so alone that she made the promise before she could stop herself. The lie slid out easily because she believed she could do it if he came back to her. Only two drinks a night, she told him; she'd been sticking to her limit all week with no trouble. She could prove to him that she'd changed, but he must give her the chance, she argued. And because he wanted to believe her, and because there was still love between them, he agreed to go away with her for a few days.

He picked her up early Saturday morning. They had made no plan of where to go; Aaron just drove, and it was not until they reached the border into New York State that Kat began to wonder where they were headed.

Aaron was quiet at first, caught up in a wash of memories as they drove over the familiar highway. He remembered all those summers in camp as a young boy, how he had come to this area his first year, scared, awkward, a city boy transplanted to the country, not very good at sports, not very used to companionship. But it was a small camp of twenty-five boys, more like a family, and it had only taken him a few weeks to find a niche. His best friend from school had been a camper for five years, and soon Aaron too felt more at home there than anywhere else. Year after year he had returned there as a camper, and then as art counselor. In the woods he found myriad subjects for his drawings, early drawings which tried only to imitate nature; in those woods he learned an accuracy of line, shape, and form that became the foundation of his later work. Today he would share the woods and his memories with Kat. He wanted to give her another chance; he wanted to hope there was a future for them; he wanted to trust her again. And so he drove toward the Catskill Mountains, rich with their resorts and their ethnicity.

When he told her where they were going, Kat understood intuitively his purpose, and she felt glad he wanted to share something again. He was offering her his childhood, he was letting her back into his life. She didn't care where they went. The wounds would heal because anything was possible now. It was a beautiful day and her euphoria made her lightheaded. As they hit the mountains, the early October foliage was a circus of color, burnt orange and red. They were silent as they drove up over highways, sunroof open, breeze zipping through the car, the engine straining under the climb. It was a day to start over, Kat thought. And then they laughed as they drove, laughed at the huge billboards advertising kosher pickles, and kosher poultry, and kosher wine, and kosher milk. When Aaron told her this was the "Borscht Belt" they laughed again, deep and free. It was an adventure, a culture she did not know, a culture alluring in its warmth, its earthiness, its ritualistic approach to a modern time, a culture where love was clean and simple, like a well-designed road map.

They spent an hour and a half walking through the camp's grounds, and then Kat said she was hungry. Aaron suggested they continue a little further up the road to Grossinger's. It occurred to him then that they could spend the night there if Kat liked. He promised her a real adventure—unlike anything she had experienced before.

They registered as Mr. and Mrs. Aaron Salzer, and Kat turned her class ring around so that it looked like a wedding band. They went immediately to the dining room, just in time for the tail-end of lunch. It was an enormous hall, more like an auditorium than a dining room, seating perhaps eight hundred people, but only a quarter full this late in the season. Kat wanted a hamburger, but on Saturday, no cooking was done; the food was kosher, and lunch was a dairy meal, with no meat. She settled

for a cream cheese and olive sandwich, and Aaron had blueberry
blintzes. The quantities of food the others around them were
consuming was astonishing to her: soup, blintzes, cheese,
smoked fish, bagels, salads, hot eggs, fruit, heavy desserts. From
time to time a waiter in white picked up a partially emptied
plate before a diner, and replaced it with an identical one
heaped to overflowing. Here, more was always better.

Overhead, a loud-speaker blared out announcements: golf les-
sons for group A on the driving range in fifteen minutes; Ladies
Swim Club from Cedarhurst at the indoor pool by one-thirty;
mahjong and bridge tournaments in the game room at two. Kat
could hardly eat for watching the circus around her. It was a
different world, a world full of quick movement and noise. There
was no elegant, silent dining here, no concentration on food.
People talked excitedly with their mouths full. Conversations
passed from table to table. Children ran wildly in circles, en-
couraged by smiling parents. There was no attention to subtlety.
She could not help but be drawn in by the verve, the honest ex-
uberance, and she and Aaron were laughing together again.
There was no doubt that these people enjoyed being alive—even
if they did it with a little too much gusto to be in good taste.

After coffee they escaped from the melee to their room: there
was a large bedroom ornately furnished, a modern bath with
monogrammed towels, monogrammed shower curtain, monogrammed toilet seat. An enormous basket of fruit and a bottle of
Israeli wine took up the entire marble coffee table in front of
the color TV, and two king-sized beds made the huge room look
almost crowded.

They spent the afternoon walking through the trees with their
burning colors, and Kat saw that there were some wounds which
could be healed only by silence. And so she told Aaron she loved
him by giving him her hand, by throwing a stone across the still
pond, by putting scarlet leaves in his pocket for souvenirs. And
when they came back to the room at dusk, she let him make love
to her. Hesitant at first, scared of the intimacy, she felt nothing
at all, no desire. She was afraid to fail, and disappoint him when
they were both so vulnerable. He was trembling with his need to

feel close, skin to skin. It had to be good. And so she pretended to feel, wanting only to see the happiness on his face, and then, kiss by kiss, and touch by touch, she grew into it, lulled along on his rhythm. She stopped being afraid. This was healing, she thought, running her hands over his shoulders. They were together again and nothing would separate them now. Nothing could come between them again.

Afterwards, there was dinner in the big boisterous dining hall, course upon course. It was a meat meal this time, and Kat made the mistake of asking for sour cream on her baked potato. The waiter's shocked expression embarrassed her to a flush until Aaron winked at her, and then they laughed like conspirators, like spies in a foreign land. Things were good. There was no wine with dinner, nor drinks beforehand, and Kat did not ask for anything, did not want to upset this balance they had found. This is enough, she thought to herself, just this.

They wandered through the immense complex of buildings, stopping to inspect the yellowing black and white photos of celebrities hanging on the walls of the lobby. In the old days, Grossinger's was the place for summer theater, summer entertainment, and even now they had a nightclub. Kat could hear its music from where they stood. It got her foot to tapping.

"Let's go look," she urged Aaron.

"To the disco?" he asked. "Not really our speed—wouldn't you rather go back to the room?" He reached out and she knew exactly what he had in mind.

"Come on," she said, pulling on his hand, pulling him toward the music.

The club was of good size, built on two levels, with a circular bar on the upper and a dance floor on the lower. A five-piece band with a singer belted out a popular song. On the upper level, around the bar, were small candle-lit tables. Hardly anyone was dancing, and Aaron wanted to leave, but Kat insisted they sit and listen for just a minute. When the band started up with the score from "Saturday Night Fever," she pulled Aaron onto the floor.

One number swung right into the next, and they danced for a

solid half-hour, enjoying themselves, despite their initial self-consciousness at being one of the only couples on the floor. After a while quite a few older couples were sitting on the sidelines, or around the bar, watching, and this pleased Kat.

"Hey," Aaron said finally, "I've got to take a breather." They sat down again, and now she looked at the bar.

"Could we have something? It's so hot."

Aaron smiled. "What can I get you?"

"Brandy?"

They sat and talked, while Aaron swigged down his enormous tankard of Pepsi and Kat sipped carefully from her snifter. Aaron had wanted to ask her about this new limit she'd set on her drinking, but he'd been afraid to bring up the subject before. Now they were so relaxed that it didn't seem to matter. All his concern seemed a bit stupid in the light of tonight; tonight reminded him of their first days together—exuberant and young and free. "You said on the phone you'd been cutting back?" he asked, gesturing to the drinks.

"Just two martinis each night. It's worked fine." She shrugged as if to say, of course, what did you expect.

"No problem?"

She shook her head and finished her brandy. "No. I just made up my mind, that's all." Why did he want to talk about it? she wondered. Some things were better left unsaid. She stood and changed the subject. "Dance?"

She was gaining confidence, feeling a bit more flamboyant now, supported by the warmth of the brandy. From the sidelines she could see one of the young waiters watching her. She felt his scrutiny. It felt good to be admired. Her red dress was made for dancing—it showed off her long lean legs. Who cared if it was sexist, the way men stared. She threw back her head and lifted her arms. She liked to be noticed. Maybe she liked being a sex object.

"Are you ready to go yet?" Aaron asked the next time there was a slow dance.

She looked up at him with annoyance. "I'm just getting warmed up," she cried. "Don't make us go."

Her disappointment was so acute that he gave in. "O.K., but sit down for a minute so I can hit the john."

She was having such a good time, they were so happy, so free, she thought she really could have another drink. After all, she hadn't had anything before dinner, and it was a Saturday night. A night for dancing. It was part of the festival air in her head, she said to herself as she approached the bar. "Brandy please. A double." Worrying that Aaron would come back and see her with the new glass, she drained it hastily and set it down. She felt it burning down into her stomach, prickling behind her eyeballs; she coughed and sat down again at their table. The waiter came over, the same waiter who'd been staring as she'd danced. He was not very good-looking she saw, he might even be ugly, but that didn't matter. He had noticed her. She looked up at him with a provocative smile.

"Can I get you anything?" he asked, standing very close to her, close enough so that their legs were almost touching.

"A refill on my brandy would be fine."

He brought it to the table just as Aaron reappeared. "Get you anything, sir?"

"No, I'm fine," he said, looking down at Kat's new drink.

She leaned forward. "Now don't worry. This's my limit, like I said. Two drinks."

He smiled. "Sorry—just an old habit. Want to dance again?"

She nodded. Now she was really quite high: she wanted people to look at her; she danced apart from Aaron, swinging her hips to the rhythm, running her hands up and down her sides. She paid no attention to what Aaron was doing. She was dancing alone. She could see the waiter watching her again, and she was dancing to him, offering her body in anonymous pantomime. When she finally looked back to Aaron, she could tell he was getting annoyed. She couldn't see why. She didn't see that he felt left out, alone, that he sensed the change in her mood.

The next time they returned to their table, Aaron again tried to entice her into leaving. The tenor of the evening shifted and clicked into place, like a motion picture frame finally falling in sync with the sound track. He felt the danger, the threat, as he watched her finishing her drink.

She wouldn't leave, she declared, squinting her eyes to bring him into focus. She was having too good a time. They had come here to dance, and dance she would. She lifted her arm and summoned the waiter. She would have another brandy.

Aaron said nothing. He sat there, just watching her, too beaten to speak. He no longer cared how drunk she would get before she was ready to call it quits. He was exhausted. He couldn't fight it any more, and when she asked him to dance again he said no in a barely audible voice. She ordered another brandy, but by now she was too drunk to drink it. She was getting sleepy, her eyes nearly closed, and so he stood, signed the check, and helped her to her feet.

He took her back to their room on an outside path, holding her up with his arm in hopes that the cool air would clear her head. Around them were stars, and crickets in the grass, and the harsh smells of autumn. He felt his anger rise at her, for it was she who kept them from enjoying all this, she who blunted it all out. He resented having to take care of her again. She had ruined this beautiful night, and he wanted to strike out, to punish her for punishing him. "Why didn't you stick to your limit?" he asked, knowing he was pushing for an argument.

She squinted up at him, unsteady on her high heels. "It's Saturday night. Limits are for weekdays."

"That's not what you said before."

"Don't be such a drag!"

"You're the drag. You're the drunk." He didn't look at her. "And you promised you wouldn't be."

Her face was angry now, and she snatched her hand out from under his arm. "I'm not drunk!"

"This is it. You broke your promise on purpose."

"I did not. Stop looking for an excuse to dump me!"

"I don't need an excuse." He looked down at her for a moment, serious beyond anger. "I love you. I don't want to leave you."

"Well, don't make it sound like I'm forcing you!" She mocked

him with a sarcastic grin. "You can't even deal with your own
guilt—blame it on me, right down to the last minute. Why don't
you admit it?" She was shouting now, her voice echoing off the
trees and cement walkways, and he didn't even try to speak, he
just watched her, disgusted. "I don't fit into your perfect ideal,
that's all—maybe if I was a good Jew and just ate too much then
you'd get off my back!"

She hurled the last sentence at him as though she were spitting in his face, and then turned to stagger off into the dark. She
was crying; she was lost. Somewhere inside her she knew she
was beyond help. Halfway up the walk she crashed into a couple
who stared in astonishment at the apparition of this well-dressed
young woman sobbing in the dark.

Kat ran in a long circle, stopping once to take off her high
heels, weaving through trees, over the grounds. She was a sick
animal, in pain; she did not know where to go; she moved on instinct. It was hard to see in the dark, hard to see around her
tears. If something or someone had been chasing her, she could
not have been more frightened or more desperate.

After a while of meandering back and forth, she recognized
the deserted swimming pool. As she rounded the corner, she
nearly ran into someone again.

"Hang on there," he said, grabbing her elbow to steady her. It
was the waiter from the disco. "Well, look who I've caught," he
said, smiling down at her. His face was ugly, she thought. He
was an ugly man. "Kinda late to be running around with no
shoes on."

She tried to think of a good answer, but she was too drunk and
too dizzy. She just stared at him, like a little girl, waiting to see
what he would do next. He led her to a lounge chair.

"Whyn't you rest just a minute," he said, sitting down beside
her. "You're a little the worse for wear."

And then somehow she began to cry again, to explain everything to a stranger, explain about Aaron, about how he didn't
love her any more. This man was easy to talk to, his ugly face listened intently, waiting. He was nice, kind, his arm was warm
around her shoulders as she shivered. She needed this kind of

companionship and understanding. Why didn't Aaron treat her like this? Why didn't Aaron give her what she needed?

Then she looked up at this man sitting so close beside her and suddenly there was something different in his face. She remembered how she had danced earlier, and how he had watched her. And she knew she was on the edge of something forbidden, something she should not do, something she might regret. The danger trembled inside her, a faint wind. She did not get up and say good night. She did not move away. She did not do any of the things a sensible woman might have done. She had no willpower to rise and change the moment, to reshape what would be. Alcohol had clouded her mind, her heart, her resolve. She sat there and sat there, and finally his hand was on her leg, and then he turned her shoulders to him and he started to kiss her. He was very strong. He made her feel his strength as he pressed against her. He made her lie down on the grass. She was under him, she was not moving, she was wondering what would happen to the back of her dress. She could feel him pulling off her red panties, the red panties that matched the dress. She could feel him pressing his penis against her, but she was dry. She was not ready. Then he was spitting on his fingers to make her wet. But she was dry inside. She was too drunk to stop him. She didn't care to stop him. He was hurting her now, pushing in like dry rasping iron, but it felt almost good to be abused, to be used. She was low. He was using her as low as she was. She wanted to throw up as he thrust against her barren dryness, twisting her breasts as though they were forgotten handles. He made no sound. After a while he got up. She felt she had been asleep. Had she been asleep? He was rough now. He made her stand up. He made her hate herself. She made her hate herself. He handed her her shoes and panties. He told her to go back to her room. She did not know the way. He pointed in the dark and then he was gone.

She was alone now, and she couldn't tell where she was in the dark. She wandered awhile and then found the right door, feeling sick, ill. But she couldn't really think about all that had happened; she knew she was too drunk to think. What did it matter anyway? All that mattered was to go to sleep.

Aaron had left the door unlocked and gone to bed. He did not move or speak as Kat came through the door. She lay down on the other double bed without even removing her clothes. The room rocked around her and she tried to go to sleep quickly so she wouldn't throw up.

When she stopped crying Aaron knew she was asleep. He went over and covered her with the spread from his bed, sitting down on the edge to watch her as she slept. Her face was smudged. He knew, for the first time, that he could not help her. She was beyond him. Now, mixed with his love and with his hate, there was pity, overwhelming pity. Grieving, he lay down beside her and cradled her body against his in a final touch, a silent good-by.

KAT HAD NO INTENTION OF TRYING BREAKFAST ON HER STOMACH, AND so Aaron went to the dining room without her. The assumption that they would leave immediately after he returned was unspoken, but clear. After all, there was nothing to keep them there, nothing to wait for.

The door clicked shut behind him. Kat lay in her bed, the red dress crumpled and sweaty as an old washcloth. She had never slept in her clothes before, and she had never felt more hung over. The quiet room accentuated the hornet's nest in her head, and the sunlight that dappled the drapes made her eyes ache; her thirst grew as she longed for the cold glass of water which she knew from experience would only increase her nausea.

Her mind raced in a tiny tight circle. Last night she and Aaron had bridged a point which could not be recouped, and she knew he had given up on her, saw the coolness in him, the detachment. She had hurt him, and he was beyond anger. She was sorry now, of course, but still, she couldn't help feeling resentful. He exaggerated everything so. He provoked her. She turned gingerly on her side.

Her body was sore, almost as though she had been in a fight. There was a sharp ache between her legs; it felt swollen there, as if someone had used her as a punching bag. She didn't understand it, and frowned to herself—certain that Aaron hadn't even steering wheel. "The point is that I can't handle this any more. Your problem is just beyond me."

"Problem?"

"Your drinking problem."

"Aaron, don't be silly." She looked over as though he had just told her he was a Martian. "I'm sorry I had a little too much last night, but I've hardly got a 'problem.'"

"A little too much!" He looked at her, shocked. "Kat. Did you want to get drunk last night?"

"Drunk? No, and I didn't—"

"But you did anyway, didn't you? You do it even when you don't mean to!"

"I wasn't really drunk!" There were tears on her face. He must hate her to speak to her this way; he must have stopped loving her. She was getting angry, and felt she must defend herself. "Anyway, what business is it of yours? You think I'm drunk when I'm not. You're always accusing me, and judging me—"

"How much you drink has a lot to do with how much fun I have," he interrupted. "That makes it my business. You get drunk a lot of the time."

"I don't think so. I don't ask for anything from you."

"Don't ask?" he repeated in astonishment. "For God's sake, do you think I hold you up while you stagger along for my own sake? Do you think I enjoy undressing you and putting you to bed? Hardly ever making love? Talking to a zombie who's so bombed she can't even hear what I'm saying, much less understand me?"

"You're exaggerating."

He tightened his jaw. "I'm not going to argue it any more, Kat."

"You're jealous because I can relax! You're so damned stubborn—nobody but you is ever right! But you're the one who's ruining things now." She was so furious with him that she wanted only to draw blood, to see him snap back at her, to know she'd hurt him the way he was hurting her. But he said nothing; they drove on, and in silence they pulled up the circular drive. Dry leaves crackled under the tires. Kat looked around her hard,

touched her last night. He'd been too angry. They'd sle[?]
arate beds. She traced the events of the disco over in [?]
and, once again, she came to a black, blank spot she [?]
explain. She could not remember what they had done [?]
second brandy last night. There was a brief memory of [?]
face, angry in the dark, arguing with her as they stood [?]
outdoor path. But that was all.

A small logical part of her brain kept on reviewing he[?]
evidence like an adding machine which must come to so[?]
total; its tinny voice concluded that she must have bee[?]
someone, someone other than Aaron.

She couldn't stand to think it, or know it—it was too awf[?]
degrading. She forced herself out of bed to get away fro[?]
idea. She would wash her face. That would make her feel [?]

In the bathroom she pulled the dress over her head and [?]
the grass stains ground into the back of her skirt. She ig[?]
them. But when she sat down on the toilet and her pa[?]
reeked with the raw rank odor of semen, a sob came up o[?]
her chest like a clot and she put her head between her kr[?]
She could not lie to herself any longer. She had been raped, [?]
lated against her will by some faceless assailant—but with [?]
own consent. She could blame no one but herself.

The outside door slammed as Aaron came back to the roo[?]
and she jumped quickly into the shower, unable to face him y[?]
She was afraid he would know by looking at her: how he wou[?]
hate her, how disgusted he would be. The steamy water helpe[?]
clear her head, and she scrubbed herself furiously with soap. Sh[?]
did not get out until he banged on the door and yelled at her t[?]
hurry.

They did not speak while she dressed and packed. They did[?]
not speak as they checked out. They did not speak even as he[?]
drove. Not until they were nearly home did Kat finally break the[?]
silence.

"I'm sorry," she said at last, clearing her throat.

"I'm sure you are." He looked over at her quickly and then
turned back to the road. "But that's not the point." He paused
and ran his fingers over the hard indentations at the back of the

taking note of details: the length of the grass, the color of the swamp maples, the pot of chrysanthemums by the front door. It was a way to slow down time, to change the inevitable.

Aaron set the Toyota's parking brake, the engine still running, and turned in his seat to look at her, his hand resting on the shift. Now she could see the pain in his eyes. And something else too. Love.

"When you've got this licked," he said, "call me. But not before."

"Just like that?" she said. "What about love? What about the way we feel?"

"I do love you. And that's why I'm going. If I stay any longer, you'll kill the love that's left."

His words moved in on her like blunt instruments. There was no escape from the meaning of this. Numbness iced down her body. Numbness and fear. "You're a hypocrite," she said in a dull tone. "A goddamned hypocrite. If you loved me—you'd be here for me."

She climbed out of the car and watched him drive away. It was as simple as that. Love and loss, she thought, synonyms for the same pain. It is as simple as that.

Eighteen

NOVEMBER MOVED SLUGGISHLY, GRAY ON THE OUTSIDE, GRAY ON THE inside. December was no better. Aaron never called. Kat thrust her pride against the raw wound whenever she considered phoning him. It was a time with none of the landmarks or signposts that generally mark the months, the events that allow you to say, "Today is Friday because on Wednesday there was a letter from Great-aunt Luce and cocktails at the Hamptons." It was a time when nothing happened, when Kat shut herself in, and took no particular notice of anything. Each day she was surprised to find herself still intact, with her grief in control. Sleeping was not much different from waking. There were no nightmares now, only a static gray space in her head. This was the second loss in a year's time, and so it moved in her like an echo, vibrating off old emotions—emotions, like weapons, she had so wanted to lay down.

She let all everyday activity go, stopped any pretense of normality, and spent most of her time on her bed, hands behind her head, studying her depression via the ceiling. It lent drama, she felt, to her pain. She pictured her life as a spiral, with grief and loss as the root, a magnetic power drawing the concentric, curved lines down into nullity; she held her life to her ear, a perfect conch shell, and listened for the hiss of its imitation ocean. Publishers called to offer free-lance work, and Kat turned them down routinely, with no apology. She even made excuses to Helena and Bea to avoid seeing them, or talking for very long. She missed Helena, but it was easier to hide than to face her. By December no one called, and she was as alone as she had set out to be.

Aaron's doubts about her ability to stop drinking had been like a dare, and during these months Kat set arbitrary and ever-shifting limits to test herself each night. It was a game—to see how far she could go—and she twisted the rules recklessly. One night: sober. The next night: drunk. She refused to think about the high stakes, or that she might finally be required to ante up. She believed there was nothing left to lose. On the nights she broke the limits and buried herself in alcohol, hate and anger surfaced like bad gases, and she toasted Aaron with a bitter heart. Never once would she admit that he might have been right. If the idea occurred to her, she pushed it away, remembering only that he had left her, hurt her. She no longer cared why. Whenever she woke up with a hang-over, his words came back at her like a taunt, but still she refused to believe and each day set out to prove him wrong.

Only Kirk broke up the monotony of Kat's existence, and she waited impatiently for evenings, when he would return from work, and they could have cocktails before the fire. With Paige abroad for a month, not due home till the holidays, Kat had him all to herself.

The Friday before Christmas, they went out to dinner; Kat's old weekend movie ritual with Aaron had been replaced by an elaborate evening with her father at Locke-Ober's, Boston's oldest and finest Continental restaurant. As they drove into town, Kat laid her head back against the velour upholstery, preoccupied with a new worry. Tomorrow, Eliot Rutledge would call her to confirm the draw against funds in her trust account for another payment to the insurance company. She played with the automatic window opener, and wondered why Rutledge couldn't just execute the transaction silently. Each month her unspoken commitment to her father turned into a nasty decision which she had to deal with on an emotional level, which she had to think

and rethink. And, of course, this was precisely what Rutledge intended; he wanted her to feel the pressure of the money and the
responsibility and the drain. Each month he tried to argue her
out of the payment, and each month she defended her position,
her father, her love.

But tonight she must put it out of her mind; dressed carefully
in her blueberry silk and her mother's sapphires, she wanted
their last evening alone together to be perfect. Paige would return tomorrow, and the competition would begin once again.

They arrived at Locke's without a reservation, but even on a
busy Friday night there was always a table available for Kirk
Sinclair, and they waited in the bar while Mario, the family
waiter, readied it. Kirk ordered cocktails for them both—his ritual of ordering for his wife now a ritual with his daughter—and
the martinis were set before them, clear and cold and dry. Kat
decided that tonight she would have two and a glass of wine
with dinner because she wanted to remember everything, she
wanted to wake the next morning and feel the sharp edge of the
event.

She sipped her drink carefully, charily, while Kirk talked of
business and the increasing problems with imports. As usual, he
was angry and frustrated and vehement; he needed a passive audience. After a while he ordered a second round. Kat watched
him, wondering how he had the mettle to keep on trying. What
made some people persevere where others give up? she wondered. He seemed almost heroic to her, with his silvered hair, the
strong planes of his face that neither time nor event seemed to
touch. There might have been a desperate bravado to Kirk, but
Kat saw only the strength of his hope; he was her last parent and
it was all she could afford to see. It did not matter if it were real
or true. It only mattered that she could reach out and touch it
now, this very moment. She moved closer to him, so close that
their shoulders touched.

At the hand on Kirk's arm, they both looked up. Mario, who
had cared for the Sinclairs since Kirk was a young man, stood
before them, his shopworn face creased into a smile, his long
white apron impeccable over the black tuxedo.

"If I did not know better," he said in his highly accented English, "I would mistake you for more than father and daughter." He laughed. "I do not wish to interrupt you young people, but your table is ready whenever you like."

The compliment brought a smile to Kirk's face, and he offered Kat his arm. They made their way into the dining room. It was not poshly done up, like the Ritz, but rather depended on a subtle, well-worn elegance broken in by scores of satisfied patrons over the years. The menu was à la carte, expensive, every item cooked to order. Great emphasis was put on detail and garnish and presentation. It was the sort of restaurant which had not abandoned the small niceties, like the finger bowl after frog's legs.

Mario seated Kat and she slipped her linen napkin into her lap as Kirk began to order. "Two more martinis, please, and we'll each have a dozen littlenecks while we look over the menu."

Kat looked up at her father in horror and started to interrupt him. She could not possibly eat a raw clam, had never been able to, not even with the cushion of a third martini—a martini, she reminded herself, which would break the limit she'd set. She leaned forward in the chair. "Dad, I'd rather not—"

He held up his hand to stop her, and Mario left to place their order.

"Tonight," he said, looking directly into her eyes, "you will learn. I will teach you."

Something in his tone swayed her resolve about her limit, and overrode the fear of a new taste. She let her objections slide away because she wanted so much to please him. If her father thought she should be proficient at eating raw things, then she would be. If her father wanted her to have another drink with him, why shouldn't she?

Mario returned with two silver platters. Kat looked down at the crushed ice with its twelve tiny clams—pristine, pale pink, and naked. How could she bite into them? she wondered silently, sipping her martini fiercely, glad to have it now. She would need it to get through this.

"First. Ignore the cocktail sauce," Kirk said as he picked up his oyster fork. "Only this," he said, spearing a wedge of lemon, "otherwise the delicacy is lost." With a twist of his wrist he separated the tiny muscle from the bone of its shell.

Kat drew on her drink, dreading her turn, feeling quite high, and thinking about cannibalism. This was nothing like steak tartare. This was still alive.

Kirk put the clam into his mouth, and chewed it up as though it were an ordinary item. "Some people prefer to swallow them whole. To me," he shrugged, "it is a tragic waste." He lifted his glass. "And then the martini. It must be a martini. No other drink will do."

It was her turn now. The two quick ones at the bar were catching up with her and she was high enough to repress her squeamishness. He was watching her, and in his blue eyes she saw something like a dare, something which said, "You will not be a woman without." And she wanted the love desperately, she wanted the approval, and the warmth and the companionship of an adventure shared. She imitated her father's precise preparations, and laid it in her mouth, that first virgin clam. It lay still as a pearl on her tongue. It did not move or squirm or beg for mercy. Silently she surrendered, and swallowed.

Kat looked over at her father—victorious, triumphant—woman enough to have eaten raw bar. They laughed together, and there was the reward of his face, his shining eye.

Around the plate she ate her way, growing more proficient as each one slid down, coming to enjoy the salty tang, the sweet snap of the muscle between her teeth, and the dry finish of the martini. It was pain and pleasure in one bite, distaste and longing, disgust and lust, a peculiar combination of contrasting sensations. Kirk winked at her, and they were bound together by her new initiation.

"Good evening, Katherine, Kirk."

Kat looked up to see Eliot Rutledge looking down at them with a careful smile.

"Hello, Eliot," said Kirk. "How are things?"

"Fine, thanks. We're on our way to the theater. Just stopped to say hello while Louise powders her nose." He looked over at

Kat, who sat and fingered an earring as she stared down at her plate of empty clamshells. "How have you been, Katherine?"

"Fine," she said, managing somehow to smile over her resentment. She did not doubt his discretion, but her father might still sense there was something between them; it was a risk, an unnecessary risk, and she didn't like it at all. She finished her third martini and gestured to Mario for another. Just looking at Rutledge reminded her, once again, of tomorrow and the impending phone call. Now that she had finally managed to set aside all distracting thoughts about the payment to the insurance company, here he was. She felt hounded, pressed to the wall. As he stood there making small talk with her father, her anger rose. It wasn't fair. Here was Rutledge getting in the way of their good time like some bad omen. His intrusion could remind Kirk of only one thing, one person: Lily.

Just as her new drink arrived, Rutledge went off to his wife, leaving Kat with a sour stomach. She wanted to start the evening over, or change the subject at least, but, a little too high to think clearly, she drew a blank. Kirk studied the menu, and then ordered them hearts of palm and lobster Savannah. He leaned back in his chair. There was an extra flush on his cheeks, a certain brightness to his eyes; Kat was glad to see he felt the impact of their martinis as much as she.

"Haven't seen Aaron in quite a while," he said, sounding offhand.

Kat looked up sharply. She'd made a point of not telling her father what was going on, so that some part of her, at least, could pretend it hadn't happened.

"Have you broken it off?"

"Yes." She sipped from her drink, and tried to look detached, grateful for Kirk's assumption that she had been the executioner.

"Don't misunderstand me, Kat. But I always felt he was not right for you." He picked up his gold lighter from the table and held it to another cigarette, setting his teeth down into the filter as he inhaled. "A nice enough boy, after all, but not really your type." He paused. "Was he?"

Despite her anger and hurt at Aaron, Kirk's words still bothered her. Confused, she tried to sort through the swirl of emotions: she shouldn't care like this any more; she shouldn't want to defend Aaron. The martinis must be muddling her.

But Kirk took her silence for acquiescence. He continued to delineate Aaron's faults as he had seen them—now that Kat was free, he felt at liberty to speak his mind for the first time. "It's really very simple," he said. "Such different backgrounds. What can you expect from a person from such a different background?"

"I'm not sure I follow," Kat said unsteadily. She wished he would just be quiet. This was not helping. She finished her drink as her father filled her wineglass with Bernkasteler Doktor 1967.

"His class." He spoke earnestly, looking at her as though she would be forced to agree because it was the only reasonable viewpoint. He was trying so hard; she could see he wasn't even conscious that he sounded like a bigot. "His heritage. His religion."

Kat put her head back and gave a giddy laugh. The idea of Aaron and organized religion struck her as comic. "Well," she sputtered. "He's hardly devout."

"I'm not talking about what church he goes to. I'm talking about what's been handed down to him—a certain sort of passivity on the one hand, and a certain aggressive quality on the other." He looked at her. "I'm sorry, I don't mean to be harsh, but to me, both are equally undesirable."

"Passivity?" Kat echoed, as she picked up her wineglass. Her chest felt hot and she wanted to launch into a brave and fine defense; she wanted to make him see how wrong he was. " 'Pushy Jew,' maybe. But passivity? Aaron? Dad, you just don't know him!"

"Come now," he said, cutting the heart of palm with the side of his fork, "surely you must admit he comes from a passive people? A people who would stand by helplessly to be annihilated, burnt, tortured? That's passive. Maybe even defective."

Kat looked down at her plate, at the pink lobster in its satiny sauce of pimento and mushroom, heaped back into the bright red shell. She put a bit in her mouth. She could not show him he was wrong without starting a fight, and she had watched too many good evenings ruined by her parents when they began to argue. Kirk provoked, and Lily responded. She didn't want that, and she also knew there was no reasoning with Kirk on a subject like this—the prejudice was in his blood, it would not be washed out by her liberal arguments. He worked with people of different religions and backgrounds and colors every day, and he had learned to be both fair and friendly. But underneath he felt something quite different. She just sat and listened; she let him go on, let it flow over her, let him think she agreed. The wine dulled her need to object. There was something about the way he spoke—this was not a hostile, hysterical tirade, but a clear, reasoned explication, studded with pertinent facts and dates and figures. Kat was overwhelmed by it all, and after a while she could not have objected even if she had wanted to. He had out-talked her. Little by little she became wound into his argument. She had lost the thread of her own moral objection. She drank more wine.

They ate. Kirk ordered another bottle of wine. Kat changed the subject, and they talked of many other things. He kept refilling her glass and it didn't seem to matter. It wasn't important that they were getting more and more drunk: her father was talking about the way he felt—about his needs, his ambitions, his desires. She stood back from the table and looked at the scene: a bottle of wine, a man and a woman speaking from the heart. Time and space were useless measurements. Words and then cognac, words and then cognac. But then, in the middle of one sentence, Kat lost her grip on the conversation: she was unable to remember what she'd been about to say. She looked quizzically at Kirk.

He peered at her, realizing she had stopped in mid-sentence. "Home," he announced, and pushed back his chair.

Later, Kat would not remember getting her coat, or leaving Locke-Ober's, or the drive home. She would remember only that when they came through the front hall to the library, laughing at one another, they found an unexpected visitor curled up in Kirk's big chair.

"Paige!" Kirk stopped on the threshold in astonishment. He regained his composure and his sobriety in an instant.

"Merry Christmas, Dad!" Paige ran over to him and he hugged her hard. Kat leaned against the doorjamb now that her father's arm was gone.

"I changed my flight so I'd be home a little sooner, as a surprise."

"A wonderful surprise!" he said. "Did you have a good time? I want to hear all about the trip—when did you get in?"

"It was great. Could we go up to the sitting room and light a fire. There's so much to tell—" She broke off, looking over at Kat in the shadow of the door. "Hello, Kat."

Kat nodded and watched Paige take her father's hand. Laughing at some story about the baggage claim, Kirk and Paige led the way upstairs. He touched a match to the laid kindling, and then went to the bar. "What will you girls have?"

"Cognac," Paige said, stretching out in the chair closest to the warmth. "It's so good to be home with all the modern conveniences. Can't wait for a shower."

Kat shook her head when Kirk held up a snifter with a question on his face. She felt sick. Now she wished she had not had so much earlier, that she'd kept her head clear. She looked over at her sister, trying to focus on her to keep the room from spinning, and make polite conversation, but underneath she was angry at the intrusion.

Paige had obviously been on a beach somewhere, during her week in Morocco perhaps. Under the ruddy light of the fire, her tan glowed against the pale sheen of her hair. Her cashmere slacks tapered to show her ankles, her silk blouse parted just enough to intimate her bust, and once again Kat was jealous. Paige pulled a long cigarette from the leather case beside her on the table, and sipped her brandy, touching a painted fingernail to the rim of the glass. Kirk crossed the room to give her a light.

Kat couldn't bear it any longer; the only way she could stay here would be to get even drunker, and she was drunk enough already. More and she would spend all night vomiting. More and she would have broken her limit past all reconciliation. She had to go to bed. She needed the oblivion of sleep. Out of the chair, she stood, unsteady on her feet. "I'm going to bed," she said, interrupting them.

Her father looked up with a frown. "Oh, come on, Kat, stay awhile. Paige's just home."

"Have a drink with us," Paige said, her eyes glinting in the firelight.

"I think I've had more than enough already."

"Enough is boring," Paige said with a smile.

"Surely one more wouldn't hurt," her father said.

"I just need some sleep. Good night." Even the promise of liquor could not have induced her to stay.

They shrugged. Kat could hear them resume their conversation as she left the room and went down the dark hall. Their laughter followed her as she pulled off her clothes, dropped them on the floor, and crumpled up on the bed. The room began its ritual spin, and she dropped one leg over the side of the bed to anchor herself to the floor. She tried not to think of all she had eaten. Pink lobster kept coming into her head. She could almost smell it. And then there were those clams. She turned carefully on her side. She had to get to sleep fast or she would certainly throw up. But laughter from the sitting room kept opening her eyes, blocking her slide into unconsciousness. Side by side with nausea was an envy that burned harsh as any brandy.

Somehow she spun down into sleep, but it was restless sleep, a sleep of nightmare. When she woke, it was with no idea of the time. It could be morning, noon, or night. She stumbled to the bathroom off her room. Too much booze, she thought foggily; she was dizzy. She must not have been asleep very long—she was still drunk, and still thirsty. She drank noisily at the faucet, but it didn't help. The nausea increased. As she went back to bed, she noticed the light coming in under her door.

She went out into the hall to turn off whatever had been left on, and saw it came from the sitting room. The door was half-closed. She heard a rustle of silk, a low murmur. Once more past slipped over into present.

She had done this before. Sometime, perhaps as a teen-ager, or as a child, perhaps out of nightmare, or fear, she had come down this dark passage, moving on silent feet toward the light, drawn to the lull of soft voices, a certain hushed laughter. There was the door; she looked around it, unseen. Firelight was the only illumination. It played unevenly over the upholstery, the drapes, the leather spines of the books. Over the two on the couch, side by side, touching, the brandy decanter on the floor beside them. There was blond hair undone, there was blond hair in her father's mouth and hands. Blond hair, gleaming in the night like a web. For the first time she saw her father naked, as he lay there, his hand on the full breasts. She knew she should not look. But she wanted to look. She wanted to know.

She backed away from the door now, holding her stomach. Was she twelve? Was she twenty-one? She could not place this in a time frame. The blond hair: Mother or Paige? Then or now? Past or present? How could she know? How could she tell? There was no set of rules, no almanac, no Bible that arbitrated this scene. Dizzy, drunk, she ran, ran in terror from what might have been.

She locked the door to her room, went into the bath, and knelt before the toilet. She vomited until her insides were as dry as stiff washcloth, and then lay down on her bed. She was shivering, but she did not cover herself. She did not sleep again. And when early dawn moved into the room with its pale gray light, she still was not sure what she had seen. For the first time in her life, she was afraid for her sanity.

"Katherine? Katherine, are you awake?"

The voice of Mrs. George came through her bedroom door now with insistence. Kat had been lying limp all morning long, unwilling to move from her bed and face the day.

It was almost noon. She had not been able to sleep, except for that one brief stuporous doze earlier in the night, but she could not just get up as though everything were normal. Could not get up and face her father and sister over the breakfast table. She wanted to hide here all day long. She turned the scene over and over in her mind, and examined it from every angle in an honest attempt to get it straight. At last she concluded that there were two possible explanations—each equally unattractive: either she had indeed seen something unspeakable, or she had lost touch with the reason and order defined as sanity.

Mrs. George's voice rapped in on her thoughts again. "Katherine! It's Eliot Rutledge on the phone, and he's most insistent. What shall I say?"

"All right," she answered in a low voice. Numbly, she picked up the receiver. "Yes, Eliot." She cleared her throat. She wanted to get it over with. No small talk. No arguing. "You're calling about the payment?"

"Of course," he said. "I wouldn't draw it without consulting you first. It must be first thing Monday morning—if you are still committed to this . . . course of action."

She was silent. He was always so formal when he spoke of it, so stiff and disapproving. For the first time since assuming responsibility for her father's debt, there was doubt in her mind. She rubbed her head, irritated and weary. How could she be expected to decide this now? It wasn't fair. It was impossible. She wanted to cry, to lie down and cry and just have someone hold her. Aaron came into her mind—but he was gone.

"Hello? Kat, are you there?"

"Yes." At the thought of Aaron something inside her snapped, a circuit breaker shut down all the power, all the electricity, in her brain. She could not cope right now. It must wait. She couldn't think about it this minute. "Make the payment, Eliot," she said in a rush. "Make it."

His breathing was steady on the other end of the line, and he took his time, he hesitated before speaking. "Are you all right, Kat? You seemed strained last night, and today—"

"I'm fine, just fine," she interrupted. Eliot was the last person she could discuss it with: if she broke down now, her credibility would be lost. She pulled herself together. "Thank you for asking, though."

"Well, I admire how you've taken hold this past year. And in a tough situation. Not many young women could have done it—even if we don't always see eye to eye." He paused. "Feel free to call on me for anything—even if it's just to talk with someone not so involved in the immediate situation."

"Thank you," Kat said, stunned, striving to keep emotion from her voice and still be gracious. "I'll bear it in mind."

"And the payment? You're sure? This is becoming quite a drain on your trust."

"I realize that. But until I see another way out—this seems the only thing."

She hung up the phone, hardly feeling the relief at having it over, numb, dead inside. Forcing herself to leave the bed, she dressed. Before she could worry about the money or her father, she had to get through today. Maybe, she admitted to herself, maybe Helena had been right—maybe it was time to start worrying about Kat.

Tonight it was Christmas Eve, with a fifteen-foot balsam fir to trim, with twenty guests for a formal dinner party—a party over which she and her father would preside. Once again, a party that was her responsibility. But she didn't care any more, she didn't see how she would get through it. Of only one thing was she certain: she must stay sober and in control. Without understanding why, she believed, finally, that this was her last chance.

Part II

DECEMBER 1980 –
FEBRUARY 1981

And I heard, but I understood not: then said I,
O my Lord, what shall be the end of these things?

And he said, Go thy way, Daniel: for the words
are closed up and sealed till the time of the end.

—Daniel 12:8,9

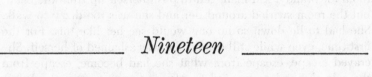

Nineteen

Down the length of the Christmas Eve dinner table, Kat looked from one blurred face to the next in panic. She was sliding, she was slipping out of control. She was drowning and there was no to help. She was drunk again and there was no one to tell her how to stop.

None of these people could offer her a solution. None of them had the magical prescription which would right her life again. They were only disinterested guests, guests with dinnertime conversations and expectations. What did people like Skip Lowell or Great-aunt Luce care about her feelings or her life? Her role was to be charming, controlled, uncomplicated. Her role was to eat roast beef and drink Bordeaux, to make sure everyone had enough potatoes.

But she could manage none of these things right now. She was too drunk. How many glasses of wine had she had? She realized with shock that she had lost count somewhere, somewhere back a long time ago. She was drunk on a night she had promised herself she would not be, a night when she'd vowed to stay sober. Aaron had said something just like that once. Confusion and fear pounded inside her; memory came washing back, all the shameful behavior that had come with drinking; burying it in one martini after another hadn't worked.

Around her, conversation continued and no one noticed her

agitation. At the far end of the table, Kirk and Paige stood up, tired of waiting, and pre-empted Kat's prerogative as hostess to terminate the meal. The guests began moving toward the living room for brandy. Kat managed to push herself up from the chair, but the room swirled around her and she was too dizzy to walk. She had to lie down so no one would see her like this. For the first time, even while still drunk, she was ashamed of herself. She craved escape, escape from what she had become, escape from the role she had so wanted to play—an escape even the booze could no longer provide.

She made it only as far as the hall closet before black spots began to descend in a shower across her eyes. Inside the closet it was dark; she shut the door to seal herself off, and slumped down the length of the wall, a rag doll among the fur coats and gloves. She would never come out. She was tired of fighting herself. Her head propped on a pair of rubber galoshes, she opened her arms to the blackness and let it take her under.

Two hours later, Mrs. George found her there. Being nearly unable to rouse her, she took her to the kitchen and forced her to down mug after mug of coffee. Kat sat very still at the circular oak table. Neither of them spoke, but the expression on the housekeeper's face was enough. Kat knew why Mrs. George had not just put her to bed. There was something important for her to do now, to face now, she was sure of it.

Kat did not move. It was after midnight, and soon the house was quiet. Not nearly sober yet, she drank more coffee. She kept looking at the telephone. Surely there must be someone who could help her, who would understand.

Of course, she'd known the answer to the question before she'd even asked it—known and resisted it with the last bit of stubborn will in her. It was impossible to admit sinking to such depths.

But in spite of pride, in spite of humiliation and the blow to her ego, Kat was afraid. There was nowhere else to go. If she went to bed now, she might be lost forever. And so, as suddenly as diving into a cold river, she grabbed the phone book and dialed the number, quickly, before she could lose her nerve.

The young woman who answered the phone said her name was Susan. She introduced herself as an alcoholic, and offered Kat two meager pieces of advice—words that sounded thin and simplistic and naïve. "Don't drink anything else tonight," she repeated in a firm voice. "And come tomorrow to an AA meeting. There's one right in Concord. At the Stratford School—11 A.M."

Kat sat in the half-lit kitchen for a while longer, trying to get control of her fear and her grief and her anger. She looked at the shining glass cabinets with their ordered stacks of crystal and china, the spice bottles in neat colored rows, the copper pots shining on their ceiling island. Why wasn't her life as simple and clean as all this? Tears came to her eyes, tears from a deep wounded place she had never opened before, and she did not try to stop them.

There was no magic any more, but it was magic that she'd wanted—just as she'd wanted her mother to admit she'd been wrong when she'd told Kat that Santa Claus wasn't real. She sobbed now, as then, with the same childish sense of injustice. She'd wanted that phone call to tell her there was a special cure, a prescription bottle with her name on the label, but all she'd gotten was oversimplified advice. What could that girl know of her troubles? She was just some anonymous voice on the end of a wire. Kat wondered what she should do, where she should go, what she would feel in the morning, now that there was no hope left.

She got up from her chair and turned out the light.

Twenty

THERE WAS SNOW FOR CHRISTMAS AFTER ALL. IF YOU LISTENED HARD, you could hear it falling with a hiss, like rain does on macadam. Kat heard it. And the throbbing of the broad-bladed plows, the clack-clack of their chained wheels, coming and going all through the night into the early morning. They were the enemies of the snow's solace, enemies of her soft mask—the mask that hid the ugly sticks and twigs, and the dead dry leaves of November. The plows were relentless, carving order into the drifts, pushing back the illusion of wildness, sanding the way for civilization, for those of intent, for those with purpose. It was a windless snow, a snow that came in straight vertical lines, a snow that had already covered the marble birdbath in the yard when Kat came to the window that morning. And underneath it all hibernated the brown earth.

She was quiet through breakfast, and through the endless exchange of gifts before the fire under the brightly lit tree. She was waiting, poised inside, for something new—a sign, a direction. Or perhaps it was only for some impetus, some sort of courage or determination. She smiled. She undid bows and paper and ornament. She looked pleased, and tried on the opera-length pearls that Kirk had given her. Standing before the mirror, she spoke of their translucence, and carefully matched size, all the while thinking that she had really bought them for herself. Her eyes looked back into themselves in the glass, frightened.

Not knowing what would happen, she went on like a mechanical doll, putting one thought in front of the other, one smile in front of the other. Her mind was a whirlpool; it eddied down around one memory and then another, unable to concentrate on the present. She thought of the toboggan slide she and her family used to go to when she was a little girl. It was always at night, and in the dark the giant slide was only a trough of ice under the moon. They would hurtle down, through time, past time, out of time—frozen into some future limbo. That was now, she thought, her fingers slowly raveling a satin bow. Time was that iced slide, leading where?

She watched the fixed rituals clicking past like the notches on a clock. A luncheon, set on the red and green Christmas cloth, of boiled lobster and champagne. She held onto those rituals because suddenly it seemed she would slide into the past and stay there. Her mind was just a piece of machinery. It could get stuck in any gear, or overheat and seize up, become a solid, immovable mass of iron. In her head the woman's voice from last night repeated the precise time and location of the AA meeting like incriminating evidence, like the court recorder at a trial. Without looking at her watch, Kat knew that the meeting was going on now, and guilt made her promise that she would at least ignore the champagne which bubbled in her hollow-stemmed glass. She could do this on her own—this was a private affair. She would simply stop drinking: a clean act with neat sharp edges and well-defined borders. This sort of diet required only willpower, and she was certain she had enough.

The champagne hissed softly, like the snow. The bubbles rose in straight neat columns, an orderly army, growing up from the bottom of the glass. Kat stared into space as she cracked open the knuckles of her lobster. When she was little her glass had been filled with ginger ale. It had been her mother's long fingers that pulled apart the red shell, while Paige tore off the eyes and stuck them on her fork like two green capers.

Kat kept wandering back to the bubbles. They looked like the

string of glass beads they'd used for dress-up as children. She
wondered how they would feel on her tongue, the cool fuzz that
crept between your molars like dry mouthwash. She picked up
her water glass, drank a sip, and then tore the strong tail muscle
into bite-size pieces; she concentrated on soaking it in the butter,
but it just didn't taste the same. It wasn't the same. Lobster without champagne was like littlenecks without martinis. She looked
at her glass with anger: why should she obey someone else's arbitrary rules?

As the switchman throws the railroad tracks for the oncoming
engine, she decided then to drink just this one glass. After all,
she knew she could handle *one*. And one would be enough. She
would teach herself to stop. Just enough to be part of the gourmet meal—but no more. Her hands were slippery with grease,
and she closed her fingers around the crystal stem tightly.

And so the afternoon brightened for Kat, as if she'd been sitting in a darkened room and now the lights had come up. She
could hear her father and Paige again. She could respond to
their laughter, could eat her lobster down to the hairy legs and
the round flippers on the tail. She had climbed back on the
merry-go-round. She was not alone.

The table was heaped high with the broken red shells, the dis-
carded bodies, the staring eyes. Kirk pushed back his chair and
stood, reaching toward Paige with an affectionate gesture. Kat
watched as her sister took his hand. What would other people
see in this? she wondered. She fought down jealousy, stubborn
as an addiction, jealousy that refused to leave her, that licked her
like a flame. And then the self-pity moved in. She was alone.
They had left her alone.

She drained a third glass of champagne. To cool this rush of
emotion, to dampen the sensations burning at her was all she
wanted, and as she stood, she looked to see if the Taittinger bottle was empty. But as she reached for it, ready to refill her glass,
a curtain drew back in her mind. Quickly, she saw the meal
replayed in flashback, with all its complicated acts. And because
she was only high, not drunk, she could not make room for excuses or evasions. Aaron's old words, last night's fear and revela-

tions: all this funneled into her head in a rush. She saw—almost as if reading it in a newspaper, the print of her actions standing out clear and black and defined—what she had done.

Without saying anything to anyone, she went to her room. She couldn't wait any longer. Fear choked her and made it hard to breathe or think. She was looking for a solid object, a solid voice, a solid thought. She was tired of being afraid and confused. Anger at the waste slowly began to stamp out the fear as she sat down on her bed and tried to stop shaking, tried to think what to do next. She couldn't go on like this. For the first time in her life, she wanted change, and needed change. She had to escape from this numb, silent blanket that weighted her down. Suddenly she knew she could not do it alone. She picked up the phone.

Not until after dinner did she announce her intention to go out. She had hibernated throughout the evening meal, caught in the eye of a private storm, picking at her food and drinking no alcohol. Now the three of them sat before the fire in the library, watching television. Paige and Kirk were on their second glasses of eggnog.

The grandfather clock in the hall struck eight.

"Well," Kat said, stretching her arms up over her head, "I'm due at Helena's in a while." Adrenaline rocketed through her veins and made her heart bounce unevenly in her chest. For a moment she felt dizzy and was afraid she would have to sit down, but she forced herself to walk blindly toward the door.

Kirk looked at her with a disgruntled expression. "In this weather?"

Of course, Helena was probably in Houston with her parents for the holidays, and Kat hadn't seen her in over two months, but she had counted on the storm to distract her father from this glaring loophole.

"It stopped snowing three hours ago," she said, leaning against the doorjamb in an effort to look relaxed. "And I've got my new tires. Don't be a mother hen."

"But when will you be back?"

"Oh, early. Ten-thirty or so," she said over her shoulder as she

left the room. It was the first time in many months she had gone
directly against her father's wishes. She would not have dared to
have done it before. But tonight was different. Tonight she was
willing to risk a great deal.

As she pulled on her coat, she went back to the threshold of
the library to say good-by. The room was warm with the heat of
the fire, the drapes were drawn against the cold night, and the
rich smell of eggnog filtered through the smoky snap of apple-
wood. Over the TV screen came the titles for Dickens' *Christmas
Carol*. Each year they sat here together to watch it. She was
looking at an old family portrait, a portrait which had endured
for years, a portrait which caught the permanence of their lives
together. This would be the first time she had left it. An overwhelming sadness she did not understand made her want to cry,
to sit at her father's feet and put her head in his lap.

She moved silently from the doorway, held by the vise of her
pain. She lifted her chin, trying to rouse the stubborn mettle
which had always been a part of her nature. As she headed for
the garage, she told herself not to be so morbid: there would be
plenty of other nights before the fire. Going to an AA meeting
tonight surely did not mean her entire life would change into
something unrecognizable.

Outside, the night was silent, all sound deadened by the high
banks lining the road. A wind had come up, and now drifts covered bushes, rocks, and fences. The new snow squeaked beneath
her tires where the plow had packed it down. At the end of the
driveway, she hesitated and looked over her shoulder one last
time. The soft blue lights traditionally strung over the shrubs
and trees at Christmas shone up from beneath the heavy wet
snow, and a muted ethereal glow radiated out into the night,
outlining the shapes and textures of branches no longer visible.
It was beautiful. Once again Kat felt herself pulled, felt the roots
of her life and of her love, drawn back to the house. For a moment she paused and considered the insanity of what she was
doing, driving out into the night, alone, to meet a bunch of
strangers. She was afraid. She wanted so much to stay.

But she was here, in the car. She forced herself to remember the black fear of that afternoon, and of last night. Surely nothing could be worse than that. She must go, if only to see, if only to prove to herself that she was still alive, not mummified in the cocoon of the past. She put her foot down on the accelerator, and skidded out onto the roadway.

Already the parking lot of the Sacred Heart Church was nearly full, and it was just eight-fifteen. As Kat had come through Lexington's empty streets she'd begun to hope the meeting would be canceled because of the weather. But as more and more men and women emerged from snow-battered vehicles and made their way into the building, she realized that exterior forces just did not daunt these people.

The AA Central Service had arranged for Rudi Heller to meet Kat here, to introduce her around, and bolster her morale. They'd even offered to have him give her a lift to Lexington, but she'd hastily made an excuse. Paige and her father were not to know where she was going; it was bad enough to be coming here.

The air in the car was getting colder and colder but she made no move toward the lighted building. She didn't want to go inside. "Oh, God," she said aloud, her breath steaming white into the cold, "why did I ever come? This's so stupid!" She struck her hand against the steering wheel, all the while trying to reason her way out, to convince herself that she could stop drinking alone. But fear banded in a tight circle around her head and kept reminding her of lying on that closet floor. At eight twenty-five, unable to bear her own anxiety and uncertainty any longer, she scrambled out of her seat and ran into the building, moving blindly, almost on instinct.

When she stopped, she was at the top of a small staircase, looking down into a basement function hall filled with the buzz of at least a hundred people. Chairs were arranged on the linoleum in neat rows and sections, and a podium stood at the front of the room, complete with microphone. It was a pleasant place —even with its exposed pipes and plain acoustical ceiling tile—

painted a soft peach to counteract the fluorescent glare of the bright overhead lights.

Moving slowly down the steps, she felt like a teen-ager at her first dance. What was she supposed to do now? How would this Rudi Heller ever find her? She must be strong; she must try to look inconspicuous. Two large coffee urns on the far side of the room drew a crowd, and Kat made her way there. At least it would give her something to do till she found Rudi, and a coffee cup would be something normal to hold onto.

As she stood in line and waited her turn at the tap, she kept watch out of the corner of her eye: what did alcoholics look like, dress like, sound like, anyhow? What class were they? To whom did they belong? One man looked like a bus driver, in blue polyester pants, and another's warped face made her avert her own. But here was a young woman with a plaid skirt, cashmere sweater, and leather boots. And there a professional-looking man in a suit. It was all confusing; it was not what she had expected.

There was a gentle touch on her arm, and she turned to a tall man, powerfully built, his black hair brushed back from a high brow. He looked to be in his forties.

"Are you Katherine, by any chance?"

With surprise, she noted his heavy German accent. "Why, yes." She moved out of line so someone could get around her. "Are you . . . Rudi Heller?"

A wide smile parted his full beard and he clasped her palm between his two large hands. "It is good you could come tonight."

"I thought maybe no one would be here," Kat said, looking at the floor and tossing her hair back from her face. "Because of all the snow." Words came through her lips like stones as she tried to talk around the incessant buzz in her head—a buzz which kept repeating that she was not really doing this, that she should leave, that she didn't belong here.

"We are always here," Rudi said, putting his cup under the tap of an urn with a Sanka coffee can inverted on it. "This is your first meeting ever?"

Kat smiled and nodded. "I'm not sure, you know," she ex-

plained quickly, "but I thought I'd come to see." She held her
cup under the tap and then added cream and sugar.

"That is exactly right," said Rudi with a smile. "There is nothing to be lost by looking us over." He took her arm and moved
into the center of the room, choosing two seats near the front.
They sat down.

"What do you do?" Rudi asked, looking at her with curiosity.

"Do?"

"Professionally."

No one had asked her such a question in a long time. She'd
done no work in so long that she felt at a loss to answer him. She
looked up to see his deep blue eyes studying her; he was thinking something but she couldn't tell what. "Free-lance proofreading, but I've done nothing for a couple of months now."

"When I came here first, I too was not working. But after a
while I was able to go back."

He didn't understand, she thought, nodding politely. She
hadn't stopped working because she was unable to—she'd chosen
to stop. But she didn't need to explain all that to a stranger.
"And you," she asked, to move the subject away from herself,
"what do you do now?"

"I am a neurosurgeon."

She tried to keep her surprise from showing on her face.

He threw back his head and laughed. "You are shocked?" he
asked with an upward twist of his eyebrows. "There are many
physicians in AA. We have the highest rate of alcoholism and
drug abuse of any single group in America."

"Have you been a member long?" she asked, embarrassed.

"This is my third year." He smiled at her expression. "It
passes so quickly. It seems only yesterday that I walked in, just
as frightened as you are tonight."

There was no way she could deny her fear and so she tried to
smile instead. At the front of the room a young woman adjusted
the mike and called everyone to order; Kat was too distracted to
listen. She had thought these people would be different. She'd
thought they would all be the same, all sloppy, all unclean, all in
sneakers with holes—all like the unemployable derelicts you saw

sleeping on park benches outside the Park Street subway station. But this church basement looked more like the waiting lounge for a charter to the Caribbean. The woman leading the meeting was neatly dressed, well groomed, and spoke clearly, if with a grating Boston accent.

On either side of the podium, blue felt banners had been hung. Their orange letters spelled out the corniest mottoes Kat had ever seen: Easy Does It; Live and Let Live; But for the Grace of God; Thy Will Be Done. What did it matter how these people looked? she thought suddenly. This was a Boy Scout troop for adults, and that was the difference between her and them in tangible terms: she would never be like them, never fit into this kind of thinking. Her education was too good, her sensibilities too fine to accept this sort of clichéd approach to life. Scorn rose in her, and she knew there would be no truth for her here. These people were just looking for a crutch and she didn't need or want one. She just wanted to get control of her life. She nearly got up and left, but there was Rudi, on her right, listening so intently. What could she say to him? No, she decided, she would just get through this and never come back again. It was easier than making a scene.

Another woman came to the microphone now, her auburn hair cut in a straight line above deep-set brown eyes, her smile crooked. She smoothed the skirt of her knit dress and cleared her throat. To Kat she seemed not in the least bit apprehensive about speaking before so many people.

"My name is Marty. I'm an alcoholic." She paused and looked around the room, gathering her thoughts. Kat felt a tingle of surprise at how matter-of-factly she had said the word alcoholic, exposing herself to everyone in the room.

"Tonight I'm here to tell you about myself. About how I couldn't stop drinking when I thought I could, about how I tried and tried until I was just plumb wore out with trying, until there was no more fight left in me, until there was only fear. That was when I came to AA. When the fear was too big for me, when it was eating me alive. When the fear was so bad I couldn't face the world without my daily ration."

Kat began picking at her fingernails, certain she was in for an hour of self-justification and self-pity from this woman. She had come here to forget about alcohol—not to dissect it, not to remember the horror. Nevertheless, she had to admit that what this Marty said about fear was true enough. The struggle of the past months had marked Kat and it was not easy to forget that intense anxiety.

"I came to booze when I was fifteen," Marty was saying as Kat tuned back in reluctantly. "It was one of those weekend parties where someone's parents are away. We drank beer all weekend and it was the first time I got drunk. It was also the first time I ever drove a car, seeing as I had no license, and the first time I was ever with a man, seeing as I didn't know what I was doing, and it was the first time I ever threw up from liquor—but definitely not the last!"

She looked around her, smiling at the memory, and a gentle empathetic laughter went through the audience; Kat didn't understand it—why were they laughing? She sat back in her seat and shook her head.

"I grew up," Marty went on, "in the kind of family where you just had sherry on the holidays. I mean, it was kept in the back of the closet in one of those cheap little decanters you get if you buy the right size of bottle, and it was always full and we never had to refill it because no one ever drank it. Who needed it? We were all going to grow up and be good neighbors, good mothers. We didn't know anyone who drank too much. Of course, as my parents' first child, I was their hopes and dreams. I was an honor student and I sang in the school choir and the church choir and I never disobeyed anybody. My mother made me wear these perfect little dresses with frilly collars like some kind of nun—but inside I was just burning to be different." She laughed aloud at herself and again the crowd responded. Relaxed even further, she put her hands on her slender hips as she spoke.

"When I got to college, I got this idea in my head—this image of how I wanted to be—of a wild crazy woman. I didn't want to be good any more. Well, this place was a teaching college, and it was real strict, but I hung around with all the Yale boys anyway,

and drank lots of their beer or their weird punches, or just anything anybody had. I loved it—it made me laugh, it made me
loose. I felt beautiful when I drank. And I got in a lot of trouble
too. The nun was gone for good!" Now the audience laughed before she could laugh at herself. "So I was wild and loose and
drunk and got kicked out of school and eventually I graduated
from somewhere else, and then I met this guy who I married
after a while. His name was Richard. He married me even
though I was crazy and drunk and wild and got up and danced
on tables in nightclubs and lay on the sidewalk in front of my
dorm singing to the moon. The years went by," Marty said,
fingering her earring and looking at the ceiling for a minute. "In
the beginning I was just one of those wives who likes her cocktails a little too much. I mean, I looked forward to my two drinks
at the end of the day. But before too long there I was with four
drinks and trying to cut down. I knew it was bad, even then. So
I'd say I'll only have two, and then after I'd had those two, I'd
say, I've been so good by only having two that I deserve a little
reward. So I'd have a third as a reward, and after a little while
there'd be the fourth as a reward for having waited for my first
reward. Pretty soon it was all those rewards that were getting
me into trouble, and I still couldn't figure out why I was so
unhappy."

Inside Kat something heavy and hard shifted. It did sound like
her. Trying to cut back, and failing. There was nothing worse,
she thought, than being unhappy and not understanding why.

"My husband, he knew I was drinking a lot and he nagged at
me to stop, so I started hiding it. I was scared he'd see all the
empty bottles in the trash and realize I was putting away a fifth
of gin a day, so I'd sneak into the basement every night, after everyone was in bed, wrap up my empty in a towel, and smash it
with a hammer. Then I'd carefully take all the little pieces and
stuff them into a Triscuit box and I'd put that in the garbage. So I
was eating a box of Triscuits a day and drinking a quart of gin,
and still nobody could figure out why I was getting so fat."

This relieved Kat—here she could draw the line. She had never been deceitful like that, she had never been so obsessive or neurotic.

"That took care of the empties, and I got more and more clever at hiding and disguising how and when I was drinking. In the beginning I always kept a full glass in the clothes dryer—ready for a quick nip—until my husband started asking if I was drinking in the morning. When he got dressed before going to work the house stank of gin. It didn't take me long to figure out that the booze in my secret cache was evaporating in the dryer, and then filtering into each load of clothes."

Again the room erupted into laughter, and Kat caught herself just in time. She couldn't laugh with them; to laugh would imply that she was a part of the group.

"Soon I came up with a new plan that worked pretty well. I'd mix up a jug of Hyponex liquid plant food using gin instead of water and keep it right on my kitchen shelf, ready for a quick shot whenever I wanted it. I figured the plant food was just good vitamins and all I really cared about was getting high.

"Nothing else much mattered. I kept getting fired—I was in TV production—because I was missing work or out of it when I was there. Eventually the time came when I got so tired I didn't even bother to look for more work. I just sat around the house with my feet up and my bottle beside the chair. And I listened to this record, a Burt Bacharach number called "Make It Easy on Yourself." And that's what I did. I made it easy on myself and hard on everyone else. After a while my kids stopped coming home till suppertime, and then they wouldn't look me in the face or speak to me. And the dishes in the sink were a mountain, and my husband had just given up. We were all a bunch of zombies. But I was the queen zombie."

Queen zombie. The phrase echoed in Kat's mind. Queen zombie. And she knew then that though the facts were different, she was hearing the truth of her own life. The fear, the numbness, the indifference about living or dying. She looked at her lap, and saw tears falling onto her clenched fists. Rudi slipped his hand over hers, and she let it stay there, grateful for the warmth and understanding. She continued to listen.

"And it went on this way for a few years—just misery, aching misery, self-loathing, and I couldn't see how to change anything —I thought, this is the way it has to be. I went on with the Triscuit boxes and the green plant-food gin, and I got to hiding my bottles and forgetting where I'd hidden them, and then accusing the kids of stealing them. I began to lose my memory. In blackouts. Whole stretches of time where I couldn't remember where I'd been or what I'd done or said. And the next morning—the terror of trying to figure it out without letting anyone know that I didn't know.

"So. That's my drunkalogue. How did it change? Well, it was a winter day, a day where the roads were covered with ice and my oldest kid called for a ride home. I'd been drinking since ten, but that didn't matter and I climbed right in the car without taking my coat or bringing a purse. But I did remember my bottle, putting it near me on the seat where I could reach it if I needed to. I hadn't gotten more than a block from home when I saw this little blur, of red, like a flash, in the road in front of me. But I was drunk and didn't know what this red thing was." She paused for a moment and swallowed to clear her throat. Both her hands were tucked tightly under her arms. "And then something in me reacted, something in me said, but in a delayed reaction, 'That's a little kid.' I tried to step on the brake, but I missed. I was too drunk. I was in slow motion. Then there was this sick thump as I ran over the red snowsuit.

"I got out of the car and ran up to this house, this stranger's house, and I was crying and telling them to call the police and an ambulance or something. I don't know. I don't remember too clearly. But I do remember standing in this stranger's foyer and looking over at myself in the hall mirror. Standing there, my hair all ratty and hanging down my back, my eyes like two black holes in my face, and that bottle, that goddamned bottle, still in my hand. And that was when I knew. I knew—it was the booze."

She paused and looked out over the crowd. "Of course, they took me to the police station, but Richard was a lawyer and he got me out on bail. But still I was up for a manslaughter charge, unless the little girl lived. I was still too drunk to know, or even maybe to care, what I'd done. I just knew I was scared. I knew that it was the booze and that I had to stop drinking or I had to die. And then I thought that I'd rather die than stop drinking."

Rudi was still holding Kat's hand. She didn't want to die. She didn't want to stop drinking. But if she had to choose? Here was this warm room, lighted with laughter. Here was a warm hand holding hers.

"We got home," Marty was saying, "and I just sat alone all night long until everyone went to bed. Finally I got up and drew all the curtains in the den, and got a white sheet from the linen closet and spread it on the floor. I brought my quart in with me and drank it down straight, and when I was good and drunk I turned out all the lights and took off all my clothes and laid myself on that sheet, my arms stretched out just as if I was waiting for the coroner. In my own head I was as dead as I could be and still breathe. I was dead inside and so I laid myself out and that was how I finally admitted to myself that I needed help.

"Well, anyway. The little girl did live. And the court made me go for alcoholism therapy. They sent this minister to talk to me who knew a lot about AA, which I thought was a bunch of Jesus freak horse crap. At first I thought, this is *not, no way, ever,* for me. But after a while I saw that they were really sort of crazy too—not just a bunch of stuffed shirts mouthing off about God. I liked the idea of crazy people—I always had, if you remember my wild and loose days—and so I went off to my first meeting.

"In the beginning I didn't take to it at all, because all this God stuff kept getting in my way. But I did hear one thing which stuck with me and that one thing kept me sober. Everyone told me 'Just don't drink today, and go to a meeting.' I was like a horse with blinders, but heard and saw this one thing and really fixed in on it, because somehow I knew my life depended on it."

Kat raised her head.

"I didn't drink," Marty said, "just took it one day at a time and it's been eight years since I joined AA. And what I learned in that time is that you *can be* wild and crazy and still not drink. And I did find a personal faith that keeps me humming, but my faith is almost beside the point in a way, because some people find it and some don't and still the Program goes on working for them. And I did find a new series of habits and rituals that replaced the old sick ones, that grew into a meaningful part of my life, productive habits, creative habits.

"All I'm really trying to say is this: if you're new, just listen to the basic facts. You do not ever have to take a drink again. Put that drink off till tomorrow, and just deal with today. Come to meetings and listen to the stories of people who fought for their sobriety and won. And if it seems we're bragging about all this terrible stuff we did—don't you believe it. We're not. But everyone needs to remember it, how bad it was. To relive it once in a while so we can know that more than anything else in life, we do not want to go back. I've come to a place in my life where I can say I'd rather die than drink again."

She smiled, and Kat felt a release, a gate clicking open. Voices buzzed up and down the aisles as Marty stepped down, but Kat sat in silence, still holding onto Rudi's hand, and he just waited, knowing that she needed to be there without the pressure of words.

After a while, she released his hand without looking over at him, and the expression on her face lay somewhere between embarrassment and apology. The rest of the meeting with its quota of speakers moved by her, but she couldn't take any more in; this first experience had been too intense. She waited, hibernating mentally, for ten o'clock; to sort out her thoughts she needed to be alone. There was so much here that drew her, so much that put her off.

"At first it is hard to hear these things," Rudi said quietly as the meeting broke and people began to gather around the doughnut table. "But sometimes one also feels relieved. For me, it was like that."

"I feel confused," Kat said. "Scared." She thought for a minute. "But at least not quite so depressed." She searched his face. "Is that all right?"

"I think it is exactly right." He smiled. "I am to be a speaker for a meeting on Thursday night. Would you like to come?"

"You mean, you'll be telling *your* life story?"

"Yes, and it is a good meeting, too." He nodded. "One speaker and then a discussion where many people talk for a short time. A group much smaller than this, in the Cambridge City Hospital."

Kat hesitated, uncertain that she wanted to go again so soon. She still was not even sure that she belonged here. "I'm not positive of my schedule," she lied, "but where would I go in case I can make it?"

Before she left, Rudi gave her the time and location of the meeting, and his phone number. The imprint of his hand was warm on hers as she went through the back doors into the clear chill air. She stood for a moment, looking at the sky. The storm had cleared and broken clouds whipped across the face of a nearly full moon. Cold snapped her cheeks, and she felt suddenly awake, alive. Hope rushed in on her and she ran back to the car.

But as she inserted the key in the ignition, she cautioned herself to slow down. After all, she wasn't even sure yet that she really was an alcoholic, or that she had to stop drinking entirely. While the car warmed up she decided to make a pact with herself: she wouldn't take another drink until she could be certain one way or another, and she would try a few more meetings.

She headed out toward Route 2, her mind playing with what she'd heard. She needed to talk it over with someone, needed to bounce it off someone trusted. But Helena was in Houston. And even if she had been home, Kat realized with a stab of fear, she might not be willing to talk to Kat. Perhaps there had been silence between them for too long. Helena might have another best friend by now—someone else to share with, someone less problematic.

At the entrance ramps to Route 2 she hesitated, slowing, wavering between east and west. Then she swung onto the left ramp, eastbound, toward Cambridge.

Twenty-one

IRVING STREET WAS DARK AND QUIET. KAT PLOWED DOWN IT, IN DE-fiance of the emergency snow regulations which made on-street parking illegal. She pulled over as far as possible into the wall of a snowbank, and set the brake. Overhead the moon was very bright, reflecting off the snow, and she kept reassuring herself that nothing traumatic could happen on a night so serene. It was a good omen.

Still, he might not be home. Or, he might not want to see her. Or, he might be with someone else.

She looked up at his windows to see that the lights were on. Holding herself very erect, she waded down the unshoveled back walk and up the steps, her mouth dry and sticky with anxiety, her tongue a big dead fish. The knocker on the door announced her with finality; there was no way to back out now.

Footsteps approached and then stopped. Kat could feel his hesitation as he looked through the peephole, could imagine the expression on his face. She was sure he didn't want to let her in, and she waited silently; perhaps he would turn and sneak away, perhaps he would pretend not to have heard her. But at last, he swung the door open slowly.

His dark hair in rumpled disarray, his shirttails loose, he wore a flannel work shirt, jeans, and the Muk-Luks she'd given him for his birthday last year. A pencil rested over one ear; he carried another in his hand. And his familiar face, so puzzled now, but still so tender. His dark eyes with their questions. She wanted to run to him, throw her arms around him, touch him. She wanted to lead them to the bedroom and undress him piece by piece. "Are you busy?" she said at last, breaking the silence.

He looked at her, uncertain of what to do in a decidedly awkward situation, before shaking his head and beckoning. "Come on in." His voice sounded unsteady.

As they passed the bedroom on their way to the living room, Kat couldn't help but look in, feeling as if she were spying on Aaron. She was checking for another woman's clothing, another woman's cosmetics and shower cap, but there was none. Over the unmade bed the sketch of her still hung. This was some weird impossible dream. Every night for nearly three months she had fantasized this reunion. They sat down in two armchairs she'd never seen before, and he looked at her expectantly. But how could she begin. "I needed to talk to you," she said finally.

"O.K.," he said. He leaned back casually, almost as if she were a stranger, here to do a survey or a census.

"You're sure I'm not interrupting or anything?" she asked as she unbuttoned her coat and shrugged it off.

"That's O.K."

Over his shoulder Kat could see the easel set up near the window. The Luxo lamp brought out the sharp details of the sketch he'd been working on when she'd interrupted. She knew she was staring at the portrait, but she couldn't help it. The woman's face drew her, stared her down. It was not her beauty which threatened Kat, it was the intimacy with which it was drawn, the texture, the detail. Here was the rival she had anticipated as she passed the bedroom door. This was no casual model posing for an afternoon's wage. Aaron knew this woman well.

"I thought you'd stopped drawing," she said, trying not to sound jealous.

"I did. But last week there was the urge." He sighed. "School just doesn't use it all up. I'd hoped it would—it would've been easier like that. Now I'm back on the fence again."

"She's beautiful," Kat said unwillingly.

"Yes. Tina's something else." He grinned and looked over at the sketch. "She's the one I worked with at the firm last summer."

"You still see each other?" Kat asked, forcing her stiff jaw to smile.

"We're good friends." He shrugged and turned back to her. "We talk a lot about school."

"How's it going?" Kat asked, hating Tina, hating his friendship with her, and eager to speak of something new.

"Some of it's boring, some's pretty good." He did not elaborate, and Kat realized he was waiting for her to come to the point.

"Well, I needed to talk something over with someone." She smiled. "Helena's away, but I knew you'd be here. Are your parents abroad for the holiday?"

"Where else?" He leaned back in his chair and stuck the other pencil behind his ear.

She sighed. "Things've been really bad since the last time we spoke—just like you predicted."

"I'm sorry, Kat," he said sadly, with no trace of satisfaction.

"I got pretty desperate, to be frank. The drinking's really out of hand, so I decided to give AA a try. I just came from there." She put her hands between her knees so he couldn't see them shake.

There was an astonished silence. "You did?" Aaron asked finally. "Why?"

"Why?" she echoed. "Well, you should understand why—you're the one who first said I had a drinking problem. I'm not sure I'm an alcoholic—" She paused and emphasized the word by underlining it in the air. "But I've decided I won't have another drink till I figure everything out. It's funny," she rushed on, "but I feel sort of happy."

"You mean that you're not going to drink anything at all? No wine? No beer?"

She threw him a puzzled look. "Wine or beer? Alcohol is alcohol and AA works on not drinking anything. Ever."

"Isn't that a little extreme?"

"Maybe," Kat admitted. "On the other hand it does seem to

work for those people, and frankly, I haven't done very well on my own, with my limits of one or two drinks. I always end up too high whatever my good intentions."

"Kat, I don't know." He shook his head. "Surely you could learn to just control yourself, if you tried hard enough."

"Don't you think I was trying that weekend in the Catskills? And all those other times?" Her eyes filled with tears. "I was always trying."

He looked down into his lap. "It's funny. I always thought you were doing it just to be stubborn, to act up. To be center stage."

"Maybe I was—at first. But not any more." She could feel herself getting angry: this was already so hard—and now to withstand his arguments. "Why are you giving me the third degree about this?" she asked. "You of all people should encourage me! You're the one who took the brunt of my drinking. Don't you remember?" Her face was perplexed and hurt.

"Look," he burst out, slapping his hand against the upholstery, "I haven't seen you in almost three months and suddenly you're here telling me all this intense stuff." There was silence, and he twisted in his chair. "I'm sorry," he said, "but what do you want? It's such a *big* problem now. When we were together, I thought you could just stop drinking so much. I thought you could take care of it yourself. I didn't know it would entail all this." He looked at her searchingly, and then stared down at his feet. "It scares me."

"But, Aaron," she said with despair, "you already knew it was a big problem. That's why you left me! Don't be scared now. Be glad."

He looked at her steadily, trying to assess her, place her, measure her, to come to terms with it all. And at the expression on his face, longing overcame her. She got up from her chair and went to kneel before him, reaching out to touch his hand where it lay on his knee. "I've missed you," she said. "Tell me it's not too late."

He looked down at her fine face, a clear frank face that let the love show. She still scared him; how could he know for sure? How could he count on her? It was too soon, too early. Nevertheless, he gave in to desire as easily as a bud opens under warm spring rain. He reached out, hypnotized, to run his finger down alongside her face. Her skin was softer than he remembered, her hazel eyes deeper. He wanted to kiss her.

His touch made Kat want to say all kinds of things she knew were better left alone; his touch showed her how easy it would be to go to the bedroom and turn out the lights. She stood abruptly. The situation was fragile, and she knew, quite suddenly, quite clearly, that they needed time. "I've got to go," she said. "But I wanted you to know." She paused. "I needed to know what you thought."

"Kat." He caught her hand. "I'm *glad* you came. I still do care. Remember that."

And then she couldn't help herself, and the question burned its way out of her like rising steam. "But did you stop loving, Aaron? Did you leave because you'd stopped loving me?"

He was quiet and then stared down at her hand, still in his. "No, Kat, I never stopped." He hesitated. "But love wasn't enough to get me through everything else. Love!" His mouth twisted in a bitter smile. "It just wasn't enough!"

Kat looked up at him and nodded. She went back down the stairs, and stood for a moment in the street under the searching white moon. For the first time, she thought maybe she understood why he had gone.

Twenty-two

SHE'D FORGOTTEN HOW BEAUTIFUL THE MORNING COULD BE. ALL WEEK long she had gone to bed early and sober, and each morning she had come awake early and clearheaded. For three days in a row she lay buried under her down puff, and enjoyed the luxury of the sun as it spilled into her room, the voice of the wind through the eaves, the feel of the fresh-laundered sheets warm against her toes. She had forgotten how the yard looked from her window seat as the sun came up, the firs throwing blue shadows across the snowy lawn. She'd forgotten the smell of bacon sliding up from the depths of the house, forgotten the hot rich taste of first coffee. This week she took joy in her breakfast eggs, their yolks quivering like new suns, joy in the tray of brown English muffins, in the luxurious pots of homemade jams.

Other things began to change as well, but gradually, a season of slow movement. Kat could not really see the changes, could not see the reasons behind them; nevertheless her life began to shift focus, and this she could feel—if without understanding it. The urge to work again came strong and hard to her, an insistent urge which would not be quieted. She called the publishers and editors she had been so cold to a few months before but they were wary now. They did not want to give her work. They did not trust her. She told them frankly that she'd been out of circulation because of a debilitating illness—and this did not strike her as far from the truth.

By the time her list of ten calls was complete, two editors had promised her assignments by the end of the week. For the first time in many months, Kat felt she had tackled a difficult task on her own and the success left her clean and exorcised—free.

But still she needed to keep busy until the work came in. And the prospect of sitting alone in the house hour after hour, avoiding bottles which, she realized now, were a significant part of every room, terrified her. She could not hide them, or throw them away. They were a living, breathing force: she had to face them, resist them, cope with them.

Lily's sitting room became her cocoon, and there she sat for hours on end, reading the time away, rediscovering how good an escape a book could be. With *Jane Eyre* and *Wuthering Heights* she resisted the pulse of the bar on the opposite side of the room—those decanters, those family heirlooms, whose call pushed at her the hardest. Perhaps she had located herself in this sitting room unconsciously, but deliberately, as a test of will. If she could do it here, couldn't she do it anywhere?

She lived on tea and cookies that first week because Rudi had told her to eat something sweet when she felt pressured to have a drink. If nothing else, it felt good to have something in her hand. Mrs. George continued to bring her trays, entering and leaving the room quietly, perhaps intuitively sensing Kat was fighting some sort of battle with these endless pots of Earl Grey and Constant Comment. Alternately proud and ashamed of herself, Kat would have liked to talk to Mrs. George about AA, but she hesitated. She wanted to be free and clear of temptation before she announced victory; to prove herself, she needed time.

Aaron came into her mind again and again, and she wanted to call him nearly as much as she wanted a drink, but here too she was strict with herself. To control one problem at a time was all she could manage now. But sometimes the loneliness was too great to bear as she sat there in her mother's chair by the fire, and then she would cry in hard wrenching sobs. She did not really understand why she was crying: whether it was for Aaron, or for her mother, or for the lost booze, or just for herself. She had given up trying to understand and just willed herself to get through each day, sensing that she was on the brink of a great change, that if she were patient and held on, her life would move across the border and through the point of transition. There was something strong in her, something like flint, something which defied the fragility she had assigned herself. It supported her during cocktail hour those first few days when she asked for to-mato juice and explained her abstinence away as a stomach-ache.

On Thursday evening, though, that excuse did not suffice; Kirk and Paige and Kat were before the fire in the den, waiting for supper, and talking in low idle tones about Kirk's day, about the possibility of more snow, about the need to take a vacation in Grenada this year. He mixed the martinis and brought one to Kat as a matter of routine. There it was in her hand. The dry odor of gin made her salivate and the glass sweated under her fingers. Kirk stood at the bar and waited for her judgment of the cocktail's quality.

She was paralyzed. Then, slowly, she looked up at him. "You'll have to taste it yourself, Dad," she said, as she twisted in her seat to look over at the fire, and set the glass down on the table be-side her.

"Is your stomach still bothering you?" he asked, crossing the room to stand beside her with a worried air. "Call Dr. Burr to-morrow and get him to squeeze you in."

Her mouth was dry, and for a moment the fire leaped high against her eyes. Again she felt that peculiar intensity of vision, a sense that the focus of every object in the room had sharpened. She made up her mind. "I never had a stomach problem." She hesitated and looked down at her hands, knotted in her lap. "I have a drinking problem, and I don't think I should drink any more."

On the other side of the room, Paige began to laugh. Kat looked over at her, silent. Kirk went to his chair and sat down, the martinis forgotten on the bar. His voice cut across Paige's laughter. "What are you talking about?"

"I have a lot of trouble controlling my drinking."

"Kat, I'd be the first to reprimand you for abusing liquor. And if you're worried—why, just cut back a bit, that's all."

"I've been trying to. For quite a while now. It doesn't work."

"That's preposterous," he said, beginning to look irritated. "Have three instead of four, or two, and you'll be all set. It's simply a matter of willpower." He stood and went to get his drink at the bar. "To call it a 'problem' is a lot of self-indulgence, and I hope you'll rethink your decision. You simply can't move in the social world and not drink at all." He turned to look over at her. "You would be a pariah."

She just stared at him, stunned by his attitude.

"Yes," said Kirk, as if the question were settled. "You've simply got to change your mind." He crossed the room back to Kat. "There's never been a Sinclair who hasn't been able to handle liquor. Why, look at your mother—she could drink the best of them under the table!" He reached down and put the martini back in her hand. "Now bottoms up, and let's hear no more of this nonsense."

It was cool against her palm. They were waiting for her to join them, and she wanted so to be a part of it again, a part of them. She closed her eyes, and there came to her again that sense of bottomlessness, of falling, of sliding, of falling over the edge out of control. She had been free of that feeling this week. She would not do this. She would not go back. She stood, feeling their eyes on her like darts, and went to the bar where she emptied her glass back into the pitcher. "I will not be drinking with you," she said, her voice shaking with emotion. "I will not be dining with you. At eight o'clock I will leave the house for an AA meeting in Cambridge."

She turned and left the room, silence surrounding her through the long dark corridor, up the stairs, into her bedroom. She sat down on the edge of her bed and shivered at the chill air. It would never be the same again, she saw now. She had made a choice.

As she drove into town that evening, coiling and turning and dodging the traffic like some angered reptile, a feeling of having been outcast began to overwhelm her, outcast like some sea animal spat up on a beach at night. Her father's respect and approval still mattered to her it seemed, and she was not sure she'd ever been without it before. Hadn't she always—all her life—tried to please him? Hadn't she been fighting for him since she'd first pushed her head out into the world? Didn't every woman fight for her father with this intensity—or was she alone, sick in this way. And what had she been doing with him since her mother died? Playing what insane game? Some answer glimmered on the rim, the very edge, of her understanding; shimmering like an iridescent slick on water, changing shape, size, form, as she looked and bent to study it. It passed quickly into something new, a candle snuffing out into darkness.

And there was anger inside her too, a slow pulse, anger at herself, anger at him. Because she had not conformed to his perfect image, he had seen her admission about alcohol as a defect—as if she were a cracked plate, or a sterile dogwood, never to bud up softly in spring, only to hold aloft pale green leaves. He had not taken her seriously; he had seen her difficulties as a reflection on him. She could not help but feel bitter at the injustice, and at the irony: she had given all she had to save him—love, money, time. Love had been an endless debt, never to be repaid. What was it, she wondered, groping in the dark for an answer, starting to cry a little in frustration, what was it that kept him from giving her what she needed? Didn't he love her enough? Who did he love more? Lily, or Kat? Paige, or Kat? An endless competition, an endless race that ended here, that left her parked on an ugly street in Cambridge, just around the corner from Aaron's house, alone once again in the dark car, afraid once again of facing strangers.

The night was cold, but there were stars, hundreds of stars spilling their white fire down into the city. For a moment she heard her father's voice, not so long ago, on a summer's evening, as he pointed out Orion. She stopped and revolved slowly on the pavement, seeking the constellation, but the stars melded together in a blur, confusing her, and she gave up.

The room was small, and warm, filled already with a haze of cigarette smoke so thick that it hung in the air like a curtain. Four long narrow tables were set in the middle of the room to form a squared circle, and Rudi waved at her from one corner. Kat went over to him, unzipping her parka, to take the empty chair to his left. He looked quite nice in a V-neck cashmere sweater and gray flannel slacks.

"I took the chance of saving a seat," he said, smiling as he gestured to the person on his left. "Do you remember Marty from last Sunday?"

Kat looked over and recognized the woman who had spoken at the meeting the other night.

"Nice to see you, Kat," she said. "How long've you been coming around?"

"Sunday was my first meeting."

Rudi reached over to pat her shoulder. "You will see this meeting is very different from the other one. Here each person speaks for a short time, and the chairman"—he pointed at himself—"qualifies only briefly." He banged his knuckles on the table and called the meeting to order.

First there was a moment of silence to do with as you wished. Some bowed their heads, some lit cigarettes. Once again Kat was struck by the diversity of the group in appearance, carriage, dress, and grooming. This meeting seemed to be made up mostly of people between the ages of fifteen and thirty. Young professionals with their briefcases and working clothes, students with their backpacks and books. And then, an old man with a golden retriever, a middle-aged woman in a wheel chair.

Rudi was reading the AA Preamble now. It was so simple, so basic, and it made it all sound easy. *Alcoholics Anonymous is a fellowship of men and women who share their experience, strength and hope with each other that they may solve their common problem and help others to recover from alcoholism. The only requirement for membership is a desire to stop drinking . . . Our primary purpose is to stay sober and help other alcoholics to achieve sobriety.*

Maybe it was easy to belong—to want to stop drinking—but it

was hard not to drink. She thought back over the week: the struggle, the temptation, the resistance. The struggle alone was convincing; if she weren't an alcoholic, why did she have such trouble keeping away from it for even a day? As Rudi launched into his story, speaking only of himself and his problems, she strained to refocus her attention. His words filtered through the mesh of her own problem, reaching her from a distance.

"In Germany," he was saying, "when I was young, we did not really know, or understand, what was happening, the repercussions. We saw only the pride of our people, lifted at last. Our parents proud again. A feeling of purpose, direction. It was a joy, a privilege to be of the ranks of Hitler's Youth. We all participated. It was not until later, at the end of the war, when I was a teen-ager, that I began to understand what had been done, what I had been a part of. And the guilt was terrible—all my friends—our guilt was like a river that could not be stopped. A national guilt. In those early years, during the trials, the occupation, the disillusionment, we all drank to escape the shame. It was a pressure—the integrity of a whole people lost, an integrity which it became every individual's responsibility to regain. But the guilt—it was too big to escape."

Helena. Kat remembered Helena talking of her mother in Chelmno, her mother's shame, her sense that she had somehow allowed herself to be victimized, allowed this rape of her life. How ironic that an emotion could be shared by victim and victimizer alike.

"I only wanted to get out. I wanted another chance," Rudi was saying. "I tried to repay my debt by marrying a Jewish girl, and then we left for America. I came here to practice neurosurgery. But guilt is not something one can run from, and although here I could sometimes forget what happened in Germany, I still couldn't run from myself. And the point was that I did not want to deal with any kind of pressure, or reality, or life, and that here there were all these things too, all these things needing to be dealt with. This was such an intense world, so vibrant, full of rushing about, with too little time, and a great deal of pressure to perform. I needed help with that pressure." He looked slowly around the room. "I had to start hiding from myself. And so I used the alcohol again as a buffer, as a way to face the world. And, in the beginning, it did help me to be more steady and self-confident."

Yes, Kat thought, turning it over in her mind, that's what it was like. In the beginning the drinks did help. They had steadied her then, to face down Rutledge, to deal with her mother's death, to mellow out the pain. The aroma came back to her, the slow easy pleasure of one drink, and the glow it left behind, a glow you could ride on. When had the glow gone? She didn't know, couldn't trace it. The memories just dissolved into a slick slide. In looking for the glow she had drunk more and more. But the insecurities only got worse—that was true, wasn't it? she thought with surprise. The liquor had cost her her work, her pride, Helena, Aaron, and worst of all, her self-respect.

And hadn't it been her own fault, just like Rudi was saying? She hadn't wanted to face the responsibility of her own life, hadn't wanted to see it, or know it. She'd wanted to stay a little girl, to be cuddled and nurtured and loved. She hadn't wanted to be pushed out into this abrupt world of adulthood with all its responsibility. If only her father had been stronger—but then she stopped herself. How much longer could she go on blaming other people? Helena surfaced in her mind again, Helena in the Wursthaus, saying something just like this. Who was to blame for that incident, the incident that had cost her one of the deepest friendships of her life?

"And because my emotional needs were so great—to perform at the operating table, to be a loving husband and father, to carry it all off—I began to need more and more alcohol. And soon alcohol alone wasn't enough, and because as a physician it was very easy to prescribe for myself, I began taking drugs. Soon I was addicted to pills, and it wasn't long before I began with a needle." He held up his hands. They were large, with big bones, and an odd puffiness which Kat had noted before but had not been able to place. "I used up all the veins in my arms so I started in on my hands. You see the destruction! These were the tools of my trade, but I didn't care. I knew inside myself that I was a failure, needing all this, and the guilt was enormous, so I drank and used the medication to get away from the guilt, and the guilt just kept me needing all those things even more. The guilt grew with my addiction instead of getting smaller."

Kat was remembering her mother now. And whose fault was *that,* she wondered idly, scanning the room, whose guilt there? All these ideas were going around and around in her head slowly, like some big ball of sticky caramel, picking up size as it revolved. Who was to blame for Lily?

The lovely face, the fine bones, the soft hair—all of it dissolving away under the weight of pills and booze. There was the last time they'd been together, she thought, in the sitting room before the fire on Washington's Birthday. Her father had been angry about something—maybe it was even Lily's drinking; he had slammed out the door and left Kat to cope. She'd tried to stop her mother, had pleaded with her, begged her, but Lily'd gone on, an engine of destruction, refilling her whiskey glass and drinking it angrily to the bottom, eating pills out of her pocket as if they were candy buttons; and when she'd passed out at last, Kat had broken down in a spasm of grateful sobbing. The ordeal was over and she could just take care of that inert dead body, could slip off the shoes and cover it with a quilt. At least Lily was safe, at least she wasn't driving off into the night, drunk and staggering, to be returned later by the police like some lost sack of mail.

But still, she wondered persistently, whose fault was that night? Was it Kirk's, for leaving her to deal with the situation? Was it her own, for being available? Was it Lily's for not being stronger?

Something happened then inside her, and she sat vibrating with emotion like a beehive. Something happened because she saw the scene in her mind with sudden clarity, as if she were looking at a picture and noticing some fresh detail that threw everything into a new perspective. Her mother had been sick. Her mother had been out of control. And maybe that was not a fault at all, but just a fact. Lily couldn't stop—any more than Kat herself could have just stopped after one or two drinks, the way her

father had so casually suggested. Why hadn't any of them seen it
before as a sickness, instead of some moral issue to be determined by willpower, or virtue? Why hadn't her father gotten her
mother the kind of help she needed? Why had he allowed her to
go on in that hell which no amount of love could conquer? Was
it too much of a blow to his ego? Was it that he felt, somehow,
without reason, that he'd failed her, that he and he alone could
rectify the wrong that had made Lily this way? Or was it an unconscious wish to keep his wife's weaknesses equal to his own,
and so control her.

And perhaps all this confusion over his role was what had
made him so angry and insensitive to her tonight, she thought,
looking into the dregs of her coffee cup. Perhaps he was only
feeling guilty for what had gone before, feeling that he had
failed his daughter as he had failed her mother. He didn't want
Kat to get better because then he would not have repaid his
debt, he would have lost control. He could not bear to let them
go, she or Lily, could not bear to take the risk that they might
not come back to him. It made her want to cry with rage, but
she understood it.

She leaned back in her chair, overwhelmed by the enormity of
all these new ideas. It had been so long since her mind had
clicked along these pathways, so long since she'd had any glim-
mer of understanding about her father, her mother, herself. And
again she returned to the question of guilt and blame and now
she wondered where her own responsibility began and her father's ended. Somewhere a line had to be drawn. But could she
define that crucial point: where does the little girl accept her
womanhood? And what does justice, morality, or fairness have to
do with any of it? she asked herself. She still needed to believe
that they had some connection to the reality of her life.

Applause interrupted her thoughts and she looked up to see
that Rudi had finished his fifteen-minute introduction. She still
could not concentrate on the meeting, and before she knew it a
topic of discussion for the remaining hour and three quarters
had been voted on. Everyone at the table, in turn, introduced
himself and spoke briefly on the subject. But she couldn't listen

to them, she was too scrambled about her own family, her life, her emotions. When would this limbo end?

With a jolt she realized that everyone was staring at her, waiting for her to speak. What could she say, how explain this confusion? In imitation of everyone else, she introduced herself, keeping her hands under the table so no one could see her nervousness.

"My name is Kat." She paused, not yet ready to say she was an alcoholic. "I'm very mixed up. This is my first week, and even though I've heard so many good things here I'm not sure about being an . . . alcoholic. I know a lot of things are changing for me because of these meetings, but it's still very hard to listen to all this." She smiled shyly, and saw with pleased surprise all the faces which listened to her with concern. "I guess that's all." Rudi touched her shoulder in a silent sign of approval.

When the meeting ended at least eight people came up to encourage her, to offer their hands, their first names, and their phone numbers. She turned to Rudi and Marty, overwhelmed by the response, and they smiled at her. "I remember my first meetings," Rudi said with a loud laugh. "Right away I attached myself to Marty. It felt so good to relax with someone in sympathy. I needed that support."

"You've known each other long then?"

"She's been my sponsor since I joined," Rudi said, poking Marty with his elbow. "And not too bad, either."

Kat looked puzzled. "Your sponsor?"

"That's the person who keeps an eye on you in the beginning and drags you to as many meetings as possible," Marty said. "The one you call in the middle of the night when you're desperate."

"How do you get assigned one?" Kat asked, looking around the room.

"Just go up to someone you like," said Marty. "Nothing formal."

"And your week, how has it gone?" Rudi asked.

"It was hard, but I didn't give in." She winked at him dramatically. "Not a drop has passed my lips!"

Rudi put his hand on her shoulder. "Good. A good beginning."

He paused. "You seemed upset when you first came in, and I wondered—"

"No," she interrupted, "not that. But I told my father and sister about AA tonight, and it didn't go over too well."

Rudi and Marty exchanged looks. "They felt threatened?" she asked.

Kat shrugged. "My family doesn't think I even have a problem."

"Sometimes the family doesn't *want* to see," said Marty. "I always tell people to ignore their families—just forget them. They can't see around their own egos or their own needs. Go to meetings and talk to the people there—they'll give you what you need, and tell you what you should hear."

Kat drew back. "I don't think you understand. My family's extremely important to me, and their opinion matters. I trust them because they know me better than anyone else."

"Still, you must've felt you had a problem to come here at all," Marty persisted. "Isn't that true?"

"Well—"

"—enough of a problem to have called Central Service, enough desperation to call Central Service, right? You're the only person who can decide if you need to be here or not. It's your decision, not anyone else's."

Kat couldn't help it now: she started to cry. First she had felt one thing, then another, then she ping-ponged back again. Anger, confusion, hostility, self-defense on all sides, everything fused together and poured out of her. Rudi put his arm around her shoulders and Marty took her hand. "Hey, look," she said, giving her a Kleenex, "ignore me. I've got a big mouth." But Kat couldn't stop. She was trying hard, still the tears kept coming, a relentless storm which battered away inside her. What was she doing in this barren room, with these strange crippled people, sobbing? She tried to pull herself together, but she simply could not—not to save face, not for propriety, not to escape embarrassment.

Rudi drew her over to a chair on the other side of the room. He didn't try to stop her from crying, but held her hand tightly instead. "Kat," he said finally, "this is always a very hard time. Everybody has trouble now. Everything you feel is all right. It's normal." He patted her shoulder awkwardly. "I remember my own first week—it was like death. Such loss and grief. But I got over it. See me now? So much better."

She looked up at him. He did not evade her eyes. She saw his concern and his caring, and then there was a touch on her elbow and Marty stood before her again.

"I'm sorry about before," she said as she laid a large blue book in Kat's lap. "But try reading some of this. It's helped me to sort things out many a time."

"Thanks." Kat blew her nose. "But I may not be here to return it—"

"It's yours," Marty interrupted. "A gift. See you both next week." She waved her hand and was off.

Kat looked down at the book and Rudi smiled at her. "Come," he said, helping her to her feet. "I'll walk you to your car."

When she got back to Concord and walked through the library door, she found Kirk there staring into the fire. The room was dark except for the flickering light, and the aroma of brandy mingled with smoke.

She sat down across from him in her mother's chair, her new book in her lap, feeling trapped. They said nothing at all, not even a greeting; they were weighted into silence, weighted under all the things each of them wanted to say. Kat no longer felt any anger toward him, just a worn-out wish to be close, to belong, to be accepted again.

The red heat of the flames moved across his face, and his hair glittered faintly silver. For an instant she saw him as an old man, vulnerable, needing love, needing care, and she fantasized her role—loving, giving, perfect communication. He turned to look at her then, and she returned to the present, to the knowledge that there was no understanding between them now. They could only move like dumb marionettes, like prison inmates on visiting day who try to touch through the Plexiglas.

"I'm sorry," she said at last, "I'm sorry for the way I spoke earlier." She had thought he'd be icy, but his eyes were hurt and glazed with tears. He said nothing. "I didn't mean to be rude." She couldn't bear his face with its defeated expression. She could have handled anger or ice, but this—it made her want to go to him, and put her arms out, so she looked away. "But you were pushing me. It was too much pressure."

"I thought you were making a mistake, and I had to say something." His voice was soft, and his hands lay like limp wings along the arms of the chair; his whole body seemed weighted by sadness—inert, without bones. "I've never even seen you drunk."

"You've just never noticed," she said, getting up from her chair and striding across the room. "I was even having blackouts." She ran her finger across the spine of a book to ease the tension, and then spun back at him, suddenly desperate. "Why can't you understand? I wouldn't know the next day where I'd been or what I'd done. I couldn't remember anything."

"But why AA? Why a bunch of strangers?" He twisted in his chair, overcoming his inertia as if a last attempt might change her mind. "*I'll* watch your drinking. *I'll* help you keep a limit. Why make your problems public?"

"Can't you see that's not enough?" She went to stand before him. "In this way," she said, crouching down to look into his face, "in this way, no one could be enough. Not you, not Aaron, not even Mom. I need a different sort of help. But don't you see —I do need your support and your love." She touched his shoulder. "I need you to tell me it's O.K."

He looked up at her. "But how can I when I don't believe it?"

"I guess you can't," she replied sadly.

She drew back and moved to the chair by the fire. As she opened to her new book's first chapter, her father stood to go upstairs to bed. She watched him leave, the confrontation over, the lines clearly drawn. He would never accept or bless this decision, and she must try not to need that blessing—she must plow on anyway to find what was right for her.

The house seemed loud around her, the mantel clock ticked like a steady heart, a branch knocked the window. Something was dying in her, and it was not dying easily. She was absolutely alone. Without Kirk, without Paige, without Helena, without Aaron. She felt a little deserted, but they hadn't really deserted her. She had alienated them all, cut them off, one by one. She touched her cheek with her hand, lightly, gently, like a kiss; she was here, she was real, at least. And somehow, she would have to make do with that. Sighing, she focused on the print of Marty's book and began to read.

_____ *Twenty-three* _____

BEACON HILL ROSE STRAIGHT UP FROM NOWHERE, FROM THE EDGE OF the Charles River, bounded on the west by the Common, by the hospitals on the east, by the rows of Charles Street antique shops on the south. The golden dome of the State House capped the crown of the Hill. The gas lamps spread their soft glow across the uneven brick sidewalks and crooked steep streets. Snow, which had fallen earlier in the month, lay humped in a gray pile along the edges of the narrow street like a long row of sleeping dogs.

Kat moved quickly through the sharp February wind. It was eleven o'clock at night and she'd just come from the Cambridge City Hospital AA meeting. After dark this part of town was not too safe, and tonight the area was deserted. There was only the sound of her heels tapping out their solitary echo. This area, once choice, with its three-tiered townhouses and ornate brickwork, was now dragged down by the bums who made their homes on the sidewalk.

At the intersection of Joy and Myrtle, she switched to the other sidewalk to avoid an old man propped against a lamppost who, impervious to the cold, swung into "Danny Boy" with drunken gusto and swigged between bars from a wine bottle. Kat averted her eyes from the caved-in face, and wondered again why Helena had chosen an apartment so far up the side of the Hill.

As she reached the top, she realized that she was not winded. Six weeks without a drink, six weeks of activity, had clearly been a tonic. The pounds had dropped away, according to the bathroom scale that morning, and even the hollows under her eyes and the shaky hands had disappeared.

But nothing else about staying dry had been as easy. Once again, she had to face life raw and unprotected, with no cushion. On top of everyday tension, there was the additional pressure of fighting the urge to drink.

During the times she was too nervous or depressed to be sure of keeping her need contained, only physical exercise sufficed. At some point in every day, she saddled up one of the mares and fled to the woods for a while. Even though the deep snow made riding slippery, she was persistent, urging the horse through drifts and across ice-covered fields. A surge of power, of self-confidence, returned to her as she trotted down the snowy trails by the Concord River and watched the pines bend like a chorus of perfect dancers, smelled the sweat from the mare's back, the soap from good leather. The weather never deterred her, not even sleet; often the animal was frisky under her in the cold air, but she was glad of the life between her knees, glad to have to reach out and take hold of something, work with it. Her muscle tone and her seat returned after a few weeks and she felt comfortable with the horse. It was what she needed. In the woods everything was clear and purely defined, with no complications—just a series of perfectly functioning systems.

At home nothing was so simple. Her father had never returned to the subject again openly, but each night he poured her martini in the evening ritual, and set it next to her chair like a dare. It was a contest between them. The martini looked as pure and basic as mountain water to Kat, and it seemed preposterous not to drink it. A small part of her gave a logical argument why she needed that drink, why she deserved it, but in fact that small persuasive voice scared her. Rudi had warned her about it, had predicted its strength and its tone, and so she resisted it and its logic with a stubborn backbone she'd not known she'd possessed. No longer did she have doubts as to her drinking problem. The void left in her daily life when she gave up booze only proved to her to what proportion alcohol had commanded her life.

This contest with Kirk hurt her as much as anything else. It was competitive when what she needed was support and tenderness. She had lost her father; how unfair that having just lost her mother she should lose him too. And then, also to forfeit the right to escape—that one solace. She had lost her last tie to her family.

Soon she had taken to spending cocktail hour in the kitchen with Mrs. George, to help prepare the evening meal. Their hours together became important to Kat, for it was like the riding—an opportunity to divert herself, to keep herself safe from temptation. And there was warmth there too, a warmth she no longer found in front of the fire with the family. The housekeeper seemed to understand intuitively why Kat was in her kitchen at the most inconvenient of hours, and set her to work on small tasks like shredding carrots, stirring the soup, or snipping the parsley.

Still, only AA seemed to offer real relief, and the meetings were almost a physical release. She relaxed a little; she asked Rudi to be her sponsor, made new friends, friends who shared her feelings and experiences, friends who were able to advise her on situations no one else seemed to understand. She had never really belonged to a club, or a group, or an organization before, having found strange people an exhausting ordeal. But now, with little choice, Kat discovered that she too could be popular and even witty, that people liked her, that she could fit in. The exhilaration after a meeting kept her going for several hours, as if she had surfaced for air and caught her breath, giddy with relief. She was coming to rely on it, to depend on it for a lift.

AA's methods, too, were truly a reversal of the way she had been taught to live. Now, each moment and each decision was tied only to the framework of the immediate, the next twenty-four hours. The future was not to be worried about. Depression was a luxury not to be allowed, with exercise the cure. Self-pity

bore the label "danger." The trick was to short circuit all the situations that in the past had led her to drink.

And tonight, as she arrived at the door of Helena's apartment
building and struggled vainly to think only of now, of going up
these stairs without worrying about what would happen at the
top, she licked her lips and wished for a drink. Fear was pushing
at her. She thought of turning back and hesitated on the stoop,
myriad excuses springing up to release her from this task: it was
late; Helena might not be alone; Helena might want to be alone;
Helena might still be angry. But that was why she was here. To
apologize. To try and bridge that terrible rupture, to stitch together the hole she'd stabbed in their friendship that night in the
Wursthaus. She'd known for weeks that an apology, or at least
an explanation, was required, but had been unable to summon
the energy, or the courage. The AA meeting tonight had "making amends" as its topic for discussion and had forced Kat to realize that she had to put the past in order. It was time to face
Helena, time to put an end to the impasse one way or another.
She had missed her too much.

She climbed the steps and rang the bell. The outer door
opened into a small dark foyer, with a narrow winding staircase,
a staircase that imitated the architecture of the streets. She
climbed to the second floor amid the odor of boiled cauliflower
and the acrid stink of litter boxes, and knocked.

Helena flung the door wide, and stood looking at her for a moment. "Kat," she said. It was a statement of fact, not a greeting. She was in a cotton nightgown and plaid bathrobe, barefoot,
her curly red hair tousled into spikes across her forehead.

"Hello," Kat said, shy and embarrassed. "I know I should've
called first."

"No, it's all right," Helena said, looking around her in a distracted fashion. "I don't mean to be so slow on the uptake. I'm
just"—she stepped back and motioned Kat in—"surprised."

It was a tiny room, made even more tiny by the clutter. Helena's clothing was strewn over chairs and doorknobs. Half-
completed sewing projects lay on the floor. The bed was rumpled and unmade. And through it all threaded a wild profusion

of plants, which grew madly in every unoccupied space. Except
for the kitchenette at the far end of the room, Kat felt that she
was back in Helena's bedroom in the dorm. She was overwhelmed with the feeling of nostalgia. It was the same mess, the
same bright things Helena chose to throw around, and suddenly
she laughed. Helena's messes were always artistic.

She perched precariously on Helena's bed, next to a pile of
books. "Is it really O.K. that I came?" she asked gingerly. "You
see I was afraid if I didn't just come tonight that I might keep
putting it off."

"It's been a long time."

There was a stiff silence. Kat waited awkwardly for a moment. She looked at her hands, which had begun to shake again.
"I know. That's why I came." She cleared her throat. "I just
wanted to say how"—she paused and fingered the zipper of her
parka—"how sorry I am."

"Sorry?"

"Ignoring you at my party, you know, the way I never called
you back those last few times." She looked up at Helena. "But
mostly that awful night at the Wursthaus."

"Let's forget it," Helena said quickly, "it's over and done
with."

"No," said Kat. "It's not. Not for me. I need to explain why it
happened."

"But it's all right. I understand—"

"No," she interrupted. "I need to talk and to really apologize.
You're important to me, and I need to make you see. I'm just beginning to realize what I've been doing to my friends. And to
myself."

Helena waited, her dark brown eyes somehow softer now, less
wary.

"I felt you were picking on me. I felt that everybody was picking on me." She smiled wryly. "It didn't matter whether or not
they were right. I just wanted to be left alone."

"Are you still seeing that weird woman?"

"Who? Bea?" She shook her head. "Not since I last saw you."

She sighed. "But I've got to do that too. I've got to straighten it all out. Everything."

"I was appalled," Helena said, picking at the button of a blouse underneath her. "I didn't know how to handle it. I probably should've kept my mouth shut."

"You thought it was disgusting and you said what you think—as always. And you were right. But I wasn't ready to hear it."

"Ready?"

"I couldn't admit it to myself. Oh, like watching yourself get fat in a mirror—you don't want to see it," Kat said. "I was so mixed up and so alone that I didn't know help from hurt. Mostly"—she shifted on the bed—"mostly I was drinking too much to see anything."

"You do see that now?" Helena asked, her tone serious.

Kat nodded, and looked down at her hands again. Her throat felt dry and scratchy, as if the effort of even talking about this were enough to make her ill. "I see it now." She paused, tears rising, pricking hot and harsh to fill her eyes. "I see that I'm an alcoholic, and that I need help." She stopped. "I've been going to AA for over a month now."

Helena stared at her without moving. Kat couldn't bear it. "Don't look like that!" she pleaded. "I need it because I can't do it alone. Why can't anyone understand that?"

There was a long moment of silence in which Helena stood, and then she went over to an armchair that had bright red wool draped across its back. "Actually," she said, picking up the skein she'd been winding when Kat had rung, "I shouldn't be so surprised. Aaron and I both thought you were in a lot of trouble."

"You did?"

Helena nodded. "But it's hard to label it like that. Alcoholism. Really," she turned and smiled. "I'm an ass. I'm sorry—anything that helps you get in control again and be well is a good idea."

Kat smiled weakly. "I guess expecting you to jump for joy was a little much," she said. "Especially after barging in like this. But I really needed to see you and talk. I've missed you." She looked away. "Couldn't we just go back and start over?"

"I'd rather go forward." She smiled and her hands flashed up and down like semaphore flags, around and around, as she wound the wool.

"Well, I've made some new friends," Kat said, after a minute. "And managed to keep away from a drink for six weeks now."

Helena frowned again as the wool tangled.

"Here, let me hold that for you," Kat offered, getting up and standing beside her. "My whole life has got to change," she said, as she dipped back and forth while Helena began to reel in the yarn. "I'm even exercising now."

"Kat the hedonist?" Helena asked, laughing. "What kind?"

"Riding," Kat said. "Every day. I have to get out of that house —just to get away."

"Move your thumb a little higher," Helena instructed. "It's coming too fast." They stood quietly then, involved with the pure action of the winding, and after a while their movements fell into a pattern, were orchestrated, synchronized perfectly. It was a ballet of winding, the tempo picking up, their arms moving faster and faster as the ball in Helena's hand grew and the strands across Kat's arms were fewer and looser. Then it was finished and they smiled at each other.

"I could use some cocoa," Helena said, tossing the ball, round and entire, into the chair. "What does your dad think?"

Kat sat down on the bed again and propped herself up against the wall, her face shadowed. "It's like a personal insult to him. He keeps putting martinis in front of me, hoping I'll change my mind."

"Well, parents see their children as reflections of themselves," she said as she poured the milk into a saucepan.

"But still, he acts like I'm talking about where to take a vacation, not an illness."

Helena turned to look at her, a wooden spoon in her hand. "Maybe it's better this way," she said. "Maybe this way it's all yours. A decision he has nothing to do with."

"The harder it is, the more I learn," she said with a rueful smile, "is that it?"

"Maybe." She shrugged. "I assume Paige is the same or worse?"

"What else? Her first reaction was that if one person at a party doesn't drink no one else can have fun."

"Well, you've always threatened her," Helena observed. "When you can't control your own life you hate to see someone else doing it right." She pointed to a shelf above Kat's head. "Get the mugs down, will you. They're hard for me to reach."

"It didn't used to be like this," Kat reflected, "not when we were little. High school was where the competition started. And then, when my mother died, we got into this thing of vying for her place." She handed Helena the mugs.

"And now?" she asked as she poured the chocolate from the saucepan.

Kat laughed. "The moment I joined AA, I had to concede that Paige'd won." She brushed the hair out of her eyes. "What about you? What's going on at Houghton Mifflin?"

"Still slaving away," Helena said, sitting in the chair again and putting her feet up on the bed next to Kat. "But I got off my duff and applied to the B-School for next year."

"*Harvard* Business?"

She nodded and sipped the hot drink carefully. "I'll know by March but I'm just praying." She shrugged. "How's the proofing?"

"Well, for a couple of months in the fall I stopped. But now I'm doing about ten hours a day."

"Why so much?"

"I just need to keep busy." Kat hesitated. "To stir me up each day, keep me from getting depressed, or self-indulgent." She smiled. "But, as you said once, proofing's hardly the most stimulating thing in the world."

"I know I'd sure be ready for a change," Helena agreed, watching over the rim of her mug.

"I've been thinking about it."

"What would you want? Have you made up your mind?"

"Maybe some regular work, like in-house copy-editing."

"When will you start to look?" Helena asked, sitting up now with an air of excitement. "Are you going to move into your own place? If you want to live on Beacon Hill, we could—"

"Hang on!" Kat said with alarm. "I'm *thinking* about it. What's the rush?"

"Sorry," she said, "I didn't mean to be pushy, but the idea of your being nearby again got me excited. I've missed you too, you know." She picked up the red ball of wool and turned it slowly in her hands. "It'd be nice to have you back."

"Be patient. With any luck we'll be next-door neighbors again."

Helena rose and moved back to the stove. "Refill?"

Kat shook her head. "I've got to get a move on. It's late and I've got a set of galleys due at Atlantic Press before five—and it's only halfway done."

Helena turned, the saucepan still in her hand. "One thing," she said, "I should tell you. Right after you broke up, Aaron came to see me."

"He did?" Kat stopped zipping her coat halfway. "What did he say?"

"He just needed someone to talk to. He was in a bad way."

Jealousy flared up in a bright painful burst at the thought of someone else comforting him, but Kat forced herself to clamp down on it.

"I wanted you to know up front, so you wouldn't think we'd been talking behind your back."

Kat swallowed. "Nothing happened?"

Helena laughed. "Me and Aaron? Have you lost your mind?"

"Close," Kat said. "I guess I forgot to tell you he's invited me to dinner in the Square on Saturday night."

"You're kidding! That's great. Maybe . . ." She lifted her eyebrows.

"Forget it," Kat said with a trace of bitterness. "He invited that woman—the one who was his boss last summer—along for protection, so it'll hardly be an intimate evening." She didn't voice her real fear. Saying it aloud would make it more real.

"Still," Helena persisted, "he could have asked anyone. He must be a little interested."

"Tell me about it," grinned Kat, pulling her hat around her

ears. "I'll call you and let you know what happens—if anything does."

Helena came over to unlock the door and gave her a big hug. "I'm glad you came by."

"So am I," Kat said, blowing her a kiss as she went down the stairs.

Twenty-four

Harvard Square was getting a facelift. Gone were the head shops and the beaded doorways of Middle-eastern sandal stores, gone the bald Hare Krishnas with their open palms and atonal chants, gone the olive-drab student activists with their leaflets, their hunger for confrontation. Now boutiques of stylish, expensive clothes filled the sidewalks with the jazzy purples and magentas of *Vogue*. The tight cut of Bonjour, Calvin Klein, and Jordache pushed aside the traditional Levi. Art food replaced health food: clever soups and imaginative little sandwiches, nouvelle cuisine and linen napkins, rare roast beef on pumpernickel —with Boursin, not mayo.

Still, some student institutions stood militant against the onrushing wave of chic clothing and dining, chic books and housewares, chic soaps and coffees and charcuterie. Elsie's, Buddy's Sirloin Pit, and Bartley's Burger Cottage poked their stubborn greasy noses up alongside the new glitter. Cambridge was an area of change, of argument, of sharply conflicting elements; from corner to corner, street to street, it was never clear which side would win the battle.

Kat walked along the sidewalk, elbow to elbow with pedestrians and shoppers. The new boutiques were an improvement, she allowed, but still she felt a wistful attachment to the old, to those well-worn student days. So much of her life, so many of

the most important events, had happened within this small
three-mile plot, this congested acre of brick and ivy. Here she
had lost her virginity, here fallen in love for the first time, here
drunk her first espresso, smoked her first dope, bought her first
backpack, seen her first Bergman film. The list unraveled like an
adding machine tape.

A dinner with Aaron seemed a chance of returning to that
past. Kat looked at her watch now and hurried along the sidewalk to the Atrium, a restaurant she'd not been to before. Rushing, she arrived out of breath and with her heart pounding, but
Aaron and his friend, Tina, were late. The world was still a
series of interconnected events to Kat, and in her heart, other
people's actions sometimes seemed a direct, ironic reaction to her
own: if she hurried they were late; if she went to a ballgame,
her team always lost; if she went on vacation, it always rained.
She sat down alone to wait and told herself not to be so egocen-
tric. When the waiter filled her water glass and asked if she'd
like a cocktail, she shook her head, wondering how it would feel
to be the only one without a drink.

The restaurant, she saw as she looked about, had been designed by some clever city architect. It was a perfect square, an
open courtyard between buildings really, its walls formed by the
brick walls of the four structures surrounding it. The ceiling was
a glass bubble, some five stories above her, supported by the
neighboring rooftops. Weeping figs grew as in a hothouse, oblivious to the seasons, stretching their bodies to the sky. Small lights
pricked out through the branches and leaves here in the evenings, every linen-draped table had a candle, and above, like a
thin slice of lemon rind, floated the moon.

Aaron steered Tina to the table with his hand on her arm, and
Kat examined her as they crossed the room: long black hair
clasped in tortoise at the nape of her neck, skin clear and
polished, eyes brown and almond-shaped under heavy full
brows. A red silk shirt brought out the tinge of pink along her
cheekbones; fashionably cut wool trousers accentuated the curve
of full hip to small waist. A long gold chain fell over her bust
and glinted against her heavy earrings. Aaron's portrait had not

exaggerated her appeal. Kat smoothed her own hair back and smiled as they sat down.

"Tina," Aaron said, "this is Kat. Kat, Tina Michaels."

"Good to meet you," Tina said, her voice of a husky timbre.

"I've heard a lot about you."

"Without Tina," Aaron confirmed with a grin, "I would never have stuck the summer out."

Tina laughed. "You give me too much credit," she said. "I've just been a draftsman too recently to forget what it's like. Working for a bunch of egotistical architects can be a nasty experience."

"You must find this place interesting," Kat said, gesturing about her. "Don't you think it's remarkable?"

Tina touched Aaron's shoulder. "I'll accept that compliment." She laughed. "This design was my first real project with the firm, and it's been a real success."

The waiter arrived for their order.

"I guess I'd like to see the wine list please," Aaron said, playing with his fork and then using it as a pointer. "Originally they'd planned on more conventional roofing. It was Tina who came up with the clear bubble approach."

"Dry vermouth on the rocks," Tina said, as she tapped her polished fingernail on the peach-colored linen. "What a waste that would have been."

The waiter looked over to Kat.

"Oh," she said with a casual glance at Tina, "I guess a virgin mary." Kat felt the focus of attention shift to her, and the waiter paused; she had done something out of the ordinary. It galled her, embarrassed her, to look like some ninny who didn't drink. But she set her chin, and thought of Rudi. "That's it," she repeated. "No vodka."

"I'll keep you company," Aaron inserted quickly. "A Pepsi, please."

Tina looked at her, puzzled. "You don't drink."

It was the first time Kat had been out in public without a drink, and it was the first time a stranger had asked why. Her pride was at stake and she wanted to explain. She didn't want to

be misunderstood about this; besides, better to be damned for a
drunk than for a temperance freak. Even more, there was a dramatic element which appealed to her. "No," she said. "You see,
it's Alcoholics Anonymous—I've just joined." She leaned back and
tried to look as if she were talking about something easy and
normal, some step of success or progress. "I can't drink because
I'm an alcoholic." She looked over; Aaron was tense, watching
Tina's face.

"You're joking?"

Kat shook her head.

Tina paused. She really did not know what to say. "Well, how
much did you drink?" she asked, curious.

"Three or four a night," Kat said, and shrugged casually.
"Once in a while, five."

Tina shook her head and laughed. "That doesn't sound like
much of an alkie to me."

"Maybe it doesn't sound like a lot," Aaron broke in, "but Kat
really couldn't handle it. At all." Their drinks arrived. He took a
long pull of his Pepsi, and looked over at Kat's virgin mary.
"That's Kat," he said with obvious pleasure, "stubborn when she
needs to be."

Tina shrugged as if the subject bored her and turned back to
Aaron. "How's school this week?"

Talk of architecture, of buildings and plans and foundations,
became the center of the evening, and the ensuing half-hour
cushioned Kat and gave her a chance to recover from the confrontation. She was rattled by the other woman's reaction and it
made her feel shut out. Aaron and Tina had so many people and
so much knowledge in common. Their mutual interests created
just that intimacy of which Kat had been so afraid; she knew
nothing about any of it, but Tina was a comrade in Aaron's pro-
fession. Tina was a mentor who could offer him advice in a warm
voice which made her seem more like a friend than a boss, and
Kat was uncomfortable with that implication. She was not used
to sharing Aaron, not used to sharing his thoughts, or his ambitions, and even though she'd known of his friendship with Tina,
she'd never seen it in action before, never witnessed its appeal.

She sat and listened, forcing a stiff smile, as she tried to look serene—but all the while an engine of despair was revving itself up inside her. She drank her tomato juice and when Tina ordered a second round, she ordered more tomato juice, and when time came for the third round, she asked for club soda because the Worcestershire was giving her heartburn. She was jealous and she was sober, and it hurt.

The waiter brought them menus, and they ordered. Tina and Aaron chose the wine. "I take it," she asked Kat, "you won't have wine either?"

"No," she said, looking over at Aaron with misery. The situation was stacked against her, she felt. Never had she felt so small or so inadequate. And to watch them talking so casually about their work, to watch them getting on a glow from the wine when she was cold as a stone—it was too much. Her internal voice began its argument, and repeated itself over and over, like the whine of cicadas in summer, a drone which eventually merged with her consciousness so that she heard it no longer: she needed a drink; she deserved a drink; she wasn't wanted here and a drink would bring her more presence; they would have to notice her. It whined on persistently—why sit like some blank lump? Order a drink and be witty, order a drink and be beautiful to Aaron again. It was at her; it buzzed in her ears like an angry insect.

She looked over at Tina. The voice inside her shrilled triumphantly: she thinks you're a bore. You *are* a bore. Get with it. One glass won't hurt anybody. In Europe even children drink wine with dinner. She kept trying to think of Rudi and his advice, but the voice kept reminding her how boring she was. She continued to fight it off, trying to hear over its noise and get involved in the conversation. Still her strength ebbed and the temptation grew. Dessert arrived. Tina was having amaretto hot chocolate—burnt almond over bittersweet. The smell was making her salivate. Come on, the voice whispered, purring now, chocolate isn't booze, you can't get high on chocolate. Order one.

And she did. She drank it down with greed, ignoring the look of concern in Aaron's eyes. She finished ahead of Tina, the taste

of almond liqueur strong on her tongue and warm in her belly.
I'm still hungry, the voice whined. Feed me. She signaled the
waiter for another, and this time got the buzz she was looking for,
the blessed relief. The table and their faces receded from her
softly, just a bit, and she wanted to laugh with triumph. She
could handle this. Rudi was wrong. She hadn't gone off on some
binge, or turned into a crazed animal.

Aaron didn't like it one bit. He kept staring at her, sending her
silent messages that begged her to stop. And because she didn't
want to alienate him, couldn't bear to lose her second chance,
she left the dregs in her cup. The evening was over anyway.

Out in the street, the cold bit at Kat's small high. A sharp wind
made conversation difficult and they huddled their way silently
to the car. She dropped Tina off first and then took Aaron home.
Pulling over to one side of the icy street, she kept the engine
running so the heater would warm up.

"It was interesting to meet her." She thumped her gloved
fingers on the steering wheel in an attempt to get the blood
flowing in them again.

"It's too bad you were so uncomfortable."

"What makes you say that?" she asked quickly, dismayed that
he had seen through her polite mask. "I wasn't. Really."

"Spiked coffee's no different than a drink—who are you kidding?" He looked at her and sighed. "I'm not trying to bug you,
but I couldn't help but notice."

"I'm surprised," she came back. "You two were off in some
other world all evening long. How did you notice anything at
all? And what did it hurt anyway?"

"Why are you jealous?" he asked, surprise on his face. "You've
got no reason to be. I told you before—Tina and I are just
friends."

"Some friend! Where does she get off judging me—telling me I
don't drink enough to be an alcoholic?"

"She didn't mean it like that!" He sighed with exasperation. "I
know it was hard and I agree she could have been more sensitive
—but you've got to be less thin-skinned. You're going to get a lot
of questions about this."

"Aaron, I just thought tonight would be different somehow. More like . . . before."

"Before wasn't enough!" he reminded her angrily. "I thought you'd changed, thought you'd learned that you can't just go back like that. But I guess it doesn't happen so fast."

"I have changed!" Kat cried in harsh defense. Anger lent her defiance and her eyes glinted in the street light. "But things aren't black or white, right or wrong. Some things are easier than others—some nights better, some worse. You can't expect me to be perfect all at once, like a doll repaired at some shop!"

He was quiet a moment, and she looked down at his hand on the seat between them, the long fingers spread and arched, blue veins mapping their course, and the soft black down against his fair skin.

"You're probably right," he answered at last. "I don't have enough patience."

She was tired of arguing and she wanted to see what he would do next, so she said nothing.

"I've got to get up early and it's midnight already." He opened the door. "Maybe I'll give you a ring mid-week?" She nodded and watched while he walked across the frozen snow to his door. The car slid into first as she let out the clutch. "Maybe," she said aloud, tears greasing their way down her cheeks. "Maybe."

By the time she unlocked the back door of the house with her key, she was so angry her head ached. Anger, flowing hot and swift from an unseeable source, anger for all she had lost, and for all she might have had. The emotion enveloped her and she lost herself in it. She was not merely angry—she was anger itself. And it was anger hissing in her ear this time, anger that led her to the liquor cabinet in the dark pantry, anger that uncorked a brand-new bottle of cognac and lifted it to her lips in one sudden swift motion. It was anger that sucked it down with a greedy tongue, anger that absorbed the sharp burn in her belly, anger that took her upstairs to bed, with the bottle. Anger got her drunk. Anger dialed the phone.

"Rudi," she said, words slipping out of her grasp, the bed doing cartwheels under her. "S'Kat."

"It's two o'clock," he mumbled in a confused voice. "What's going on?"

"Wanted lil' talk with my pal, Rudi. Tell him." She was trying to enunciate carefully.

"You're drunk," he said, alert now. "Are you drunk?"

"Not drunk," she said, shaking her head vehemently, as if he could see her. "Jus' called to say AA stinks. No good. No help. Called up to say"—he could hear her sucking from the bottle—"g'by. No more meetings."

"Go to bed, Kat, and I'll call you in the morning. I'm not interested in talking to you now." He hung up the phone and it clicked over into a dial tone.

She couldn't remember how to hang up the receiver and when it began to buzz its loud rhythmic alarm in her ear, she stuffed it under the pillow. She took one more long hard pull on the bottle and then passed out on top of the bed, propped against the headboard, still in her coat and shoes and hat.

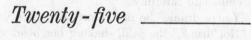

Twenty-five

THE ALARM WAS BUZZING. IT TOOK A WHILE BEFORE KAT REALIZED she must turn it off, for this was a deep sleep, a drugged sleep, a sleep which incorporated waking noises and sensations right into the dream. In her dream Kat was with her mother, out in the car, parked by the side of some long wooded road: they were arguing, Kat was asking her not to go, shouting and pleading over the buzz of the seat belt alarm.

Finally she opened one sleep-furred eye, untangled her arm from the pillow, and reached over to push the button. It still buzzed, vibrating on her ears, her heart, her sleep. Again she tried the button, and when this failed, she banged the clock down hard on the bedside table. It buzzed on. In desperation, she slid off the bed onto the floor, and, with her eyes still mostly closed, she followed the cord to the wall socket by touch and jerked it loose.

The noise poured on. Kat shook her head to clear it and stretched her eyelids wide at last, realizing for the first time that it could not be the clock that was buzzing. It was not the steady growl of her alarm, but a syncopated rhythm of two different tones. Back on the bed, she now took in the phone receiver just under the edge of her pillow, and she hung it up slowly. The room clicked into silence.

The clock, still in her hand, had frozen at five-ten. The room was dark—even though the drapes were not drawn—and the glass panes of the windows mirrored back a black early light. Her head throbbed relentlessly, and to move her eyes brought violent stabs of pain, but she did not lie down again. She was very hot, and looking down she saw her coat still buttoned up to the chin, scarf neat in the neck. Her shoes were on, even her hat. Her back ached, her head ached, her mouth ached. The world ached around her and she closed her eyes, wishing for some kind of sleep or death, some kind of warm haze to obliterate the shame and the guilt, this terrible failure.

But there was the half-empty bottle. She studied the label for a while, and then, trying to pretend some kind of normalcy, got up and took off her clothes, put on her bathrobe and slippers as if it were bedtime. Dizzy, at the sink with her mouth full of toothpaste in an attempt to wipe away the obvious remains, she threw up, then numbly rinsed the vomit down, relined her brush with paste, scrubbed, dashed her face with water. She could not remember ever having felt worse. The warmth and comfort of her bed seemed the only way to survive.

But she would not allow herself the luxury; punishment was requisite, and punishment was consciousness, punishment was to know, to see, to hear all that had gone before—to think it through. Down the stairs then, down into the kitchen, kettle on the burner. Copper pots shone dim orange in the darkness and everything was silent. She poured boiling water over a teabag, and went to the breakfast nook, creeping through the dark house like an early morning snail.

It was not dawn yet. Kat sat down on the cushions in the bay window seat which overlooked a yard full of shadows. It was the time when the light comes stealthily, sneaking in on the observer little by little, but slowly and steadily all the same, so that suddenly one sees dawn is here when only a moment before it was dusk. And as it changes, objects are revealed, like a shuttered and draped room whose dust covers are removed one by one.

It looked as if it might snow—swollen, heavy clouds buoyed by the half-light, with not even a strand of pink from the sun which was rising, hidden somewhere behind their masses. It was a mysterious time of day, a mysterious season, with its shadow and bark, with its shadow and trunk, a time of possibility. The house waited to be wakened, and the earth waited to be revealed.

Kat felt as a stranger in the house at this hour, every object and piece of furniture taking on new dimensions in the dark, each shrub and tree in the yard a different shape of shadow. She tucked her feet beneath her Indian-style, the steam from her mug warm and humid against her face. A pheasant crossed the crusted snow, his tail feathers dragging behind him elegantly in a narrow train, his bright colors a flare against the half-light like the brilliant shower of a firework on a summer night. The trees stretched their bare limbs against the sky, brittle bones of winter, knobby ends, gray on gray.

There was corn scattered over the old crust of a snowdrift, and the pheasant bobbed up and down as he pecked. And then, for an instant, he paused in some silent alarm with his neck outstretched. His profile was etched against the coming light as he hurried back into the black lines of trees, camouflaged again.

But that picture caught at something inside Kat. Her mind was loose, turning over the old rocks and stones of memory, and in that arc of neck she had seen something, seen that curve before. Like a swan's neck, like the arm of a dancer, like a thread of blown glass. Searching for the memory, she could not place it. Her mother came to her instead, her mother curled in this seat after nights of insomnia. Kat touched the cushion with the tip of her index finger: had she looked out on this very same scene, seen the same pheasant at his dark early breakfast?

She missed her mother. It was a simple fact. And yet, here she was at 5 A.M., sitting in the dark, the house around her full of its life and its memories; here she was, hung over and defeated again. She'd missed her mother, and she'd been unable to admit it, really to grieve over the loss. Lily was always alive in Kat's mind; could grieving bring her back? No. It had seemed better to sit in her seat, view her scene, wear her perfume, use her life— no, *live* her life, for wasn't that really what she had done? Live her mother's life to make her live again. You're a fool, she thought, resting her head against the cold pane of glass. Frailty, illness, dependence on her father—they were all her mother's traits and Kat had used them and then tried to lay them down. But the old habits and rituals were tenacious; they did not want to be set aside or exorcised. They had grown into her personality and her life and she had not seen it. No longer did she control them—they controlled her. Last night she'd been dead drunk, nearly mad with rage and disappointment. This morning she barely knew why, could barely trace those emotions, much less give them a name or a source. How to go on? How to tell Rudi? How to change it all?

She had let Rudi down, and now it would hurt to hear his voice and his disappointment. Inside her there was only limpness, and no strength to do the telling, the necessary confessing. But neither could she lie. She'd never been any good at lying. She had enough trouble with reality. You are a coward, she said to herself. Can't lie. Can't tell the truth. When will you grow up?

A few flakes began to fall outside as she sipped the last of her tea. It was only the beginning of the storm, only the start; clouds dominated the sky like a great woolen giant and they promised more.

In the kitchen Mrs. George banged her pots and pans with brisk breakfast clatter. Outside, a dog ran past the window. The rest of the world was waking. Day had come. Kat went to her bath to shower and dress, to be ready. At nine o'clock, after more tea, still having spoken to no one, her head throbbing and hands shaking harder than ever before, she dialed Rudi's number. Her heart pounded with anxiety, but she had no choices left.

He picked up, sounding crisp. She could visualize him over a breakfast table, in the middle of his paper, still wearing a bathrobe.

"It's Kat," she said. "I didn't wake you?"

"Not this time," he said after a moment.

"Pardon?"

"It was last night you woke me. This morning I'm already awake."

"When last night?" she asked quickly. "I didn't call you last night."

"Yes, you did—don't you remember? Sometime after two o'clock. You must have been in a blackout."

She began to cry with shame. "Rudi. I'm sorry. Here I get my courage up to call and tell you about last night, and then you know it all already." She leaned her head on her hand, and tears slid down into her palm.

"Not all, but enough. Now stop crying."

"I've let you down. I've failed you—"

"Me!" he interrupted with astonishment. "Not me, Katherine. It's you you've failed. I'm not your father or your priest. Don't confess to me."

She was quiet a moment. "I tried, Rudi. I really did. But it was too hard—"

"—did anyone promise it would be easy?" he interrupted again. "Stop feeling sorry for yourself. You are not the only one who's had trouble with sobriety. You just must work harder."

"Harder how?" She was desperate. "How can I change? I can talk all I want, go to meetings till I'm blue, but nothing ever changes."

"It will change. It will get better. But only if you stop complaining. Stop expecting it all to land in your lap. You've got to want to stay sober, that's what makes it work. If you have to cry, then cry. But for God's sake come to a meeting when you're about to take a drink. Don't give it a chance to get you."

"But it happened so fast—"

"Not so fast that you couldn't have called me."

"It was late."

"You can call me anytime when you are sober. Never call me when you are drinking. I'm not interested in the midnight ravings of a drunk."

"Sure," she said, her voice choking off again. Everything seemed so impossible.

"Last night you said you weren't interested in AA any more. What about this morning—will you still pick me up tonight?"

"I think I need a vacation."

"It's up to you. But you can't take a vacation from alcoholism."

"All right," she said, reluctantly. "I'll see you at eight."

They hung up. Her mind circled around and around in a maze of questions, but still there were no answers. Family pictures floated before her: a photo album of memory, scenes of flesh and bone, interaction upon interaction, love, loss, hate, and temper. Her mother, a shining, soft blondness, a woman masked, but dead now, dead on the road, her life drained away. A victim of excess. That was the truth.

Then it came to Kat: she must untangle these strands, must understand and take action—if only just a motion, a mere lift of the hand on one gray winter morning. Last night was unthinkable and she must never repeat it. She had felt like this too often, and she was tired, tired of making herself promises and then breaking them, tired of being controlled by something else. She wanted to be sure, to be safe; she wanted to wake without shame, wake clean and pure, knowing there was nothing elusive to remember or to be unearthed from some dark corner of her unconscious. She sat up straighter on the seat. She didn't want to go on like her mother, buffeted by events she couldn't control, much less understand, and she didn't want to spend her life waiting for that final blow, anticipating it with every fiber of skin and each last inch of nerve.

Rudi wasn't going to let her run from this one, she thought, as she wiped away her tears and looked out into the swirls of snow. He expected better of her and she would do better. She still didn't understand how she would do it, but suddenly that didn't seem to matter any more. She would manage it because she wanted it, and that was enough.

Part III

MAY 1981 – MAY 1982

Keep thy heart with all diligence;
for out of it are the issues of life.

—Proverbs 4:23

Twenty-six

IT WAS A HUMID RAIN, AN EARLY MAY RAIN, A RAIN MADE FOR greening. It slicked down the new bright leaves, and trickled into the throats of half-opened crocuses, and turned last year's mulch a rich fragrant brown. It was the kind of day when the earth smells clean, just bathed, cracked out of its heart of ice and snow, and ready to begin a new season of blossoming. It was the kind of day when you begin to forget about winter.

Kat was ready for it, this new spring, with all its buds and promises, for on this wet morning she would move out of her father's home at last. It was a leave-taking, a break with family, a break made for the first time really. Going off to college cushioned by high school yearbooks and old stuffed animals had been more like a vacation or a temporary stay with friends of the family. Now she chose to be on her own and to do for herself, under no one's hand or eye. Her new apartment on Beacon Hill was only two streets over from Helena's, a studio with huge bay windows and the original parquet floors, but more important, it was all hers.

So much had happened within the small confines of the past four months—so many departures and beginnings—that each day on waking Kat wondered if her life were really her own. This life was not the same as the one she had led before; still, she was the same person, with the same weaknesses and hesitations. For the first time she saw patterns in her emotions and actions and understood them as a series of interconnecting spirals. How it surprised her to discover that simply by changing one response, or one action, or even a few words, she could sometimes shift the way her life would happen, or change the way a scene would unfold. It seemed to her now that there was a certain necessary morality to living: to be responsible for her own troubles, to stop blaming others and whining like a spoiled child, to be grateful for what she now saw, despite its burdens, to be a very privileged existence.

She had gotten in touch with Bea Daniels because she felt she owed Bea an explanation. The memory of their relationship was a wound in her mind and to exorcise or heal it she must face her down and bring them back to the friendship she had originally welcomed. Kat had called her the week following her lapse with Aaron and Tina at the Atrium. Bea had been coming to Boston to work with an editor at the *Atlantic,* and she and Kat had met in the Square for a long lunch with talk well-spaced over several courses of well-spiced Indian curries. Kat had been so tense that her hands were shaking again, and she kept sipping her water, hoping for courage. But in the end, it was Bea who brought it up.

"It's the sex that's bothering you," she said, "isn't it?"

Kat didn't answer, but flinched at the mention of that dark bedroom in this sunny public place.

"When I woke and you were gone I should have known. But then I kept calling." She shrugged. "You kept putting me off. It was pretty obvious."

Here was opportunity then, winking up at her like a lighthouse shaft in the night. Now she could clarify; now she could explain her silence; now she could fashion a future for the friendship. But there was pain in this reaching out. It was humiliating, searing, to admit her weaknesses, to admit she had been defeated by her own problems. Still, she did it, put her hand out into the fire. "I made a mistake that day," she said.

Bea looked at her.

"I said yes when I wanted to say no. I knew I should be saying no. Then I was ashamed later, and I didn't want to face you."

"Why did you say yes to begin with?"

"I wanted to make sure you'd come up with those contacts. I wanted you to like me."

Bea's brow line tightened as she put down her fork. "So you were just using me." She looked up at Kat, angry. "You set me up."

Kat twisted her napkin under the table. "I'm sorry if it looks that way," she said. "I never, consciously at least, meant to." She stopped and sighed. "All right, I guess there's more to it than that. It's just not clear-cut in my mind. To be perfectly honest, I was very drunk that day—I wasn't capable of saying no, or making a rational decision. I was so drunk that nothing really mattered at all. I didn't care what we did—then. Just afterwards. Maybe that was using both of us."

Bea looked neither convinced nor forgiving.

"Listen," Kat said, hearing herself begin to sound a little desperate. "I was drinking very heavily. All the time, not just with you." She stopped, unsure of what to say next. In the past three months, she had learned not to tell people that she was an alcoholic unless it was absolutely necessary. All too often it provoked remarks and jokes, or arguments she couldn't deal with very well yet. But this seemed to require something different: Bea was wise, a woman to be trusted. "To be honest, I was drinking alcoholically—totally out of control," she blurted out, and then looked up to see Bea's face clear.

"Of course," she said, "it all fits. The weight, the nerves. The way you needed to get to that bar." She looked over at Kat with concern. "Why didn't I see it then, I wonder? I was worried about you sort of intuitively, but I couldn't put my finger on it." She sighed and wiped her mouth on the napkin.

Kat nodded miserably. "Well, I hid it pretty well then, I think. But I've been dry now for over three months. I joined AA."

Bea didn't look surprised. "My ex was a member." She nodded and sipped her wine. "It didn't work too well for him though. Or maybe he didn't work hard enough at it—I don't know. He kept slipping up, going on benders. Another reason I left him."

"That sounds familiar," Kat said. "I think you told me that before—in the Ritz bar maybe. I don't need to explain much to you then, do I?"

"Definitely not," Bea replied. "Here's the way I see it: you can learn a lot from AA, but you've got to put it to work for you. It's no good unless you use it."

"Yes," Kat answered slowly. "At first I didn't see that, but now I do."

"You know their motto 'Easy Does It'?"

Kat nodded. It was on a banner in every AA hall she'd ever been to.

"My modification is: 'Easy Does It—But Do It!'" She laughed. "I'm always rewriting," she said, beckoning for the check. "So. Are you still living at home?"

When Kat admitted she was, Bea urged her once again to get a place of her own and stop stalling. "Enough excuses," she said, "get moving." And perhaps it was there, at that table, that Kat had made up her mind, decided to lay down guilt and fear simply by refusing to think about them. She began to look for an apartment that very week.

Of course, it was Helena who went hunting with her, checked out the ads and the realtors, laughed at the horrible pits they inspected. She kept Kat from sinking into a discouragement which might have paralyzed her or prevented her from carrying out the plan. Kat leaned on her and on her love because, although she hated to admit it, she had no choice. She needed Helena. It was the first time in years that she'd allowed someone to look after her, and it was a hard role reversal, this learning to take help when it was offered, or even to reach out and ask for it. It was learning to accept the risk of rejection.

At the same time, she began a search for full-time employment, a job which would push her through regular hours and strict discipline, a job which might lead her to the career she'd prepared for in college. She needed to feel good about her work again. Bea had wanted to help her, to set up introductions to some of her associates, but Kat had refused. This she wanted to do herself, and she would not use Bea's strings, or her father's, or even Eliot Rutledge's. In and out of publishing houses she tramped, both trade and text, and magazine establishments as well. She answered endless questions, filled out form after form, and bit down on her frustration when she got nowhere. There were so few places to apply in the Boston area. Then one morning as she drove herself into town, she decided her approach to the problem was wrong. The hell with personnel, and following channels. You had to have gall, she thought, you had to march in on some editor you barely knew or had never met and make him, or her, believe in you. But how to do that, she'd asked herself, in a sweat at the very idea. A nice trick when you barely believe in yourself.

But in the end that was exactly what she did, acting confident and aggressive. And she'd gotten a job. A good job, as an editorial assistant at *Boston* magazine. It should lead to the editorial position she was aiming toward; it had possibilities. Now she accepted the typing and the secretarial duties because she was willing to be realistic. The very same week, an apartment on the choice side of Beacon Hill became free. She took one look and signed the lease.

Telling her father had been more difficult than anything else, an ordeal during which he said nothing—his icy silence more expressive than words. But Paige had looked upset at Kat's announcement. What did that mean? she'd wondered later, surprised by her sister's reaction. Paige was still a locked door in Kat's head, and she had stopped trying to pry it open for one simple reason: it hurt. Sometimes, Kat thought, sometimes it was better just to block out the hurts you could do nothing about.

It was solid AA practice to "turn over" everything you could not control or change to the responsibility of a "higher power," but Kat still felt that God belonged to someone else. She just delegated her obsessions and neuroses to some general unknown face: on Tuesday, a frumpy matron riding the streetcar in a veiled hat was awarded custody of her nausea and fear about the new job; on Friday, the Hood milkman, driving up a suburban street, took over her worry about leaving Kirk. It didn't mat-

ter where the problem went, provided it was hers no longer. Life
got simpler: there were no more hours of contemplation and despair. She acted on what she could, the rest she left behind—a
good and durable habit.

AA seemed like a miracle to Kat during these months. If she
stuck to their simple formulas for coping with daily problems,
everything became easier. Somewhere in her heart she'd always
thought she would be depressed for the rest of her life. But for
the last four months she had been happy a good deal of the time.
For four months she had been free. Rudi and Marty's advice
influenced her more and more, as she began for the first time to
achieve a balance between her emotions and her actions. Before,
life had been an unmanageable swamp of emotion, but now,
there were simply emotions she could afford and those she could
not: anything that led to a drink she must eradicate. Rudi told
her to stop being so intellectual, to stop worrying whether AA's
principles could meet the intellectual requirements of a Harvard
grad, and settle for being a responsible adult instead. In some
ways he was only telling her what Aaron and Helena had tried to
say a year earlier, but she was ready to hear it now.

She took Rudi's suggestions almost indiscriminately, blindly,
without caring why they worked, but only that they worked. It
was a time bathed in the magic of sobriety, of a new life evolv-
ing, of magnificent change.

The break with her past, with her father, with the house, was
inevitable. First Rudi, then Marty, then Aaron and Helena, then
Bea—all of them told her to get out. When the day arrived, wet
and rainy, when she'd looked out the window to see the earth
opening beneath the warm wind, she'd almost moaned aloud. It
was going to make the move even more difficult. Kat could just
see Aaron hefting cardboard boxes soggy with rain, trying to
keep furniture from getting wet.

Since the fiasco at the Atrium she and Aaron had both seen
that they needed time and a carefully measured distance before
trying to begin again; for two months after that they'd met for
lunch a few times, but had not allowed anything more involved
or intimate. He'd stood back and let her reorient herself. In April

they'd gone to the movies, and when he'd offered to help her move out, she'd accepted. It was ironic, but appropriate, that he should be the one. And she'd needed the help, because there was a great deal to be moved. Determined to be surrounded by familiar objects, she was taking the bulk of her bedroom in Concord. Other furnishings, purchased at Bloomingdale's, would arrive later in the week. Well, she thought, as she swung out the door and down the stairs, she would not let this weather stop her.

Kirk was stirring sugar into his tea when she came down to the breakfast nook; the spoon grated against the bottom of his cup. She kissed him good morning on her way to the sideboard to fill her coffee cup. Against the window, the rain came down more insistently now, and the lawn grew a dull soggy brown.

"You're up early for a Saturday," Kirk observed, as he spread apricot marmalade out to the very edge of his English muffin.

"Aaron will be here soon," Kat said. She took bacon, eggs, and toast, because the fortitude and discipline breakfast represented were important today.

"Why's he coming around?"

Fear began to unfold inside her like a rose. He was not going to let her leave easily. He was going to make this hard. It didn't surprise her that he had forgotten what today was. He did not want to remember. It hurt him to remember.

"Aaron's helping me move into my apartment," she said, fiddling with her coffee cup. "I told you last week."

"Yes," he said absently. "That's right. You did tell me." There was silence for a while as he stared out the window into the rain. She wished he would say something, and allow her to be close to him again. But there was nothing she could do—nothing short of offering to stay.

"The day's so bad. I should think you'd wait." He looked over at her, his blue eyes hard and set, and she flinched. She knew that expression—it meant he disapproved and was determined to change her mind. "Everything will get wet," he said. "You're going to ruin all that furniture."

"I'll cover it with plastic." She lifted her chin and set her cup back into its saucer with a louder clink than she had intended. "I'll make sure nothing's damaged."

"That won't work!" he said, angry now because she hadn't acquiesced. "You didn't plan this very well—a bad day and no one but you two to move it all. I suppose this was his hare-brained scheme?"

She refused to be put on the defensive about Aaron. "My lease starts today," she said, deflecting the subject. "And work on Monday. I want to be settled in. I'll be careful of everything." Her tone was so brusque it was almost insolent.

"It's your life." He pushed back his chair and moved out of the room with a clipped stride.

Kat slumped forward and leaned her head on her hand. This wasn't the end of his argument. She could tell. There was more to come. More anger, more bitterness, more pressure.

The morning moved by so slowly it hurt. Kat wanted to be up and out of there before she could feel what she was doing, but there were so many boxes, so much to lift, so much to heft over stairs and into the U-Haul. Piece by piece her childhood room was coming apart: the snowscape over the foot of her bed that had moved her into sleep each night for eighteen years; the mirror over the dresser that had watched her first attempts with lipstick. And as each piece went by, she felt as though her childhood was passing out, was being given away. She was growing up now, this very moment, at some stupendous, forced rate. And when the room was stripped bare it held more than ever before— it opened a floodgate of old ghosts in Kat's head. Its nudity made it possible to remember the room in all its stages, this room which had grown up with her, this room, a dear old friend. When she was five it had bunkbeds and kangaroo wallpaper. When she was twelve it had twin beds and a dressing table with a sprigged skirt. It all came back now, echoing out of floor boards and empty walls.

Her father patrolled the halls, and watched each piece go by; it made Kat feel both uncomfortable and guilty. She kept closing

the door to the bedroom, but the double bed with its antique
brass headboard was not easy to hide or to move quickly. It was
the last to go, and Kirk met them as they were carrying it down
the stairs to the truck.

"You're not taking that?" His face was angry. "It's far too big
for a studio apartment. Don't be ridiculous—take one of the twin
beds from storage in the attic."

The three of them stood on the stairs. Kirk blocked the way,
and the weight of the double mattress dragged at Kat's arms.
She knew why he wanted to stop her from taking this bed—it
was a symbol of all she would become once she was out of his
house. He knew she would sleep in this bed and make love in
this bed. Aaron shifted now under the weight, waiting.

"I need my bed," she said to her father.

"You can have any bed!" he said, exasperated.

She cut him off. "I need my bed," she repeated, "and it's
heavy. Let's go, Aaron."

They lurched forward and Kirk had to give way under the
presence of their weight. Kat did not look at her father as he
pressed himself against the wall to let them pass.

A half-hour later, short of breath, Kat finished filling the truck
with loose bedding, clothes, and lamp shades. She looked at
Aaron. "Be with you in a sec," she said as he got into the truck
and started the engine. "I just have to say good-by."

"Are you O.K.?" he asked. "Do you want me to come?"

"No," she said, "I can do this by myself. I'll follow you in my
car."

In the kitchen Mrs. George had nearly finished preparing
Kirk's lunch. "So," she said, and her face creased into a ring of
smiles, "are you ready now?"

Kat nodded and tried not to cry. "Please make sure the bedroom is redone with that set from the attic—and cleaned and
polished and done up fresh." She paused. "I just don't want Dad
looking at the room empty like that."

"I promise I'll take care of it," Mrs. George said, putting her
arm around Kat and walking her to the door. "Now go along."

"What about dinner tonight?"

"Katherine," the housekeeper interrupted, "your father's a grown man and I've been running this house for twenty-eight years. Get to your own work—all those boxes!"

"Right," Kat said, giving her a kiss. "Maybe I'll see you soon." She turned quickly on her heel, and left the room before she had the chance to ask more questions, or get any sadder. Kirk was on the back steps, pulling off his gardening gloves, his faded khakis stained with dirt, his old sports shirt sweated out beneath the arms and in a dark arrow down the back. This was the time of year he loved best: there were beds to be groomed, bulbs to be repotted, and on rainy days, a wealth of odd jobs in the green-house.

"Well," Kat said, wanting to hug him but sliding her hands into the pockets of her jeans instead, "I've got to get going. Aaron'll be waiting in town."

He looked out over the lawn. "Rain's a good fertilizer," he said.

"Come visit me as soon as I'm set up," she pressed him.

He looked at her; now she could see the stone-hard anger that flinted from his eyes, and her whole body trembled under the force of it. She'd wanted him to kiss her good-by with tears in his eyes, wanted him to say he'd miss her. But there was only anger.

"I'll call you soon," she said, as she quickly turned to go down the steps. "I left the new phone number on your desk." She waved and headed toward the car in a hurry.

The engine turned over and she lifted her head to see Kirk in his stained shirt and pants, as he stood there on the steps alone. He was her last parent. He was still her father, despite his faults and angers. She wanted to run back to him, but she knew she should leave. Random thoughts flickered down her mind like water through a sieve, thoughts of loss, of desertion, of death.

It was impossible. Brake set, engine left running—she ran from the car, needing to try one last time. Emotion blurred judgment, emotion sucked her back into the old patterns, back to encircle him with her arms, back to tell him nothing had changed. She was still his little girl. "Daddy, please," she said, feeling the solid safety of his body against hers.

But he was a tower of cold black rock. He didn't move. He didn't raise his arms to hold her. He didn't even look at her. It was then, as she slowly turned away from him, that her own anger rescued her, that anger gave her the strength to withstand the rejection. Putting the car into reverse she backed out the drive, wishing for a drink, for relief, for oblivion—anything to end the pain. Her throat ached from fighting the tension, and she began to cry.

"Damn him, anyway," she said aloud, gritting her teeth as she drove down the slick road through a haze of tears. "I won't drink over him. I won't." She would call Rudi, she would talk to Helena, she would ask Aaron to hold her, but she wouldn't give in.

And maybe by tomorrow she would begin to feel good about her new apartment, her new work, and her new life. Maybe she would begin to feel free. It hurt now. This leave-taking, this unbinding, tore at her, flesh from flesh, but by tomorrow, by next week or next month, she might draw down deep on her own hidden source, and take root.

---------- *Twenty-seven* ----------

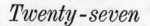

HEAT LIGHTNING FLASHED UP PURPLE, GREEN, YELLOW—A MULTI-
colored bruise against dark clouds, clouds which hid the sunset.
There was no thunder, no sound except the wind moving against
the trees, the call of birdsong at dusk. Kat and Kirk sat on the
back patio in wooden-slatted garden chairs, watching the sky in
its colors as if it were the Fourth of July. They pretended to read
but really they were just watching, listening to the night coming,
and wondering if it would storm. It was August, a muggy New
England summer.

Yesterday's phone call from Eliot Rutledge had prompted Kat
to come to Concord to look for answers, or maybe it was absolution. The insurance company wanted her answer, he said: would
she renew her father's loan, or should they foreclose. She'd
paused and rested her head against the wall, tired of other people's problems and other people's debts. It had been over a year
since she'd taken this on, and in that year so much had changed
for her. Her independence from Kirk had taught her that solving
his financial problems was not her duty, and now she felt sick-
ened by it all. She'd told Rutledge she would go to Kirk and discuss it; she would explain what she had done and why, and why
she could do it no longer. Rutledge had been pleased but Kat
only felt empty, as though something was over without being
finished.

She had not seen her father in over a month; in fact, since she moved out of the house in May, their contact had been limited and brief. Although frequently she asked him to visit her on Mount Vernon Street, he'd always been too busy. He would meet her for dinner at a restaurant but he refused to acknowledge that her apartment even existed. She knew what it all meant, she recognized these obvious signs of disapproval, and they hurt. In her mind, she saw the relationship with her father as an endless white landscape, a cold land leached of color where nothing ever grows or flowers, where nothing ever moves or bends with the wind, where there is only stark white acre upon stark white acre, unremitting, unforgiving.

So as not to starve for love and laughter, she had forced herself to move in new directions. Her work was at the core of every day now, not planning Kirk's dinner or creating dry martinis, and she'd discovered how truly capable she was. Her boss was giving her more and more responsibility, and less and less typing. A natural ear for language, and years of writing papers at school paid off as she pushed words around with her blue pencil, edited grammar, rearranged structure and paragraph. Often she stayed late or brought work home with her, and she began to scout for material and good writers in hopes that successful pieces brought in under her name might stimulate interest among the senior editors.

It was an exacting job, a taxing job, and she loved it. She loved the efficiency and the occasional inspiration she could bring it, she loved the feelings of competence and excellence—to see her boss's face when she turned in a letter-perfect piece. For the first time since college, she belonged: she had a purpose and a goal and a future. A night course at the Harvard Summer School in "Journalism as Literature" seemed another good way to increase her general knowledge, and as long as she was there, she began to stay late to catch the lecture series immediately following hers on the history and culture of the Jewish people.

She did not want to waste what little free time she had in Concord; at home, she knew, there would be only isolation, frustration, and silence. Instead, springtime came to the city and she let herself be carried by its small surprising beauty. Each night she opened her windows to sit on the fire escape, and looked down onto the gas lamps of the Hill, feeling gentle warm air on her arms. And, in the mornings, there was the scent of lilacs from some hidden inner garden.

There were bicycle trips with Aaron and Helena to Martha's Vineyard, Saturday picnics in the Arboretum with her new friends from the magazine, and long Sunday afternoons at Plum Island, where, hidden in the dunes, she and Aaron baked in the sun, made lunch of cheese and bread and cherries, and kissed with fruit-stained mouths. The defenses between them were coming down. They built sandcastles against the tide; one afternoon Kat told him, bit by bit, all she had hidden while in the haze of her alcoholic fever—all about Bea, all about her father and Paige, all about the blackouts, the self-loathing—and he didn't disown her or push her away or cease to love. He was tolerant. He forgave. He wanted the wounds to heal, and so they went down to the water and washed themselves in the balm of the salt, in the cold magic of the Atlantic.

AA still filled two evenings a week and provided Kat with the support she needed to stay away from alcohol. During the first weeks in her own apartment—that period of crisis—she had replaced her father's love and approval with the affection and approbation of her friends in the program. She was proving to herself that she could change her life, and by July she was stronger, a little more independent, a little more self-confident. Decisions were easier; being alone was easier—and she hadn't given up anything except booze. Her life apart from AA fleshed itself out and increasingly she found major amounts of support in her new friends, in Helena, and in Aaron; in late June she and Aaron began to sleep together again, but there was no question of their living together; they were intimate but independent.

The sky lit up a deep magenta and the trees, top heavy with summer's leaves, were outlined in violent color. Kat shifted in her chair, and wondered who or what made this happen. A scientific explanation just didn't seem adequate tonight, just didn't match the spectacle before them. This was another way

AA had marked her life, but this she discussed with no one. Although she had declared herself an atheist to Rudi when she'd joined the group, all the talk about "higher power" had made her seriously consider the question on her own for the first time in her life, and she realized now that her atheism was simply a refusal to consider possibilities. Everyone she knew in AA had a different definition of their "higher power," from the traditional, to the Great Pumpkin, to the tooth fairy. It was so unfashionable to think about God that it seemed almost anti-intellectual to Kat; nevertheless, an idea persisted in her mind—some creative pattern which governed the helter-skelter of everyday life, a sense that events moved by themselves on some predetermined starlike course.

"It's bizarre—all these colors," Kirk said, leaning his head back against the chair and flicking open his lighter. "Only other time I've seen anything like them was during the war."

"Where was that?" she asked idly, brushing her fingers through the grass.

"Some island in the Pacific. No name for it, just an island. After—" He stopped and settled his teeth into the cigarette filter.

"After what?" Kat looked over at him and the marsh peepers started up in a soft throb of sound. "I thought you were on a carrier."

"They sent me there for punishment. It was after Alex was killed. You remember him—he gave your mother and me those brass bookends in the bedroom."

"Yes," Kat said, "I always wondered where they came from." Quiet, she waited for him to continue. Then, "How did he die?"

Kirk drew slowly on his cigarette. "In an aircraft attack. I was coming through a doorway onto the bridge. Alex was behind me. He saw them over my shoulder, coming in low, and he pushed me flat. He took a full hit in the chest." He paused and flicked the butt out of his fingers into the grass where it lay like a small red eye in the dark. "I was crazy with the thing. He got what should have been mine and he was my best friend, my only friend on board. When I got insubordinate with my C.O. they sent me to the island—alone, on a recon, to sober me up. The place was a nest of Japanese. The feel of that night around me, hot and wet—you could feel it on your face. And darker than I'd ever seen before. No lights of civilization or people. But there were flares, colored flares, every once in a while. That's how I saw the Jap sentry—in the light of a flare. We were almost face to face, and I had to kill him. I got his throat in my hands. I was so scared I just kept squeezing and squeezing." He stopped for a minute and then cleared his throat. "When he didn't breathe any more, I went onto the beach and vomited. I was twenty."

There was silence for a time. "I've never heard that story," Kat said finally, thinking that she was only twenty-two.

"I don't think about it often."

"But you kept the bookends," she said in a soft voice, reaching over to touch his arm.

"When I got back to the ship I finished the letter he'd been in the middle of writing to his parents. I told them he was dead." He lit another cigarette. "The colors just reminded me."

Kat couldn't quite believe he'd told her this, her reticent, closed father, the man who never communicated. She could not doubt that pain in his voice, and she wondered how, now, she could tell him about the loan. He had shared himself and to tell him would be to ruin this moment. It would hurt him, it would bring him pain. And she knew in that instant that she was not strong enough to fight this, there just was not enough willpower in her to fight this urge to protect him and preserve this moment of love. And she hated him for that, and she hated herself. She was trapped. Once again she would pay the ransom. Once again she would pay the price she had set. The loan must be renewed; for now, she saw no other choice.

Twenty-eight

Kᴀᴛ's ᴀᴘᴀʀᴛᴍᴇɴᴛ ᴡᴀs ᴜɴᴜsᴜᴀʟʟʏ ʟᴀʀɢᴇ ғᴏʀ ᴀ sᴛᴜᴅɪᴏ ᴏɴ Bᴇᴀᴄᴏɴ Hill; in a newly renovated townhouse at the very crest of Mount Vernon Street, it was a long L-shaped room with floor-to-ceiling windows which faced south. To the right of the entry door, at the far end, was a marble fireplace, and on either side of it Kat had placed two easy chairs; the glass coffee table between them had a terrarium for a base—cleverly designed by Helena. A tuxedo-roll love seat, covered in a soft pattern of green and yellow cotton, bounded the third side of the table, and several large dracaena flanked the sofa's back, creating a natural wall which separated the living area from the rest of the apartment.

The polished wood of a round teak table was the centerpiece of the dining area, to the right of the living room, where Kat had hung her snowscape and her favorite Monet print on opposite walls. An oriental screen drew the line between dining room and the small kitchen, which was built into the wall at the bottom of the room. The alcove created by the foot of the L served as the bedroom, just big enough for her brass bed, dresser, and night table. Large brass stands on either side of the foot of the bed held asparagus ferns; it was rather like sleeping in a forest, for she had also chosen bed linens of greens and taupes.

The force of her taste on each part of the room was strong, and she had created a comfortable warmth. The built-in book-

shelves by the fireplace were filled with her favorite volumes
from college and the leather-bound set of Dickens her father had
given her as a Christmas present two years ago. At the windows
there were no draperies, but instead, with Aaron's help, she had
installed natural wooden blinds which allowed the sunlight to
spill in unchecked.

It was a beautiful apartment, a home of color and warmth.
And so it was with a feeling of gladness and of security that she
returned after leaving her father on Saturday night. She walked
through the door, took off her shoes, and went to sit on the fire
escape to think things out. She was resolved in mind, if not in
heart, to renew the loan. It bothered her to back down once
she'd decided to have it out with Kirk; nevertheless, there was a
need to be realistic. She would just have to wait.

On Monday she instructed Rutledge to notify the insurance
company, and then forced herself to put the entire matter from
her mind. The rest of the week moved by quickly once this decision was past, and she turned to other things.

She took no lunch hour at work on Friday, and left early
enough to prepare a special surprise for Aaron. Since auditing
the course in Jewish history and culture at the summer school,
she'd been intrigued by the idea of preparing him a Sabbath
meal. All week long Helena was on call as consultant for every
last detail, not really surprised by Kat's fascination—ever since
college she'd been pestering Helena with questions about being
Jewish. When Kat asked for transliterations of the Hebrew
Sabbath blessings, Helena asked her when she was planning to
become a member of the tribe, and they'd laughed.

It was a meal such as she'd never made before. First came the
challah—the traditional Jewish bread—which she had gone home
early to set out to rise. Up to her elbows now in flour and egg
yolk and honey and raisins, she was surprised to find what hard
work making bread was. The dough was sticky in her hands, and
the fruity smell of yeast filled the room. Pushing it away and
pulling it back, leaning into it with all the strength in her arms,
using the hard heel of her palm to work it. It was changing
shape now, becoming less sticky and more of an elastic mass. She

was sweating in the late heat of the August afternoon. Under the surface of the dough there were little blisters rising—a sign that it was time to let it rise again. She divided it into four chunks of equal size, and began to roll them into the sixteen-inch-long ropes. Each one flattened evenly under the spinning motion of her palms; she used to do this with clay when she was a little girl, and it reminded her of that—and then, too, she was thinking about the meal and its rituals. Though religious, they were rituals of the home, she realized, and in this they were unlike the Protestant rituals she'd been raised with, which had mostly been conducted in church. And this was why the Jewish traditions appealed to her, and this was why Judaism itself appealed to her: it was the warmth that drew her, a Friday evening meal where a family came together in harmony to bring in the Sabbath. A mother who blessed the candles and a father who blessed the bread.

She braided the four long strands of dough, shaping them into a beautifully curved and woven loaf. With a sharp knife she cut off the bottom third and rerolled it into three strands. These pieces formed the braid which crowned the four-strand loaf. After another hour's rising it would be ready to bake. She covered it with a towel and set it aside on the cutting board.

The outside buzzer rasped through the apartment. She pressed the release catch for the outside door, wondering why Aaron was an hour early, but when she opened the door, it was Kirk who stood opposite her. He was still in his business suit, briefcase in hand.

"Hello," she said with surprise. "I wasn't expecting *you.*"

"You've been asking me all year. Now I'm here," he said.

"Come on in," Kat said, beckoning. She shut the door behind him, secretly pleased.

He stood in the middle of the apartment, looking up and down with a critical eye, and she went into the kitchen so she wouldn't have to watch his face. "Can I get you a drink?" she asked over her shoulder as she slid the pot roast into the oven.

"That would be nice." He settled back into a chair by the fireplace.

"What do you think?" She poured the mix of gin and vermouth and rimmed the glass with lemon peel.

"Pretty small."

"Bigger than most."

"And expensive, no doubt."

"But what do you think of how it looks?"

"You've made it very attractive," he said finally, as he accepted his glass with a nod. "Very homey."

"So," she said, smiling as she sat down on the couch. "How was your day?"

"Actually that's why I came." He sipped his drink. "I've just been with Harry Rollings at Security New England Insurance."

She looked into her glass of tomato juice, pressing it hard between her palms, and told herself to stay calm. She waited.

"I know what you've been doing." His voice was rigid.

"Doing?" she said, very low.

"With Security." He lifted his glass. "You picked up my debt and paid the extra interest." He kept his face controlled and expressionless. "When they renewed again with no penalty, much less no interest hike, I knew something was going on." He twisted his wedding band on his finger and then looked over at her directly. "Why?"

"I love you. I wanted to help," she answered, leaning forward. "Isn't it obvious?"

"It should have been obvious that this kind of help would be the last thing I'd want." He stared at her. "If you'd asked me, I would have told you. In fact, you did ask me once and I did say no."

"I thought it was just your pride—"

"*Just* my pride!" He stood, suddenly angry. "Isn't my pride enough reason? What have you got if not your self-respect? Lose that and you've lost everything important."

"But what would you have done if I hadn't stepped in?" She was beginning to feel angry and defensive: after all she had been through, after all she had given and given up, his ingratitude was monstrous. She wanted to be thanked, to be loved for her gift. "You would have been bankrupt."

"It was my crisis, mine to solve." He put his glass down with a sharp click. "I don't know what I would have done—but something. I would have found some way, made some move. Now look at it—no better off for all your help."

"No better off!" Her voice turned rigid with suppressed rage. "You still have the company! I gave you everything I had! What was the sin—loving you too much?"

"You didn't have the right!"

"The right! Isn't love justification enough?" Suddenly the sarcasm was heavy in her voice, the hate oozing out of her, sticky, sweet, like honey from a pot. "Or was it too much love when Mother gave it all those years? Did she have a better right than me?" She moved forward to the edge of her chair. "You took it from *her*, you lived off *her*—what's the difference who? You took it then, you take it now—that's the point."

His anger ignited in a short static burst, and he rose from the couch in an involuntary motion—as if to put his hand across her mouth and stop her words, as if to put his hands on her throat and choke them off. And with that motion she was suddenly afraid: arguments over cocktails, anger beating its symphony off the walls and into their hearts. Once Kirk had provoked and Lily had accused; now Kirk provoked and Kat accused.

"It's not your business—you aren't your mother! You're not my wife!" He was shouting, his fists knotted into tight painful balls.

She covered her face with her hands. He had said it. It was true. It was all true. She had been lying to herself. She lifted her head to face him. "I didn't do it for you," she said, her voice dull with the insight. "I did it to save my family. I wanted to keep Mother. I wanted to keep you." She started to cry, deep sobs of recognition. "I did it to keep me."

Her father stood in the middle of the room, limp, stunned, like a patient who has undergone electric shock therapy. He sat down beside her on the couch, his face palsied with exhaustion. "I know you were trying to help." He took her hand.

"What will you do?" she asked, her bottom lip quivering.

"I don't know."

"I'm sorry."

"I know," he said. "I understand that."

There was a knock at the door.

"I'm sorry," Kat said, wiping her face. "That must be Aaron." He nodded and she crossed to the door and opened it.

If Aaron was surprised to see Kirk standing there, he didn't let it show, but instead crossed the room to shake hands. "Mr. Sinclair." He nodded with a smile. "Didn't know you'd be here for dinner."

"No, no," Kirk said, holding out his hand. "I just dropped by. I'm on my way now."

"All right," Kat said, still dazed, wishing there had been more time.

He picked up his briefcase and looked at her. "Come home for dinner soon." He kissed her on the cheek, and she clung to his arm for a moment.

"Soon," she repeated, watching his back go down the stairs. She closed the door and put her head against it, then turned to Aaron. "Please just hold me."

"What's been going on here?" he asked, guiding her to the sofa.

"He found out." Her voice was muffled by his chest. She wanted to hide against him forever. "He knows about the loans. We fought."

"Can't say that I blame him." Aaron put his feet on the coffee table and lifted her face away from his shirt.

"Thanks for the sympathy!" She started to cry again.

"Look—the choice should have been his, no matter why you did it. Sooner or later he was going to find out and be mad. He's not stupid."

"I was selfish! It was a mistake!" She sighed and shrugged. "I am sorry." She paused and looked up at him. "But I can't change what I did. What can I do?"

"Apologize."

"I already did." She got up and went to stand before the window, forcing herself to stop crying.

"So now you live with it."

He was right. It sounded easy, but it wasn't. There was the

guilt, and that endless desire to help, to be needed, to be loved. These things wouldn't vanish just because she understood them; they were old stains, they would not be bleached out. But some relief lay in the new clarity: her father was no longer her responsibility. There were no more games to play, no more strategies to be planned. There was no more emotional blackmail. She was free.

"This is my crash course in growing up," she said, turning from the window and going back to stand beside him.

Aaron nodded. "What are you going to do?"

"I'm going to make dinner, that's what," she said, going over to the oven and checking her roast. "I'm going to bake my bread and get on with my life." And so she brushed the loaf with a wash of egg yolk and poppy seed and slid it into the oven.

Aaron watched Dan Rather while Kat set the table with Dansk stainless, Boda candlesticks, ecru napkins with deep brown stitching. There was solace in small tasks. Yellow daisies and tiger lilies in a brass bowl brought out the colors of the room, and the warm smell from the oven filled the air.

When everything was ready, she called Aaron to dinner. He turned off the television and came to stand beside her. "It's beautiful," he said, putting his arm around her waist. "You did all this just for us?"

"*Just* for us?" she repeated, with a smile. "What else is there? Now you sit down while I light the candles." She struck the match and held it to the wick, feeling self-conscious and wondering if he would laugh. He was watching her from his seat. In Hebrew she chanted: "*Baruch ata Adonai . . .*"

"What are you doing?" he asked in amazement.

"It's the blessing over the candles. Helena wrote it down for me, and I spent the whole week memorizing it."

"Do you know what it means?"

"Something," she said as she sat down, "something like Praised are You, O Lord Our God, King of the Universe, Who hast sanctified us with Your commandments, and commanded us to kindle the Sabbath lights."

"Impressive," he said, smiling, but clearly confused. "But why are you doing this?"

"I don't know." She shrugged. "I just liked the idea of it. I thought it might be fun for us to do. I'm losing one history—maybe I'm looking for another."

"It is fun," he said, looking shy for a minute. "But I'm kind of embarrassed—I barely know this stuff myself. We didn't have any of it at home."

"Well, there's always time to learn," she said in a teasing way.

"So, Rabbi, when are we allowed to eat?" he asked, lunging at the bread.

"Just a minute." She snatched up the knife. "I've worked long and hard on this challah and it's not going to be devoured without the proper blessing."

"You *made* this?" he asked, astonished.

"Helena's mother sent the recipe. It was fun." She motioned to the two-foot glossy brown loaf and laughed. "That's a lie," she said. "The truth is, I saw it in last month's *Gourmet* magazine—but it's still authentic." She motioned with the knife. "Now you bless it."

They sat down to eat and it was as intimate and loving as she had planned. They finished their coffee and dessert slowly, waiting for the candles to burn out as tradition dictated. Aaron took her hand in the darkness. They went into the bedroom and lay down on the cool sheets, with the rustle of ferns around them.

"I love the meal you made me," he said, stroking her face, "I loved the whole thing. Even if I don't know all the blessings." He turned her toward him and began to kiss her. "D'you know what a mitzvah is?"

She shook her head.

"A mitzvah"—he kissed her—"is a good deed. A good thing. And there's one Jewish custom I do know."

"What's that?" she whispered.

He paused a moment, and then pulled her to him. "It's a mitzvah to make love on the Sabbath."

Twenty-nine

THEY HAD BEEN OUT ON THE OLD POSSUM TRAIL FOR ABOUT AN HOUR when the wind picked up and it began to snow again, feathering down over Kat's black ski sweater and her bright red cap. The woods were quiet, and they were in quite deep now. It was the weekend before Christmas, and the holiday ski traffic had not yet hit New Hampshire; they had last seen someone on the cross-country trail an hour ago. Around them were only trees and shrouded rocks, bushes, and iced-in streams. Snow was filling the ski tracks of the person who had come this way before them, erasing this last sign of civilization, making their glide even smoother and faster. Fir trees arched above the path, bent low with their arms full of snow, arched close together to make a vaulted ceiling of some king's Great Hall. Even the winter birds were silent this morning, and in the gray light was only the wooden swoosh and clack of skis moving along the track.

This was hard work, Kat thought, kicking her left leg out behind her and using the opposite pole to balance the motion as she leaned forward on her right ski. It was a bit like flying, and it reminded her of something, something past but not forgotten. Push and glide, push and glide—like skating, she thought.

When she was a little girl she had skated nearly every winter afternoon until dark, on a nearby pond. Each night her father had come down to call her home to supper; he would skate across the pond to tell her, his face alive in the cold air, his blue eyes happy. He loved the freedom and the speed. He would skate with her, hand in hand, in the fading light. How she had loved him, her small hand firm in his big mitten, how they moved together like birds, or dancers. She threw her head back, held herself erect and proud. It was a ballet on ice, a ballet of love. They had wings when he lifted her above his head, when he spun her and twirled her. She had been a little girl, but he'd made her feel a woman, a strong delicate thing of grace and speed. And that was love as she had known it then, love on the ice, as the light went grayer and grayer, as the lights in nearby homes began to prick through the trees with irritating brightness; that was love, pure and simple, uncomplicated, love in motion, love in tandem, love spinning itself out in a dark that had never seemed cold.

The snow was coming thicker, blurring Kat's vision, but she pushed on, exhilarated by the glide of good wax on this fresh dry fall. Somewhere, sometime, all this had changed: her father had changed; she had changed. They had both grown up, become less connected. Her father was sorting out his problems alone now, she reflected. Since their confrontation about the loan, he had told her that Sinclair Shoe was declaring bankruptcy—but he did not volunteer what *he* would do, how he would go on or with what. And she had not asked. Over and over during the past four months she'd had to force herself away from his problems; despite her anxiety for him, she'd kept herself clean, out of it all. What kind of life could he have now? she wondered sadly, lifting one ski off the ground so as not to slide over a rock in the path. How could he survive when so much of what he loved was disintegrating beneath his touch—first the business, and soon, she felt sure, the house.

Around the next bend, she stopped to catch her breath. Aaron slid up behind her and, unable to stop quickly enough, caught hold of her as a bracing post. He pointed to a ledge of rock at the side of the trail; sidestepping, they went up the small incline on their skis. Kat pulled the thermos of hot chocolate from her

knapsack and poured a cup to pass back and forth between
them.

"How come?" Aaron said, when he had caught his breath, and
swallowed a mouthful. "How come you're so much better at this
than me?"

"Not better," Kat said with a smile. "More co-ordinated."

"Yeah, well," he said, draining the cup. "This time I get to
lead."

"O.K.," she said as she screwed the top back on the thermos,
"but get going. I don't want to get cold and stiff sitting here."

She slid down the small slope back onto the trail. Grumbling,
he bent to adjust his binding and then he struck off in the lead.
"Bend your knees and lean over the skis," she called. "Push into
it. Didn't you ever skate when you were little?"

"I was a city kid," he shouted, "remember?"

"So work at it," she shouted back. "Concentrate."

That's what Rudi had said yesterday, she thought, stretching
forward into the motion, concentrate. Concentrate on AA.
They'd been arguing about her trip north and her upcoming ab-
sence from the usual Sunday night meeting. Rudi had pushed
her to attend a meeting while she was in New Hampshire to re-
place the one she would miss, but Kat had wondered what she
was supposed to do—leave Aaron in front of the fire after dinner
by himself? Which was more important, Rudi asked, a romantic
evening, or her sobriety? She'd wanted to say a romantic evening
was, but instead closed her mouth with a snap and promised to
make an effort to go.

Inside, she'd resented it, resented Rudi's implication that if she
didn't get to at least two meetings a week she was going to get
drunk. It was hard not to believe what he said though, because
he, after all, had showed her what a sober life could be like. And
under no circumstances did she want to lose that life, or to risk
this new happiness. Nevertheless, she didn't want to go to a
meeting in New Hampshire either—not unless she felt she was
endangered and about to give way to temptation. But Rudi kept
telling her—

With a crash she plowed right into Aaron, who had stopped to refasten his binding in the middle of the track, and they both tumbled over into the snow.

"What were you doing?" she snapped grumpily, trying to sit up without success.

He looked over at her and started to laugh. She had snow in her hair and eyelashes, her hat had fallen off, and a small branch from a pine tree stuck out over one ear.

"I'm skiing with a reindeer," he snorted.

"You think I'm funny-looking?" Kat demanded, catching up a handful of snow. Their skis were tangled together, Aaron's legs trapped beneath hers, and she began to wash his face with her mittenful. "Taste good?" she asked gleefully as he sputtered beneath her.

"Rat!"

"But a loving rat," she said, and bent to kiss him. His face was very cold against her cheeks, but his lips and tongue were an oasis of soft warmth. It was a long kiss. Around them snow settled in a silence broken only by the hiss of their breathing.

"It's really coming down." He sat up. "Aren't we awfully far out for this kind of storm?"

"Relax." She tried to stand up, using her poles for leverage, and this time succeeded. "These trails are clearly marked."

"But we're in the woods."

"Aaron, I promise we won't get lost. *Really*. There's nothing to be afraid of."

He didn't look convinced.

"Let me lead now." She settled the straps of her poles over her wrists, and moved past him. "We're not in a raging blizzard in the Himalayas. We'll finish this loop of the trail in another hour and then it's fifteen minutes back to the lodge—I'm getting hungry anyway." With that she was off, moving along the path with a quick snapping stride, and he had no choice but to follow the bright red cap, as it wound its way through the snow.

English-cut rare roast beef and Yorkshire pudding were the inn's specialty, and Aaron and Kat had three helpings apiece. At nine o'clock they began a cribbage war before the fire, but Kat's

yawns, coupled with the fact that Aaron skunked her game after
game, soon sent them up the three flights of stairs to their small
room at the back of the top floor. It was very cold. Kat washed
up quickly and put on her flannel nightie. The soft double bed
that took up the entire room was not too warm either, so she
huddled and shivered, and hoped Aaron would hurry. Finally he
came back from the bathroom down the hall, snapped off the
light, and pounced on her.

"Off with that thing!" he said, burrowing under the pile of
quilts and pulling the nightgown over her head.

"Cut it out!" she protested, laughing despite herself. "It's
freezing in here!"

"All that's missing is cold cream and curlers." He threw the
gown onto the floor and climbed on top of her. "Let me be your
blanket."

"Forget it." Kat pushed him off. "I'm much too sore from skiing, and my thighs are killing me."

"You're right," he agreed as he flopped back on the pillow. "I
am exhausted."

They lay quietly for a while, hugging and getting sleepy and
watching the snow pile up against their window. The air in the
room grew even colder, and they snuggled close against each
other in the warm pile of quilts.

"What're you thinking?" Aaron asked after a while.

"Rudi. Going to a meeting up here."

"I thought you'd decided not to."

"I did."

"Well?"

"I can't help it—I dread telling him I didn't. He'll make me
feel guilty."

He sighed. "Why? Why should you? Did you feel like drinking tonight at dinner?"

"No," she agreed.

"Were you in a state of crisis? Were you torn up about it? No
—you were having a good time, right?"

"Right."

"So why not trust yourself?" He kissed the nape of her neck.

"You can control the problem—you've proved it for almost a year now—and with work you'll continue to control it, but that doesn't mean you have to spend the rest of your life in AA meetings. It means going when you want to, or need to. And making up your own mind."

"The Program says you can never trust yourself or your own judgment again. It was my judgment that got me into trouble to begin with—remember?"

"Kat, your judgment is what took you to AA in the first place. Your judgment is what keeps you sober day after day. Take credit for your progress—you've come so far." His voice was beginning to sound angry. "I'm so proud of you, proud of how you've taken hold. I trust you again, and I resent the way they're always putting you down." He paused then and in that moment she suddenly did feel proud, felt that perhaps her sobriety was no mysterious miracle from God, but something she had accomplished herself, after all. The wind was shaking the window panes, bringing up the smell of tomorrow morning's bread from the kitchen, and she was suddenly happy.

"Kat," Aaron said, breaking the silence of her thoughts. "Marry me."

She sat up straight in the bed, the quilt falling away from her body, her nipples erect in the cold air. "Are you serious?"

He nodded.

"Where and when?" she laughed, bouncing up and down on the soft mattress.

"I'll assume that means yes," he said, starting to smile.

"I wish we could do it at home," she went on, "but I don't suppose Dad would like that." She paused. "How about Appleton Chapel, in Harvard Yard?"

He looked doubtful. "But who'd officiate?"

"That is problematic," she agreed. "I take it a minister is out?"

"You take it right. And no self-respecting rabbi would marry me to a shiksa." He lay back on the pillow and crossed his arms behind his head. "How about a justice of the peace."

Kat made a face. "Oh hell—let's figure this stuff out later." She rolled over on top of him and kissed his mouth, and then his neck, and then his ear. "Right now I've got more important things to do."

"I thought you were too sore," he joked, as her tongue painted a long wet line down his chest, down his abdomen, as her head disappeared under the quilts. "Yes," he said, as she drew him into her mouth. "Oh yes."

Thirty

THIS YEAR IT WAS A SIXTEEN-FOOT BLUE SPRUCE, AND PAIGE SWORE under her breath as she stabbed her finger again on a prickly needle. "Shift that blue one a little to the right," Kirk instructed, "and, Kat, take the clear gold one up higher."

The girls were perched on twin stepladders. "Hand me some tinsel, will you, Aaron?" Kat called. "As long as I'm up here I'll start it." As he fed her the shining chain, he planted a kiss on the back of her knee. "Hey!" she said, laughing. "Knock me over and you've had it!"

He was so rambunctious, Kat thought, as she looped the shiny garland up and down; his enthusiasm made the holidays just that much more enjoyable—new blood in an old tradition. It was his first Christmas and it was obvious he was enjoying it. She looked around her, and there came a rush of warmth—the room lit softly, the fire reflected in the wood of Lily's piano, the tree fragrant and majestic. The family was working together tonight, without argument or friction. Yes, she thought to herself, as she climbed down the ladder, this is a good time of year.

Kirk was busy at the bar on the other side of the room, whipping together his mysterious blend of eggs, cream, and liquor. Eggnog was also a Sinclair ritual on Christmas Eve, consumed by the quart while decorating the tree. Tonight Kat would have to refuse for the first time since she'd been allowed to try it at

the age of fourteen. An urge to leave the room came over her as
she realized the difficulty of resisting this particular temptation,
but she forced herself to sit down on the couch: the rest of her
life could not be spent running. The fragrance of cinnamon and
nutmeg drifted across to her as she watched Kirk approach with
his tray.

"The cup in the left corner." He gestured with his elbow.
"That one's for you."

"I really can't." She sat up very straight, but inside was the
sensation of having been cornered again and trapped. "I'm
sorry."

"This one." He gestured again impatiently. "I made it without
any Bourbon. It'll probably taste lousy but I thought we'd give it
a try."

She picked it up, so stunned that she didn't even remember to
say thank you. She took a sip, and found it to be only a shadow
of what she was used to, but she reminded herself sternly of last
year, and her unexpected nap atop the boots and scarves on the
closet floor. Last year she'd had to call AA to be rescued. She
looked up and saw Kirk still before her, waiting, as he used to,
for her verdict. "It's really pretty good, Dad," she said. "Make
sure you remember how to do it."

Aaron had already finished his cup. "And I used to hate
eggnog."

"I'd better make another batch," Kirk growled as he headed
toward the bar in an attempt to hide his pleasure.

Aaron came over and sat beside her. While Kirk's back was toward them, he nuzzled her ear. "Your father's in a pretty good
mood," he whispered. "Must be Christmas rubbing off on him.
I'm having a great time."

"Chanukah's neat too," she whispered back. "I'm glad we've
done both." Kat had given Aaron a brass menorah on the first
night of Chanukah, and each evening as the sun set, they'd lit
the candles and chanted the blessing she'd taught him. Even tonight, the eighth night, before they'd come here to Concord to
decorate the tree, they'd stood, hands linked, to watch the
straight line of little yellow flames burn so fiercely into the dark.

"Could we go out into the hall for a sec," he whispered again.

"What for?"

"You'll see," he said, insistently, pulling her to her feet.

In the dark vestibule, he backed her against the wall and began to kiss her.

"That's not fair!" she protested. "You taste like *real* eggnog."

"Want me to go brush my teeth?"

"No," she said wistfully. She hesitated. "Look, I don't really regret having baby eggnog for a minute, and I was amazed at Dad—it's the first time he's acknowledged that I don't drink. It's just," she hesitated again, "it's just sometimes I feel sad. I've lost something, and there's no getting around it. I've had Sinclair eggnog every Christmas for eight years. I know I'm better off without it, but still, it somehow feels sad. Tonight it hurt a little, that's all."

It was funny, she thought to herself, she'd said this very same thing, had talked about the grief she still felt at forcing her love for drink to die. It was like losing a good and cherished friend.

It had been her first AA commitment, the first time she'd gotten up to tell her story before an audience. Rudi was the chairperson and he'd called her as soon as the meeting was open because he knew how nervous she was. She'd thought it would be hard to talk about some things—like the sordid details of her drinking past—but it wasn't because she had faced all those details. And because she talked honestly she could see these strangers' faces responding. Always shy, never even in high school had she gotten up before a crowd. But it was like flying— scary, exhilarating, that sense of power as she shared herself. When she spoke of her mother's death, a young woman in the front row began to cry quietly, and after the meeting ended she came to Kat and thanked her.

Kat had not hesitated to say that sometimes staying sober was still hard, that—although she had been dry almost one year now —there were days when a drink seemed like it could only help. On those days the idea of alcoholism sounded nonsensical.

On their way home in the car, Rudi had complimented her on the fine job she'd done. "But that business about being sad," he told her, "that would disappear if you went to more meetings."

"Don't you think it's normal to feel sad?" she asked in surprise.

"Sometimes, but it can be dangerous. A sign that something's wrong." He swung the car onto Route 2. "Did you get to a meeting in New Hampshire?"

"There really was no time," Kat said quietly.

He said nothing for a moment. "You're looking for trouble—cut yourself off and you will start to drink again. We've seen it time and time again."

"I'm feeling pretty secure right now."

"That is when you run into problems—when you become self-confident and complacent."

She made up her mind. She would not sit through this passively any more. She would declare herself. "Rudi," she began, choosing each word with deliberate care, "you've been with me from the start, and you're a good friend, but I don't agree with what you're saying. I don't believe it's true for me—it's just dogma." She twisted in her seat to look at him earnestly, blood going hot and quick through her veins. "You can't know what's right for me. The only reason you're telling me this like gospel is because once someone told it to you. How many meetings I go to is up to me—only I can know what I really need."

"You must trust AA to know what is right for you," he said tensely, his eyes on the road.

"Rudi." She sighed. "When I was a little girl I did what my parents said, and I trusted their judgment. I had no other choice. But now I do have a choice. When you grow up you have to start using your own judgment, and that's what I'm beginning to do. I used to drink to get away from the burden of trusting myself and making decisions. It was a terrible mistake, but I'm not dumb and I've learned a great deal. I'm just trying to grow up and be an adult. I'm not going to lie to you and promise to follow rules that don't make sense to me. I'm not saying your way—three meetings a week, or three meetings a day for that matter—isn't right for you. I'm just saying it's not right for me. And I don't need another parent right now."

"Can't you see that as your sponsor I'm obligated to try and change your mind?"

She looked out at the road, the river glistening in the dark with the lights of the city. "But arguing with you all the time only makes coming to meetings harder, not easier. Maybe it'd be better if we were just friends."

He pulled up in front of her apartment building and set the hand brake. "I too have found the past months frustrating," he agreed sadly. "I felt perhaps I was not doing things right. I didn't seem to be reaching you."

"Rudi, you were reaching me!" she said softly, putting her hand on his arm. "It's just that I don't always agree with what you say."

He sighed. "Then that is that," he said, with a nod of defeat.

"Rudi, I needed you very much in the beginning and I still depend on you—but in a different way. I still need a friend I can call in the middle of the night." She leaned over and kissed him on the beard.

"O.K.," he said thoughtfully. He began to grin. "We are both stubborn people. I hope this time that we are both right."

"See you next week," Kat said over her shoulder as she got out of the car. Climbing the steps, she felt clean and free for the first time in months—and they had still parted as friends. For Kat, AA had been like a giant Virginia Reel: reaching out her hand to one stranger after another, she pulled them forward as they pulled her; it was an interlocking dance of fluid protective motion. But now she had returned to the spot on which she'd begun, only to face her first partner—herself. Now she must be as self-reliant as she'd claimed she wanted to be, and suddenly that frightened her.

But here was Aaron's weight against her and that was a comfort. He was kissing the end of her nose again. "I thought maybe we could tell your father tonight," he said.

"Oh, Aaron, I don't know." She bit her lower lip. "It's so complicated and tonight's kind of a family thing. And if we tell him we're getting married, then I'll have to tell him I'm thinking of converting—you know he can be a little anti-Semitic, and it could get sticky, especially on Christmas Eve. Would you mind awfully if we waited?"

"I can see your point."

She patted his shoulder, and wished her father was a more tolerant man. His dislike for Aaron had faded into a quiet acceptance of the inevitable, but Kat felt sure that, even with time, he would never react with such equanimity to the possibility of her conversion. Kat herself was not entirely resolved about the idea, and hard as she tried to fight it, her father's projected reaction was a part of her ambivalence. It had all happened so unexpectedly—in trying to decide who might marry them, she and Aaron found themselves in the midst of an inevitable discussion. All sorts of questions they had never even considered before came up: which holidays would they celebrate in their home? In which traditions would they raise their children?

When Aaron had facetiously suggested that the obvious solution was for Kat to convert, the idea had seemed a poor joke. But she continued to think about it. And, on a gut level, she wanted to be married in a religious service. Over the carrots in the grocery store she was wondering what such a conversion entailed. On the street corner waiting for the bus, she was feeling a beat of excitement. In an odd way it seemed she had been leading up to this all along; all this time she had been borrowing the Jewish rituals and making them an integral part of her life with Aaron. To take a step which would formalize what they were already doing seemed as natural to her as taking the marriage vows which only formalized what they already felt. She believed that conversion would give them a solid base to step off on, and common ideas around which to raise their children—a tradition of family warmth which was visible and demonstrative and could be passed along. At first Aaron had cautioned her to slow down, and think about it, but she could see that he was pleased in spite of himself. Even he had not anticipated his own reaction.

Conversion was an involved process requiring instruction with a rabbi. Next week she would begin this preparation, and, as she pointed out to Aaron, if she found in her heart that this was wrong for her, she would simply have learned a great deal. Un-

derneath though, she continued to return to the question of her
father. Would he refuse to participate in the ceremony if she did
this?

Mrs. George touched her elbow to tell her the roast beef was
on the table, and Aaron and Kat turned to go into the dining
room. "I was thinking," she said, catching up his hand. "If I convert—can we really still have some of my holidays too?"

"You mean Christmas?"

She nodded anxiously.

"Easter I might have a little trouble with," he said with a grin,
"but Christmas at your house doesn't have anything to do with
religion anyway."

"No," she agreed. "We've never gone to church or anything.
It's just a time to be together at home."

"You don't have to give up anything you want to keep," he
said. "It's all up to you."

The fire was a collection of coals now, odd-shaped, intense
with heat, and Kat slipped off her shoes and spread her toes toward the warmth. Aaron had left and she was alone. The living
room was lit only by a circus of red, green, orange, and blue
bulbs. Each light silhouetted its branch with a pool of warm
color, each ornament reflected that color outward, and the tinsel
made a great halo of illumination around the tree. It was the
symbol for all the Christmases she had ever known, and although the type of tree changed with the years, they might all
have been the same—all Douglas fir, all balsam, all spruce—the
same tree year after year. It was the center on which they had
anchored the holiday every year: buying the tree, decorating the
tree, putting packages beneath the tree, and sadly, dismantling
the tree on New Year's Day. Even if her parents had been
fighting, there was the tree—solid and stable. Even if Lily were
depressed—there was the tree, full of its life and joy. How many
times had she hidden in this room as a little girl, crawled right
into the safety of the tree's branches and lain there surrounded
by packages, looking out at the world from within its special cocoon.

Behind her, Kirk came into the room and moved quietly to the bar. She heard the soft chink of ice against the glass. A stinger, no doubt, she thought to herself.

"Would you like something," he asked, "some juice or club soda?"

"I'm fine, thanks."

He came and sat down beside her on the sofa. "When you were little," he said, "I used to come in every Christmas Eve at midnight just to sit with the tree for a while. Before Santa came." He lit a cigarette and laughed softly. "It was the last moment of peace before morning."

Kat laid her head back against the cushion. "Tell me how old the star is." Every year she asked the question and she never tired of the answer.

"Probably fifty years. Your mother's parents always had it on top of the tree. They bought it on their honeymoon in Venice. The man blew it while they watched."

"Where's Paige?" she asked then, more to make conversation than out of curiosity.

"In bed already," he said, "and frankly I'm starting to worry about her."

"Why's that?"

"She floats from day to day—not accomplishing much." He tapped his cigarette. "I think she tries to escape an awful lot, and now George Burr is giving her Valium! Between that and alcohol . . . ironic to tell you all this."

Kat was silent for a minute. "It sounds a little like Mom," she said with a frown.

"You're damn right it does! I'm telling you, Kat—she's too young for this. I wish you could talk to her."

"Me?" Kat said, incredulous. "I haven't been able to talk to Paige since we were kids."

He drew in the last of his smoke and flicked the butt into the fire. "But you're such a good example," he said. "You went through a very tough time when your mother died, and you've managed to snap out of it—although I'm not saying I exactly agree with your methods. But I do have to admire the way you found a job, and made a life for yourself. Taking control. I can respect that."

"Thank you," she said in a small voice. There was so much she wanted to say; how much she wanted to reach out and hug him. But she knew his openness would capsize quickly at the first sign of too much emotion from her, a delicate sailboat in too much wind. She controlled her voice. "I think things'll get worse for her and then she'll either give up or start to fight back. But she's a strong person."

"Is she?" he said. "You were the one who really had things put together, not Paige."

"Me?" she echoed in surprise. "But it was Paige who could always take anything in stride. I was just the crybaby."

"She put on a good act, covered up the insecurity." He lit another cigarette. "Are you sure you can't talk with her?"

Kat sighed. "I'd talk to her in a minute if only she'd come to *me*. But if I try to draw her out, it'll just make things worse." She laughed. "You should know better than anyone what happens when I try to interfere."

They sat there in the dark for a little longer, separate in thought but united for once by their common worry. When Kat finally went up to bed, she left her father still watching, still waiting for the magic of the lighted tree.

Thirty-one

AARON DOUBLE-CLUTCHED INTO THIRD WITH A ROAR, AND ACCELER-
ated quickly as the road hooked to the left. Leaning into the
bend, he watched the tenseness on Kat's face from the corner of
his eye. During the past year he had learned that she could handle stress like this; nevertheless, he worried. The changes she
had wrought in the patterns of her own life sometimes struck
him as miraculous—even now—but he had come to see that anxiety was by far the hardest emotion for her to cope with; often he
had protective urges he couldn't prevent. But he did make certain Kat did not know of them because he realized intuitively
that she needed to feel trusted. Besides, he thought to himself, it
wasn't as if he felt particularly relaxed about confronting Kat's
father with their wedding plans either.

She reached over to wind one of his close-cropped curls
around her finger. "Nervous?" she asked.

"A bit." He shrugged, then looked up at Paige in the rearview
mirror. "Still alive back there?"

Paige raised her head an inch off the seat. "Barely."

Kat looked back with a touch of sympathy: her sister really
did look horrible—hair tangled and dull, skin drained of color.
Being hung over was a feeling Kat knew too well.

She turned forward in her seat with a sigh, pleased once again
to be clearheaded on New Year's morning. Last night had been

her first experience at a really big party without the cushion
drinking used to provide, and she'd handled it well. With Helena
and her new boy friend from the B-School, they'd gone to stuff
themselves on quiche, salad, and rich Bavarian torte. She and
Aaron had danced and talked, and at midnight, when everyone
else had champagne, Helena produced a bottle of ginger ale
wrapped in a towel; a year ago Kat might have felt angry at
being singled out, but last night it just seemed funny.

Later, when they had come home, and climbed the stairs to
Kat's apartment, the glow of the party still wrapped about them,
they'd found a surprise waiting—Paige. Propped against Kat's
door in the hallway, collapsed, hysterical, reeking of musty
scotch, she was like a frantic wounded bird. Half an hour later
Kat still had not discovered what the problem was. She'd only
been able to gather that Paige had left a party in the Back Bay
after a violent argument with some woman—which accounted for
the deep scratches along the length of her cheek—and then
walked all the way to Kat's, in the dark, alone.

Kat could feel herself growing more and more angry at this in-
vasion, even though she knew she ought to be sympathetic. Finally, she drew Aaron into the bedroom. "Why should I put myself out now?" she hissed. "She's never come to me before."

"I agree," he said, looking her dead in the eye. "Other people's
irrational behavior is no picnic." He paused. "But if you love
them, you cope."

Tired, they tried to convince Paige to settle down on the sofa,
and eventually she did pass out—but not into an easy sleep. She
muttered and thrashed out her dreams. Kat and Aaron slept on
the edge, always waiting for the next explosion, always aware of
a third presence in the apartment. By morning Kat had a hot resentment simmering. Over the breakfast table Paige was silent
and sullen—oblivious, Kat felt, to the disturbance she'd created.
She ate her eggs angrily, wondering if she should tell her sister
how she felt.

"I know you're pissed off," Paige said casually at last. "Just
stop acting so self-righteous."

"It was an imposition," Kat flared back. "I don't like it when you're out of control—it reminds me of Mom."

"Well you should know all about that," Paige snarled. "You love playing out that fantasy."

Kat looked down at her plate. She couldn't defend herself against the accusation, but it occurred to her then that maybe her father was right. Maybe Paige was really in trouble. "We'll take you home after breakfast," she said, feeling helpless, believing there was nothing more she could do.

As long as they had to drive Paige to Concord, they decided the day had come to break their news to Kirk. When Kat called, her father seemed genuinely pleased that they were coming and suggested that Aaron watch the Sugar Bowl with him. After breakfast, they'd warmed up the Toyota and begun the drive to the country.

But as they neared the house, Kat's tension only got worse. She looked out the window and watched the bare forest blur by her, replaying the scene to come in her mind; each act was different, but every conclusion the same. The fantasies rolled off the assembly line in her brain, growing progressively more disturbing: he would be cruel and turn to attack Aaron; he would become so angry as to forbid the marriage; he would refuse to participate. Despite her determination to remain controlled, her palms began to sweat, and nausea bumped against the back of her throat.

They pulled into the drive and she stood for a moment to look out over the grounds. A succession of warm days had melted the snow, and everything was flat and bleak. She wished she did not have to go through with this, she wished it were over. But mostly, she wished her father's opinion didn't matter so much, wished that his disapproval wouldn't alter how she felt about the wedding and the conversion. But that was asking for magic.

In the library, Kirk had his feet on an ottoman, and was reading the paper. He got up out of his chair and kissed Kat hello. "Game's just about to start." Paige passed through the room without a word and went upstairs.

"Is she all right?" Kirk asked Kat, raising his eyebrows in a gesture of worry.

She nodded. "Hung over."

"A good thing you were home last night!" He sat down and flicked his lighter open with an angry click.

Aaron settled himself on the couch. "Kat tried to talk to her this morning, but she was pretty defensive."

"What did she say?"

"She didn't want to talk about it." He took a pretzel from the bowl on the coffee table. "So what are the odds here?" His question was a clear effort to distract Kirk, and it worked. When Kat left the room to look for Mrs. George, they were making a bet, arguing over the point spread. Aaron's dark hair was rumpled and he was just starting to go through the elbows on his sweater —so different from her elegant father. She liked the way they looked together, drinking beer before the set. And another fantasy came to her then—a father and son fantasy. She shook her head to clear it, and the tension began to hum once again in her stomach. She had to get rid of all these fantasies.

Mrs. George was in the living room on a stepladder, in the midst of dismantling the Christmas tree. Kat stretched up to give her a kiss. She took off her favorite red ball and laid it carefully in its box, but she was really too distracted to get organized about stripping the tree. First one ornament, then another, drew her attention, and she took nothing down.

"Is everything all right?" Mrs. George asked finally. The housekeeper came halfway down the stepladder with an expression of concern. "You seem—preoccupied."

"No, I'm fine." She smiled hesitantly, wanting to tell, wanting some approval before she had to run the gauntlet with her father. But she couldn't. It wouldn't be fair. Her father should be the first to hear.

Mrs. George looked at her cagily. "Oh—a mystery!" she said as she pulled the star from the top of the tree and handed it down carefully. "A surprise."

"Yes," Kat said. She forced herself to concentrate on this task because it was a way to diffuse her anxiety. They unraveled the tree layer by layer, as if it were some rich and gaudy woman they were undressing. Still the time dragged for Kat, despite their chatter about the holidays, her apartment, her work, and soon the tree was almost bare, except for a few lone strands of tinsel.

Aaron appeared at the doorway. "Half-time," he announced.

"Go along you two," said Mrs. George. "We're finished here anyway."

They went back to the den, hands laced together. Kat felt shivery and cold, and Aaron put his arm around her. Cheerleaders strutted across the screen, and the bands all marched in dead-pan harmony, an army of tin soldiers lifting their chalk-white feet.

Kirk looked up as they came into the room and sat down again, still holding hands. They turned to face him on the sofa. "Kat and I have some news," Aaron said. "We've decided to get married."

There was a small tight silence which exploded inside Kat's head, a silence that was slow motion, and lasted and lasted. In her father's face she read an instant of reaction, but it moved too quickly for her to read it. When he got up and crossed the room, she did not know what he was going to do. Her head felt tight and hot and she wondered if he would strike them, or leave the room. No, she saw, that was not it. He was offering Aaron his hand.

"Well, congratulations," he said. He kissed Kat on the cheek. The heat drained from her head and she could see clearly once again. Her father's face was friendly, but still she didn't trust it.

"So." He sat down again. "What are the plans, Kat?"

Aaron took her hand again. Concentrate, she told herself, concentrate on finding the right words, the words to make him understand. The silence was becoming awkward. "Our plans are still up in the air," she said finally. "Because we're doing this a little differently than you might expect." Her mouth dried up and she thought of paste, the glue she'd used as a little girl to make collages and red cutouts. "That is, we'd like to be married by a rabbi." She paused. His face had not changed. Perhaps he did not understand what that meant, she thought. "I'm going to convert. I'm going to become . . . Jewish." There it was. She had said it. The word was out. Now he must see. She wanted to run, but rushed on instead, needing to wipe out the shock she saw in his eyes. "I've been doing some studying on it. It feels right to me, so much of the way I think—the intellectualism, the approach to family, the traditions—" She stopped short in confusion; she wasn't breaking through to him, and now he wouldn't meet her eyes at all. "And as for Christ, well I never did believe—" she trailed off. He looked right at her, smiling, but their eyes did not meet. He hid behind his smile, he would not let her see his feelings.

"So, anyway, that's the current plan." She looked over at Aaron. "What do you think, Dad?" she asked anxiously.

"What do *I* think?" he said, sounding surprised. "I really couldn't say. You make these decisions for yourself, Katherine. Life is hard and it'll get harder as you two go along. Anything that helps to weather the storms together is a good thing. Now," he stood and lit a cigarette. "I'd say we need some champagne."

He left the room to unlock the wine cellar, and Kat turned to Aaron weakly. "What do you think?"

"He took it very well."

"*Well?* He didn't even react!"

"He reacted—and then he left it up to you. He just decided not to get angry and not to interfere."

Strong feelings of disappointment were arcing through Kat, and she fought back the urge to cry. He had accepted it all, but without coming to meet or support her. He'd refused to let them touch, had just turned aside and left her with the decision. She hadn't found the words to make him understand. It occurred to her then that maybe there were no words which could have done that. Maybe it was just asking too much.

Aaron pulled her into his arms. She could hear his heart strong against the curve of his ribs. His voice by her ear. "You thought he was going to fight for you, didn't you?"

She didn't answer. Her eyes were closed and somewhere within there was a sensation of something being jarred loose, a mooring cast loose, a sensation of light, a departure. Here was the independence she had sought, but it seemed like rejection. She had wanted him to stop her, to cry out, to prove his love by binding her to him. The ideas were moving hard inside her now, tumbling together and coming up in new combinations; the ideas were falling in new patterns and coming out of the old chrysalis into the light. Behind her eyelids she saw the sun on a leaded glass pane, dust motes in the air, a strong summer storm, roses bent wet against the earth. It was like being born, and it was like giving birth. There were no words to move her father, there would never be words to do it. It was not language, nor habit, nor ritual alone that held what she was looking for. In the end there was only the emotion which drew you together or did not. Trying to capture that emotion and bind it with words or symbols was as impossible as trying to catch the water spouting from the end of a hose. But to go without those words or symbols, to let so much pass untouched, unmarked, was equally impossible. She opened her eyes and there was Aaron. There was the emotion, this love, this unending friendship. This was what she had chosen. It was her decision.

Her father came back to the room with a silver tray: Moët & Chandon on ice, and a carafe of sparkling water for Kat. "I've been thinking," he said, as he popped the cork and began to pour. "We could have the wedding right here. What time of year did you have in mind?"

"Well, late May," Kat answered, looking at Aaron uncertainly.

He smiled. "The gardens will be in early bloom—you could do the ceremony in front of the rhododendron hedge."

"I like it," Aaron said, turning to Kat and squeezing her hand. "I can't think of anything, or any place, better."

Kat was wondering privately just who was going to pay for everything. It would be easy enough to pick up the tab herself, but she hesitated about saying this to her father, especially in front of Aaron. "We're not planning anything elaborate," she said finally, testing him, trying to see how he wanted to handle it.

"That's good." Kirk twisted his champagne glass in his fingers and then looked up matter-of-factly. "Frankly speaking, I can't manage anything particularly elaborate."

She looked over, ready to release him, but he lifted his hand. "Now hold on a minute and let me finish. I want to give you a nice party and I'll be able to—because I'm starting in with Teddy Eliot. You know he's been needing someone to help him run things since Skip decided to be a fool and move to New York." He stood and refilled his glass and Aaron's. "Anyway, your wedding's important to me, and I can handle it—within reason."

So Sinclair Shoe was gone at last, Kat thought. Her father was beginning a new life—and he had done it on his own, she realized, surprised at her own small sense of loss.

"After running your own show, how will it be?" Aaron asked.

"I think I'll enjoy the change," Kirk answered. "A relief to take a back seat. I need to simplify my life these days." He looked over at Kat. "I meant to tell you—I'm planning to sell off the forty acres down past the stables to a developer in the spring."

And that would save the house. Somehow this did not surprise her, for there was sadness in his eyes. But there was also the straight line of his back and shoulders. He had simply compromised instead of being defeated, she thought. He had faced what he had to do, and dealt with the problem. Slowly she leaned forward, put her glass down, and went to stand behind him, her face next to his, his cheek rough against hers. The tears which pricked her eyes would have embarrassed him and she was glad he could not see her.

"And your parents?" He patted Kat's cheek with a hand cold from his glass. "What do they think about all this, Aaron?"

"They're out of the country right now," he said, "so we're waiting till they're back."

"Perhaps they would like to stay here in May?"

"That's a nice idea," Aaron said, sounding very pleased. Kat went back to the couch and snuggled up next to him. There was so much emotion, so many contrary feelings going through her, that she felt her bones would melt under the friction. Would she

have the courage to make that move, in legal, public ritual, away
from her father; would she have the strength to take up her own
elusive power of womanhood. She looked over at Kirk's lined
face, and wondered for the first time if she were really ready to
let him go.

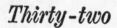

Thirty-two

PEOPLE WERE ARRIVING. THEY STRAGGLED ACROSS THE WIDE LAWNS, dressed for the weather in lightweight linens and silks, armed with hats for the already strong mid-morning sun.

Stretched out on her bedroom's window seat in nothing but her new satin panties, Kat watched them drift across the grounds like brightly colored ribbons. The trees brushed against the screen, painted with the new, soft green of May. But all the beauty in the world could not lessen her anxiety. This was her wedding day.

Across the room, the free-standing cheval mirror caught her decadent and lazy pose. It distracted her from further contemplation and she crossed the room to the mirror, turning from side to side to study her reflection. This was what she was. Everything was told in a body, she thought; even the fifteen pounds she'd dropped this year had left faint stretch marks, even the supple lithe tone which had come from exercise could not change the fullness of hips and buttocks. Only her breasts, her small, smooth breasts, had not changed with the years.

And there was her face, with its few deep lines. She looked down hard into her own eyes. Here she could confront the fear and uncertainty. It was important to examine these feelings openly, to dissect and understand them before she went any further with this day. Was she just nervous, or was it all a mistake?

Who would she become now? Having decided to keep her own name, she could not be Mrs. Aaron Salzer, nor could she any longer be Miss Sinclair—and she hated the self-conscious battle flag of *Ms.* No, in declining the custom of taking her husband's name, she placed herself in limbo.

In the mirror, her eyes still gave no quick answer to her questions, and when she tried to brush a curl back into submission, her hand shook. It had shaken like that before. She had stood there that day too, and looked into her own eyes for an answer.

It had been a strange day, a day of beginnings and endings, of gain and loss. The mikvah, the ritual cleansing bath, was in a small, well-kept house attached to the synagogue. It was here, on a cold, rainy April day, that Kat had gone to be converted by her rabbi. The attendant, an immigrant woman with a heavy black mustache, spoke little English and took her silently to an immaculate bathroom where she was instructed to undress. It was foreign to her, with its shiny purple and silver wallpaper, its jug of bargain-brand shampoo in the shower. A list of instructions by the mirror told what was required: no woman was to enter the bath before her period had ended, she was to shower first, to wash her hair as well, to brush her teeth. Sitting naked on the toilet seat, still wet from the shower, Kat clipped off all her fingernails with the manicure scissors. The ritual required purity. Nothing must stand between the convert and what she was doing.

Opening the door abruptly, the attendant startled Kat and then shuttled her, still naked, into another room with a flight of six steps. They led down into the pool of green water. Clutching the rail, Kat moved slowly down into the bath, over her ankles, over her thighs, into her crotch, up against her breasts. Then she waited, the water tepid and strangely soft against her skin. In a distracted fashion she wondered why it was green; perhaps disinfectant ensured cleanliness, just as the bath was required to circulate through intake and outflow pipes constantly. Under the water she could see her hands were shaking hard. She was afraid.

It was so primitive, so irrevocably physical, so far from the

ethereal Cross and still white aura of her Protestant upbringing.
In her mind, an irrational idea took root: God would strike her
down for this; she would be punished for such pagan blasphemy.
But then she stood up straight and forced herself to stop quivering. There was no way to make such a departure without some
pain, there was no growing accomplished without stretching,
no change that was clear-cut, black or white. This was what she
had chosen: to convert here, rather than in a ceremony at the
temple, to feel her choice not only with her mind but with her
body.

The rabbi stood to the side of the open door where he could
not see her, and the attendant positioned herself on the stairs to
make sure all the rituals were observed. When he asked if she
were ready, Kat nodded her head.

And then she began. There was the downward plunge into the
still water. She opened her mouth and eyes, as she had been
taught. The world was green and undersea and tasted of lime.
On the surface again, she recited the first blessing in Hebrew:
*Praised are You, O Lord Our God, King of the Universe, Who
sanctified us with Your commandments and commanded us con-
cerning immersion.*

And then, two more times, down into the water—water for
healing, water for purifying, water of this unorthodox baptism
she had chosen. And then up, up again to the air, for the final
blessings. Her mind was strong and clear, her voice was strong
and clear: *Praised are You, O Lord Our God, King of the Universe, Who kept us in life, sustained us, and enabled us to reach
this moment.* The rabbi asked her a few questions; finally, he
gave her the Hebrew name she had chosen, her link with the
people of Israel.

It was finished. She stood there, stripped down, wet, and suddenly glad. The panic was gone; the uncertainty was gone. The
attendant bundled her into a towel, and Aaron was waiting for
her when she emerged, clothed, her face soft with pleasure. And
she could admit then that she had done it not only for herself,
but for him too, for the love of him.

Maybe today would be like that, she thought, still gazing into the mirror, maybe this anxiety would disappear once the marriage ceremony was finished. But to move from this house, forever, to lose those soft round years of childhood, forever, to draw a definitive line between one part of her life and another. It was her wedding day, and she was sad instead of happy, confused instead of certain.

"Kat, what're you doing?" Helena asked, bursting into the room. "It's time to get going. Stop daydreaming." Ordinarily Helena would have been the maid-of-honor, but to shut out Paige was more than Kat had wanted to deal with; nonetheless Helena had come early to help her get ready.

"I've only got my dress and shoes to put on—it shouldn't take long."

"But I've got to finish your hair," Helena said over her shoulder as she went to the closet and took out the dress. "Paige had plenty of extra pins." The dress was a rose-tinged ivory silk, designed for Kat in New York when nothing in the standard bridal shops had suited her. Everything she'd seen had been too virginal —with empire waists which hid the body and veils which masked the face. Kat was determined to be herself, and that meant being a little elegant, a little sexy. She wasn't eighteen any more.

The dress slid over her head with a rustle and Helena began to button up the long sheer bodice of Valenciennes lace. It was only lined with a wisp of silk camisole. The full-length sleeves were a continuation of the lace on the bodice, tightly pegged down the arm. Recognizing that her collarbones—not her cleavage—were her strong point, Kat had the neckline cut shallow but wide, so that it just caught the very edge of each shoulder. From the tightly fitted waist the silk fell down against the curve of her hip, and flared out into a full circle at mid-thigh.

Her tan skin glowed against the transparent lace, and the soft easy lines of the dress accentuated her slender body. She looked comfortable and natural, and nothing like the fantasy mannequins in *Bride's* magazine. On her head she wore nothing, leaving her auburn hair free to curve around the miniature orchids Helena had artfully tucked into her curls.

"You look spectacular." She hugged Kat carefully and then handed her the violet, magenta and lilac orchids Kirk had picked this morning from the greenhouse; he'd left them long on their stems so that Kat could simply lay them, tied with a satin ribbon, across her arms.

"I wish we had more time."

"Well, we don't," Helena said, hustling her out onto the landing where Paige waited for them, her lilac crepe de Chine throwing a lovely color up onto her face. Kat had picked out the dress with her; she wanted to make sure it had a reasonable neckline. Paige wore her hair simply, drawn away from her face and down her back, and carried a small bouquet of violets.

"You look beautiful," Kat said, kissing her on the cheek and for once feeling no jealousy. "But I wish I weren't so nervous."

"If you weren't, you'd be nuts," Paige said, and they all laughed.

As they went downstairs Kat's stomach began to slip and slide, and she wondered if she would be sick. Kirk was waiting for them at the french doors which opened out onto the garden. He looked very handsome in his morning suit. Once again Kat felt a sharp tug of loyalty. He drew her to him by taking her hand. She could tell from his face that he thought she looked lovely.

They stood at the threshold and looked out over the scene. It was as lovely as he had promised. The gardens, where a hundred and fifty chairs had been set up for the ceremony, were in full fragrant bloom: a field of daisies with their sunny faces, jonquils and daffodils in a yellow sea, the deep periwinkle blue of the tall iris, the rosy throats of rhubrum lilies, and clouds of white baby's breath. It was overwhelming, and against it all, against the pastel beauty of the gardens, was the twenty-foot hedge of ancient rhododendron before which Aaron and Kat would stand to make their vows. It ran the length of the property, marking the boundary, and in the past week this green-leaved wall had opened itself to the warm spring wind, had flooded out into a deep blood-red, a violent artery of color.

There were no cut flowers or arrangements anywhere because Kat had trusted her father and relied entirely on the natural beauty of the grounds. He had helped her to plan it all, had been able to tell her precisely which flowers would bloom and when, which colors would be visible and from where. They had walked the grounds together after she had come home to stay for the week before the wedding. She'd wanted this time and space to be near him, to share quietly anything he might want to share, and yesterday they'd spent several hours together, completing the single planting they'd planned: a magnificent stone urn filled with the deep purple, yellow, and blue of birds-of-paradise. It was to be the centerpiece of the patio, where luncheon would be served after the ceremony.

Kirk tightened his grip on Kat's arm as he heard the piano, moved up against the living room windows, begin the quiet processional she had chosen. Paige moved out the door and down the aisle. Kat looked down at her father's hand. Yesterday his nails had been thick half-moons of dirt; today they were cleaned and polished. Yesterday they had worked in the earth together, the sun had been warm on their bare heads, the smell of damp earth had been rich and strong. There was so much Kat had wanted to say: she wanted to talk of love, of being a little girl skating on the pond, of being close to him. Still, she had learned to control the frustration of loving with no way to show it, no way to say it, and she was silent too. But as their hands touched, carefully moving the long sculptured necks of the plants, she wondered what he was thinking. She watched his hands instead of asking. They were strong hands, hands made to burrow in the earth and bring forth something beautiful. And she saw then that simply to work with him this way was a communion in and of itself. She must accept this as enough.

"I was wondering," he'd begun, as he tamped the earth down around each stalk, "if there's a place in this ceremony where they ask who gives the bride and all that?"

She shook her head. "Is it important to you that there is?"

"No. I just wanted to be prepared."

"If it is important, I could ask the rabbi to include it." She hesitated; it was so awkward to discuss the Jewish service with her father.

"It's fine," he repeated. "I've got to get more soil."

She watched him go, shirt stuck to his back with sweat, knees of his pants dark brown with wet earth. He wouldn't have asked if it didn't matter, she thought to herself. But she was afraid to call the rabbi and anger him with such an unorthodox idea. Still, if it mattered to her father, it mattered to her—she would not shut him out.

She'd made herself go into the house to call the rabbi, who'd been shocked and put off by her request. Perhaps he felt she was showing some ambivalence toward her conversion, but Kat didn't really care what he thought—she just wanted him to agree to it. And so she was persistent and pointed out that this was still a marriage of two cultures: there was no way to erase who she was or where she came from. It was a reasonable request, and it required nothing antithetical to the Jewish beliefs; it was a small piece of inoffensive Protestant ritual with no reference to Christ. After all, she argued, the Reform branch of Judaism was based on an ability to be flexible, and to adapt when new situations required it. "Some things you can't wash out of a person," she'd said. "I want him to give me away."

And so now she stood, about to go forward on her father's arm. Paige had reached the head of the aisle, and the music pulled them forward. Kirk stepped out, but Kat hesitated, still on the threshold.

She looked up into her father's face, into his eyes, and there was a connection between them, a moment when everything unsaid before was said. He touched her without reservation, he gave her love without defense.

"Come, Kat," he said at last. "It's your turn."

They were moving into the music then, moving down through that bus station of faces, and Kat felt a smile come through her anxiety and bloom out onto her face. And there was Aaron, his face shining down on her, his hair unruly, waiting for her to join him. And she knew then that this was right, that each step forward was right. Aaron was waiting for her there, waiting under the blood-red rhododendron.

Paige came forward to take her flowers and the rabbi opened his prayer book. "Who gives this woman to be married to this man?"

"I do," Kirk said, holding onto Kat's hand tightly for one last minute. The service was silent; there were no words here; everyone waited for him to take his seat. Aaron reached for Kat's hand, though she had not yet released her father's. For a brief second they stood, silhouetted in unity: all three together, all three as one, linked by her hands.

She turned to her father, laid her hands on either side of his face, kissed him. In her heart she had let him go; in her heart he would be always hers. For a moment she stood alone under the straight fall of noontime sunlight, touching no one. Fear and hope beat inside her like inspiration—a vision of the moment, beyond memory, beyond dream. And then she nodded to the rabbi, ready to begin.